One Night WITH THE BIKER

ROYAL BASTARDS MC

KATHRYN C. KELLY

One Night With The Biker by Kathryn C. Kelly
Royal Bastards MC
Published by Makin Groceries Media
24200 SW Freeway, Suite 402, Box #353
Rosenberg, TX 77471
www.katkelwriter.com
www.deathdwellersmc.com

One Night With The Biker
Royal Bastards MC, Kansas City, KS Chapter
By Kathryn C. Kelly

PRINT ISBN: 979-8-88630-0321

7TH RUN PARTICIPATING AUTHORS

Crimson Syn
Kathryn C. Kelly
Verlene Landon
Angera Allen
Barbara Nolan
Chelle C. Craze
Eli Abbot
Nicole James
Quinn Slater
Elizabeth N. Harris
A.J. Downey
K.L. Ramsey
Roux Cantrell
Heather Dahlgren
JA LaFrance
Madalyn Judge
Ciara St. James
Emma Creed
Posey Parks

Jena Doyle
Kristine Dugger
J.A. Collard
Isabella Starling
Claire Shaw
Kathleen Kelly
Rae B. Lake
J. Lynn Lombard
Kyla Orinick
Dani Rene
Kris Anne Dean
Elle Boon
Thetta James
D. Williams
Shannon Youngblood
Elise Gendicke
Letha Gene
April D. Berry
Nicola Jane

ABOUT THE ROYAL BASTARDS MC

Welcome to the Royal Bastards where loyalty is King and Code is the only way to survive.

Founded by Author Crimson Syn in 2019, the Royal Bastards MC is a world all of its own.

This club is not for the weak-minded or easily disturbed. These 1%ers are vicious, ride hard, and love raw. Our stories are dark, cold-blooded, and created to trigger the best of you.

If you dare travel down our dark twisted roads, hold on tight!

PROTECT: The club and your brothers come before anything else, and must be protected at all costs. **CLUB** is **FAMILY**.

RESPECT: Earn it & Give it. Respect club law. Respect the patch. Respect your brothers. Disrespect a member and there will be hell to pay.

HONOR: Being patched in is an honor, not a right. Your colors are sacred, not to be left alone, and **NEVER** let them touch the ground.

OL' LADIES: Never disrespect a member's or brother's ol' lady. **PERIOD**.

CHURCH is **MANDATORY**.

LOYALTY: Takes precedence over all, including well-being.

HONESTY: Never Lie, Cheat or Steal from another member, or the club.

TERRITORY: You are to respect your brother's property and follow their Chapter's club rules.

TRUST: Years to earn it...seconds to lose it.

NEVER RIDE OFF: Brothers do not abandon their family.

Thor, you were such a sweet kitty, gracing our lives for thirteen years. One day, we'll meet again at the Rainbow Bridge. We love you.

One Night
WITH THE BIKER
ROYAL BASTARDS MC
KANSAS CITY, KS

CHAPTER ONE

REESE

Each time a woman headed my way, I expected her to slide into the booth across from me and introduce herself as Ainsley Valois. And each time a woman nodded to me but kept walking, I asked myself what the fuck was I thinking. I'd let Louisiana, our chapter's RC, talk me into a fucking blind date.

What did that motherfucker do? Directed me to a Cajun restaurant, when my tastebuds firmly laid with barbeque.

Grabbing my brew, I gulped the last bit of it, set the mug down and drummed my fingers on the table. One fucking thing I hated was tardiness. My mystery woman was a half hour late and I was ready to fucking bail. I'd prefer listening to Louisiana schooling my ass on his state's culture than continuing to wait on a chick who couldn't tell the fucking time.

A girl headed in my direction and my fucking tongue nearly dropped to the table. She was stunning, drawing the attention of every red-blooded male in the place. Dark hair cradling her face and cascading down her back. Smooth, olive skin revealed in a jean miniskirt and a crop top. Luscious tits, a small waist, hips that flared just right, and long legs perfect to wrap around my back.

As she drew closer, though, I winced and turned my head away. Disappointment surged into me. She was young—too fucking young for me. Women had been my pastime for years and—

"Are you Reese?" She glanced at my embroidered name patch and nodded. "You are."

Her eyes were whiskey colored, her lips pink. Inches away from me, she was even more gorgeous. My cock jumped and my nostrils flared. A delicate floral scent wafted to me.

"Ainsley?" I put no inflection into my voice. Nothing to give away the lust punching me in the gut.

Smiling, she held out her delicate hand. "Nice to meet you."

Her slender fingers gripped my big paw in a firm handshake, then she slid into the booth across from me.

"Don't be cross with me. I'm so sorry I'm late. Nova has been on my ass since I told her I was stuck in traffic."

Nova was Louisiana's side piece, and the link to my blind date. Out of respect to his ol' lady, I'd never met Nova. I was complicit just knowing about his bullshit. Motherfucker couldn't bring her to the Devil's Pit—our clubhouse—with his ol' lady running the fucking bar. Jinx would slice his dick off.

"Lou Lou reiterated I had to be on time."

I lifted a brow. "You call Louisiana 'Lou Lou'?"

Settling her elbow on the table, she leaned closer. "He says we can't call him Louisiana or Keir," she confided, referring to his given name. "What with his ol' lady and all."

Lou Lou? Sounded like something a favorite aunt called her adorable nephew. Wait 'til I got back to the fucking clubhouse. The next time that motherfucker warned me about the pronunciation of New Orleans, I'd punch him in his fucking mouth.

Ainsley cleared her throat. "Right? I mean, he does have one, doesn't he?"

"An ol' lady?"

She nodded.

If I hadn't ratted him out to Jinx, I certainly wouldn't open my mouth to this girl. I thought she and her friend knew Louisiana's marital status. Apparently, he didn't confine his fuckery only to Jinx. I shrugged. "You tell me."

"I say yes, but Nova says no."

My waitress bounced to the table, tits jiggling underneath her tight purple top. She frowned at Ainsley, sniffed, and glared at me. When she'd brought me my second beer, she'd offered to blow me out back. As much as I once liked a hot mouth on my cock and balls, Monster hadn't even stirred.

Now, he was hard as stone. For Ainsley.

"I've always wanted to go to Mardi Gras," she chirped, smiling at Mira, the waitress. "And I love those green jeans. You should find a gold-colored belt."

"There's an idea," Mira agreed, thawing. "My boss wants me to wear these ugly gold shoes. I won't be caught dead in those things, so I might take your suggestion. Would you like a drink?" She listed sodas and other non-alcoholic offerings.

"I want a Hurricane," Ainsley announced, set her purse on the table, and proceeded to pull out her ID.

Scowling, I scrubbed a hand over my face and reached for my beer, too late remembering I needed a refill.

"See? Twenty-one as of June 30th."

Mira glanced from Ainsley to me and smirked. "Hurricane coming right up. Do you need another beer, Reese?" she purred.

I didn't miss Ainsley's frown at Mira's blatant flirting. But, fuck, young chicks weren't my thing. I couldn't wait to get my hands on Louisiana. What kind of fucking joke was this?

"Yeah, babe," I answered, ignoring Ainsley's clenching jaw. "I need more than that."

I *definitely* didn't dig jealous bitches, young or old. My cock deflated and my grief returned. Trinity had been so fucking perfect. I should've had her on the back of my bike as my woman rather than just a club rat I fucked. In the last weeks of her life, I'd taken steps to make that happen and ordered my brothers to keep their dicks away from her. Though Razor as Prez and Jester as VP outranked me, they'd backed away from her, too.

I just hadn't been able to bring myself to commit, then she was killed, and I missed her every fucking day. Six months later, I still mourned her.

"Whatever you want I'm willing to give, Reese," Mira cooed. "In the meantime, your drinks are coming right up." She winked at me, swept Ainsley with another look, and sashayed away.

Silent, Ainsley saved her ID, placed her wallet back in her purse, and zipped it closed. Her movements were jerky.

The date was already a bust. She was too fucking young; she had my fucking attention more than I liked; and she was the jealous type.

No reason why I shouldn't light into her and send her packing.

I opened my mouth, but her glare fizzled my anger.

"I'm not here for a great romance, Reese," she started. "I'm here for a good time and nothing else. You're a biker, so I *especially* don't want long-term with *you*. I've had enough of them to last a fucking lifetime. But this is what I'm not doing: sitting here simpering and watching pathetically, while other women fall all over you, you eat that shit up and arrange a cock suck or a quick fuck in front of my face. You want Mira as your date for the evening?" She slid out of the seat and stormed to her feet; her whiskey eyes narrowed. "Be my guest and have her."

I didn't think. I acted out of instinct, grabbing her wrist and halting her. Our gazes met, clashed, and my heart pounded. The angry flush on her cheeks, the indignation in her eyes, affected me in an indescribable way. The feel of her delicate wrist, her furious pulse pounding against my fingertips, sent a bolt of electricity down my spine.

"I'm sorry," I heard myself say, when I never apologized to anyone. I owned my motherfuckery. "Stay." She said she only wanted a little fun. I convinced myself that she spoke a truth I could accept. "I'm always a beast when I'm hungry."

"Lou Lou should've warned me. I would've brought raw meat to throw at you until we were served our food."

"Sassy little bitch."

She smiled and relaxed. "Survival tactic."

Chuckling, I released her and nodded to the booth. "Sit," I ordered.

"How can I deny such a heartfelt request?"

Huffing, she slid back into her seat, and I followed suit. Mira walked up to the table, carrying a tray with our drinks.

"Can I have a word with you?" she asked, placing her hand on my bicep once she set our drinks in front of us.

Ainsley wrapped her pink lips around the straw and took a delicate sip, the promise of heaven in her eyes. I wasn't sure if she was trying to tempt me so she'd be my sole focus or if she was hiding a powder keg of anger in the gesture. Straightening, she darted her tongue out and licked her lips, her expression suddenly unreadable. One minute, she offered me a glimpse of passion, and the next I didn't know what the fuck she was thinking.

"It won't take long," Mira pressed.

"I'm not interested," I told her, unable to take my focus away from Ainsley long enough to impart that.

"Asshole," Mira hissed, and stomped away.

"I vote for no tip," Ainsley said. "At least, *I'm* not tipping her. You do what you want with your half."

"So you're one of those 21st century chicks? Splitting checks. Opening your own doors. Getting yourself off. No swallowing."

"You're a biker. Modern or traditional, you likely aren't a gentleman. Besides, we're in the here and now, so that makes you a 21st century man, Reese."

I could listen to the way my name rolled off her tongue for hours.

"However, I was always taught to pay my own way, especially on dates." She shook her head. "Not that I've had many. My older brother gives new meaning to overprotectiveness."

I took in her beautiful features again. "I can understand why. If you were my little sister, I'd fuck up any motherfucker who looked your way."

"Oh my god! That is such a cave man thing to say."

"Although I appreciate your independence, I'm footing tonight's bill."

She glanced around the restaurant with its wooden beams and floors, Mardi Gras colors, and photos of crayfish—crawfish according to *Lou Lou*—steamboats, and buildings I didn't recognize but I presumed were somewhere in Louisiana.

"I will bet you a hundred bucks this food isn't authentic." She sipped her drink again. "The minute I taste a Louisiana dish, I know if the chef has ties there."

"Interesting. What makes you such an expert?"

"My mother was born and raised in New Orleans. My father wasn't, but they made it work." Sadness flickered across her face. "They loved each other until the end."

"How long ago did you lose them?"

"Eleven years ago. In a month. But my brother stepped up to the plate and took care of me like I was his own. He's about your age. Fifteen years older than me."

Ouch.

"You're younger than I expected, though," she continued. I was coming to realize Ainsley was very chatty. "Lou Lou told me you were his age."

"That motherfucker! I'm not fucking forty-two. I'm thirty-one."

She shrugged. "It doesn't matter." Her gaze fell on my cut. "You're a biker," she reminded me again.

"Tell me about your brother. What's his name? What does he do? Where does he hangout? I know a lot of motherfuckers, even those not connected to the life, so I might know him."

"Does it matter?"

"Fuck yeah! I wouldn't want a bullet in my ass if he sees us together. He sounds quite protective."

"He is," she admitted, sighing. "But he's not here. He's out of town and I'd like to push him back to the sidelines."

"Agreed." Ainsley sounded loyal to her brother, despite her frustration at his overprotectiveness. She knew Louisiana was a part of the Royal Bastards MC – Kansas City, which meant she knew my affiliation, too. Heaven forbid, her brother was somehow associated with the Bloody Scorpions. She wouldn't knowingly cavort with the club's enemy because I would be a foe of her brother as well. Assuming, of course, she knew all that much about that fucking club or any of his dealings with them. I returned to the topic of the restaurant. "Where would you like to eat?"

"Aren't you hungry?"

Her question reminded me of the lie I'd blurted to get her to stay.

"Starving."

She laughed, a happy, rich sound that touched my soul and lightened the darkness always chasing me. "You're so full of shit."

"I felt like an asshole and didn't want you to leave," I admitted. "Where do you want to go?"

"We're here now. Let's order."

Once I summoned Mira, I nodded to Ainsley so she could go first.

"Your tip has gone down dramatically because we haven't gotten our warm French bread and butter," she started. She tossed her menu aside, leaned back, and folded her arms. "Remedy that, then we'll order."

Surprised laughter escaped me. Once Mira stormed away, I shook my head. "You're going to get our food spat on."

She picked up her menu and flipped it open. "Nova will bail me out because if that woman spits in my food, I'm beating her ass."

"The face of an angel with the tongue of a devil."

She smirked. "My brother would be furious with me if I end up arrested. He has this totally awesome future planned for me. His life's goal is to see me safely married and far away from KC. Dude has my entire wedding planned. Huge budget. White gown. Veil over my face. The works."

"Well, Miss 21st Century Woman, how very old-fashioned. You are aware a white gown and veil implies purity?"

"Who the hell would fuck me with my brother threatening castration?"

Ainsley

Reese Sinclair was the answer to my prayers. I definitely owed Nova and Lou Lou for choosing a man that I could fall hard for if I allowed myself. Unfortunately, Roman would classify Reese *and* Lou Lou as mortal enemies. My best friend's man knew the danger he placed himself in—Reese didn't. But desperate times called for desperate measures. In all fairness, I hadn't realized my blind date would be one of Lou Lou's brothers. I thought it was a friend outside of the life.

On the other hand, this *was* Lou Lou.

I should've known better than to trust him with setting me up on a date when I really didn't trust him with Nova. His sudden absences without explanation; his insistence we couldn't call him by his road name or his given name; the out-of-way places he took us; and so many other signs that indicated he had another woman. He knew Nova was my best friend and the daughter of the local Bloody Scorpion president. Sometimes, I believed he strung her along for that reason. That dickhead would find humor in sending me on a date with an enemy of my brother's club. *Fucking asshole.* I did not.

My brother meant the world to me, even when I wanted to wring his neck.

Upon the deaths of our parents, Roman dedicated his life away from the club to me. He moved back home, helped me with my homework, learned to cook, and handpicked club girls to babysit me when he couldn't allow me to tag along. He could've easily sent me away and turned his back on the grieving ten-year-old I'd been. But we were close, my parents, brother, and I. Just as our father had been a Bloody Scorpion, Roman had only just become a full patch member, when our parents were shot and killed.

Roman obsessed over my safety. He'd tapped a councilman's son to marry me. The guy was planning to move to New York, a perfect distance between me and trouble in Roman's eyes. Except I couldn't stand the arrogant fuckhead he'd chosen for me and I had yet to accept.

However, every guy *I* chose wasn't good enough. If I couldn't have my dates at the clubhouse, Roman went with me and sat at the fucking table. He wanted someone *he* deemed worthy of me. He definitely didn't want me with a biker.

This weekend, Roman took his flavor of the month away, and I made my move. I had one opportunity for freedom and rebellion. One chance to have my V-card punched without Roman ever finding out.

Reese continued gaping at me. Long enough to allow all the bullshit swimming through my head and threatening to pollute my date.

"You're a virgin?" Reese managed finally.

I nodded. "It isn't a crime against fucking humanity," I grouched.

His gray gaze fell on my mouth, and I licked my lips. I tried my best not to clock his rippling muscles and full sleeves. The intensity on his face should've repelled me, but it drew me like nickel to a magnet. A square jaw gave way to a strong chin and firm, unyielding lips.

I sipped my Hurricane again. It tasted like shit—too much syrup—but whatever.

"Does Louisiana know?"

"Nova probably clued him in. I certainly don't announce my sexual inexperience to random dudes." I shook my head and sipped again. "It isn't their fucking business."

"That motherfucker definitely knew," Reese said flatly. "I thought he was looking out for me."

"He told me that you lost your lady friend a few months ago. He thought I'd cheer you up."

Ignoring Reese's curse, I went in for another sip.

"He had no fucking right bringing up Trinity Parker."

I gasped mid-suck, sending the drink down the wrong way. Luckily, Reese believed my reaction stemmed from the liquid, not the fact that the woman Reese was mourning was my brother's ex, whom he'd killed when he discovered her affiliation with the Royal Bastards.

Chapter Two

Ainsley

Amid my choking at hearing Trinity's name, Mira arrived with the bread. I checked for phlegm, or anything disgusting, and would continue to do so every time she set food on the table.

Once my coughing subsided, I decided to push aside Roman's fuckery and enjoy myself. I could pretend I wasn't about to throw my life away in hopes that my brother would take an ol' lady. The times he tried never worked out. He moved the first one in with us a year after our parents' deaths. That girl hated me. Later I discovered he suspected as much, set up cameras, and saw her punching me in the stomach.

Her body was never found.

Then, there was Trinity, who was apparently immensely popular. My brother thought he'd found 'the one'. Until someone tipped him off that she was a Royal Bastards' club rat and in love with one of the brothers who snubbed her each time she pressed for more. The day she came to the house, I tried to warn her away. We got into a huge argument. Unfortunately, Roman walked in.

He ignored my pleas for her life and dragged her away. Nova told me he'd sent pieces of her back. It fucked with my head so much, I'd taken a leave of absence from school.

I pushed that horror aside, too. My brother was my protector, but a brutal motherfucker to everyone else. Cognizant dissonance and pretense were my best friends until reality smacked me in the fucking face.

I leaned back and allowed Mira to set a steaming cup of gumbo in front of me. The French bread and butter had been perfect, the fried alligator bites and crawfish tails ordered as appetizers were crispy and spicy.

Just as I finished my gumbo, Reese pushed his aside.

I swiped my napkin across my lips. "I cannot tell you how happy I am you didn't ask for potato salad in your gumbo."

Reese snorted. "Louisiana swears that's how it's done in those parts."

"Louisiana is a liar. The only person I've ever met who did that is him. Usually, you get a dollop on the side to counteract the gumbo's spice."

He leaned back and clasped his massive hands, resting them on the table. "So does the food pass muster?"

I tilted my hand from side to side. "Eh. I've had worse."

"But you've had better."

"Yep. From my own kitchen." I would've loved to cook a meal for Reese. An impossible dream that filled me with sadness. I'd soon be all married up. Stiffening my spine, I pasted a smile on my face. "What do you think of the food?"

"So far, so good," he answered. "Left up to me, I would've blown this joint for barbeque."

"You should've told me. I like barbeque."

His smile lit up his face. "Now she tells me."

"You didn't choose this place?"

"Louisiana picked."

An agitated breath escaped me and I shifted in my seat, resting my elbows on the table and leaning forward. "You don't have to answer if you don't want to. I hope that you do." I'd try a different question, since he'd evaded the first one. Pursing my lips, I met his gaze. "*Is* Lou Lou married?"

"What gave you that idea?"

That was a yes. First, he'd punted the response back to me. Now this. Answering a question with a question was classic diversionary tactics in my eyes. I'd play his game.

"He disappears for days at a time. He prefers to call Nova, instead of the other way around. When she does call him, it's always at specific times. They rarely go on real dates. If they do, I'm usually involved as if I'm running interference. If he doesn't live at the clubhouse, Nova doesn't have any other address for him. We have to call him *Lou Lou.* Every time she mentions commitment, he storms away, then breaks up with her, then lures her back with promises and pretty words. It sends my bullshit meter into overdrive. Nova falls for it every fucking time. Is he married or not? I say yes."

"What do you intend to do with any information I give to you? Take it to your friend? Messengers are usually fucked up."

"I don't know," I admitted. "I've known Nova since we were kids. She's two years older than me, but she's a romantic."

"And you aren't?"

"Nope. I have no place for romance. My brother has a revolving door. His two attempts at relationships didn't work. I've witnessed my fair share of shit that I'd love to erase. If I see his hairy ass as he fucks a random woman on the sofa once more, I'm going to fucking scream."

"Don't scream, sweetheart. Get a fucking bat and whack his ass *literally*."

I giggled and Reese smiled. His wink made my heart flutter.

"He gave you the bedroom?" he asked when the moment passed.

"Our family home has three bedrooms and two bathrooms. According to him, privacy is only for a special woman. Before I moved to my own place, I made sure to stay awake when he was out and look at the camera when I heard him to make sure he was alone. If he has a girl with him, I stay in my room until she leaves."

"Good idea." He cocked his head to the side. "My turn to ask you a question."

"Fuck off," I said with a laugh. "You never answered *my* question."

"I did. In so many words. A direct answer might give you information that makes you culpable if this ends badly. Say he *is* married. You don't tell your friend, shit goes sideways, and she discovers you knew the score. What then? She'd blame you for withholding the information."

"I think he's married and I've told her so."

"That's your gut feeling?"

"It is, but Nova doesn't believe me."

"Always follow your instincts, Ainsley."

"Fuck, I knew it!"

"So now what?"

I didn't know *that*. Nova adored Louisiana. They'd been in their cycle of misery for two years. "What's your question?" I asked irritably.

"You said you want a night of fun with me, but I doubt it's the usual. So what did you have in mind?"

"Conversation for starters."

"Yeah, I noticed you like to talk as much as you like to eat." He lifted slightly and pretended to check me out. "For such an itty-bitty thing, you sure the fuck can scarf food."

"Oh, hush," I teased, waving my hand between us to dismiss his words.

"You want dinner as well." Reese nodded to the empty gumbo bowls. "What else?"

"Dancing and dick."

REESE

It escaped me how Ainsley continued shocking me. She intrigued me, though I knew it was temporary. When I took an ol' lady, I didn't want someone so young and bubbly. I wouldn't be responsible for extinguishing her light. Nor would I put her at risk. As long as a Bloody Scorpion walked the fucking earth, my brothers and I and anyone associated with us was in danger. I had a personal vendetta against Roman Mac.

I wanted that motherfucker's head hung as a trophy for what he did to Trinity. It was senseless, and I wouldn't rest until I'd spilled all his blood.

Ainsley and her desire for one night of fun would've been perfect for me. If she wasn't a fucking virgin. From what I heard, virgins grew attached, and that was a complication I neither needed nor wanted.

"Let me get this straight, Ainsley. You asked your friend to set you up for a night of fun and fucking? A no-strings attached v-card punching?"

She considered my words, then nodded. "That's about the size of it."

"She said I have the perfect motherfucker in mind?"

"Not immediately. She called me two or three days ago and gave me the details. She said I have the entire weekend, so if I wasn't comfortable giving it up on our first night, we could meet again tomorrow night."

"I could've looked like Venom and you would want to fuck me?"

The idea annoyed the fuck out of me.

"Bomb ass movie. Wrong idea. Nova knew I wanted a handsome guy of my choosing as my first."

Quite the roundabout way of complimenting me. "Of your choosing? What the fuck does that mean? You didn't choose me. She did."

"I disagree. She connected us. The decision is mine."

She was hiding something. Secrets shadowed the depths of her eyes. I wanted to uncover every mystery she kept from me. Bare her beautiful skin slowly and trail my tongue over every inch.

My nostrils flared.

"I like you more than I should, Reese," she said softly. "I've never participated in the actual act, but I've seen more than my share of fucking." Leaning back, she jutted her chin out. "I want...I want a man like you. Everyone I know fears my brother and my life is about to drastically change. This is my last chance at a semblance of control."

That sounded ominous. "What does that mean?"

"I owe my brother my life, but I'll never have the freedom to choose my own boyfriend, so I will agree to marry the man he picked out for me."

"*What*?" My one word snarl drew the attention of nearby patrons. "You can't piss away your fucking life out of guilt. Absolutely not."

"My brother deserves to live his life without me underfoot." She wagged a finger at me. "We just met, so chill."

Chill my ass! "He did what he was supposed to do. More than that, that motherfucker *chose* to do it." I drew in a deep breath to calm myself. Ainsley Valois was a fucking handful. "What about school?"

"Something happened a few months ago and I took a break. I want to be a preschool teacher. I have a job at a nursery."

"Ainsley—"

"If this is too much, I understand, Reese. If you feel as if I'm just using you for dick, I understand that as well. I like you a lot," she repeated as if I'd already forgotten her confession from two minutes ago. "Too much." Vulnerability crept into her face and she swallowed. "But it's so complicated. More than I can explain."

"Try me. I'm a good listener."

"If I wanted you to hear," she retorted.

"Your prerogative, princess. Here's mine. I'm not fucking you unless you swear to me you won't throw away your fucking life."

"I can always lie."

"You could, but I'd be madder than a motherfucker, and you don't want me to lose my fucking temper."

"What? You'd punch me? Kill me?"

"I don't hurt women," I snarled, "but I have no problem fucking up a motherfucker who wouldn't deserve you."

Her eyes rounded. Now, she was getting the fucking picture. "You couldn't kill Dayton Morgan. Do you know the hell that would bring to you?"

She was planning to marry that pompous fuckhead? Fuck, I'd want someone else to fuck me too if I was set to become the bride of fucking Frankenstein. She sounded so alarmed, I decided not to tell her I meted out justice and retribution to whoever deserved it. Their status in society didn't matter. If they fucked up or crossed a line, they died.

I swallowed my chuckle. The enforcer mentality survived and thrived. That had been my position for years until the Trinity situation and my brothers decided they wanted me close so I wouldn't go off the deep end.

"How many times have you been kissed?" I asked crossly.

"A few."

That knowledge worsened my mood. "Ever sucked dick? Had your pussy licked? Anything?"

Clamping her mouth shut, she glared at me. *Sonofabitch.*

"With Dayton," she finally pushed out.

My eyes almost popped from my fucking head. "You kissed Dayton," I decided, because she sure as shit couldn't be telling me she'd allowed him to touch her any other way.

A blush stole into her cheeks. "He asked me to go down on him to make sure he could properly teach me. But he said he doesn't eat pussy, so he didn't return the favor." She looked at me warily. "He gave me very high marks in my oral skills."

Color me stupid, I didn't think I could get anymore fucking appalled. How wrong I was. I searched my brain trying to remember which clubs dealt with any of our local politicians. We didn't fuck with council members. We aimed higher. But I needed someone to help me fuck up Dayton Morgan. If I paid an ally of ours with ties to local leaders enough money, I'd take care of her problem.

"I'm going to call an Uber, Reese," Ainsley said.

"I'll give you a ride," I said harshly, then regretted the words at the filthy images of her riding my cock rising in my head. "Just say the words."

"You're not compromising on this, are you?"

"Give me your phone," I ordered.

"What?"

"You heard me."

She sniffed but did as I instructed. Once I had her phone, I saved my contact information, then called my number, so I'd get her shit. I held the phone out to her.

"I don't fuck around with another man's woman," I barked. "Wouldn't want it done to me, so I won't do it to another motherfucker. But it's my way or no way, Ainsley."

She snatched the phone from me. "I haven't accepted his proposal yet." She drew in another breath, opened her mouth, then snapped it shut.

"And you won't," I decreed.

She glowered at me. When I lifted my brow, she gave me a sullen look but shook her head.

I wasn't sure what the fuck came over me or where the fuck I intended this to go, but for now, Ainsley belonged to me and that was all that mattered.

CHAPTER THREE

REESE

After unlocking her door, Ainsley grabbed my hand and guided me into her dimly lit apartment. I closed and locked the door behind us, then allowed her to tug me through the living room, where outlines of a sofa, chair, and tables were grouped on one wall. Picture frames sat on one of the end tables, but I couldn't see the actual images. A breakfast bar separated the living room and compact kitchen, all of which clipped through my brain at the same pace Ainsley pulled me to a door at the end of a very short hallway. She opened the door, flipped on a light, and stepped aside, so I could enter.

It looked like the fucking Easter Bunny hopped his ass in here and farted pastels. Yellow ceiling, green floor, pink wall, blue wall, lilac wall, and a striped wall with a combination of those five colors. I appreciated how big her bed was. I hated all the fluffy fucking pastel-colored pillows piled on it.

"I don't have anything other than water to drink," she said, shifting from foot to foot. She hadn't removed her cowboy boots, her barely-there crop top or her little denim skirt. "I should've told you on the way here."

"It's okay. I'm not here to drink, babe."

She nodded. Pursed her lips. Drew in a deep breath, walked to me, and dropped to her knees. Her fingers went to my zipper, but I stepped back.

"What the fuck are you doing?"

"Getting the dick suck out of the way. Dayton says guys always start off with that."

I needed to fucking kill Dayton on GP.

"Nova hates him. She thinks he's a prick and is only using me."

I agreed with her friend, but I kept my mouth shut and held out my hand to her.

Although I saw her confusion, she accepted my help and stood. She was nervous. I could see it in her eyes. I threaded my fingers through her silky curls, leaned in, and brushed my lips over hers.

That quick taste wasn't enough. Taking her face between my hands, I dipped my head again. This time, I coaxed my tongue between her lips and swept into her mouth, enjoying the way she melted into me. I grunted, roaming my fingers over her belly and sliding underneath her crop top. Her bralessness pleased me greatly. My hands cupped her tits and I thumbed her nipples to hard little points.

She gasped into my mouth, and it vibrated through me. Our kiss deepened, turned hot and passionate, sloppy even, but I didn't give a fuck. I tore my mouth from hers, long enough to remove her top. Her tits were round and firm with pretty pink nipples that I couldn't wait to feast upon.

"Undress and meet me under the covers," I told her. Boots were a fucking vibe killer because they were a bitch to remove. She was nervous enough. I didn't intend to stick my dick anywhere in her before I got an affirmation that she really wanted to do this. That's as far as my chivalry went.

She sat on the edge of her bed and removed her boots. *She* struggled with them, so they would've been a fucking nightmare for me. When she stood again, her fingers hovered at the button on her skirt.

Pretending not to notice, I turned my back to give her privacy, then whistled as I removed my own clothing. I took my time unholstering the guns strapped on my sides and laying them on her dresser, then setting my cut carefully on top. I didn't care where anything else landed.

My cut was sacred.

Finding her in bed and under the covers didn't surprise me. Her gaze fell on Monster and her eyes widened. He rose proud and wide. If we went through with this, I'd make sure to get her nice and wet before I buried myself inside her. At the thought, precum gathered on my dick tip.

Since I'd never fucked a virgin before, I kept my mouth shut. I didn't want to add to her anxiety about my size or where I intended to put my lips.

I slipped underneath the covers and pulled her into the crook of my arm, allowing her to adjust to being in the company of a man without clothes.

"Seeing and doing are two different things," she started.

"They are," I agreed, keeping it simple.

"I didn't think I'd feel so shy at being naked in front of a man." She tipped her head back to look at me. "Dayton just wanted my top off. He'd intended to come on my tits, then decided he needed to train me to like the taste of cum."

I stiffened and tightened my hold on her.

"I might like it better if he'd warned me first, you know?"

"Stop talking," I ordered.

"You're so fucking bossy."

"Ainsley, shut the fuck up. I'm trying to give you a little tenderness but you're ruining the fucking mood."

"I talk when I'm nervous."

"You talk just to fucking talk."

"Is that a bad thing?"

"In the big picture? No. Now? Fuck yeah."

"Can we talk for a bit? That can be tender, too."

I wasn't winning this one unless I put a gag in her mouth. "As long as it isn't about Dayton."

"You almost sound jelly, which is insane. I'd classify that as insta-love. You might decide to stalk me."

I grinned. "That will never happen, sweetheart. I feel the same way about jealous chicks, so I can assure you jealousy is an emotion that never afflicts me."

"That means you'll never let your guard down enough to care what a woman does."

"Probably not."

She squirmed against me and the hard point of one of her nipples pressed into my side. "Did you, um, did it matter what Trinity did?"

"Louisiana shouldn't have brought her up. That's my personal business."

"Did you love her?"

"No," I said honestly. "I don't believe in fucking love, Ainsley. Just like you."

"I don't believe in romance. I'm a big advocate for falling in love."

"You can't have one without the other."

"I can argue that point."

"Not in the fucking bed!" I snapped. "Every time you move your luscious body, my cock jerks. He needs relief."

"I can ask why you refer to your cock with a pronoun, but I don't think you'd appreciate that conversation."

"I sure as shit wouldn't. He also has a name, if that makes you feel better."

She roared with laughter. "You named your dick?"

Chuckling, I turned on my side and faced her. "Have you changed your mind, sweetheart?"

"No, Reese," she whispered.

"Then trust me to take care of you."

"Lou Lou really built you up. He said you've been celibate for six months and before that you didn't sleep around much."

"I wasn't aware he had such an interest in my dick."

She ignored that. "I'm not on any birth control."

That didn't make sense if she knew she wanted to fuck. "I brought condoms." Not going to lie and say I wasn't disappointed I wouldn't fuck her bare, but I appreciated her honesty.

"Nova helped me research and understand the rhythm method. She said sex for the first time is uncomfortable enough without condoms and said I might have an allergic reaction to them. Anything from anaphylaxis to gastrointestinal, skin, and respiratory."

"An allergic reaction?" I'd never heard of such bullshit nor could I believe Ainsley bought into that. Just what the fuck was her friend trying to accomplish by making Ainsley afraid of condoms? "I'm clean, but there are other reasons for protection."

"Nova wouldn't lead me astray. She wants my first time to be memorable and enjoyable. She's like a sister to me and is really the only woman I have to talk about stuff like this."

I wasn't keen on trusting a chick who fucked around with a married man. Louisiana's age and experience gave him an advantage over such a younger woman. Still, she was an adult with free will, which she used every time she saw him. I refused to fucking believe she didn't have an inkling that he had a wife. Jinx meant everything to that stupid motherfucker. Nova must've had signs about his marital status.

"She said you'd appreciate it too," Ainsley went on, unaware of my racing thoughts. "Condoms take away from a guy's pleasure."

"But add to our peace of mind. I'd think you'd want such assurances, too."

"Nova swears by it, and she hasn't ended up pregnant. There's a failure rate of less than five percent when done correctly. We counted and recounted my calendar. My period ended three days ago, so I won't be fertile for another two."

"I don't know anything about the rhythm method," I confessed. "That means I'd have to trust your word and, fuck, failure means a baby."

"My brother would kill me, so I agree. Failure isn't an option. You can trust my word because I trust Nova's. She's always looked out for me."

"Are you sure about that?"

Admittedly, I wanted to bury myself balls deep in Ainsley without any barrier. Even if *I* didn't know or trust Nova, Ainsley did. Louisiana also felt something for her to allow their affair to last so long.

"We don't really know each other, Reese. A condom would make it even more impersonal."

"Your logic is ass backwards."

"Maybe, but it's how I feel."

"Remind me to slap your fucking brother when I see him."

She snapped her brows together. "Why?"

"STDs are a thing. He should've warned you about diseased dicks."

"Yours isn't. Lou Lou showed me your last test."

Fuck that motherfucker. I couldn't get too angry because it would ruin the vibe, but I couldn't wait to see Louisiana. He must've gone to my room and snapped a photo of the test I'd taken a few weeks ago. I hadn't fucked in six months, but I got checked annually.

A warning ran through my head. This was a bad fucking idea, but for now, I let it go. We'd spend the night talking instead of fucking. I pulled her closer and kissed her again. She had the sweetest mouth of anyone I'd ever met. One day, I'd spend hours just kissing her.

Trailing my lips down the column of her throat, I turned her onto her back, inhaling her delicate perfume. I licked between the valley of her breasts before worshipping both those beauties with my tongue. She gasped and sighed, slipping her fingers through my hair, her touch igniting my blood. I slid lower, careful not to spook her before I kissed paradise. As badly as I wanted to finger fuck her, Ainsley was skittish.

I settled between her thighs and kissed the delicate skin on each side. I should've kissed up her legs, but the scent of her arousal drove me insane. If I didn't taste her, I'd lose my fucking mind. The moment I wrapped my arms around her thighs and sniffed her seam, she lifted onto her elbows.

"Wait! If I would've known you eat pussy, I would've taken another shower." She tugged on my hair. "Let me run and—"

I swiped my tongue against her slit, cutting her off mid-sentence. A moan replaced her words. I licked her again. She tilted her hips up.

"Spread your legs wider, baby," I directed, releasing my grip on her.

She complied without question, then slid her fingers over her clit.

Growling, I speared my tongue into her pussy and alternated between licks and sucks.

She grinded against my mouth, tweaking her nipples, her head thrown back.

"Oh god, oh god, oh god," she chanted as her orgasm washed over and she went wild against my tongue.

I was so fucking hard and hot for her, if she turned me away now I'd have to rub one out before I left. Rising over her, I poised my cock at her entrance.

"Are you sure, Ainsley?"

"Yes, Reese," she said hoarsely.

That was all I needed to hear. I slid partially into her, hoping she'd lost her hymen years ago through exercise, a doctor's exam, or something random. She hadn't, and I swore under my breath. I didn't know how to fuck a virgin, so I drove into her as I normally would and went still at her intake of breath.

Goddamn it, she was tight. My spine tingled at the way her pussy walls gripped my cock. Giving her a moment to catch her breath and get her bearings allowed me to do the same. I captured her lips again as I moved my cock in a slow in-and-out motion. She placed a tender kiss at the base of my neck and wrapped her legs around my hips, opening herself to me.

Her slick heat drew me deeper, urged me to powerful thrusts. Moaning into my mouth, she moved to the rhythm of my hips.

"Fuck, baby," I murmured, the only words I could manage. I wouldn't last much longer. Determined to tip her over the edge with me inside her, I slid my hand between us and found her clit, caressing her.

"Oh my god, Reese, that feels so good." She licked her lips, her eyes glazed. "You feel so good."

Her eyes rolled back in her head, and she released a wail, falling apart under me and tipping me over the edge. As I spilled my seed inside her, the pressure that had been building in my balls and at the base of my spine released and left nothing but bone-deep satisfaction.

Afterward, I drew her into my arms again.

"That was amazing," she said groggily. "I can become addicted to you."

I wanted to clean her up, but I hated to move away from the warmth of her body. I hadn't fucked since the day before Trinity's death and I'd been awake since the early morning hours, so I allowed my exhaustion to claim me.

Piss awakened me. More specifically, *needing* a piss. Sometime during the night, Ainsley had stolen all the covers. Now, they were tangled around her legs. Smiling and shaking my head, I carefully tugged my arm from under her head and went in search of the bathroom, wondering if I'd find fucking unicorns and rainbows on the walls. Only two other doors stood in the hallway. I opened the closest one first and found a closet filled with towels, bed sheets, and an extra comforter.

Behind the second door, I hit the jackpot. Once I relieved my bladder, I headed to the kitchen for a bottled water. A half empty case sat on the counter, so I took one and drank the entire bottle within seconds. Turning to go back to the bedroom, a picture frame caught my eye. The words 'Best Big Brother' were chiseled at the top of the wooden frame.

Bending to better see the man who wanted her to give up her fucking life on a motherfucker like Dayton Morgan, I blinked. Squinted. Blinked again. Fuck, I even straightened and bent again.

A tall man with skin slightly darker than Ainsley's smirked toward the camera. Even from the photo, his smirk mocked me and my nostrils flared.

Roman Mac was Ainsley's brother. I wasn't sure how since they had different last names, but it didn't fucking matter. Whether she knew my club and her brother's club were archrivals, I didn't know and I sure as shit didn't give a fuck. She could've mentioned that her brother was a fucking biker.

I stormed back to the bedroom and went for my guns. Roman killed Trinity and she was an innocent victim. An eye for a fucking eye. It was only right I took Ainsley from him.

I stalked to her side of the bed, lifted the gun...and couldn't do it. She was sweet and soft in slumber. I doubted I could've pulled the trigger had she been awake. She was an alluring combination of hellcat, chatterbox, and angel. Trinity needed avenging, but I couldn't use Ainsley to do it.

Brushing my lips over hers, I backed away and dressed quietly, hoping she didn't awaken. I'm not sure how I would've responded in such a confrontation.

I didn't know where my disappointment came from. She was just a random girl. Even if I'd seen her again, the relationship would've fizzled eventually.

They always did.

The evening I'd spent with Ainsley slid through my mind. When I'd asked for her brother's name, she hadn't answered.

Fuck.

She knew our clubs were mortal enemies. It was why she hadn't turned on the light in her living room when we'd arrived.

I glowered at her. Before I shook the fuck out of her, I snatched up my keys and walked out of her bedroom. A big photo on her living room wall grabbed my attention. It wasn't Roman or his father or even Ainsley as a child. It was her mother, a pretty black woman with gorgeous brown eyes.

Ainsley was biracial. I would've pegged her as Latina or Greek, not half black. Not that it mattered. She was my enemy's sister. If she was a fucking Navi, it wouldn't have changed a thing.

Without another word, I left and went to my bike. Before I rode away, I texted Ainsley.

I'd also block her because I never wanted to hear from her again and I refused to tempt myself if she ignored my order and called me anyway.

CHAPTER FOUR

ROMAN

Shoving Kylie away from me and throwing the covers aside, I stumbled out of bed and made it to the bathroom for a piss. Once I washed my hands and threw cold water on my face, I gazed into the dingy bathroom mirror. Bloodshot eyes stared back at me. Stubbly jaw. Unkempt hair. And just general fucking exhaustion.

Taking Kylie away was supposed to be a fuck fest and a break from all the bullshit. She wanted me to put her on the back of my bike as *mine*. I wasn't sure I wanted that or could give myself to her or any woman ever again. Not after the way Trinity played me for a fucking jackass.

She'd ripped away the small piece of my heart not reserved for my little sister. I don't know who the fuck sent me the video of her and Reese motherfucking Sinclair, where she was proclaiming her love and begging that fuckhead for a shot. *Two* fucking days after she claimed she carried *my* goddamn baby. If I could kill that two-timing bitch again, I would.

Not only had she fucking played me, but she'd made me Reese's sloppy seconds.

Cunt.

Clenching my jaw, I scrubbed a hand over my face, then splashed more water to cool my temper and to wake the fuck up, so I could call Ainsley. She hated when I went on benders, but somehow always knew. The kid was brilliant.

She had a bright future ahead of her. I knew she disliked Dayton. I couldn't stand that prick either, but shit kicked off on a dime. Since Trinity's death, the Bloody Scorpions and Royal Bastards had been circling one another, seeking the perfect opportunity to strike and resume our deadly feud so I needed Ainsley safely away.

Dayton swore he was smitten with Ainsley and would keep her safe for me. If I survived and Ainsley still hadn't warmed up to Dayton, I'd kill him and bring her back home.

And if I bit it? That was a real concern of mine. Ainsley might be stuck in a loveless situation, although I was counting on that asshole to romance her and show her how special she was to him.

A ringing phone peeled in the morning's silence. Immediately, I knew it was Ainsley based on the ringtone, *Wind Beneath My Wings*. Seized by worry, I rushed to my nightstand, but she'd already disconnected.

Fuck! It was just after seven on a fucking Saturday morning. Ainsley slept in until eight or nine. Kylie's big blue eyes popped open, and she shot into a sitting position, her auburn hair a mass of tangles and curls falling around her.

"Church bells woke me up," she mumbled and fell back against her pillow.

Grabbing my phone, I snickered. "Nope, babe. It was just Ainsley."

"*Just* Ainsley?" She snorted. "If only."

I stiffened. No one fucked with my little sister and came away unscathed. Before I issued *one* warning to Kylie, since I liked her, my phone rang again.

"What's wrong?" No use for pleasantries. She wasn't calling me so early for shits and giggles.

Her sniffle traveled through the line and my heart seized.

"What's the matter, Ainsley? Talk *now*," I roared.

"I just...I just had a nightmare," she said hoarsely as if she'd been sobbing for hours.

"A nightmare?" I asked skeptically.

True, they plagued her from time-to-time, but she hadn't had one in months.

She sniffled again. Ainsley wasn't a crier, so what the fuck happened?

"I shouldn't have called. It's...it's nothing. I just...I just...I can't accept Dayton's proposal."

Fuck, she was back to this shit. I thought we'd settled the argument.

"I don't love him, Roman. I...*please* don't make me. I moved out to give you space to live your own life. I swear I won't interfere...just...*please*. I want love." A little sob escaped her. "Romance. Passion."

Distaste roiled in my gut. "Passion?" I barked. "That has to do with fucking. Generally, a lot of fucking and before you have a fucking ring. It's not happening, Ainsley. Dayton likes and respects you. He'll make an excellent husband and give you everything I can't—"

Hysterical laughter broke through her tears. I couldn't imagine what the fuck had her so upset. I knew Ainsley. She was a snark, but naïve as hell, which was partially my fault. Kylie, *Trinity*, bitches older than her, had grand ideas of romance. Not Ainsley. Until I ignored her pleas not to kill Trinity, she'd been a top student. She was a responsible young woman and took no bullshit.

"Are you on the rag, Ains?"

Another sobbed escaped her. "No."

Fuck, this was bad. She didn't hand my ass to me on a platter for a question she deemed personal and none of my fucking business.

"Is Nova still there?" She'd told me she was spending the weekend with Ainsley.

"She's asleep."

I squinted. One reason Ainsley demanded that big fucking bed was because of her girls' nights that sometimes turned into slumber parties. The small apartment didn't have room for an air mattress, although I'd recently ordered the manager to find my little sister a bigger place for the same price. Motherfucker was still salty that I painted Ainsley's bedroom floor green. But she'd wanted it, so she got it.

If Nova was really in that apartment, she would be next to Ainsley and awake because of the sobs. A fucking apocalypse couldn't awaken my sister. Nova was a notoriously light sleeper. When I took on the responsibility of Ainsley, I, unfortunately, became responsible for her best friend whenever she visited. That kid still pissed me off regularly. Case in point, when she hit on me and pitched a bitch because I turned her down and asked her if she was out of her fucking mind.

"I have to go, Roman."

"Put Nova on the phone."

"I told you she's asleep."

I scowled. "Wake her the fuck up."

"No."

I gritted my teeth. "I need to get breakfast, Ainsley," I grumbled. "I'll hit the road afterward." In the meantime, I'd send a couple brothers to watch Ainsley's apartment.

Something was up, and I'd bet my bike Nova wasn't there and hadn't been there.

If Dayton wasn't with me, I might suspect he'd charmed his way into Ainsley's bed. But he wanted to escape the watchful eye of his father and the press for an evening at a casino. He was twenty-five and sheltered, with more political aspirations than his father.

"Stop thinking," Ainsley ordered, sounding more like herself. "Nothing's going on. I told you I had a bad dream. That's i-it."

I might've believed her if she hadn't stuttered over that last word.

"Don't leave because of me, Ro," she said quietly. "I'm fine. I just…" She huffed and I swore another sob wrapped around that release of breath. "I'll marry him. I love you. Bye."

"Wait, Ainsley—"

She disconnected.

"Fuck!"

"Dayton Morgan will make Ainsley miserable," Kylie said around a yawn. I'd forgotten I had company. "He's an abusive asshole who loves to force his cock down a woman's throat."

I blinked. "Excuse me?"

"It's true. I'll bet you ten dollars he's made Ainsley suck his dick."

"You're a fucking liar." The alternative was that motherfucker played me and turned me into a fucking fool. That was a mistake. But if he forced Ainsley to give him a dick suck? *That* was a death sentence. "Fair warning, cunt, don't fuck with my little sister. I will rip your fucking head off and pitch it into the Missouri."

Her eyes widened. "I don't have no problem with Ainsley."

"Your earlier comment suggests otherwise. *Just* Ainsley? If only," I reminded her in case she'd forgotten. "Now, you're lying about her almost fiancée."

"That came out wrong. I just...I like Ainsley, but your entire life is wrapped around her and the club. You're pushing her out instead of letting her figure shit out on her own. She's a big girl and she's not afraid to ask for what she wants. If she needs your help, she'll ask, Roman."

"Stay the fuck out of my family business. I'm doing what's best for her."

"If she doesn't want it, it isn't best," Kylie snapped.

"You've put this shit in her head."

"I did not! She barely talks to me because you fuck everything you see. In her eyes, I'm just your latest pussy to fuck."

"You are," I snarled. It was too fucking early in the morning for all this bullshit. I'd gotten up for a piss, not more fucking problems. "You give good head and have a hot pussy. There's nothing else I want from you."

Bursting into tears, she yanked the pillow from the bed and lobbed it at me, then stormed to the bathroom and slammed the door shut.

Fuck!

I hurriedly dressed, grabbed my smokes, then headed to Dayton's room. That little asshole had some explaining to do. I probably should've questioned Kylie further instead of flying off the fucking handle. Except Ainsley and the entire situation was a sensitive subject.

Eleven years ago, Royal Bastard motherfuckers targeted our father and sprayed his fucking car, not realizing he only took the cage when he and Mom went out. She was killed, too. Ainsley slept through it all in the back seat. She'd had an ear infection and Mom plied her with Tylenol to help the pain. The medicine coupled with her ability to sleep through a fucking earthquake guaranteed she hadn't awakened.

Somehow, the bullets had missed her. The coppers thought when Dad slammed on the brakes so suddenly, Ainsley tumbled to the floor and missed getting hit. When I arrived, she was just awakening. I don't think she saw our dead parents, but I was pretty damn sure that day invaded her subconscious and fueled her nightmares. She always spoke of a lot of blood and holes in Mom and Dad and the smell of burning tires.

That day changed my entire world and I don't think I ever recovered. I'd been so fucking happy that Ainsley survived, I swore I'd dedicate my life to her until the day I trusted someone else to do it for me.

Anger made me pound on Dayton's door. "Open this motherfucker up, Dayton," I demanded, not caring if I awakened the entire fucking motel. If I wasn't so worried about Ainsley, I'd kick the door in. Couldn't do it now because I didn't want to end up in the tank. "Dayton!"

"Jesus, what?" Dayton demanded, cracking the door so only his long fucking nose poked out. He didn't remove the privacy latch.

"We need to talk, Pinocchio."

"It's not even eight in the morning, Roman."

I tried to push my way in, but he resisted just as fiercely, aided by that fucking latch. "Open the door. I'm paying for the room, asshole."

A green eye replaced the long nose. "Fuck!"

"Dayton?" a female voice purred. "What's going on? Come back to bed, baby. I want to suck you off again."

Disbelief, fury, and outrage warred for space inside me and came out in a furious growl.

"I can explain," Dayton said quickly.

The moment he removed the latch, I shoved the door open and slammed his ass against the wall. The waitress who'd served us last night at the casino swept her gaze over me and smiled.

"I can explain," Dayton repeated, walking into my line of vision with his hands raised in supplication. "It isn't what you think. It's just a paid fling." His Adam's apple bobbed. "Don't tell Ainsley. Please, Roman. It would break my heart to lose her."

The chick cackled.

"I-I just want some experience to know how to please her when we get married."

Motherfucker faced me, so he didn't see the waitress roll her eyes and shake her head. She knew something about Ainsley.

I smiled at Dayton and patted his head. "I understand."

Face-to-face, he looked decent. Ainsley found him nice-looking. I assumed she hadn't seen his profile.

"Pre-wedding jitters."

Dayton nodded. "I love your little sister so much. She hasn't even accepted my proposal." He rocked on his heels and scratched his jaw. "It's *pre-engagement* jitters. I love her," he reiterated.

Motherfucker's nose grew by ten inches. It would be the first to go, followed by his lying fucking lips.

I transferred my gaze to the woman glowering at motherfucker's back. "Dayton mentioned Ainsley?"

She clamped her jaw shut and turned away.

I dug a grand out of my wallet. "Money's yours if you tell me what you know, babe."

"She knows nothing!" Dayton cried. "I thought you liked and trusted me. I thought—"

"I need my car repaired," the waitress cut in. "Make it two and I'll talk."

I only had five more on me. "Take it or leave it," I told her.

She held out her hand.

"Talk first," I ordered.

"Ainsley got dark hair and, uh, like amber eyes?"

"Enough! Shut the fuck up now," Dayton ordered.

Elbowing him in the fucking head, I watched as he dropped like a sack of shit, then I lit a cigarette. "How do you know how my sister looks?"

Turning on her back, she stared at the ceiling, revealing a luscious rack. Fuck, I wouldn't mind motorboating those beauties. She heaved in a breath and her tits jiggled.

"He got a video of her," she finally confessed.

A video sounded innocent enough, but her tone suggested it was something I wouldn't fucking like.

"I don't think she knew he was recording her. It's just a short clip where he comes in her mouth when she wasn't expecting it. She gagged, he ordered her to swallow, and then the video ends."

Dayton stirred, wiggling on the carpet like a fucking worm. Ainsley was a woman now, which still blew my fucking mind. Neither here nor there. I didn't want her with a biker because I didn't want her caught in the crossfire like our mother had been. I hadn't wanted her with one of those high school freaks because teenaged boys had big fucking mouths, and I tried not to kill women and anyone under eighteen.

In my eyes, absolutely no one was good enough for her. And, yet, Cyrus Morgan swore to me his candy ass son would be perfect. The kid had a clean record, earned good grades, and came from excellent stock. Most of all, he had money, connections, and was headed to New York. Cyrus even claimed Dayton hadn't had many girlfriends because he didn't want to bring shame on his future wife.

Corny and pathetic, but whatever. He'd sounded so perfect for Ainsley. I didn't want to believe the waitress. Just as I hadn't believed Kylie.

Unfortunately, when I ordered him to unlock his phone and show the clip in question to me, I discovered the truth. Seeing was worse than hearing because Ainsley was on her fucking knees and topless. I knew she didn't have a shirt on because the camera captured them from a side angle. Presumably so he'd have an excellent view of his cock sliding in and out of her mouth.

He tightened his grip on her hair, held her head in place, and smirked at the camera before coming. She jerked away and gagged. In response, he grabbed a handful of her hair, tipped her head back and ordered her to swallow his jizz.

My blood threatened to melt my fucking veins and boil through my skin. Rage was too mild a word for what I felt. Somehow, I calmed myself. That fucking coward would go into hiding and I needed to keep my focus where it belonged.

I walked to the waitress and handed the money to her, then set the phone back on the nightstand. The heat of Dayton's miserable gaze followed my every move.

"I can explain, Roman," he said again.

I'm surprised my smile didn't crack my fucking face. "She's your future wife. I have no place in your relationship." I widened my grin. "Especially your intimate moments."

Puffing out his chest, he hopped to his feet and dusted off his expensive trousers. "Right, right. I knew you'd understand. Maybe you can get one of the club girls to give her tips. She can't suck cock to save her life. And, just so you'd know, I didn't touch her pussy. I only eat special pussy and since I'm marrying Ainsley, she don't cut it. I also like that the white veil will mean something on the wedding day." He finished with a clap to my shoulder.

He'd bleed to death if I cut his cock and balls away too soon. I still rearranged the order of his dismemberment: Fingers, hands, lips, nose, tongue, balls, cock.

"What time are we going back to the casino?" he asked.

"Change of plans." I didn't want anyone to say we'd been together today. "I was an asshole to Kylie and I want to spend the day making it up to her. You're on your own today."

Grinning, he winked at the waitress. "I intend to fuck your mouth raw, babe."

She glanced at me. I didn't know if she'd finger me when he turned up missing, so I shrugged and smiled as if I didn't have a fucking care in the world.

"I have a thing for bikers," she said, staring at my cut. "Do you and your girl want to join us? You can fuck me while Dayton fucks her."

Dayton's eyes lit up. "You're my kind of woman, babe."

I needed to add eyeballs to my list. "Kylie likes her cunt eaten—"

"Fuck yeah," Dayton crowed. "I'll eat that hot box. Tell him, babe." He winked at me and puffed out his chest. "I drowned in her pussy juice and licked her asshole."

"You tongue fucked my ass," she agreed.

He patted my back again. "She thought the way Ainsley gagged was the funniest shit she ever saw. Said I should've slapped her across her face. That's how she learned to suck good dick."

I nodded to her. "Can you come with me? I just remembered I have a few more Bennies in my room."

She jumped out of bed, unashamed of her nudity and the dried cum on her thighs. As she passed Dayton, he grabbed her and kissed her.

"Whenever you're ready," she said.

"My rooms five fucking doors away. Get a sheet."

"My friend works night shifts here. She said the cameras on the floors are down. Only the one by the front desk works."

"Don't take too long," Dayton called as I led the waitress into the hallway.

Inside my room, I found Kylie back in bed, her eyes red and swollen. When she saw the waitress, she sucked in a breath.

"Roman—"

Ignoring her, I sat on the edge of the bed, pulled Dayton's slut closer and buried my face in the valley of her tits. Her skin was soft and warm, even if the scent of that motherfucker's cologne turned my stomach. Behind me, Kylie released a sob. I trailed my hand along the waitress's curves down to her pussy. I fingered her clit and licked between her tit crevice. She gasped. When I sucked one of her nipples into my mouth, she cried out. Grabbing her waist, I deposited her on the bed.

"Ride her mouth, Kylie," I ordered.

Swiping her cheeks, Kylie scrambled into position, opening her pussy lips and revealing her swollen clit.

"Don't suck it," she breathed. "I like my clit licked. I come quicker."

The waitress giggled. "Okay."

Kylie's strong leg and thigh muscles allowed her to hover slightly above the waitress's lips. Her tongue darted out and swept across Kylie's slit. Hesitantly at first, then faster and relentless, sending Kylie into a frenzy. Throwing her head back, she relaxed against the waitress's mouth and grinded, her D-cups bouncing, the headboard slamming against the wall, her screams filling the room.

Her orgasm left her weak and breathless. She fell to the waitress's side.

"My turn," I said, whipping my cock out.

Kylie lifted her head. "What? No! I can eat her out, then suck your cock, Roman."

The waitress smirked at her, her lips and chin glistening with Kylie's juices. "He wants some new pussy, love," she cooed. She tried to kiss me when she reached me, but I turned my head. "You want a cock suck first?"

"Yeah, babe."

She dropped to her knees. I jerked a handful of blonde hair into my hands. Ignoring her yelp, I shoved my cock down her fucking throat, unconcerned at her gags. She teased my little sister? Laughed at her humiliation?

Ruthlessly, I pounded her mouth. Not giving an inch. Not caring about the sting when she sank her nails into my ass cheeks or her paltry punches. I decided her last act of kindness would be to make me come, so I eased out of her mouth and met her gaze.

"Make me come and then you can go."

Sniffling, she nodded.

I thumbed her tears away, unmoved. My nostrils flaring, I slid my dick between her lips and allowed her to suck me off. When my orgasm bubbled up, I yanked her head back and came in her miserable face, then shoved her away.

"Bastard!" she hissed, hopping to her feet and swiping an arm over her mouth.

I didn't bother with a reply. Her fate was decided. Conversation wasn't necessary. Grabbing her throat, I looked into her eyes the entire time I strangled her, then let her body drop to the floor.

Once I scrubbed my cum off her face with soap and hot water, I laid her on the bed and nodded to Kylie, who'd been staring at me the entire time.

"Clip her fingernails, then wash the tips off."

While she followed those orders, I went to the bathroom and got Kylie's coke. I filled two glasses with rum, dumped the coke in one of them, then brought both out and set them on the nightstand.

Poor Dayton, so coked out he accidentally killed a woman, then couldn't live with himself.

Kylie was already finished with her tasks. She was sitting on the edge of the bed, a dazed expression on her face.

"Go to Dayton's room, fuck him, then tell him you want us to party together," I told her.

She stumbled to her feet. At the door, she looked back at me. "What did he do to Ainsley?"

Smiling, I shrugged, my only answer.

She left without another word.

Chapter Five

Ainsley

"Knock, knock." Nova pushed open my bedroom door, tray in hand. She'd been at my apartment since yesterday when I called her and gave her a head's up about my brother. A little while ago, she'd prepared a bubble bath with Epsom salt and ordered me to relax while she saw to a meal. "I made my famous hamburger soup just for you."

Not gonna lie. Her hamburger soup was fire. Any other time, I'd slurp it up without hesitation. But since I woke up to find Reese gone with just a single text, I hadn't had an appetite. From what I gathered, he'd gone to the kitchen for water and saw Roman's picture.

Nova snapped her fingers in front of me. Her fake nails were polished blue and decorated with silver stars and moons.

"You have to eat something," she chided. "Roman will be home soon. One look at you and the game is up. He'll know something more than a nightmare went on and, frankly, I don't want to be on the receiving end of his fucking accusations."

I looked at the bowl of soup. Curlicues of steam rose up, wafting a delicious scent into the air. Tears slid down my cheeks again. I wasn't sure why I called Roman yesterday morning. After all the subterfuge, I'd nearly blown my cover. But my brother loved me. We were each other's only family and he knew the right words to make me feel better.

"I'm marrying Dayton and moving to New York like Roman wants," I said hoarsely. "The entire reason I went on the date was to have agency over my first time. It's done. I slept with a guy I chose and now I can move forward with my plans."

That thought only made me feel worse.

Scowling, Nova put her hands on her hips. "I'm sorry the guy walked out after he promised to call you or whatever, but it isn't the end of the fucking world. Whether you marry Dayton or not, you can have any dick you want."

Swiping my cheeks and sniffling, I glared at her. "What are we doing with Roman while I pitch pussy?"

"The same fucking thing we would've done with him if Reese had kept in contact. Deceive your sainted brother."

"My sheltered existence has me so upset," I lied morosely. I couldn't admit to deep disappointment. I'd awakened, expecting to find Reese next to me. My plan had been to cook him a huge breakfast, soak in a hot bubble bath to ease the soreness between my legs and possibly make love with him again. "Where am I going to meet another guy before I marry Dayton and move to New York? I don't think Roman's going on a run anytime soon."

"What's wrong with you? It was supposed to be *one night*. Now, you're talking about finding another dick because some old dude jetted on you?"

"Lou Lou's older than Reese," I said stiffly.

"Roman's older than Reese."

"What are you talking about?" I cried in confusion. Nova was jumping from one subject to the next that had no bearing on the Reese situation. "Didn't *you* tell me I could have another dick? And what does Roman have to do with anything?"

"Nothing, Ains," she huffed. "Just forget it. As usual, your spoiled brattiness is driving me insane. Luckily, Roman and I adore you and would do anything for you."

"I know. I don't know what I'd do without you. I trust you with my life. With everything."

"It's nothing, babe. I promise, although sometimes I wish I had someone like me to lean on. My mother walked away and never looked back."

Whenever Nova brought up her mom, guilt surged into me thanks to Roman's role in that situation.

"She should've stayed until Daddy straightened up or beat her to death if it meant staying for me."

"You don't mean that, Nova," I said gently. "You were an adult. You could've left with her."

"I think not. Leave with her and give up my place here? Are you insane? Why would I give up my life and status as Boom Boom's baby girl to hide and struggle with her?"

That was all kinds of fucked-up. "You might've had to struggle and hide, but you would've been with your mom."

"And you would've been alone," Nova replied.

"You shouldn't have sacrificed yourself because of me."

"I didn't. I stayed for the most important person in my life. *Me*. If I hadn't stayed, I would never have met my sexy Cajun daddy."

"Your sexy Cajun..." An image of Louisiana rose in my head. He had pretty turquoise eyes, even though they always seemed a little wild. His dark hair and dark beard were okay but couldn't compare to Reese's panty melting good looks.

Nova was becoming someone I didn't recognize. Whatever was going on, I hoped we got past it soon. I missed my good friend. Perhaps, though, I'd overlooked the reason why she'd gotten so attached to Louisiana. She still felt as if her mother deserted her. Maybe, if she healed that deep damage, she'd put everything else into perspective.

"Why don't you seek out Carol and try to repair your relationship? The last time Boom Boom beat her, she almost died. I know it hurt when she left, but you're older. Surely, you understand why she did it."

"There's no greater love than a man who sacrifices himself for another," Nova spat. "And a mother's love is supposed to be all-consuming and unparalleled."

"I wish I knew the right words to make you feel better—"

She glared at me. "You wouldn't know shit. Roman spends his fucking life protecting you. Before that, Nicolette and Mac did. You can't relate."

"I'm sorry," I said quietly, not knowing what else to say. We couldn't bring up Carol's name at the club, so Boom Boom probably prohibited Nova from discussing her mother, leaving an open wound inside her. "Remember how we once talked about moving in together?" I waved my hand around the room. "I want a bigger place, but you can move in sooner. It might be easier if you weren't surrounded by memories of your mother."

"Why the fuck would I want to live with you when I have my own trailer on club grounds? Daddy isn't always the best, but he looks out for me and makes anyone who crosses me suffer."

That almost sounded like a warning, but I knew my overwrought emotions made me feel that way.

"Enough about me," Nova said briskly. "Let's get back to you and Lou Lou's friend."

"There's nothing to get back to. I felt a connection to him but it wasn't mutual." I glanced away, still inexplicably hurt over his treatment. "I'll survive."

"Are you going to eat the soup I toiled in the kitchen to prepare?"

"I'm not hungry," I said hoarsely.

Sighing, Nova took the tray and set it on my dresser, then she sat next to me and took me in her arms. "This isn't you talking, Ains. It's your pussy. He must've fucked you so good that you can't bear to give up his cock."

I smiled. Leave it to Nova to cheer me up.

"That's what kept drawing me to Lou Lou at first. Even when I hated that motherfucker, my kitty was willing to say *hello* to his cock anytime he asked."

"You're so silly," I said around giggles, but instantly sobered when I remembered what Reese revealed about Lou Lou.

My muscles tautened and I tried to pull away.

"Okay, what now, Miss Ma'am?" Nova demanded, tightening her hold on me.

One thing about best friends. You couldn't hide from them.

"How do you feel about Lou Lou now?"

She separated us and frowned. "You know how I feel about him. He's my world. He's the one. I'd lose my mind if we break up."

"You're twenty-three. He's forty-two."

"You're an ageist now?"

Though it was a coward's way out, it was the easier route. "You don't know anything about his life outside of the fact that he's a Royal Bastard. Your father's enemy. My brother's enemy. Fuck, the enemy of the entire fucking club." I grabbed her arms and searched her face. "Suppose he just got with you to thumb his nose at the Bloody Scorpions? Suppose he's just using you?"

Jerking away, she got to her feet. "Just because you're so fucking miserable doesn't mean I am. Shame on you for trying to ruin my happiness."

"I'm not! Reese said—"

"One minute you're sobbing behind his dick and the next minute you're quoting him?"

"Louisiana is *married*, Nova." What kind of a friend would I be withholding the information when she was in so deep? "*You've* got to tell him to kick fucking rocks before he sends you away."

The more I spoke, the angrier she became. Her glare cut through me, so I didn't see her fist until it landed on my jaw.

"Fuck you, Ainsley," she snarled in a wobbly voice. "You're my best friend and I expected better than you carrying hearsay and falsehoods back to me." She turned, stalked to my dresser, and swiped the tray off. On its way to the floor, the soup spattered on my wall and rained on the dresser before the bowl shattered.

The noise didn't drown out Nova's furious slam of my front door.

REESE

Beer in hand, I stood outside the Devil's Pit. The early August evening was warm and slightly humid, with the golden hues of the sun casting shadows on the asphalt. A light breeze rolled off the nearby rivers, offering some relief from the heat.

Ironic our tail gunner had bike problems and needed assistance back to the club. Cursing, Bolt finally freed the chain that had snapped and then twisted. He was a lucky motherfucker not to have eaten asphalt.

He got to his feet and wiped his fingers on his jeans, trailing motor oil over the denim.

"Have yet to hear about your hot date," he said, studying each chain link. "You seeing her again? It seemed to have worked. You're out amongst the living instead of cooped up in your room."

I sipped my beer. "There's nothing to tell."

"Is she a good cock sucker?"

"Wouldn't know." More beer to wash away the bitterness of betrayal. "She didn't suck my cock."

Bolt frowned as the heavy wooden door opened and Louisiana strolled out into the bright afternoon sun. I glowered at him. Ignoring me, he settled an arm around my shoulder, but I shrugged him off.

"Don't be like that, Sarge."

I grunted and sipped more of my beer.

"What's crawled up your ass now, Reese?" Bolt asked, shaking his head. "You've been an emotional bitch since Trin's death. The blind date was supposed to help you."

"Tell him who the fuck you set me up with, asshole," I ordered Louisiana. "No, excuse me, *Lou Lou.*"

That wiped the smirk off that motherfucker's face.

Shaking his head, Bolt looked at Louisiana. "You're taking that, bro? That's a fucking insult."

"It's what his bitch calls him."

Bolt lifted his brows. "Fuck, you got a side piece? Jinx will rip your balls off and shove them down your throat."

Unconcerned, Louisiana shrugged. "I won't risk my fucking wife over that cunt. She's just a fuck. Wanted to knock her up and send her home to her daddy with her belly full of my kid at first. Had it happened as planned, I would've loved to have been there when she explained that."

Bolt hooked a thumb in a belt loop and rocked on his feet. "Who might her daddy be?"

"Boom Boom."

"Sonofabitch!" I tossed my empty bottle into the trash can near the door before I used it to bash Louisiana's head. "Not only are you fucking the enemy's daughter, but her old man is the fucking *president* of the club? Have you lost your fucking mind?"

Louisiana released a wad of spit. "That's how I feel about Nova Wren. Fuck her. We haven't been able to prove it but I know those motherfuckers took out Kenneth and stole our guns two years ago. I want justice for my kid brother and I'll use anybody to get it."

As angry as I was with Ainsley, she was innocent. For that matter, so was Nova, but I didn't know her, so she wasn't my concern. "So what the fuck did Ainsley do, motherfucker? Why did you fucking set me up with Roman Mac's kid sister?"

Bolt whistled and scratched his long gray beard. He shook his head at Louisiana. "Boy, even for you that's low."

"You fucked her, Reese," Louisiana said without heat. "It must not have mattered."

"I didn't find out until after." I narrowed my eyes. "How the fuck did you know...never mind. Nova."

"She tells me anything I want to know, although she pissed me off when she called me. Jinx had just left. Otherwise, she'd want to know who was on the phone."

I didn't want to hear about Nova, Jinx, or Ainsley. For that matter, I didn't want to hear about Trinity. Since I left Ainsley's apartment yesterday morning, my mind had been on her. The few times I thought about Trinity, I lacked the overwhelming guilt and grief that I usually felt. Turning, I opened the door and walked into the clubhouse. It was early evening, so only about fifteen members milled about. A few at the bar, some by the pool tables, and others on the sofa pushed against the wall. Our emblem was painted on the wall near the pool table that separated the short hallways for the male and female pissers.

A couple years ago, Jester convinced Razor to switch from white light bulbs to red. He liked that red sheen cast over everyone as if we cavorted in hell. Before anyone noticed me, I walked to the staircase that was located right past our storeroom and went up. Down led to the actual pit, suitable for riding out tornadoes and dust storms, and perfect to fuck up enemies.

I hurried to my room and slammed the door behind me once inside, not wanting to run into anyone. If Bolt hadn't needed my help, I wouldn't have left the room except to eat. Not only had the motherfucker sponsored me years ago, but he'd been like a father to me, so instead of calling Louisiana, our RC, he hit me up.

I walked to my window and gazed out. Our clubhouse was right near the river bend where the Kansas and Missouri rivers met, known as Kaw Point. Located near downtown, this confluence was a key landmark for Lewis and Clark during their 1804 expedition and remained an important part of our geography and history.

The scenic location blended natural beauty with an industrial backdrop. The Devil's Pit was located in one of the warehouses, where just beyond was Kaw Point Park. Lush green trees framed the meeting of the muddy Kansas River and the wider Missouri River. The park itself featured walking trails, open grassy spaces, and an amphitheater with a breathtaking view of our twin city's skyline. Kansas City, Missouri was just across the water.

Beyond the park's natural beauty, the surrounding area had an industrial feel. Rail lines, warehouses, and old brick buildings were scattered nearby, reflecting KC's deep ties to shipping and commerce. Bridges crisscrossed and connected Kansas and Missouri, while the riverbanks provided a mix of wild vegetation and urban infrastructure.

Seeing barges or boats navigating the river or opening my window to hear rushing water had always brought peace to me. Or, like now, when I just stood looking out without opening the window. Except I felt no calm.

Sunshine glimmered off the water. Days like this, with cool air and a cloudless blue sky, were made for riding.

My door opened. I didn't have to turn. I already knew who it was.

"You could've fucking told me, Louisiana."

Sighing, he closed the door. "I'm sorry, okay? I thought you'd get a kick out of it, too."

"That stunt left me fucking vulnerable to attack from the Scorpions, asshole. Suppose one of them had seen us together? Then what? You want to put your fucking life at risk, be my fucking guest. I resent you gambling with mine."

His boots pounded toward me. "Ainsley's a cool chick," he whispered. "A little too trusting. Shocking, considering she's Nova's bestie and Roman's sister."

Spinning, I narrowed my eyes. "If you're thinking about playing some type of game with her, I will fucking kill you. You already did enough fucking damage. Ainsley's cool for now, until you're done with Nova." He talked about her constantly. I knew so much about her, I'd pick her out from a crowd, though we'd never met. "Who I honestly believed you liked."

He winced, leaned in closer. "I do. Kind of." He blew out a breath. "You outed me to Bolt. What the fuck did you expect me to say? It started off the way I said. I want to avenge Kenneth. But fuck, I really care about her now. I was hoping you'd hit it off with her best friend, so we could double date sometimes. Nova thinks I'm hiding her."

"You are, fuckhead."

"If she got to know my best friend, she wouldn't feel so fucking isolated."

"She'll just push for more. By the way, you never answered my fucking question. What did Ainsley do that made you want to involve her in your game?"

"She didn't do anything, Reese. She didn't want strings attached and you just needed a pick me up."

"Are you stupid or are you dumb? That contradicts every goddamn thing you just spouted."

"It's complicated. Okay? I have my own fucking guilt where Trinity is concerned. If you hadn't been with me and she was with you instead—"

"It doesn't matter. Give me a straight answer about Ainsley."

"Since she said she didn't want anything serious, it made the date an easy sell to you. I was hoping...I don't know, Reese." He sighed. "As I said, I was hoping you hit it off and ran interference for me with Nova because they're best friends. That's it."

I believed he hid his true motives. "There's something called free will, fucker. I didn't have that because you didn't give me all the fucking facts."

"I thought she'd tell you herself. Ainsley can hold a conversation with a rock. She fucking loves to talk. And ask questions. And *talk*. It was up to her to confess."

"Spoken like a true asshole."

Shame crossed his face before he rallied. "You feel the same way since you're so pissed with her, you don't want to ever talk to her again, but you haven't thrown me out the fucking window."

"Don't tempt me," I grumbled, and faced the window again. "Why the hell would you have Nova report to you about Ainsley and me?"

"I didn't. She called me because she punched Ainsley."

"That bitch did *what*?" I roared, spinning to face him again.

"She told Nova I was married." He folded his arms. "I assume you told Ainsley."

"She asked. I told her to figure it out. That still didn't give Nova the right to lay her hands on Ainsley. If she's too fucking blind to face the truth, that's her business. That bitch definitely shouldn't blab Ainsley's private life out of spite."

Louisiana jammed a cigarette in his mouth and lit it before continuing. "It isn't out of spite. Ainsley spent the fucking weekend crying and not eating because she woke up and found you gone."

A stone dropped in my gut. I was agitated over the situation, not because I'd walked out on her. I didn't even know her. Yet, just as I didn't want her to throw her fucking life away on her brother's behalf, I hated the thought she cried over me. It didn't matter that I never wanted to see her again or hear her voice.

The smell of burning tobacco floated to me on a wisp of smoke from Louisiana's cigarette. "Before the argument, Nova prepared a nice bubble bath for her. To help with the soreness."

"I still might break your fucking face. You sound too goddamn amused."

He huffed and smoke whooshed my way. "Why the fuck are you so angry? You got easy pussy for the cost of a dinner. She wanted to fuck. A warm, wet home to stick your cock in was almost guaranteed."

I snatched a handful of his shirt and yanked him to me. I was three inches taller than

Louisiana with more muscles and a faithful workout routine. "If you want to disrespect Nova that way, that's up to you. Don't ever do it to Ainsley. *Ever*." I had one better. "As a matter of fact, don't talk about her to me ever again. I don't want to hear her fucking name. Am I clear?"

"Yeah, Reese," he said, finally realizing how on edge I was.

"Yo, Sarge," someone shouted through the door. I preferred Reese. Sarge sounded like a mutt's name. "You in there?"

"Come in, Marquis," I growled, and he peeped his head in. He was one of our newer members, a college dropout and a low-level drug dealer. "Warrior brought you a present."

By the glee in his voice, I knew it was a Bloody Scorpion. Corralling and torturing those motherfuckers always brought me joy.

"In the pit I assume," I said.

Marquis nodded.

I lifted a brow. "Who the fuck is it?"

"Roman Mac."

CHAPTER SIX

REESE

At the top of my bucket list was separating Roman Mac's head from his fucking body. It topped my wish list, my to-do list, and any other fucking list I missed.

I loathed him. Before he murdered Trinity, it was just a general hatred because he was a Bloody Scorpion. The war between our clubs began long before I patched in and would ride on long after I bit it. I wasn't sure of the actual origins. It just was, like birds flying free and shit traveling through a sewer.

The pit was comprised of three rooms and a bathroom. The biggest served as a shelter, the smallest as a prison. But I walked into the square one, smack in the middle of the other two, its four concrete walls equal in length and width on all sides. It was cold and stark, with a bright light when we wanted to see our enemy. Like now.

Roman sat on the lone chair in the room. He was chained and bloody, one eye almost completely shut. His nose was bruised and misshapen and he had a hole in his shoulder that looked as if it was on its way to an infection.

He lifted his head. His brown eyes burned with the same hatred embedded in me.

The heavy door opened and Louisiana walked in, carrying a phone.

"Warrior says the thing's been ringing constantly. It's his sister." He looked at me with meaning. "She's called him about ten times, Reese."

Snatching the phone, I walked to Roman. His hair was long. He liked to wear it in a ponytail. At the moment, it was grimy and coated with blood.

"I'm going to redial her and I want you to tell her everything's fine."

Roman spat a stream of blood. "Fuck you."

I leaned into his face and grinned. "This is how it will be, motherfucker. Call your sister or I'm sending someone to get her and throw her ass in here with you." Never would happen. "Then, maybe, we can enjoy the fucking show as my brothers take turns in her pussy." They'd die. "So what's it going to be?"

He met my gaze again. "I'll do it on one condition."

"Don't think you're in a fucking position to set conditions," I sneered. Motherfucker had a lot of nerve.

"Just don't tell her where I'm at," he said, ignoring me. "And you can cleave my head in two if you promise not to send any part of me to her."

"Cleave your head in two?" I pretended his request didn't affect me. I pretended I could still kill him and leave Ainsley all alone. She'd probably marry Dayton Morgan. "That's creative."

"It's what I'd do to you if the roles were reversed," he said without flinching.

I grinned without humor. I still didn't know how Warrior had gotten the jump on him. The phone started ringing again and the song registered.

"I'll talk to her," he said.

Swallowing, I answered and clicked on the speakerphone.

"Hey, Ains."

A moment ago, he'd sounded as if he was in unbearable pain. Somehow, he got the strength to affect a normal tone.

"Where are you, Roman?"

"Once I dropped Kylie off, I remembered some club business."

"Are you stopping at my apartment before you head home?"

I hated hearing her fear and sadness. Ainsley was smart. She knew something was up.

Roman swallowed. "Don't think I can tonight, sweetheart."

"Is it true about Dayton?"

Sighing, Roman shifted and the chains jingled, but either Ainsley didn't hear or she ignored the sound. "Yes, I fucked up Dayton, Ainsley. You should've told me what that motherfucker did to you. He's lucky I found out so far from home."

I straightened, wanting details, but Ainsley's sob threw me for a loop.

"He's a city councilman's son. You'll go to jail and leave me all alone."

Roman tipped his head back. "You're a survivor. You don't need me."

"I do! Everyone needs someone. I love you. You're an overbearing jackass, but I love you so much."

His grin made him wince and blood seep from the cut. "I love you too, Ainsley. Stop crying. Everything's going to be fine. Why the fuck are you so emotional? You've cried more these last two days than you have at any time except when Mom and Dad were killed." He deflated and the energy he'd found seemed to leave him. "Let me talk to Nova."

"She left, and the next time I see that bitch I'm throwing hands, Ro. She punched me because we had a disagreement."

Roman jerked against his chains. "She did *what*?" he demanded, having much the same reaction as me.

"Where are you, Roman?" Ainsley demanded hoarsely. "Why do I keep hearing chains? And just because Dayton wanted me to practice blowing him for when we're married doesn't mean he had to die."

My growl matched Roman's.

"That motherfucker did more than that." He strained against his chains again.

More? What the fuck did he mean *more*?

"Oh my god, asshole! Did you torture the information from him? Why would you do that and risk jail?"

Glancing away, I smiled. No matter her mood, Ainsley loved to talk.

"It doesn't matter, Ainsley. I took care of it."

"Yeah, well, if Kylie doesn't shut the fuck up she's going to get you sent to jail forever."

"That's the least of my fucking problems at the moment."

"Are you in trouble?" she whispered.

He swallowed, glanced away, and dropped his head. "I love you, sweetheart. Always remember that."

"No, God, no! Let me talk to them," she said wildly, truly hysterical now. "Please, please, please."

"Ainsley, sweetheart, listen to me."

I don't think I ever saw so much regret on a man's face. It was the look of someone who knew the end was near and would extinguish life yet to live and loved ones left behind.

Somehow, he calmed her enough to make her hear him. My insides were roiling and my hands were shaking. I almost wished Warrior had taken Roman Mac out himself instead of doing me the favor of bringing him to me to avenge Trinity.

"I have to go, Ainsley."

He nodded to me to disconnect. The call ended with her screams. I wanted to redial the number, but I wouldn't, and I couldn't call her later. Not only had I blocked her, I'd deleted her number before I had a chance to memorize it. Eventually, I would've caved, if only to demand answers. I'd thought it best to have no way of contacting her. Ainsley was an entanglement I didn't fucking need. Now, I regretted my haste. I could always ask Louisiana for her number, but pride would prevent me from doing that.

"Just get it done, Sinclair," Roman ordered.

It made sense that he knew my name. We were enemies. It was best to know everything about them.

"Your sister's name is Valois, huh?" Louisiana asked from behind me. "Why the different names?"

Roman turned his head. He didn't intend to answer any more questions, especially about

Ainsley. I could demand answers, but it would do no good. He was as good as dead anyway. Why give up information about his little sister?

He finally gave into the darkness calling to him and his eyes slipped closed, his chin tipping to his chest. He was even more helpless than before. Killing him would be a breeze.

Except...

I sighed.

"I take it you've had a change of heart," Louisiana guessed.

Roman was an enforcer in the club. Icing him would be a huge blow to their morale.

"What if he was the one who killed my brother, Reese?"

Louisiana was right. I couldn't let a piece of ass sway me. I had a job to do. Top of that list was killing any and all Bloody Scorpions I ran across.

I unholstered the gun at my side and pressed it to Roman's head. Ainsley's screams rose in my head. I put my finger on the trigger, and...couldn't do it. Just like when I'd thought about shooting Ainsley. Then, I hadn't been able to extinguish her life when she'd looked so innocent and gorgeous. Now, I couldn't take away her only family. Maybe that made me a traitor to my brothers. I didn't know.

One less Scorpion meant one less threat to us. Yet, even with that, I returned my gun to the holster.

"You fucking asshole."

I refrained from pointing out that it was *his* fucking games that put me in Ainsley's path. "If you don't want to help me, then leave. Either way, shut the fuck up."

"How the fuck do you plan on getting this motherfucker out? Any of our brothers will do the job you don't have the balls to do."

Thinking fast, I removed my serrated tactical knife from my boot and lifted one of Roman's hands. I'm sure the motherfucker would prefer to lose his hands if it meant returning to Ainsley. Putting him out of commission wouldn't only make him useless but could save his miserable life. Turning him into an invalid was a fate worse than death. As far as the Bloody Scorpions were concerned, being disabled made you a fucking burden to your club. Burdens were dealt with via bullets, so chances were, he wouldn't be on this Earth much longer, regardless of if he survived his impromptu amputation.

It was a win/win for me. My enemy would be dead, and Ainsley couldn't blame me for killing her beloved brother. On the off chance he made it, my guess—hope—was that he'd retire and live the rest of his life protecting Ainsley.

Some would argue—likely the entire membership—that killing him was the only answer. Assuming Roman survived, he could always get prosthetics and learn to shoot a gun, but I'd cross that bridge when I got to it.

The chances of him living that long were slim.

When I finally got his chains out of the way, I brought the blade down. It took two hard swings to chop off his left hand, the knife slicing through muscle, tendon, and bone with ease. The squirting blood indicated his heart continued to pump.

For how much longer, I couldn't say, and I didn't particularly care.

I took a moment to relish the feeling of his blood on my skin, imagining what it would feel like for his brain to be splattered everywhere. If Ainsley wasn't in the picture, I'd likely be disgusted at having his DNA tainting my skin but feel unmatched satisfaction. I'd celebrate his death by drinking and fucking, once Roman's body was chopped into tiny pieces.

Alas, Ainsley had ruined me for Roman's retribution, and doing something so vicious to her brother would leave me guilty. A conscience could be so bothersome, especially it made me sympathize with my enemy's sister. So much so, that I decided to spare the fucker.

Pussy made a man do stupid things.

"Wrap his wrists." I wiped off my blade, then returned the knife to my boot. "I'll be back."

"What the fuck are you doing?"

I dangled Roman's severed hands. "Saving Ainsley's brother."

The trek from the pit seemed longer than normal. Razor had talked about installing cameras and microphones in the torture chamber so we could watch our prey as they wrestled with the last hours of their lives. I'd had motherfuckers beg me to spare them. Offers to pay me. Offers to suck my cock. My toes. My fingers. A man lost all fucking dignity when he fell into his enemy's hands.

Warrior spotted me first and whooped, which started everyone else's cheers. Congrats were thrown my way. Roman Mac was fucking notorious. He took no prisoners and showed no mercy.

I hoped like fuck I wasn't making a mistake.

"I need a body bag," I announced after I downed the glass of rum Warrior handed me.

Razor pushed his way through the guys. Motherfucker was sixty if he was a day, but he wore it well with thick salt-and-pepper hair that matched his thick salt-and-pepper eyebrows.

"We don't transport body parts," Razor said in his gravelly voice.

Holding up Roman's hands, I nodded. "We don't, Prez," I said easily. "But he has a sister. He's her only family. Figured we could bring her his body and let her give him a proper burial."

By the time I carried him through the clubhouse, he'd already be in the body bag. I'd cut holes near his mouth and nose, so he wouldn't smother. No one would know. I intended to carry him Fireman style.

Razor snatched one of the hands, held it up to study it, then stuffed it in his pocket. My guess was he wanted to practice skinning with his razor. He snatched the other one and it disappeared into the other pocket in his cut.

"Let me see his fucking body, Reese," Razor ordered.

Sonofabitch.

If Razor noticed the rise and fall of Roman's chest, I'd have some explaining to do.

"Did you find out why he killed Trinity?" Marquis asked.

"Wasn't interested," I said, and immediately regretted my words. I'd spent six fucking months mourning her. No wonder my brothers gaped at me. "Just wanted to get my lick in," I quickly added.

Razor narrowed his icy gray eyes and cocked his head. "What the fuck's going on? I smell a load of bullshit."

"Nothing's going on, Prez. His sister is twenty-one years old. She deserves to know what happened to that asshole."

He looked me dead in the eyes. "That motherfucker breathing or what?"

"Barely," I admitted. I wasn't a liar. From time to time, I embellished, but I didn't flat out lie to my president when he asked a direct question about an enemy club. Shit like that would get *me* fucked up. "By the time we get him to her, he'll probably be gone, which is why I want the body bag."

I'd wanted the body bag to sneak him out. My amended plan sounded just as good.

Prez clapped my face between his big hands, harder than necessary. "Then you should put a bullet in his head and make sure he ain't breathing."

"I want him to die slowly," I replied without flinching.

My words weren't a lie, per se. More like another amended plan.

Jester inserted himself next to Razor and studied me from head to toe. I kept my face passive.

"Trinity was his favorite slut," Jester decided, looking at Razor and nodding at me. "Should be up to him how he avenges her."

"He's a Bloody Scorpion," Bolt said with disgust, glowering at me. "Roman Mac's entire fucking existence is a crime."

"He's probably already bled to death," I said.

That was true. He'd lost a lot of fucking blood.

"So, what's wrong with shooting him in the goddamn head to finish the job?" Warrior demanded.

Murmurs rippled through the crowd. Some saw no harm in my actions. Most agreed with our president.

Fuck my life.

I shoved a hand through my hair and gritted my teeth. "Look, I fucked his little sister before I knew who she was. Saw his picture on her counter the next morning. I left and blocked her fucking number. Haven't talked to her since."

Nope, not since before we fell asleep, early yesterday morning.

"If he's alive, you're risking all of us for a twat," Razor boomed.

"He no longer has hands, Prez," I argued, trying to ignore how annoyed I felt at how crudely he referred to Ainsley. "If he somehow survives, his president will probably finish him off. What good is a crippled enforcer?"

I hoped that was how Roman met his end. Despite not putting a bullet through his skull, he deserved death. But I no longer sought to be his executioner.

More whispers, the opinion still divided, but a few more had joined my corner.

"What good is a living Scorpion, boy? Cripple or fucking robust, he should be dead," Bolt snarled, his disappointment cutting through me.

I might no longer be a devastated teen under his care, but it'd be a blow if he stopped seeing me as a surrogate son. Not the end of the world, though it *would* warrant a night of drinking my sorrows away.

Hearing some people agreeing with me gave me the confidence to address Razor once more. "I don't ask for much, Prez."

Razor scratched his leathery jaw. "First time in memory you're asking for anything, Reese." After studying me for a moment, he walked up to me and thumped my shoulder. "Take him to his sister. Seeing as how this is such a big favor, you better not ask for nothing anytime soon. If that motherfucker survives and takes out one of our boys, I'm killing that bitch. This time, there won't be no fucking intervention. I'll let you live the rest of your days knowing you played a role in her death. What's her name?"

"Ainsley."

"Roman Mac's sister, you said?" Razor asked, grinning at the ripples of laughter running through the crowd. "Dark hair, whiskey eyes?"

I nodded.

"You planning on seeing her again?"

"Not after tonight when I drop her brother off. I plan to wear a mask and a jacket over my cut."

"Then go. Get that motherfucker out of here before I change my mind, Reese."

I didn't have to be told twice.

Ainsley

I never knew how many of the memories surrounding my parents' deaths were real and how much I conjured from my overactive imagination. My mother's scream, followed by gurgling, haunted my nightmares. Just before I always awakened, blood bloomed on the side of my father's head. Then I'd fly forward and bounce to the floor in the back of the car.

In my waking moments when those thoughts invaded me, I always lifted my head and watched as my father shifted the car into park. I'd hear my mother's voice asking what were we waiting for, then I'd lay my head down and close my eyes again. My mother's scream, the sound of Harley pipes, and tires screeching always awakened me. I went flying because the car ramped from zero to Mach 1 in seconds.

I was there when my parents were killed. That was the only definitive knowledge I had about that day, then Roman was there, pulling me out of the bullet-riddled car and into his arms.

I'd clung to my brother. Though I was sheltered, it wasn't as much as some ten-year-olds. Partly because of who my father and brother were and partly because my mother believed in the power of an education. She believed in knowledge.

That day, I knew my life had changed forever, but I also knew I had my brother. Roman's love and dedication to me and the memory of our parents never wavered. And I loved him just as much. It was why I'd made the decision about Dayton.

My rebellion, my one night with Reese, was all for nothing. Dayton was dead. I didn't have to marry him. Roman had taken care of the problem.

Except he'd been taken away from me. Once he disconnected our call, I tried to contact Reese, not realizing he'd blocked me until then. I would've begged him for help in finding Roman. Yes, they were enemies, but I'd hoped he'd do this for me.

My call to Lou Lou went straight to voicemail. I supposed he'd blocked me too because of Nova. As usual, she'd run straight to him with what I said about his marital status. And as usual, he fucking lied to her.

It didn't matter. None of it mattered because Roman was gone, too, and I was completely alone in the world.

I knew I had to find the strength to go on. Somehow. My mom had been amazingly strong in the face of many adversities. Dad was there as much as possible. They'd want me to go on. More than anything, I wouldn't allow all Roman's hard work in raising me to go to waste.

I covered my mouth to hold in my sob. But Roman was right. I'd cried the entire fucking weekend and for what? Reese walking out couldn't compare to my devastation now. Mom always advised me to cry over the big stuff. This was it. Reese could fuck himself for all I cared.

My virginity was gone, Dayton was dead, and I had to face life without Roman. Or, anyone, really, because fuck Nova, too. Throwing hands because she was a stupid bitch was a hard pass.

The pounding on my door matched the pounding in my head. I didn't want to disturb the neighbors, so I stumbled forward and looked through the peephole.

Louisiana stood on the other side. I couldn't drum up any anger, so I opened the door. Louisiana stepped aside. Four men wearing skull masks brushed past me. Carrying Roman. They dumped his body on the floor and a scream escaped me.

Louisiana clutched my arms. "He's breathing, Ainsley."

It took a moment for the words to sink in. Afraid to hope, I met his turquoise gaze. He nodded, and I hurried to my brother, touching his nose and his cheeks. Lifting one towel-wrapped hand then the other.

"Do you know how to contact any of his brothers?"

"Yeah."

"He needs a doctor."

"I'm going to call an ambulance," I said, reaching for my phone, but he cursed and snatched it from me.

The other men shifted. He glared at them.

"Wait ten minutes," he ordered.

"But—"

"Ten minutes," he gritted, pocketing my phone.

I hopped to my feet and lunged for it, but he grabbed my wrists. One of the guys made a noise, but I didn't care who.

"How can I call anyone if I don't have my phone?"

"You'll get your phone back tomorrow. I'll have Nova bring it to you."

"Tell her to leave it at the door. Unless she comes with an apology, I don't want to talk to her. I need my phone to call '911'."

"I'll call," he barked, his nostrils flaring.

One of the guys cleared his throat.

"Why'd you tell Nova I was married?"

"You mean why did I do the job you should've done?" I retorted, wanting them gone so I could see to my brother. I didn't trust they'd really call an ambulance.

"Stay out of my fucking business, Ainsley."

"Gladly, Louisiasshole."

Scowling, he shoved me away. The moment they left, I'd go to the neighbor's and make the call. Fuck him.

"Most of the club wanted Roman Mac dead," Louisiana said. "He's alive because of you. I'm going to call a fucking ambulance, Ainsley. Give us the courtesy of getting away before those motherfuckers swarm the neighborhood."

"Fine."

"Why is he a Mac and you're a Valois?"

I explained why, so he'd leave and take his scary friends with him. "After our parents were killed, he didn't want to take any chances with my life. From then on, he gave me our mother's maiden name. Mac is unusual because it doesn't have a second part."

"He did it to protect you."

"Yes," I answered, although he hadn't asked a question.

He backed toward the door and the other men followed suit.

"See you around, Ainsley," Louisiana said.

"Yeah, you too." I closed the door and hurried to the bathroom for more towels.

Chapter Seven

Ainsley

It was exactly fourteen days since I'd met Reese, and I couldn't believe how my life had changed in two short weeks. Since then, I'd lost my virginity, lost my best friend, almost lost my brother, moved back home, and spent every waking hour fussing over Roman.

He should've been awarded a prize as the worst patient to ever exist. Granted, he was in pain and losing both his hands was absolutely horrific, but instead of gratefulness that his life was spared, he was angry and refused to say more than a few words to me. As if it was my fault he was now what he called a handicapped burden.

I left him in peace as much as possible, which didn't help *my* mood. I had no one to talk to, so when he sent me to the clubhouse to see Boom Boom, I didn't hesitate to grab my keys and almost skip out of the house.

The moment the guards sent to watch over our house saw me, two prospects hopped on their motorcycles to serve as my escort. Ever since the ambulance picked Roman up, Bloody Scorpions closed ranks to protect my brother and me.

I texted my thanks to Louisiana, but he never responded. He left me on read, so I knew he hadn't blocked me. So many times, I prayed Reese would call to check on Roman, on me. I wanted to hear his voice again and feel his lips against mine.

Whenever those thoughts overtook the memories of our evening together prior to the lovemaking, I chalked my feelings up to Nova's assumption. It was my pussy talking and nothing more than lust and desire. Then, I immersed myself in caring for Roman and shoved Reese out of my mind.

Sometimes, I wondered how Roman's brothers knew about his injuries. They found out somehow and arrived in time to escort the ambulance and me, since I followed behind in my car. The first two days were touch and go. Roman had been shot, beaten, and lost both his hands. By the time he was brought to surgery, infection had set into the gunshot wound.

Right around that time, Dayton's death hit the news cycle. Reportedly, he'd killed a waitress, then OD'd on cocaine. Purposely or accidental no one knew. Except *I* knew it was all bullshit. Roman had killed him.

Ever since Louisiana and his masked men brought my brother to my apartment, I'd felt so alone. Devastated. Frightened. My nightmares also returned. I always awakened drenched in sweat and fearing my heart would beat out of my chest.

The only reason Roman even agreed to let me move on my own was because they'd been almost non-existent for months. Inside me had settled down and I found peace. I'd gotten a job, a car with Roman's help, and a tutor to help with my grades. My future seemed so bright. Then, my brother killed Trinity and that began another downward spiral.

At the clubhouse gate, Spike waved me through. I grimaced. The sea of bikes and cars indicated a crowd. It was a Friday evening, so of course it would be crowded. Once I parked, I hurried inside, nodding at the brothers who greeted me. They clapped me on the shoulder and asked about Roman. Those who hadn't visited promised they would. I darted between the big bikers, ol' ladies, hang arounds, and club girls, adept at weaving my way through the crowd because I'd done it since I was a child.

The loud music, the indistinguishable chatter, the roar of laughter blended together and became white noise. At first, it had been a coping mechanism as a grieving kid. Dad had taken us to family events. Roman brought me as much as possible, so I was always with him.

Finally, I reached the hallway that led to the offices. It took longer than expected because of the sheer number of people concerned about Roman.

As I passed the conference room to get to Boom Boom's office, he called my name.

"We're in here."

Damn it! Boom Boom wanted to see me in the conference room and not his office. I knew what that meant. Nova pulled rank and went to her father to make me talk to her again. She'd gotten me into trouble before with her dad. I could do without his shouting today. I could always threaten to expose her and reveal she was dating a club enemy, but I wouldn't do that. Those club enemies spared my brother.

Stiffening my backbone, I peeped into the conference room and snapped my brows together. Nova sat to the right of Boom Boom, but all the club officers filled the other chairs.

My stomach knotted and a wave of nausea slid through me.

I greeted Boom Boom first, then said hello in ranking order. Roman drilled three things into me—rank meant everything, never disregard an officer, and never disrespect the club's colors.

Boom Boom tasted whatever concoction he'd wanted tonight, then set the glass aside again. His black gaze never left my face. I once told Roman that Boom Boom reminded me of Count von Count from *Sesame Street*. He hadn't been amused.

"Would you care to explain why you've shut my daughter out, Ainsley?" Boom Boom demanded.

Annoyance swirled into me. This show of force wasn't necessary just so Nova could have her way. "We had a falling out," I said calmly.

"She tried to apologize on several occasions and you rebuffed her each time."

That was news to me. She'd tried twice.

"She's over here, Ainsley," Boom Boom barked, pointing to her. "You've known each other most of your lives and this is how you treat a friend?"

If only my eyes could chop that heifer into tiny pieces. A glare had to suffice. I didn't want to chew her ass out until we were alone.

"Apology accepted, Nova," I said sweetly.

"I'm so sorry, Ains," she said quietly.

"Yeah, *no*. You hit me for no fucking reason, then you swiped that fucking soup off my dresser."

Nova got to her feet and rushed to me. "It's just that I didn't like what you were saying."

"Then you could've cursed me. Walked out. Told me to lose your fucking number—" Like Reese had. "You could've done any of the above as long as you kept your motherfucking hands to your motherfucking self," I yelled, my brother's influence showing itself at the wrong time. But I was so furious she'd put me in this predicament and I was angry at Roman's treatment. I jabbed her chest. "Punching me is a hard no. I would never raise my hand to you." I wagged my finger at her. "And let me tell you this, wench, you're so fucking lucky you shocked the fuck out of me because you would've left in an ambulance."

Fuck. I'd just threatened the president's daughter. He could kill me for that.

"Is that truly how you feel, Ainsley?" Wizard asked. He was the VP or the Treasurer. I didn't know since a denim jacket covered his cut. The only constant was Boom Boom. Roman complained about the high turnover rate and how the other officers were constantly voted out.

He hadn't complained to me. I'd just overheard one of his conversations.

Bones, Vector, and Price watched in silence, officers, men who Roman considered his friends. Men who'd visited him over the past days and talked to me. Now, their look of dislike and disapproval shocked me.

Boom Boom lifted a brow. "Well, is it how you feel, Ainsley?"

I folded my arms and lifted my chin. "Yes."

"I could have you beaten. Killed," Boom Boom added darkly. "I love Nova. I thought you did, too."

"Love is meaningless when violence enters the equation," I said sullenly, not knowing when to shut the fuck up. "If Nova loved me we could've agreed to disagree, Boom Boom."

"This isn't about *you*," he retorted. "It's about my princess."

I sidled another glare at her. Boom Boom got to his feet. He was massive, related to the *Jolly Green Giant* and the fee-fi-fo-fum dude that lived up Jack's beanstalk. One swipe of Boom Boom's hand and I was done for.

"Daddy, wait," Nova cried, inserting herself in front of him to stop his advance. "She didn't mean it. Don't hurt her."

He shoved her out of the way. It took effort to hold my ground. But I kept my arms folded and tightened my muscles to hide my shaking.

Nova grabbed his arm again. "She came because you need to talk to her about Roman."

He shrugged her off. The room wasn't that big, but his advance took forever. He stopped in front of me and Nova began to chant, "I'm sorry."

While he was so furious, I knew better than to look Boom Boom in the eye. He'd take it as a sign of disrespect. Out of the corner of my eye, I saw his hand arch toward me. Even if I'd had time to react, I would've forced myself to stand still.

His backhand sent me to the floor. He sank his hands into my hair, jerked me to my feet, and hit me across the other cheek. I saw him coming, but I didn't know what to do, so I acted on instinct and scrambled back, stopped by the wall behind me.

This time when he leaned down, he grabbed my arm and yanked me to my feet. By a miracle, he didn't pull my arm out of the socket. He marched me to his chair and shoved me in it. Blood leaked from my nose, so I swiped my arm across it.

I wish I could've held my tears in, but I was in pain and scared shitless.

"Come here, Nova," Boom Boom ordered.

She stumbled toward her father. When she reached him, he punched her and then kicked her. My hands flew to my mouth.

"You stupid cunt," he snarled. "Bringing this bullshit about this uppity slut to me. You hit Roman Mac's sister?"

He hit her again and I screamed. At her sobs, my heart broke. Boom Boom was insane. He did anything for laughs and often performed dangerous stunts to impress everyone. All the times Nova crashed at my house, and then my apartment, rushed through my head.

He picked her up and shoved her to Kite, who ripped her shirt away and bared her breasts as well as the bruises blooming on her belly. She wasn't even struggling. She just hung her head.

Kite looked at me. "I can make them fuck, Prez."

"Not tonight," Boom Boom said, normal again. Not a psychotic woman beater.

No wonder Nova wanted things to work out with Louisiana.

"Take Nova away, Kite. Just come in her mouth."

I dry-heaved.

Kite shoved Nova out the door, then all eyes turned to me.

"I like Roman. He's damn good and gets motherfuckers," Boom Boom said. "If you tell him about your time here, you'll get worse than Nova."

I nodded vigorously.

"Tell me about the Royal Bastard who brought Roman to you."

"I don't know much." My voice trembled.

"Is Nova involved with him?"

"No! Of course not. She'd never betray you."

"I heard otherwise. The calls logs from her last phone bill shows an unfamiliar number answered by an unfamiliar motherfucker. If you're lying to me, I'll give you to Kite and let him fuck every hole you have, then I'll make you disappear. Royal Bastards are our enemies."

"I know, Boom Boom."

He walked to the safe in the corner, opened it, and pulled out five straps of hundreds. "Make that last until Roman's back in circulation. Send his hospital bills to me." He threw them at my head. They hurt when they hit and left me slightly dizzy as the money smacked the floor. "Now, crawl on your fucking knees, get the money, and get the fuck out of my club."

In spite of my pain and fear, I cursed Boom Boom to hell and back, but I gathered the money, stood, and rushed to the door.

"Ainsley?"

I halted.

"Answer me!" he yelled.

"Yes, Boom Boom?" I said tiredly.

"I hope you're proud of yourself. You got yourself beat and Nova hurt."

I begged to differ.

"Next time, know your place and shut your fucking mouth. If you would've accepted Nova's apology, all this could've been avoided."

"I understand. I m-m-mean I know. I'm sorry."

"Finally got it right." Boom Boom laughed. "Remember, don't open your fucking mouth to Roman. He's rabid about protecting you. Wouldn't want no hard feelings between us."

I didn't know what to say, so I whispered, "yes, sir."

"Get out."

I ran all the way to my car.

CHAPTER EIGHT

ROMAN

Staring at the ceiling in my bedroom, I watched the fan blades spin on the axis, wondering how much longer I could hold in my piss. A man could only take so much humiliation. I couldn't even piss like a guy. I had to sit my ass on the toilet like I had a pussy.

I tipped my head back and blinked. Pain traveled through my entire body, radiating from the stumps formerly known as my hands to my shoulders and all the cuts and abrasions I'd suffered. If I hadn't checked myself out, I probably would've still had a drip to ease me.

They'd done all they could. I would've remained in the hospital for fuck all except bills. Which I couldn't afford at the moment. I had to swallow my pride and call my president with a voice activated device Ainsley set up.

Boom Boom had been an abusive asshole to his ol' lady, but he loved his kids—especially Nova—and he liked Ainsley. Whatever I might've done or didn't do wouldn't reflect on her. She was a kid and that counted for something.

Soon, she would return with the cash Boom Boom wanted to give me to tide me over since I'd be out of commission for a few months. I never considered myself a quitter, but I'd never burdened anyone else with my needs. Especially my little sister.

She fed me, combed my hair and kept me shaved, while Kylie came every afternoon to wash me off. I still wore bandages where my hands had once been and the surgical stitches remained in my shoulder where I'd been shot.

Ainsley didn't deserve my fuckheadedness. I should've been happy to be alive, so I could find a suitable husband for her and get her somewhere safe. Living without my hands was more humiliating than if they'd just killed me. For that matter, I didn't know why they let me fucking live.

After I watched Dayton OD, I called Boom Boom and brought him up to speed. He knew my location and knew when I'd arrive back in town.

Kylie and I made sure we didn't leave anything behind, then walked the fuck out and went to my bike. I was so fucking glad I'd used an alias. It wouldn't do any good if I'd left any evidence, even trace amounts of DNA on the bodies. Dayton wanted to party, but he hadn't wanted to be seen with me. A plus for me.

About an hour from home, Kylie needed to pee, so I pulled up to a convenience store. She took forever. As she was walking out, all hell broke loose. Warrior and his band of Royal Bastards ambushed me.

After the deaths of my parents, shit between the clubs quieted. Boom Boom held off avenging them because of Ainsley. She was in sixth grade and I sure as shit didn't have time to homeschool her.

Two years ago, Wizard took out Kenneth, kid brother to a Bastard who went by the stupid name of Louisiana. Supposedly, Kenneth's death avenged my parents. The Bastards hadn't responded. I thought they were planning a massive attack against us, but Boom Boom claimed they were running scared.

When I killed Trinity, I refueled the war between the clubs. She was under their protection, and they wanted revenge. Within weeks, two of our guys were killed.

Once Warrior took me, I expected to die and hoped they'd dump my body. Whether it was ever found didn't matter as long as they didn't send pieces of me to Ainsley. It would torment her but she could live the rest of her life without knowing my fate if they spared her the gore of my dismemberment. I'd also asked they not hurt Kylie. She hadn't done anything. My crime. My punishment.

They'd taken me to the Devil's Pit and thrown me in their cell, and I knew they'd brought me for Reese Sinclair to finish me. Had he asked why I killed that two-timing cunt, I wouldn't have answered. Deep down, I felt as if the Royal Bastards sent her to gather intel. Or to set me up and do exactly what the fuck they'd done—ambush me.

My nose itched. I rubbed the bandage over it, but nothing compared to using fingers to scratch.

If Ainsley was here, she'd hurry to scratch my nose. She was wasting her life because of my bad decisions. My little sister's conversation would've cheered me up and filled the well of emptiness. She'd throw away her life catering to me, so I preferred if she hated me.

Without warning, my window slid open, and I lifted my head. Knife between his lips, Louisiana slid in, landing as silently as a cat.

"Scorpions are crawling outside. You may have gotten lucky and dodged them, but when they find my body, they'll suspect it was one of you."

The asshole smirked at me and took his knife in hand. He walked to the edge of my bed and stared at me like I was a freak show.

"In my mind, I'm lopping your head off, motherfucker," I growled.

"Only place you can do it, Roman," he said around laughter.

"Just kill me and get it over with."

"Can't." Louisiana walked to the side of the bed, pocketed his knife, and folded his arms. "Promised Reese I wouldn't."

"Remind me to thank him," I sneered.

"You should. He saved your fucking life, so you wouldn't be taken from your little sister."

I hadn't been sure if I'd dreamed talking to her and hearing her screams. I had my answer.

I lifted my head to glare at him. "Why are you here?" I gritted.

He stared at me, hatred burning in his eyes. Even if I hadn't killed his family member, one of my brothers had. That made me a lifelong enemy.

"Trinity was a cheating cunt," he announced.

Fuck. "You sent that video."

"I took the video. Needed something to do with it. Why not send it to you?"

I laid flat again. "You could've shown it to Reese."

"Negative. Every time Reese thought about taking the next step with that cunt, he got cold feet. Something held him back. Instinct. One day, I had free time on my hands and decided to follow her. You could've knocked me over with a cotton swab when I saw her all loved up with you at one of your club functions."

"You have big balls, spying on us on our turf."

"I have a big cock to go with those balls," he retorted. "I wasn't worried about being seen. Trust me. I could slip in and out of any place I please." He turned and began walking around my room.

The distinctive sounds of a nosy motherfucker reached me. Shit sliding on my bureau. Keys jingling as they were moved. A picture frame returned to its place.

As an enforcer, I'd honed my senses to keen awareness. I'd learned to pick out sounds and see in damn near total darkness.

The automated voice on the alarm system alerted me to someone opening the front door. Ainsley was home.

"Can you get the fuck out so my sister won't see you? She's been through enough."

The asshole slipped into my closet just as I wrestled my way to a sitting position and my sister walked into my room.

"Hey, Ains—" Bruises marred her face and dried blood stained her lips and chin. "What the fuck happened to you?"

She sat the straps of money on my dresser, then rushed to me and launched herself into my arms, sobbing into my neck. Fuck hands. My arms wrapped around her.

"Tell me what happened, Ainsley. Who the fuck hit you?"

She didn't answer.

"Sit back and look at me."

She did, and I flinched at her battered face.

"Talk to me *now*," I snarled. "I'm not fucking playing. You have three fucking seconds to tell me what happened."

It wasn't as if I could do anything *now*, but when I was fitted for my prosthetics, there'd be hell to pay.

"I can't tell you, Roman." She swallowed. "Can you call B-B-Boom and...B-B-Boom B-B-Boom," she amended. "Tell him I need Nova's help. Please, you have to help her."

"What's wrong with Nova?" She hadn't been around. I figured it had something to do with her fucked-up behavior. "Why didn't you ask her to come with you?"

"Knock knock." Boom Boom's voice traveled down the hallway and Ainsley almost fell off the fucking bed.

"Hide me," she cried, as panicked as she was when she had her nightmares.

"Roman?"

He was closer. She dove behind me and cowered.

"Came to check on you, boy," he said, standing in the doorway but not coming any farther. "Thought I saw Ainsley come into the house. Wanted to say hello to her."

I gave him a half-smile. "Didn't you say hello to her at the club?"

He burst into laughter. "Just fucking with you. Wondering if you still had a brain since you no longer have hands."

I ignored him. "Can you send Nova over later? Ainsley needs help. I'm a handful."

Nodding, he scrubbed a hand over his chin. "Reckon you are. Nova pissed me off. Let Kite work her over. She's my baby girl and I love her to death, but I don't like bullshit."

"Neither do I," I said with a cool smile. I never thought he'd turn his crazy on his own daughter once we convinced his ol' lady to leave before he killed her.

I pursed my lips. Well, shit. I'd been so instrumental in her decision that I'd funded her escape. If Boom Boom found out, he'd put a hit out on me. What better way than to frame the Royal Bastards then to have them kill one of the club's top enforcers?

Boom Boom tried to peep around me. Had my bed been at a different angle, the overgrown motherfucker would've seen Ainsley trying to crawl up the back of my shirt.

Fuck, I could only imagine how that worked out for her nose.

"Came to spend a little time with my favorite enforcer."

I forced a yawn. "As much as I'd like to humor you, Prez, I can't. I'm exhausted. Another time."

He met my gaze, glanced around the room once more, and backed into the hallway.

"Not yet, Ainsley," I whispered, wanting to make sure that motherfucker left before she unfolded herself from behind me.

My closet door cracked, and an eye surveyed the situation. I still didn't know why that motherfucker decided to darken my door. He'd betrayed Trinity out of loyalty to Reese. I doubted he was that delusional. He shoveled me a load of bullshit that he expected me to accept.

Ainsley began wiggling and Louisiana closed the door again. I needed to install locks on the windows pronto.

Fuck. A handless motherfucker couldn't install anything. He was at the mercy of stealthy enemies that slipped past his brothers.

Huh. Doubtful. More like those brothers looked the other way when the enemy slipped in.

Ainsley stumbled to her feet and thrust her fingers through her hair. Her face was swollen. I heaved in a breath.

"It's good to see you sitting up, Ro. Since it's almost six, I think I'll order a pizza. I'll feed you a slice then eat my own."

Lifting a brow, I folded my arms. Fuck, I shocked myself. I'd been so lost in pain and self-pity, I didn't even try to see what I could and couldn't do without hands.

"Gonna tell me what happened, sweetheart?"

I never had to draw shit out of her. Although she flipped on a dime and her mood went from cheery to quiet without warning, she told me whatever I wanted to know.

"Why did Boom Boom slap you around, Ains?"

"It's nothing compared to what he did to Nova," she said woefully. "He humiliated her and…and…he gave her to Kite and told him just come in her mouth. That's her father!" she sobbed.

"What did he do to *you*?"

"I told myself to keep quiet, then Nova…I was being a mean bitch to her because I'm so upset that she fucking punched me."

Ditto.

She told me what set Boom Boom off. "I shouldn't have said it, Roman. But I was so lost in the moment. All I saw was Nova." She hung her head, a study in misery as she explained the entire story to me, including Boom Boom's threats. "He's your friend and her father," she said for the countless time. "What kind of a man does that?"

A dead one.

Ignoring my bandages and pain, I lifted my arms to her. She snuggled against me, and I missed the days when she was a little kid. In the meantime, I needed to get motherfucking Louisiana the fuck out of my house.

"Go upstairs and take a bubble bath. I'll use that voice activated ball to call one of the guys and send them for Chinese food. They need to come in and help me into my pajamas anyway."

Ainsley spent too much time in my room, in spite of my grumpiness, for me not to respect her and wear jeans and a T-shirt during the day.

She stumbled toward the door.

"After your bubble bath, you need ice for your cheeks." She needed it now, but *Louisiana...*

She'd hear us talking and come to investigate.

She paused at the door and turned to me. The sight of the damage Boom Boom inflicted turned my stomach and gave me a new purpose. If I took out the president, I'd be marked for death. I had to get creative again.

"I'm not too hungry," she said, fidgeting. "I'll take a bath and then feed you. I won't be long."

"It's fine, sweetheart." It wasn't yet, but it would be. "I'll survive."

She searched my face.

"What, Ains?"

"Have you ever missed someone and wanted to talk to them, but couldn't?"

That was an odd fucking question. She could've meant Nova, but I knew she didn't. I tried to think of which one of my brothers would ignore my rule and sneak around with Ainsley, when all those motherfuckers knew I didn't want her with a biker.

I'm almost certain my father wouldn't have married Mom if he knew his lifestyle would lead to her death.

Swinging my legs over the bed, I stood up and swayed like a fucking pussy. Alarmed, she rushed to me and gripped my arms until I felt steadier.

"I'll call one of the guys," she said.

Disappointed in myself, I sat on the edge of the bed. "I'm fine, Ainsley. Go do what you need to do to feel better." I certainly couldn't fucking help her. "Close my door. I need a little privacy."

Her shoulders slumped, but she nodded and did as told.

When Louisiana walked out of the closet, his blazing anger shocked me.

I'd kicked a motherfucker to death once. Louisiana had a blade and probably a gun, but one good blow to the head would do the trick.

Fists balled, he started pacing.

"What? You don't get enough attention at *your* fucking club?"

He halted. "What?"

"You've heard more than you needed to. You shared that you wanted Trinity fucked up by my hand because you're such a sterling friend. What more do you want?"

"You were flat on your fucking back when I climbed through the window. You've been reinvigorated."

I shrugged.

"Are you killing that motherfucker?"

"To whom do you refer and what's it to you?"

"Boom Boom and nothing. Just curious."

"I'd never kill my own president," I lied with a straight face. Unless he crossed one particular line. He had.

"Then you're a pathetic jackass," he said flatly.

Anger burned me. He was another score to settle. "I've been called worse."

"I should just kill you."

"Dump my body out the window when you do."

"I want you to fear me. I want you to shake and tremble as I imagined my little brother doing. I'd leave your fucking body right here, fuckhead."

"Ainsley would find me," I said patiently.

"She needs to grow the fuck up."

I clenched my jaw. Ainsley made a mistake when she allowed her temper to get the best of her. I knew better. I couldn't back up threats with actions for the time being so I'd bide my time.

"You and your fucking den of depravity," he whispered, low. "I should kill you like the fucking mongrel you are. You're not killing Boom Boom because you're just like him. You killed Trinity."

Despite the offense, I offered another shrug. It was the best show of nonchalance I could give. "You aren't much different," I said with a small smile. "Who revealed her dirty little secrets?"

"I wanted you to die when you were in the pit. When Reese didn't pull the trigger, I almost did. I hate you and your entire fucking organization. I'll see you dead by hook or crook and this time Reese won't be able to save you."

He backed to the window and slipped out as stealthily as he entered. It was ten minutes before I realized the picture of Ainsley had been stolen from the frame.

CHAPTER NINE

REESE

My father had been a huge football fan. I'd entered Chiefs Kingdom as a tyke and never left. Whenever I visited Chiefs Nation, it reminded me of the person I'd once been, the oldest son in a family of five with a school janitor mom and a truck driver dad.

We hadn't had a lot, but we'd always had clean clothes, hot food, and a lot of love. Until it was stolen from me by smoke and fire. I'd slept over at my best friend's house and escaped the wrath of flames. Bolt and Ma Siller took in my traumatized thirteen-year-old self and added me to their brood of six. All three of his daughters were married. One of his sons was killed four years ago in a motorcycle accident and the other two remained in the club.

I'd gotten the Siller family into football and it was a tradition that continued to this day. Arriving back at the club fresh off a Chiefs win left me stoked. I'd spent the weekend at the house with Ma, Bolt, Knight, and Baron because I didn't want to be at the club, thinking about Ainsley and how she'd looked when she opened the door to us.

Letting Roman Mac live had been the right call no matter how much it galled me. So many times, I'd thought about going to check on her. Then, I remembered Trinity and how I allowed her murderer to walk free because of a girl I'd fucked once.

I'd pull out Trinity's picture, study her face, and wish I could've gotten over my hesitancy. My guilt was the hardest part. Trinity died because of me. I'd kept her at arms' length and Roman was my enemy. Then Ainsley would intrude again on my complicated feelings for Trinity, until it was a never-ending loop.

If I could only fuck Ainsley again, I'd get her out of my system. Whenever I took an ol' lady, I didn't have my eyes turned toward marriage or children. I didn't want a wife and I sure as hell didn't want kids. My little sister was three when she died. With ten years separating us, I felt like an adult over her. As much as I mourned my parents and my eight-year-old brother, losing that mischievous brat was what almost drove me over the edge.

Perhaps, that was why I always held Trinity at bay. Maybe, she could've gotten past the wedding vows. Kids? No. Every time I fucked her, I made sure to put on my own condom and didn't let her near them even after we finished.

Or, maybe, I couldn't take her as my ol' lady because she'd fucked so many of my brothers, and I wasn't sure she wouldn't have declined anyone if they offered her enough money.

Ainsley and I hadn't discussed much. Her mission had been to fuck. My expectation was to fuck her, so it fucking escaped me why the fuck I walked into the clubhouse after the game and wanted to talk to her.

I wondered if I threw a word out and told her to talk about it for ten minutes, could she? I wondered how she was holding up or whether she knew I made Louisiana call Nova so he could return Ainsley and Roman's phones that same night. We'd let him go. If she decided to talk, not having a phone wouldn't stop her. She'd gone to the fucking hospital where I'm certain questions flew at her from all directions.

Jinx sidled up to me and wrapped an arm around my waist. "Hey, babe," she said in a loud voice over the din rising around us. "What's up?"

Usually, she kept her currently blue hair in a long braid. Tonight, it was loose and free, framing her face. She was thirty-one. Same age as me. Our birthdays were two days apart. We'd dated before Louisiana took her. I couldn't give her what she wanted, so when he told me he wanted to take her out, I stepped out of the way.

"Heard the boys won."

"You're so full of shit. You know you watched that game."

"Possibly," she said in a sing-song voice. "Anyway, guess who stopped by?"

My first thought was Ainsley, which I immediately dismissed. Razor would've handed me my ass and possibly thrown her into the fucking pit. Then I would've gotten killed trying to protect her.

"Who, babe?"

"Delilah. She's down to fuck." Beaming a smile as if she'd done me a great favor, she dug in the valley of her tits and produced a slip of paper. "Call her *tonight*."

Pocketing the number, I grunted. "Last time we fucked, she accidentally bit my cock. That shit hurt for fucking days."

"Ouch."

"Yeah, easy enough for you to be so dismissive. Wasn't your cock in the vise of her chompers."

"True, given that I have a pussy. However, the Novocain hadn't worn off."

"I beg your fucking pardon?" I didn't mean to sound so fucking outraged, but who sucked cock with a numb mouth? Especially *my* cock. "Strikes one, two, and three." I snatched the number from my pocket and handed it back to her. "If she can't properly protect Monster, then fuck her."

"I can't with the dick names."

"Better than Bear. According to Louisiana, you gave his cock that name."

"I didn't think he'd actually use it!"

"Your mistake, babe." I tugged out of the arm she still had around me and pulled out my billfold. "Bring me a beer. I'll be at the pool tables." I handed her a twenty. "Keep the change."

"Such a big tipper."

"You flirting with my wife, Reese?" Louisiana asked, stepping between us, the severity on his face shocking me. He put his arm around us and drew us closer. "Can't leave you alone for ten minutes."

Sniffing, she rolled her eyes. "A digital watch where you can actually tell the time properly will be your next gift from me. You've been gone for hours. As usual."

"Sure haven't. My bike's outside and I haven't been on it today, babe."

Skepticism crossed her face.

Bending, he brushed his lips over hers. "Do you see how crowded it is tonight? You lost track of me. I've been here. Mainly outside."

"Okay. I'm sorry, babe. I—" She gulped, glanced at me, and shoved her way behind the bar.

"The way you gaslight her is fucked up," I shouted over the noise to make sure that motherfucker heard me.

"She bought it, so it worked." He nodded toward the door. "I need to talk to you."

"Jinx is bringing my beer."

"This is about Ainsley," Louisiana gritted.

"What about her?"

He indicated his ears, then arced his hand toward the crowd of bikers and chicks. Holding up a hand, he walked away, returning a few minutes later with two beers and nodding his head toward the door.

Outside, I drank deeply, enjoying the fresh air after the press of bodies inside.

"What about Ainsley and how do you know?"

Louisiana flicked his lighter until the reefer caught and then inhaled before passing it to me so I could hit it.

"I went to their place," he started.

I snatched the joint and inhaled again. "You did what?" I asked on an exhale of smoke. "You could've gotten fucking killed, asshole."

"Please." He reclaimed the joint and relit it after several flicks of his lighter. "My intellect outweighs a Bloody Scorpion's any fucking day of the week."

"What about Ainsley?" I demanded. The fuckhead hadn't gotten killed, so I wouldn't argue and point out why it had been such a bad idea.

"I went there to tell Roman he should kiss your ass every day for sparing him."

"You offered my ass to that motherfucker? Next time don't be so generous."

Snickering, he held out the bud to me.

"What about Ainsley, fuckhead?"

He studied me, then smiled. "Nothing too urgent. I took a little memento for you." Smiling, he pulled out a photo of Ainsley and handed it to me. "It was in a frame that said 'Best Little Sister'. Sweet, huh? Twinsies. Well, not really since hers said 'brother.'"

I didn't care about the frame. Louisiana had stolen her picture for me.

"I'll put it in my desk as a memento of our date."

Eyeing me, he sipped his beer. "I thought maybe it would be a souvenir from the time you got the easiest pussy ever."

"Ainsley isn't easy and if you say that again, I'll rip your fucking tongue out."

"I'm just kidding, Reese. I did you a solid. Enjoy it."

He grabbed the joint from my hand and walked away. I knew in my fucking bones something was up.

Chapter Ten

Ainsley

8 weeks later

With just several days before October arrived, the crisp air of late September carried the scent of fallen leaves and distant barbecue smoke. The late afternoon sky stretched wide and blue, though wisps of white clouds occasionally streaked through it. As I sped away from the Bloody Scorpions clubhouse on the northwestern edge of the city, a golden glow shone over the streets.

Trees turning shades of gold and rust dotted stretches of land, especially where the surroundings were more open. Strip malls, gas stations, and local diners, some with their signs advertising fall specials—pumpkin spice coffee, barbecue platters, or Friday night football deals—zoomed by.

Heading to the Royal Bastards clubhouse, I wasn't sure what to expect. Would they stop me at the gate and question me? Maybe, there wasn't a gate and it was easy to access. If they were like the Bloody Scorpions, women were always welcome.

Unfortunately, my reputation might've proceeded me if they asked for my name and recognized it in connection to Roman. I didn't know what he'd revealed while he'd been so gravely injured. Reese warned me not to contact him again. Perhaps, he'd alerted his brothers to my identity.

God!

Would they kill me?

I just didn't know and I couldn't care. If Roman, or God forbid *Boom Boom*, discovered my secret I was dead anyway. My brother might not actually kill me, but I would be dead *to* him.

"Ains, it's okay." Nova's soothing voice washed over me.

Time wasn't my friend. It was closing in on me to find a solution to the situation I'd gotten myself into. Nova had invited me over to her place, located on a back lot on club grounds. We were supposed to spend a girls' weekend filled with ice cream, pizza, manicures, and Rom-Coms once the football game ended. I was a fanatic. Nova hated organized sports.

As I listened to her talk about Louisiana and her annoyance that he'd ghosted her, I'd thought about Reese. A regular occurrence, especially considering my current state. I'd blurted the truth to Nova, remembering she was the only girl who I truly trusted with my deepest secrets.

Immediately, she'd agreed with me that Reese deserved to know the truth and insisted we go to the Royal Bastards' clubhouse with all due haste.

"If you go through with your plan, it's a whole process," she'd said breezily. "You'll need to have counseling, then schedule the procedure, then recovery. You have *two fucking weeks*, Ainsley. Then, Roman will be home. It's best to have all your facts ASAP. If Reese is willing to do right and stand by you, then fuck Roman."

I'd snapped my brows together.

"I don't mean it in a bad way, Ains. But you're twenty-one. A grown woman. I mean, is getting knocked up by Roman's op a shitty way to repay his dedication to you? Def, but it is what it is."

"You aren't helping my guilt," I'd grouched.

She shrugged. "I'm not trying to make you feel guilty. Facts are facts."

"You helped me with that stupid rhythm method calendar, Nova."

"Oh. Right. I must've gotten it wrong."

"Obviously, you did."

"You're so fucking spoiled, Ainsley." She'd rolled her eyes and plopped down on the edge of her bed. "Always relying on Roman or me to help you figure out shit. Must be nice having a big brother who'd die to protect you."

"I can do without your bitchiness, Nova. You said you used the rhythm method because of problems with birth control. Remember? That's why you suggested I don't take pills."

She'd snapped her fingers. "Right. I did say that. I suppose you took my advice about condoms, too?"

"Yeah."

In short order, she demanded we get going. I tried to talk her out of accompanying me, even though her insistence I needed moral support reminded me why we'd been friends for so long.

Before we left, I made one last attempt at finding another way to contact Reese, hoping we didn't have to breech that fortress. When I begged her to give me her phone so I could call Reese, she'd declined. Another solution I had was for her to call Louisiana, then hand the phone to me and I'd beg *him* to call Reese.

She shot down each idea I had. She didn't think Louisiana would answer because he'd been pulling away from her for weeks now.

"I'd prefer to go to the 8th circle of hell, then to go to that clubhouse," she'd said woefully. "Lou Lou will swear it's because I want him and won't believe it's for moral support for my bestest friend in the whole wide world."

Her use of our childhood term warmed me.

Then, she'd hit me with another argument. According to her, Boom Boom searched her phone now, something I knew based on what he'd asked me that day at the clubhouse. Even if she deleted the number once I called, they'd still appear on a bill if he requested a detailed statement. Although I couldn't argue her logic, especially after what I'd witnessed, I wondered how she'd explained away all the previous calls between her and Louisiana.

"Daddy wouldn't have time to look over all those records," she'd said, waving a dismissive hand.

That tracked with Boom Boom saying he'd only looked at the call logs for the month. We never talked about the scene in the clubhouse. A week after that horror, she came over. Our respective bruises were fading. Still, it surprised me when she smiled and greeted me as if nothing happened.

I'd followed her lead. Between the two of us, Boom Boom had been the most reprehensible to her. I didn't want to push the issue and traumatize her further. We talked on the phone every day and visited once a week.

After Boom Boom's visit to the house, my brother's hostility toward me had receded. Before he left a month ago, I would sometimes catch him staring at me and I wondered if he'd somehow discovered my date with Reese Sinclair. Roman's departure pissed me off for a couple reasons. I wouldn't have given up my apartment if I knew he had a run to go on. The bigger issue was Boom Boom and Wizard, who'd ordered my brother to accompany them to *wherever*. They'd made special accommodations and had someone drive Roman in a van.

If he didn't video chat with me daily, I would suspect something was up.

Two days before Roman left, I knew the truth. I was pregnant with Reese's baby. Roman's leaving was a blessing in disguise because of the morning sickness that he chalked up to nerves over his departure. Today, he told me he'd return in two weeks and I finally decided I needed to talk to Reese.

When I confirmed my pregnancy with three at-home tests, my kneejerk solution was abortion. Reese didn't want me. He definitely wouldn't want our baby.

Despite Boom Boom's violence, I was calming down again. Mainly because Roman allowed me to help him. My brother seemed to have gotten his sense of self back. I couldn't be a pansy and fall apart.

"Do you know Scarlett O'Hara was almost named Pansy?" I blurted into the silence of the car.

Nova sat in the passenger seat, staring out the window. The closer we got, the more our tension grew. I felt so bad for dragging her into my mess. Now, she shook her head and laughed.

"Only you would know that. Why the fuck would you know anything about *Gone With The Wind*?"

"Mitchell is better than Shakespeare." I *loathed* Shakespeare. If *War and Peace* had been the alternative in high school, I would've chosen it. *David Copperfield.* A book handwritten by Medieval French monks. They couldn't have done worse with their 'thees,' 'thous,' and 'shalts,' than The Bard. "I campaigned for *Lady Chatterley's Lover*. Roman wasn't amused, neither was the principal, or my English Lit teacher."

"I still maintain your brother should've allowed you to go to public school like the rest of us," Nova grumbled. "Still, you chose *that* book."

Jumping onto I-70 as GPS directed, I huffed. "I intended to list a bunch of grievances if I could've given my book report, but I stand by my decision. *Romeo & Juliet, MacBeth, and Hamlet* would've been bad enough. *Titus Andronicus*? No, ma'am. Stupid, stupid name with stupidly over-the-top violence. I discovered all I wanted to know about that crap since I was the only one who didn't choose it."

"Wait! Is this the class where the teacher put you dead last to give your report?"

"Yep. He skipped over me then because he said we ran out of time. Remember? And that stupid report was a major part of my grade."

Nova snapped her fingers. "Didn't you fail the semester and Roman asked why?"

"And I confessed." I giggled. "Like magic, I received an A+. Didn't even have to stand in front of the class and give the report."

"So, wait! That teacher lived? Roman didn't fuck him up for fucking with you?"

Sniffing, I glared at Nova, losing my good mood. "Roman isn't a savage. For your information, the teacher transferred. According to Roman, it was somewhere out of state."

"Okay, stupid. Believe that if you will. I guarantee that dude was bug food."

I flipped her off.

Our surroundings soon shifted from suburban to urban and industrial. Warehouses, train yards, and aging brick buildings hinted at KCK's working-class roots. Old factories and rail lines gave a glimpse of the city's industrial past.

The closer I got to downtown, the more traffic I encountered. I swore the scent of barbeque drifted through the car's vents and my mouth watered even as nausea swirled in me.

Nova shifted. "You know what I haven't stopped wondering since I found out about the little biker that Reese parked in your garage?"

I wrinkled my nose. "Eww."

"Oh, grow up. Would you prefer if I said the load he dropped in you that has the potential to fuck up your life?"

"I'd prefer if you called it my baby!"

"Why even think about it like that? It's the enemy."

"Are you out of your fucking mind? This is an innocent child."

"Made by the seed of an enemy, stupid. Which, by the way, is completely fucking insane. What the fuck did you say to Reese Sinclair to make him fuck you raw?"

"The same fucking thing you must've said to Louisiana so he'd fuck you at all."

"Not bare! Louisiana went without a few times, but then he had an abrupt about face about our lack of protection. I've tried many times to change his mind about a baby. He's a fucking fanatic about my period. I think he knows my cycle better than me."

"Stop thinking of my baby as an enemy."

"You've already claimed it?" She sounded appalled, so I sidled a quick glance in her direction. She stared at me, mouth open. "*You're* the one who's insane."

"Shut up. I was with Reese once and ended up pregnant, based on your fucking *stupid* advice."

"I didn't fucking think you'd actually convince him to do it, idiot."

"What are you talking about? You know I didn't want Roman to find out and he has connections everywhere to keep watch over me. I trust *you*. I Googled options and came to you. You told me to do it this way so I wouldn't have a shitty first experience."

"Yeah, whatever, Ainsley. I don't know what you say to get your fucking way all the time. Never mind. Men are stupid. They rush to cater to idiots like you."

The skyline of Kansas City, MO rose in the distance, but I couldn't enjoy the stunning view of the city. "Don't call me another name."

"You're carrying an adversary. A foe. We both know Roman will never accept it. The thing in your belly has Royal Bastard blood."

"Stop referring to my baby as the enemy," I reiterated. "*Or* a thing. Didn't you just fucking tell me you wanted Louisiana's baby? That kid would've had Royal Bastard blood, too. What the fuck would *you* have done as the daughter of the Bloody Scorpion's president?"

"It didn't happen, so I have nothing to worry about."

"Only because Louisiana had sense."

"You're such a fucking cunt, Ainsley. He wanted me pregnant, then he changed his mind, so obviously he saw something in me."

"Doubtful, bitch. You were a bitch then and you're a bitch now. I don't see what Louisiana fucking saw in you."

"That's fucking rich," she said bitterly. "Little Miss Chatterbox that Louisiana found so hilarious. I'm surprised he didn't offer to fuck you himself."

I gritted my teeth. We'd had this argument before, just one of many over Louisiana. I never thought he was attracted to me, though at one time I thought he liked me as Nova's friend. Until Roman ended up in their hands and Reese allowed him to live. "Louisiana cared about you a lot, Nova. But he had a wife. He's married. Eventually, whatever was between you had to end. I wish you'd walked away."

"He loves me. He wanted me to have his baby," she insisted. "I refused, then when I changed my mind he denied me. He either pulled out, wore a condom, or wouldn't touch me because he said I was fertile."

"Who knows why he did that." I searched for an excuse that made her feel better and opened her eyes. Roman came to mind and I hit up on what he might do. Granted, he kept a lot of club politics and business away from me. I was a child of the club, though, and I knew my brother quite well. He was fiercely loyal to his colors. "Maybe, uh, maybe, Louisiana started the affair as a way to humiliate Boom Boom." I forced a laugh. "What better way to do it then to impregnate his daughter?"

"You've never liked Louisiana if you think he could do something so fucking low down and devious. On second thought, he would never have offered cock to you. I mean, look at you and look at me. I'm a blonde bombshell. You're you. Average. Cute, but not overwhelmingly gorgeous. Nice body, but mine's better. Yet, you have two hot guys twisted around your fucking finger." She laughed merrily. "If I didn't love you so much, I'd fucking hate you and plot your downfall."

A chill slid down my spine. In my emotional state, Nova's words sounded like a threat. To me, to my baby, or both. She had punched me, though I excused her because of Boom Boom's treatment. Now, I wasn't so sure. She was rabid in her insistence that this innocent child was an enemy. I didn't know if she lashed out because of frustration or trauma. Maybe jealousy toward me for whatever reason.

Except we grew up together and we'd always looked out for each other.

"Did I tell you I tried to fuck Roman four months ago?"

"You did *what*?"

"Apparently, *I* did nothing because *we* didn't. Anyway, he was at the club and I told him I needed the light bulb in my refrigerator changed. While he was seeing to it, I stripped and tried my best to seduce him. He would've fucked me if it wasn't for *you*, chick."

"Your reasoning has lost me." Once we got back to her place, I'd light into her over the fact she'd tried to sleep with my brother. What if I wanted to have sex with Boom Boom?

Bad comparison. Roman was quite handsome. Boom Boom was a cyclops. Or something, since he still had both eyes.

"How is it my fault Roman didn't have sex with you?" *Yuck*.

"He said I was your best friend and he watched me grow up. He told me it would be gross abuse and he considered me a child under him."

"All true, so how the fuck is his honor my fucking fault?"

"You're so fucking dense, Ainsley. He's fucked some of those club sluts who are my age. He didn't do me because of you."

It was that and because of Trinity, but I'd clue her in later.

"I don't accept that blame," I said firmly. "I don't control Roman's penis." So gross talking about his private parts. "You should applaud the respect he has for you and I."

She snorted.

"What did you want to ask me, Nova?" Changing the subject was best. I'm not sure what bee was buzzing in her britches this time, but hopefully our weekend together would smooth things over.

"Was Nicolette really your mom? If so, what color do you think your baby will be? You and

Roman def aren't *real* bi-racials. What happens if the baby is brown skinned like your mom? Stepmom? Not-mom? My guess is she couldn't have kids and your dad hired a surrogate."

I breathed in and out, trying to cool my blood. I was so fucking happy I'd left my gun at home. Roman insisted I keep it nearby when I was alone in the house. I think I would've shot the fuck out of this stupid bitch.

She knew the shit I'd endured when Mom was alive, because she looked so different than the other ol' ladies. Mom and Dad once had a huge argument because she'd overheard him say how happy he was at the color of Roman and me. Dad revealed he'd had to get special permission to even bring her to the club, which I found fucking horrendous. He should've walked away from those motherfuckers then. Except he said he'd met Mom after he was already a high-ranking full patch Bloody Scorpion.

Roman and I rarely discussed our heritage. It just was a part of who we were. My guess was he didn't think about it too much, unless *I* got shit over it, then he went ballistic.

Most of the time, I didn't consider myself one way or the other. While my parents were alive, that was different. But it was just easier to lean into my ambiguity.

"Of course, you'd have to keep the baby for it to be any color, right?" Nova went on. "I know you're leaning toward making that little problem go away."

The anger roaring in my ears almost drowned out the voice of the GPS. I would've missed my exit.

"First," I snarled through clenched teeth, my fingers so tight on the steering wheel they were turning white, "this baby isn't a problem. It's a child, no matter what I decide."

"Fucked up, but okay."

"Second," I spat, ignoring *her* fucked up comment, "I only want a healthy baby. It doesn't matter how it looks."

She made a face at me. "You're so fucking sensitive, Ainsley. I didn't mean anything by the question. I'm genuinely curious."

"Curiosity got the cat's ass beat to death. Remember that before you open your fucking mouth again."

She huffed. I considered a detour to the river, where I'd shove her ass in and ruin her hair and makeup. Nice dream…

"Your destination is on the right," the GPS announced, and my fantasy died.

REESE

It was quiet for a Saturday afternoon because a good many of our members went to the *Kansas Speedway*. Razor, Bolt, Warrior, Jester, and a bunch of the guys loved car racing. Football was my thing.

I'd once dreamed of a career in the NFL. As club life sucked me in, those ideas fell apart.

I leaned back in the stool where I sat at the bar, took a sip of my beer, and gazed at the TV. The Chiefs were playing a regular season game against a division rival and were down by three with fifty-seven seconds on the clock before halftime. My boys would rally. They always did. I wasn't a fair-weather friend, so even if they lost, my support never wavered.

Our quarterback threw a Hail Mary. The ball hung in the air and my breath caught. Our running back and their safety were neck and neck, then that motherfucker shoved our guy and jumped, catching the fucking ball and running it in for a touchdown.

"Goddamn it!" Louisiana shouted.

"Where's the fucking flag?" I waited for a pass interference call or for the officials to review that play. But nothing. The head coach didn't even throw a challenge flag. "Motherfucker!"

"Turn that shit off, Jinx," Louisiana yelled.

She looked at me and lifted a brow. I nodded, still fuming.

"We should've gone to the racetrack," Louisiana complained, swiping his pint of gin from the bar counter and drinking. "I can't believe that shit."

"Fuck, me neither. Sometimes, I wonder what those coaches are thinking."

"Yeah, bro. Paid millions and offer a whole lot of nothing."

"Come on, you two. It isn't the end of the fucking world," Jinx said.

Two weeks ago, she'd dyed her hair pink. I wasn't sure why the fuck she was suddenly fascinated by these crazy shades.

"I know one thing that'll ease my disappointment, babe," Louisiana said.

Leaning against the bar, she grinned. "Really, Big Man? I'd love to hear it and then I'll see what I can do."

He grabbed her throat and yanked her halfway across the bar for a sloppy kiss. When he released her, she scooted back and slid off the bar.

I shook my head. "One day, you're going to jerk her head off her fucking shoulders, asshole."

"I won't!" Louisiana protested. "Tell him, babe."

"I trust my man, Reese. Stop being such a worrywart."

"That's worryfart, babe."

Chuckling with them, I flipped off Louisiana and drank more of my beer.

"Soooo, Reese," Jinx started, leaning against the bar again. "A little bird told me you might ask Candy out again."

"Yep."

She clucked her tongue. "Don't be like that. Did I choose good this time?"

"At least she didn't bite my cock when she sucked it."

"You two assholes are just alike. Always more concerned about your dicks than substance. Did you like her? Was she pretty to you?"

"Come on, babe. Lay off Reese. He obviously doesn't want to talk about it."

"He had the date last Thursday, then went on a run the very next day. This is the first time I've seen him." She batted her lashes at me. "At least humor me."

I could humor her without going into detail. The truth of the matter was I took Candy out, forced myself to pay attention to her, and forced myself to fuck her. Partly because I'd been sick to death of Louisiana constantly bringing up Ainsley. Whatever Nova told him about her, he passed on to me. He ignored my order to shut the fuck up about her and keep that shit to himself.

Even if I'd considered dropping by her apartment to see her, his constant barrage of information turned me off. Two weeks ago, he finally obliged me, though I suspected he hadn't brought her up because he wanted to protect himself rather than my sanity.

Yet, my date with Candy left me annoyed and unfulfilled. Worse, I'd felt like shit ever since, confirming I'd lost my fucking mind in the months I'd grieved for Trinity.

Why else would I feel as if I betrayed...fuck, I couldn't even bring myself to say it, I was so fucking humiliated. My feelings weren't even directed at Trinity, a woman who'd been killed because of her connection to my club, who'd died brokenhearted because I'd been such a motherfucker.

Thankfully, the run cleared my head. We were diversifying our interests and had made a deal with a smaller club located in a neighboring county to serve as one of our distributors. A few months back, Marquis made the case for allowing him to create a meth lab since he knew how to make that shit.

We hadn't put it to the members yet. Razor wanted exact numbers, not estimates. It seemed as if he was putting plans in place to go in that direction. I understood Razor was trying to create barriers between our club and the lower-level stuff. On the other hand, I doubted he'd trust such a small club with our level of distribution. My thought was, Razor intended to test Marquis's drug making abilities and have the smaller club distribute the merchandise for us. A test for them, a loss leader for us. If the plan failed, we wouldn't lose an exorbitant amount of money.

"What do you say, Reese?"

"Huh?"

Louisiana snickered. "Told you, babe. Motherfucker's mind was a billion miles away."

"It was." I drained my bottle, then set it on the counter and grabbed the fresh one Jinx had waiting for me. "What's up, J?"

"A double date. Keir and me, and you and Candy."

I smirked at Louisiana. "Keir, huh? What did you do, brother?" If he pissed her off, she used his given name. "Forgot to take out the garbage?"

Draining his gin, Louisiana lowered his lashes. Jinx glanced away. An uncomfortable silence descended into the sudden tension.

"What's going on, you two?"

"Nothing, Reese." He slammed the empty pint on the bar top. "Some slut's been blowing up my phone. I told her to lose my fucking number. I danced with the bitch once at a party."

Jinx's nose reddened and she swallowed. Holy fuck! This was serious shit for Jinx to look so vulnerable.

"Her name is Nova," she said tightly. "And why did she send you a naked photo if you only danced with her *once*?"

My knowledge of Louisiana's affair with Nova made me just as culpable because I helped to deceive Jinx, while laughing and joking with her every time I saw her.

"Jinx, babe, I don't know why this girl sent that photo. I didn't even give her my number. She must've had one of those magnetic readers and stole my information."

I squinted.

"They have those?" Jinx asked suspiciously. "I thought it was only for bank cards."

Louisiana shook his head. "Some people store credit card information on their phones and a bunch of other personal shit that magnets suck into the readers. Suddenly, all your information is in fucked up hands. Including phone numbers and email addresses." He looked at me. "Tell her, Reese."

Predictably, Jinx turned her hopeful eyes toward me. I wanted to bash Louisiana's fucking head in for putting me on the spot. Unable to meet her eyes, I focused on my beer and gave her a curt nod.

"I just love you so much, Keir," she said quietly. "After I cut your cock off, I would be devastated if you ever cheated on me. You're one of the good guys, babe."

"That's why you love me, babe." He reached across the bar and grabbed her arm. "When you got me, you got the best of the best. I'm not a typical motherfucker with an ol' lady and a bunch of bitches on the side. That Nova cunt? Fuck her."

"Reese? Louisiana?"

At the sound of one of the prospects calling my name, I swiveled in my chair. "Yo?" I said as Louisiana turned, too.

"Two chicks are asking for you. A girl named Ainsley for you." He nodded to me. "And a Nova for Louisiana."

CHAPTER ELEVEN

REESE

To say all hell broke loose was the fucking understatement of the century. I couldn't wrap my head around Ainsley being at the clubhouse because Jinx launched herself over the bar top, punched the fuck out of Louisiana, and jetted outside.

I didn't want her to fuck up the wrong girl, so I left Louisiana on the fucking floor and ran after Jinx. She might've seen a nudie of Nova, but I'm not certain she'd have the presence of mind to take in her features.

Outside, Jinx skidded to a halt and glanced between Nova and Ainsley. "Nova?" she snarled.

Tossing her hair, Nova smirked. "No wonder he doesn't want you—"

Jinx's punch to Nova's mouth cut her off. Nova reeled back, but came up swinging, barely missing Ainsley. If she hadn't held up her hands and ducked, she would've gotten the punch meant for Jinx.

Over my fucking shock, I rushed to Ainsley and yanked her away from the other two as they circled each other, throwing punches and insults. Placing myself in front of Ainsley, I grabbed the girl closest to me, which just happened to be Nova.

"Let go of me!" she snarled, struggling in my arms.

"Calm the fuck down," I ordered.

Louisiana entered the melee. Jinx's fist careened toward him but he caught her arm and trapped her against him. "Enough, Jinx! Enough. I'm not putting up with your jealous bullshit."

"Fuck you. You're a liar and a cheating asshole." She began struggling again. "Let go of me."

My deceptive composure amazed me. I was so aware of Ainsley that my skin prickled and my body reawakened for the first time in weeks. "I need to talk to Ainsley. Stay away from Louisiana and his woman. Understand me?"

Nova heaved in a breath. "I'm his woman. He told me so."

Fuck, I didn't give a fuck. While I felt sorry for how pitiful she sounded, she wasn't my top priority. I didn't even know her. I just knew *of* her.

Louisiana threw Jinx over his shoulder, ignoring her furious screams and ineffective punches. He pointed at Nova. "Get the fuck off my club's property, cunt. Don't ever show your fucking face again."

"Hey!" Ainsley peeped from behind me. "You're an asshole."

"Stay out of it, Ainsley!" I gritted.

She glared at me, but watched Louisiana carry Jinx away without another word.

"Wait!" Nova called. "Wait, Lou Lou. Where are you going?"

His look promised murder.

"Louisiana! Wait." Nova began sobbing. "You promised...Why are you ignoring me? I wouldn't have come with Ainsley if you'd answered my calls. You didn't even respond to the nude photo."

He didn't answer. He just carried Jinx inside and left Nova crying in my arms.

"You lied to me, Nova," Ainsley accused.

"Oh, grow up, Ainsley," she snarled around her tears. "Life isn't only about you. I needed to see Louisiana and you were my ticket in."

Ainsley opened her mouth, but I shook my head. I wanted to know why she'd come. I didn't have time for a bitch fight. I especially couldn't allow Razor to find her here. Roman Mac's life was spared because of Ainsley. He knew who she was and would just as soon kill her for when the next time arose.

The prospects on duty—two at the gate and two patrolling the property—had gathered around to take in the scene with infuriating interest. I nodded to the one who'd summoned me.

He jogged over. "Yeah, Sarge?"

Setting Nova on her feet, I nudged her toward him. "Watch her until I'm done with her." I pointed to Ainsley.

Licking his lips, he swept his gaze over Ainsley. It was so fucking hard not to pluck his eyeballs the fuck out of his head. Which pissed me the fuck off. I wasn't a jealous fuckhead. I wasn't possessive. And I wasn't a stars-in-his-eyes pussy who turned into a pussy-whipped wretch.

Grabbing Ainsley's arm, I dragged her into the clubhouse. I didn't see Jinx or Louisiana, but I feared for his fucking life with all the glass breaking and wood splintering. As I climbed the stairs and drew closer to my room, the noise increased. I understood why Louisiana wouldn't take her to their house. Unless he tied her up, she would've attacked him on the way there. And if he *had* tied her up, well, I'd be pulling out my leathers and white gloves for his fucking funeral.

Once I unlocked my door and turned on the light, I released Ainsley. Slamming the door behind us, I stormed to her. She wasn't wearing make-up today, but she was still stunning. Thick, dark lashes ringed her whiskey-colored eyes. Eyes that could touch my fucking soul and crack it wide open.

Her smooth olive skin, high cheekbones, a straight nose, and full lips haunted me.

"You have two fucking minutes to tell me why you're here, Ainsley."

She opened her mouth, but I raised my hand.

"I told you to lose my fucking number."

"Did I dial it?" she snapped, her eyes flashing.

"It would've been better than showing up at my fucking clubhouse, smart ass."

"You blocked me! What did you expect me to do, asshole?"

"Fuck all! I don't want to fucking see you. If I did, I would've come to you. Get out of here. Don't fucking come back. Lose my number. Forget my address—"

She thumped my shoulder. "Fine. Fuck you, by the way. You didn't even let me explain."

"That Roman Mac's your fucking brother? No explanation needed, Ainsley. I saw all I needed to see."

She heaved in another breath. It seemed as if she was holding herself together by a thread. She looked so fucking young and vulnerable. The stark pain and misery in her eyes almost undid me. But we were on two different sides, and it would never work. I wouldn't leave my fucking club under any circumstances and she couldn't be a part of my life here. Even if I didn't question her loyalties, Razor and the rest of my brothers would. If one thing went awry, I would be looked upon with even more suspicion than I had been since I released Roman Mac. I allowed him to live.

I stiffened my resolve. "Go."

She twisted her hands together. "I'm pregnant," she whispered. "With your baby, Reese."

The announcement slammed into me with the velocity of a speeding bullet. I searched her face, looking for signs of deception. Hoping she was fucking with me. She wasn't. Her fear and panic was as real as my disbelief.

"You fucking told me you weren't fertile. You had three days."

The detail I remembered went over her head. Thankfully.

"I-I c-counted wrong. It was wrong. I was wrong."

"You're going into your tenth week, and you've just decided to tell me?"

She blinked. "T-ten weeks? You...you...That was a quick calculation."

Because she lived in my fucking head. I couldn't tell her that. Whether I was obsessed because I was a stupid fuckhead, because I'd taken her virginity, because she was young and bubbly and my complete opposite or because...

Frustrated, I scrubbed a hand over my face. It could be for any reason. None of which concerned her because it was about me, not her. And I'd overcome this pathetic bullshit without her.

"We're getting the fuck off track. I assume you're here because you want child support."

"The baby isn't even born yet."

"Stop calling it that!"

"It's not a fucking fish," she yelled. "It's a baby."

My gaze dipped to her tits and my cock hardened. They were bigger and more luscious in her tight little sweater.

"I don't want anything, Reese. I came because…" Her voice trailed off and she glanced away. "I came because Roman's on a run and he'll be home in two weeks." She hung her head. "I wanted you to know because it was only fair."

Turning away from her, I stormed to the window and glanced at the river. "You wanted me to know because you thought that would change my mind about us."

"That isn't true."

My nostrils flared. I could always tell her the baby might not be mine, but I knew the truth. Apparently, Nova hadn't mentioned Ainsley's pregnancy to Louisiana. Maybe, all the information Nova fed to Louisiana was wrong. I didn't even know Roman Mac had gone on a run.

Not much he could do without hands, so I was suspicious about that. They may have taken him away to kill him. Razor said if the situation was reversed and a bunch of Bloody Scorpions dumped me at Ma Siller's house, he'd put a bullet in my brain. He'd think I gave up club information or somehow betrayed the Royal Bastards to survive.

It made sense that Boom Boom would feel the same way.

"I suppose Nova put you up to this?"

"She didn't know until today when I went to her place for a girl's weekend."

Well, that explained why she hadn't told Louisiana.

"I thought you should know, Reese."

My name rolling off her tongue curled around my insides. I glowered at the horizon beyond the window. Hopefully, she left. I didn't know if I could withstand her sweet chattering.

"I-I-I don't know what I expected from you. When I talked to my brother today, the enormity of my predicament hit me. He'd hate me."

I didn't think anything would turn that motherfucker against Ainsley. My life would be so much fucking easier if they were enemies.

"Boom Boom would kill me."

Hyperbole. Roman wouldn't allow Ainsley near his president if she was in danger.

"I've thought of every way possible to keep our baby."

Our baby. I flinched. I'd made a baby. With Ainsley.

"I'm going to abort it."

From the moment she'd made her announcement, those were the words I wanted to hear. Now that she'd said them, my insides twisted and I recoiled.

"Is that what you want, Ainsley?"

"I have to do what's right for all of us."

"Don't you mean the two of us?"

"Three, if you include the baby. But it's four. I have to consider my brother. I don't want him marked for death. I'm already worried sick about him because he doesn't have hands. I don't know why they insisted he go on a run. I don't know if they want to kill him or he wants to kill them."

Turning, I cocked my head to the side. "Why would he want to kill his club brothers?"

Her gaze flickered over me before she glanced away again. "I'm just talking, Reese," she said softly. "I'm worried about Roman is all."

Something else was up, but she was upset enough. I refused to add to her stress. I crooked my finger at her.

She walked closer but remained at arm's length. I searched every curve and angle of her face, seeking answers, trying to uncover the mysteries of the universe.

"Do you want to get rid of the kid?" I asked slowly, succinctly.

A tear slid down her cheek and she shook her head. "No. I didn't know my definitive answer until now. But deep down I know I want to keep it."

I didn't know what the fuck came over me. Except *Ainsley*. She'd bewitched me. I couldn't give her the answer I knew she wanted and tell her that we'd make it work. No matter how I spun it, it couldn't and it wouldn't.

People in my life meant a lot to me as well. If Bolt discovered Ainsley carried my kid, he'd be so fucking disappointed in me. They didn't care if I'd fucked her. A kid was a different story.

She was here though, and I'd ached to hold her in my arms again. I jerked off to her photo almost every night and pretended I was fucking Ainsley as I drove into Candy that one time.

Taking Ainsley's face between my hands, I dipped my head and slanted my mouth over hers. Standing on tiptoes, she wrapped her arms around my neck and groaned against my lips. Seizing the opportunity, I swept my tongue into her hot depths, absorbing her little sounds, tasting mint and sweetness and Ainsley.

I slid my hands under her sweater, grunting in approval when I discovered her bra-less.

Grinning, I forced my mouth away from her. "You like your beauties as free as I like my balls."

"I need new bras," she breathed, nuzzling her lips against my neck. Her fingers gripped my cock as it pressed against my jeans. "My boobs are bigger because of the baby and I haven't gotten any new clothes."

I yanked the top from over her head, wrapped an arm around her waist and carried her to my bed. Her wedges pleased me. They were much easier to remove than the boots she'd worn on our date.

I wasn't sure which part of her I wanted to taste first. Her feet, her nipples, or her clit. She was so fucking delicious.

A warning seeped into my lust-fogged brain. It was getting late. Ainsley needed to leave before Razor and the guys returned. I needed to check on Jinx and Louisiana. Tasting Ainsley would have to wait.

And, maybe, just *maybe*, fucking her would cure me. She didn't protest when I removed her wedges and her jeans. She didn't comment when I stretched out over her, still fully dressed. She opened her legs, inviting me in.

The scent of her desire hit me, and I paused, breathing her in, my nostrils flaring, opening wide. I slid my fingers into her hot hole, testing her readiness. Her pussy was sopping. Undoing my fly, I pulled my jeans down far enough to free my aching dick.

Thrusting into her, I stopped myself from taking her mouth again. A strangled moan left me, and I halted, ready to come at the sheer pleasure electrifying me because I was inside Ainsley again.

She arched her back, slid her hands to her breasts, and tweaked her nipples, just as she had our first time together.

"You like your tits played with, huh, baby?" I said roughly, my cock throbbing inside her.

Her eyes glittered and the skin bared to me flushed. She nodded. Tilted her hips.

Groaning again, I closed my eyes and started moving, hoping to control myself. Hoping I could drown her out since I was fucking her.

Her pussy walls gripped my dick and I shook. Her little fingers slipped under my T-shirt and skated along my spine.

"Fuck, Ainsley." I gave up the pretense. I couldn't hold back. Once I came, I'd tell her I'd support her, but no one could ever know her baby belonged to me.

I thrust into her as deep as I could, pulled out to my dick tip, then pushed into her again. Her silky smooth pussy burned me from the inside out, scorching every fucking nerve I had. Little noises escaped her and drove me insane. Somehow, I got control of myself. I didn't want to hurt her or the baby.

"Reese," she gasped, meeting my thrusts with her own grinds. Her hands moved from my back to the nape of my neck. "Reese, I've dreamed of this."

She couldn't dream of shit with me and she couldn't take away my fucking control. I wasn't a sad sack. I'd do right by my kid, but once I came, that was it for Ainsley and me.

Grabbing her hips and lifting myself to my knees, I widened her thighs and fucked her hard. Trying to fuck away my thoughts of her and my desire for her.

This. Was. *BULLSHIT*.

Fuck her. I wouldn't make her come. I wouldn't allow her to come. I'd nut and put her out. I slammed into her one final time and jerked my cock out, finishing on her belly, then collapsing at her side.

"You have to leave," I said when I caught my breath. I pulled my jeans up to cover my cock, not fastening my fly or buckling my belt. "I'll get a towel to clean you up. I don't want anyone seeing you here. Especially my president."

She studied me, but I kept my poker face in place. She swallowed, but didn't protest, cry, or argue. Instead, she sat up and wiped her stomach off with my comforter. My bed was crumpled, though still all made-up.

Her lips were swollen, her cheeks were flushed, and her eyes were soft and passion glazed. Perhaps, if I hadn't looked at her when she got to her feet and saw her breasts bobbing and her skin flushed, I could've allowed her to leave. I stormed to my feet and pulled her back on the bed, burying my face between her thighs and devouring her pussy.

I used my fingers to hold open her lips and tongued her clit, her screams music to my ears.

I slurped her juices, licked and sucked her cunt, speared my tongue into her hole, not stopping until she begged me.

I was frantic, unable to satisfy my need for her. Latching onto one of her tits, I caressed the other one, egged on by her cries. This time, when I buried my cock in her, I didn't halt for her or for me. I fucked her the way I'd dreamed about it. Without mercy or coordination, just by instinct. Her passion matched mine, measure for measure.

When my orgasm neared, I caressed her pussy. The moment she cried out, I let loose and emptied inside her. Before I pulled out, I allowed my heartrate to slow and my pants to subside.

Next to her, I pulled her into my arms, soaking up the peace while it lasted.

Chapter Twelve

Ainsley

Laying in Reese's arms felt more right than anything I'd ever experienced. I felt safe and desired and beautiful. When I turned on my side, he spooned me just like the heroes always did in my favorite romance novels. His big body pressed into mine, a wall of solid muscle and strength.

Whatever else I'd expected, it wasn't this explosive passion. He chinned some of my hair aside and nuzzled my neck. Goosebumps rose along my skin. I shivered, sighing dreamily. He splayed his huge hand over my belly, and I knew he was thinking about the baby.

"I don't have a doctor yet," I said, giddy and lost in a haze. "I wasn't sure who to ask since Roman takes care of everything. If I went to my regular doctor, she'd rat me out. We can always choose one together, Reese."

Sighing, he moved his hand away and gently pushed me out of his arms.

"Get dressed, Ainsley. We aren't a couple. We're having a kid together. That's it."

"What?"

Reese got to his feet. It dawned on me that he was fully dressed. He hadn't even removed his boots, while I'd shed my clothes with abandon. He tossed my jeans and underwear at me.

"Put your fucking clothes on and *go*. Give me your number so I can unblock you."

"You don't have my number anymore?"

He shrugged. "I deleted it."

"I see."

That cut me deeply. He'd wanted to erase me from his life with such totality that he didn't even want my number in his contact list. Swallowing, I glanced around.

Reese's bedroom was rugged but surprisingly comfortable, despite its rough masculinity. The large, industrial-style window framed a view of the river, breathtaking even from my spot on the bed.

The walls were made of exposed brick, and their deep red and brown hues gave the space a gritty, lived-in feel. His steel-framed bed sat against one wall, the dark leather headboard worn from years of use. The bedding was simple but comfortable—a thick, slightly rumpled black and gray comforter, and an extra throw blanket, stitched with the club's emblem. I couldn't see the sheets since he hadn't bothered to pull the covers down.

A heavy wooden dresser held a few personal items—a flask, a collection of lighters, and several photos. Motorcycle helmets, a leather jacket, and a pair of well-worn boots rested near the doorway.

Reese's voice broke into my contemplation. "Call me tomorrow and we'll meet one day next week."

"But—"

"I'll ask the chick I'm fucking if she knows of an obstetrician."

Since Roman's accident, I'd cried buckets. I didn't have any tears left in me. Even if Reese was a motherfucker.

He thrust his fingers through his hair. "Don't fucking look at me like that. I didn't make you any promises."

I got to my feet and pulled on my panties. "I didn't ask for any, so fuck you." I jerked on my jeans, then looked around for my wedges. "I'll find my own fucking doctor, dickhead. Don't ask that bitch anything on my account."

"That's nice. You don't even know the woman."

"I know *you*. She has to be a bitch since you're the fucking cunt."

A dark look settled into his face. Not caring, I flipped him off and opened my mouth to call him whatever name popped into my head.

Before I could, Nova barged in. "How could you, Ainsley?" she cried, red-faced and furious; bruises and cuts marred her face. "I'm suffering and you're in here fucking." She raised her cell phone and snapped a photo, then showed it to me. "This is the memento of where your loyalties lay. I'll look at it for the rest of my life and know the truth. You aren't a real friend! If you were, you would've saved me from having to watch Louisiana leave with *her*."

"How the fuck do you know what a real friend is since you've never shown yourself as one?" I snarled, fed up with her even more than I was Reese.

She took a step toward me, but Reese inserted himself between us.

"Jinx is Louisiana's wife, Nova. Obviously, he's chosen her. You set yourself up for this bullshit by bringing your ass to the club. What the fuck you aren't doing is blaming Ainsley and you're sure the fuck not running up on her."

Folding her arms, she lifted her chin and ignored Reese. "Take me home, Ainsley. You're not spending the night at my place. You're too much of a pathetic cunt for my company. I hope you choke on your vomit."

Reese frowned and looked at me. "You're sick?"

"Thanks to your cum," Nova said viciously. "Which you completely deserve. How the fuck do you fuck once and end up with a baby in your belly, stupid?"

"Nova, I'm losing fucking patience with you," Reese snarled.

"As if I give a fuck!"

"You fucking should. There's only one cunt in here." Reese glared at me again. "And I'm looking at her, Nova. You're pathetic, needy, desperate, and whiny. I wouldn't fuck you with another motherfucker's cock. I can't imagine what Louisiana saw in you."

"It isn't what he saw," Nova said coldly. "It's what he felt and what I gave him. Young pussy and good head." She smiled at me, then winked at Reese. "Try it for yourself and find out."

"I'd prefer hacking my cock off with a slipknot than putting it anywhere near you. Listen well. If you keep fucking with Ainsley, you'll also be dead."

His strident defense unwillingly impressed me. I wished I could've pushed away my amazement and appreciation, but it settled into me and wouldn't let go.

"Reese?" One of the guys who'd been outside when we arrived peeked in. His gaze fell on

Nova and relief flooded him. "We've been searching all over for her."

"I'm beating the fuck out of you," Reese barked. "No one comes upstairs unless they are with a member."

"I'm sorry," the guy said. "We were helping Louisiana with Jinx because she was still fighting him so bad. We had to get her in the back of the van because he didn't want her to jump out of a car or off his bike." He pointed at Nova. "In the midst of that, she disappeared."

Reese stormed to him and knocked him on the side of his head. "One of you should've kept eyes on her at all times! I don't give a fuck what the fuck else you have to do. You don't allow a strange bitch to be alone in the fucking club."

"I'm sorry!"

"You sure the fuck are, Chi Chi."

"Razor and them are on the way back." He gave Reese a pleading look. I almost felt sorry for him. "Don't tell him about my mistake. He said if I fucked up one more time, that was my ass."

Not caring about their club business, I spied my wedges, so I scooped them up, sat on the edge of Reese's bed and started putting them on. Nova took a step towards me, but Reese snatched her and shoved her away.

We both blinked at him.

"I was just going to apologize to her," she said, staring at him.

"You're not doing anything except staying the fuck away from her."

"You don't have any say," she told him. "She's my best friend."

"I'd hate to see your fucking enemies," I grouched. "You don't get to shit on me, then fucking apologize because you've gotten over your anger. Nor do you get to run to that fuckhead maniac and have him beat the shit out of me because you're his daughter until he decides you're his fucking punching bag!"

Nova paled. I didn't give a fuck. I was so done with her.

"I'll take you to the fucking clubhouse gates since you came with me. Boom Boom isn't there, so I'm safe. But lose my fucking number. Don't call me."

"The next time he'll kill us."

I jumped to my feet. "Simple," I said with a stomp of my foot to emphasize my point. "Don't tell him that our friendship is over."

"He asked me about you after our argument at your place, Ains. I swear I was respecting your wishes, then he wanted to know why you hadn't been around and why I wasn't at the house helping you with Roman."

Reese snatched a set of keys from his nightstand. "Come on. I'll escort you to the clubhouse so you can drop her off."

We both looked at him.

"We have to leave. Razor will arrive soon."

"Razor?" I asked.

"My president," Reese answered. "I don't feel like explaining why you two are here. No, fuck. I couldn't explain it, so don't fucking argue. Get your shit and let's roll out."

I didn't want to meet his president either. Everything was in such an upheaval, I still didn't know who knew my actual identity. Roman was somewhere, though I didn't know his exact location. Besides, if I got into trouble, it wasn't as if he could hop on his bike and ride to me.

"Whatever," I spat and stormed past that motherfucker and that bitch AKA my baby daddy and my former friend.

CHAPTER THIRTEEN

REESE

Near the Scorpions' clubhouse, Ainsley waved at me to pull over and blew her horn when I ignored her and blazed on by. She was out of her fucking mind if she believed I'd trust her with Nova.

I couldn't react upon hearing Boom Boom beat Ainsley. I wasn't well acquainted with the latest crop of prospects. We opened our ranks every two years. Sooner if motherfuckers wiped out, turned in their patch, went to prison, or got out bad. Razor firmly believed the more members, the more money, but last time we had prospects, three of them decided against joining within six months.

The dude who came after Nova could report every fucking thing to Razor. I didn't know if he feared Prez or respected him. Either way, it boded ill for me.

When Ainsley stopped her car at the gate, I gunned to the dead end and circled back, slowing my ride to make sure she hadn't turned in. Nova was just opening the passenger side door and getting her bitchy ass out of Ainsley's car. Satisfied, I rode to the intersection and idled my bike until she paused her car beside me.

She rolled down her window and flicked on the light. "Are you out of your fucking mind?"

Obviously. It was insane to be in enemy territory and alone with only my holstered guns, my knives in my boots, and my questionable wits. "It's dark, Ainsley." I couldn't admit the truth and panic her any more than she already sounded. "They can't see my cut."

"Reese—"

"Let's get the fuck away from the clubhouse," I told her. She looked ready to chastise me for the next hour. "I'll escort you home."

"*Reese—*"

Ignoring her, I rode off. I took care with my speed. I didn't trust Ainsley not to put the pedal to the metal to keep up with me. City driving was so fucking different than the open road with nothing but the wind in my hair and miles of freedom ahead of me.

Once or twice, she tried to swerve around me, but I sped up and jumped ahead of her. If she kept that shit up, I'd spank her ass for endangering herself. And the baby.

Fuck. The baby. My baby. I was still trying to wrap my head around that news.

When we finally reached her neighborhood, I thought she was shitting me. It was a quiet tree-lined street with nice houses in a well-kept area, fit for families with moms, dads, and two point five kids. Not bikers with blood on their hands. But it *was* where she lived because she turned into the driveway of a charming home that blended a traditional style with modern touches. The exterior soft beige brick and light gray siding gave it a welcoming feel and brought me back to another time in my life, when I hadn't been a biker but a regular kid with parents and siblings.

The memory of my little sister running around a neatly manicured front lawn with patches of green grass that stretched up to a porch like this one, swarmed me. A large oak tree stood off to one side, its branches spreading wide, dripping leaves in autumnal colors.

A neatly paved pathway led from the sidewalk to the front door, framed by a pair of symmetrical bushes, perfectly pruned and trimmed. Near the porch, my little sister would've loved the wood and iron bench sitting under the tree.

Ainsley killed the engine and exited her car. Outdoor lights illuminated her, the paved driveway that led to a two-car garage and the pathway to the front door. Right before I turned in behind her, she ran into the middle of the fucking street, forcing me past her, so I wouldn't run her over. Apparently, that's what she wanted because she hurried to the curb, three houses down.

"Roman has cameras," she said frantically. "He hasn't asked me about my comings and goings. Either he's too busy to check footage or he hasn't seen anything alarming."

"Let's go to your apartment."

"I don't have it anymore. I moved back home to take care of my brother."

I released a frustrated sigh.

"Whatever you want to say, tell me now."

I didn't want to say anything. I wanted to protect her. Unease sat like a stone in my fucking gut. Besides, I wanted to question her and I couldn't do it in the middle of a fucking street. I'd camp close by and keep watch on her house. Tomorrow, I'd take her to breakfast and figure something out.

Her phone began ringing and her lips turned down. "That's Roman. I have to get inside, so I'll see you around, Reese." Spinning, she answered her phone and sprinted away from me. "I'm going inside now, Ro. You won't believe..."

The rest of the words were lost to me because of the space she'd put between us. I rode the short distance to her house, watching as she slammed the car door and disappeared into the residence without looking back, though she must've heard my Harley pipes.

She was pissed with me. That much was clear. Not that I blamed her, since I'd thrown in her face a woman I had absolutely no interest in. Frankly, it shocked me how easily she gave herself to me again.

Maybe, the baby had her hormones out of control and she needed a fuck. She'd given into me because she felt a certain attachment to me. When I saw headlights coming toward me, I realized I was in the middle of the fucking road, so I steered my bike across the street from Ainsley's house.

Lighting a smoke, I wondered how many cameras Roman had installed around the house. Normally, they were pointed at entryways and installed on doorbells. I could understand if he felt the need for more. Fuck, this was a job for Wave, our tech guy, but he'd probably tell Bolt. I didn't want to alert Razor, Jester, or Warrior to Ainsley's vulnerability. I didn't trust them not to scoop her up to make her pay for my perceived crimes or her brother's.

Either way, it wasn't good for her. She'd pay for the sins of Roman and me, when her only crime was loving him and sleeping with me.

I flicked my cigarette away, wishing I'd brought my fucking flask. I was just debating on if I wanted to go back to the clubhouse for a couple supplies when Ainsley's door cracked open and she peeped outside. Apparently satisfied, she opened it fully and walked out, carrying an overnight bag and running to her car.

"Ainsley?" I called.

Startled, she looked in my direction, remaining still until I reached her.

"Where are you going?"

"To a motel," she responded. "I don't want to stay here alone."

I tried to grab her bag but she tightened her hold.

"What did Roman say to you?"

"None of your business. Please, get out of my way, go back to your girlfriend, and let me handle my own business."

"What motel are you going to?"

"Refer to my previous answer," she gritted.

I needed to talk to Razor, convince him of my loyalty and that Ainsley wasn't a threat.

She tried to shove me, but I didn't move. She was no match for my muscles.

"I'm going to shoot you if you don't fucking move, Reese."

"Shoot me?" I asked skeptically.

She pushed her jacket aside to reveal a holstered gun at her side. Was that a fucking .357 Magnum?

"You don't think my brother wouldn't teach me how to defend myself, do you?" She shoved her hand through her hair. "I just hope I don't have to use it."

"Did Roman tell you to leave?"

She glowered at me.

"At least tell me that."

"For future reference, take a page out of my book and listen to these instructions. Don't volunteer information I don't want to know and don't ask questions that won't be answered. You'll make my life easier."

"You're not going to shoot me, Ainsley," I said with confidence. "I'm not a threat and you wouldn't fire that gun in cold blood, which it would be if you retaliated just because I won't allow you to leave until you answer me."

"Reese, I'm not going to allow you to control my life at your whim. I'm tired and hungry. That's the only reason I'm giving in. During my conversation with my brother, I overheard Boom Boom..." Her voice trailed off and she shivered. "I'd prefer..." Shaking her head, she stopped again as if she couldn't bear to continue. She closed her eyes for a second, then looked at me and forced a smile. "If any of his brothers come around, Roman will call me."

"Not if he doesn't know you're gone." I glanced at the garage and the bright light shining on us. "A camera is there?"

She flushed. "I may have embellished the number of cameras we currently have," she mumbled. "There is a doorbell camera. After I moved out, he was rarely here. He thought about selling the place. He also hated the exorbitant fees of the monitoring service so he was in the process of installing another type of system."

My Ainsley was back. Ask her one thing and she'd tell everything.

"Let me bring you somewhere safe."

She pursed her lips. "No." One word full of defiance and steel. "Go away, Reese."

"Ainsley, just trust me, please."

"Nope, jackass. You led me to believe our one-night stand could be the beginning of a friendship if nothing else. Then, you snuck away, all up in your feelings, without even giving me a chance to explain. Old news. More recently, you fucked me and then told me you'd ask your girlfriend for recommendations for an OB."

"I didn't say girlfriend."

"Semantics, fuckhead."

"I want to talk to you," I said, desperation creeping into my tone. I never had a woman deny me especially when I asked so sweetly. "In private."

She made an arc of her hand. "We're in private. Only you and I and the sky are outside right now."

"Suppose one of the Scorpions sees you or recognizes your car, Ainsley? You'll be alone and vulnerable."

She touched her side, where the gun was. "I can defend myself."

"You don't have only you to think about now."

"I can defend *us*. Better?"

I tried a different tact. "Have you ever killed a man, sweetheart? Your first kill can fuck with you if you have a conscience. You're pregnant. You don't need that stress."

"You're so fucking unfair," she whispered, but this time when I went for her bag, she allowed me to take it.

I took her hand and started toward my bike. Of course, she resisted and forced me to stop.

"If you're taking me to your girlfriend's, I will fucking kill you."

Unable to stop myself, I caressed her jaw. "You have a very low opinion of me if you think I'd do that to you."

"I'm not your girlfriend, so you're doing it to her if you're sneaking around with me."

"I don't have a goddamn girlfriend."

She huffed. "I'm tired and I'm hungry," she reminded me. "As long as it isn't your *woman friend*, can we just go to wherever? I'll talk to you if you swear to leave me alone afterwards."

"We're having a baby together."

"Listen up, motherfucker," she said, losing her temper. "You're not fucking with my emotions. We were having a baby together earlier too when you reverted to dickheadedness, so fuck you."

"If I had a hundred bucks every time you said 'fuck you', I'd be rich."

"By the time my baby's eighteen, that'll probably reach billionaire status because you're you."

"Can you just give in?"

"Gave in twice. Not doing it again."

She yawned and rubbed her eyes. Smiling, I pulled her into my embrace, but she held herself stiffly. I considered throwing her over my shoulder like Louisiana did to Jinx earlier. Not wanting to injure her or the baby, I dismissed the idea. She'd fight me every step of the way *and* she was strapped.

I applauded Roman for his foresight and Ainsley for her self-preservation. Some chicks would refuse to carry for any number of reasons. While I respected their decision, this life wasn't for the weak and faint of heart.

Despite Ainsley standing like a statue, I tightened my arms around her. "Does it matter if I have one woman or twenty? *You're* having my baby."

"I'm not putting myself through baby mama drama."

I laughed. "You're the baby mama."

She pulled away from me and thumped my shoulder. "Exactly. The baby and me would get the short end of the stick. Your girlfriend is your primary concern. If she told you to forget about your baby or she was bouncing, you'd throw it aside."

Ainsley dropped her guard for a moment and I saw her vulnerability. I hurt her. Regret welled inside me. I wasn't a man used to giving in to women. Normally, I didn't have to. They fell into my bed with a snap of my finger or a winsome smile.

"Some chicks see it as a challenge when a man tells them they're involved with another woman."

"Good for them. I'm not one of those chicks, which I'm sure you know. Otherwise, you wouldn't have told me about her. I'm not involving myself in other woman drama."

Fuck, I might've played myself. "Suppose I told you I embellished the truth about another woman?"

"Then I'd call you a stupid, immature fuck face, not worth my goddamn time if you'd resort to those games. Instead of manning up and saying I don't want to be involved in the pregnancy, you resort to throwing another girl in my face. You're not jerking my emotions around like that, Reese. I deserve better."

She did, and her words shamed me. "Am I ever going to win an argument with you?"

"Not if I can help it."

I grinned. "Thought so," I murmured, more than happy to take up her challenge.

CHAPTER FOURTEEN

ROMAN

The moment Boom Boom returned to the small room where they'd been playing cards, I knew something was up with Nova and Ainsley. Barely concealed anger blazed in his eyes. He sat at the table where I'd been talking to Kite and Wizard, watching as they drank, forcing myself to be content with the few times they lifted a bottle to my mouth. Ordinarily, his glances annoyed me. Or the former me.

Current me was in a fucked up position because I couldn't defend myself if and when guns started blazing.

We'd arrived on the outskirts of Salt Lake City a couple of hours ago at the Mother Chapter of the American Scorpions. Boom

Boom thought an alliance should be inevitable. I wasn't sure why, besides the obvious, because the club was in the middle of nowhere. To me, they seemed like a fucking rip-off of a club that had been destroyed in a rivalry years ago.

Though the president wasn't at the clubhouse yet, we were given food, alcohol, and rooms where women waited for us. I hated sharing a room with Kite. I couldn't caress a woman's body, sink my fingers into her pussy, or tangle them through her hair. Kite made a production of doing all the things I once enjoyed. My chick rode my cock until I shot my load and left me unsatisfied, missing all the things I once took for granted.

I couldn't shake my uneasiness or sense of doom. Rendered scorpions decorated the walls. A huge American flag and a club banner hung from the ceiling. Two huge, covered terrariums sat on each side of the room, decorated with Halloween props of fake skulls.

The terrariums looked empty, though Wizard claimed a scorpion lived in each one. Since I knew nothing about this club, I wasn't sure.

Maybe that's what had me so uneasy. We were in an unfamiliar clubhouse and I was unarmed.

For the first time in memory, I didn't know what to do. Kite roomed with me. I couldn't call Ainsley and tell her to get the fuck out of our house for her own safety.

Immediately, he'd know that *I* knew what those motherfuckers did to Ainsley. When they disappeared, I would be the first one the club pointed fingers at if I aroused suspicions.

"How's Nova?" I finally asked. That cunt was on my list, too. I'd check it twice for the naughty and the nice, then fuck them all up. None of those assholes had been nice to my little sister. "She hasn't called much while we've been away."

Steepling his fingers and resting them on his chin, Boom Boom leaned back. "She and Ainsley had a falling out."

I remained impassive. "What about?"

He scrutinized my face, glanced at my handless arms, studied my neck. "That isn't important."

I refused to ask why. I wasn't interested, and if he wanted me to know, he'd fucking tell me.

"But you know what is?" He folded his arms. "That slut you have for a sister carrying Reese Sinclair's baby."

"*WHAT*?" I exploded, not even caring he called Ainsley a slut. His statement was so outrageous, so fucking unbelievable, that I could only say that one word. It felt as if my heart momentarily stopped and I wanted to vomit. No fucking way...impossible...Ainsley wouldn't. I began shaking my head in denial. "No. That isn't true. Nova's a liar. Ainsley would never betray me that way."

"You're calling my daughter a liar, fucker?"

"Yes," I snarled. "Yes, the fuck I am." My arms jerked with the need to pound my fucking fists. I settled for stomping my foot like a fucking toddler. "Nova's a goddamn liar. How fucking dare she spout that bullshit."

Boom Boom stood, so Kite and Wizard followed suit. I remained seated. If they intended to shoot me for disrespecting that cunt, I wouldn't show them a modicum of respect. Slowly, Boom Boom brought his hand to his side. My only regret was leaving Ainsley to fend for herself before I found a man worthy of her.

They'd foisted this trip on me at the last minute. They'd brought me there to watch me because I sure the fuck couldn't do a motherfucking thing without hands.

Instead of pulling a gun, Boom Boom took out his cell phone. Once he found whatever he sought, he laid it on the table and slid it to me.

Ainsley stood next to that Royal Bastard, her hair disheveled, her mouth swollen. I'd fucked enough women to know the afterglow. Seeing it on Ainsley turned my stomach. But knowing it was because of Reese Sinclair ripped my heart in two.

Betrayal sliced through me.

I studied the picture closer and searched my mind. Since Ainsley got tits, I dismissed them. I couldn't face that she was growing up and I didn't want another motherfucker looking at her. As her big brother, I certainly wouldn't.

Still, we'd gone to Galveston a few summers back. She also liked crop tops and tight clothing. I didn't like it, but she'd challenged me to arm wrestling. If she won, she could wear whatever she wanted. If I won, I dictated her clothes.

I accepted the challenge, knowing she'd already won. I always allowed her to beat me in our arm-wrestling contests.

Looking at the photo until the battery saver kicked in, I admitted her breasts were bigger. Even after two and a half months, I forgot I didn't have hands. Like now, when I hung my head and wanted to cradle it. The weight of the latest information made it overwhelmingly heavy.

How could Ainsley do this?

"You aren't the reason your life was spared," Boom Boom said, breaking into my heartache. "She is. Her pussy saved your life."

My nostrils flared. "If that's the case, I would've preferred to die," I spat, the words spewing from all my hurt and anger.

"She's a whore," Kite uttered.

"A slut," Wizard added.

"A cocksucker," Boom Boom said.

They looked at me expectantly. As livid as I was with Ainsley, I wanted to hear her side. She must've had a reason for sleeping with Reese. Maybe, they had called her and she'd sacrificed herself to save me. That made sense.

"Don't you agree, Roman?" Boom Boom pressed.

"Ainsley loves me," I said, refusing to disparage her to anyone, but especially these motherfuckers. "My guess is she fucked Reese in exchange for my life."

I blew out a heavy breath, disgusted at the thought, but feeling better about the situation.

Wincing, Boom Boom shook his head. "Nova says otherwise. Ainsley had already fucked Reese."

A cold feeling slid into me. I was so fucking angry with Ainsley. I'd make her watch while I castrated Reese and then let him bleed to death. If she really was pregnant, she was getting rid of it.

"You know what you have to do, Reese," Wizard said, his smile icy.

"Yeah," I said heavily, then revealed my plans.

"Reese does have to die," Boom Boom agreed. "But so does Ainsley."

I jerked as if I'd been shot. He was ordering my sister's death? Of course he was. She'd betrayed us all by sleeping with a Royal Bastard, and an officer at that.

He sat down again, so the other two took their seats as well.

"When will you be fitted for the prosthetics?" my president asked.

"In a month." Or not. I'd gotten myself out of my funk for Ainsley's sake, not knowing of her deception. "The appointment's set exactly two weeks after we return from our run."

"Good." Boom Boom lit a cigarette, then picked up the deck of cards that lay forgotten in the middle of the table. "Your first assignment when you're fully functional again is bringing me Ainsley's head."

If my agreement to that fucked-up task got me home alive, then so be it. I could never kill my sister, but as of this moment, she was no family of mine.

Chapter Fifteen

Ainsley

I didn't have many friends outside the club, and I'd always considered Nova my best friend, even when my parents were alive. Looking back, I didn't know if our forced proximity bred familiarity and, in turn, what I believed was a loyal confidante. As kids, we had no choice but to be in each other's company because of our parents. My dad was the VP for as long as I remembered. To me, my father's death destabilized the club. Roman never confirmed that the one time I brought it up, but I wasn't an idiot. Before Daddy's death, the officers weren't voted out the way they were nowadays. He worked so closely with Boom Boom, it seemed logical that Nova and I gravitated to each other.

Understanding she currently acted out of a place of trauma and putting myself in danger on her behalf warred within me. I worried what she'd give as my reason for not spending the night. Everyone knew Roman was on a run with the officers. Because he was gone, they'd removed the guards from our house, in spite of his protests. He wanted them there to protect me.

But I couldn't handle Nova's bullshit after the stunt she pulled. After the damage our friendship already endured, she'd used me to see Louisiana on his home turf, then barged into Reese's room and finished showing her ass.

Tightening my arms around Reese's trim waist, I leaned into the turn he made. Being on the back of his bike felt so different than all the times I'd rode on the back of Roman's. He'd taught me how to enjoy rides—he'd taught me *to* ride, shoot, and throw knives. Having a bike of my own wasn't a goal, though. I preferred fast cars, loud music, and football.

I'd learned how to shoot because Roman insisted. He'd also insisted I learned how to get away from attackers. But I'd never had to shoot to kill and hoped I never would. Would I hesitate to shoot if it meant saving my life? No. It was survival of the fittest and I considered myself quite fit.

Would taking someone's life haunt me? I think it would depend on the circumstances.

I always preferred peaceful resolutions to any type of violence. Nor could I imagine sitting up all night with my gun in hand, stressing about one of Roman's brothers breaking in to seek justice for whatever story Nova spun. My guess was she'd blame her injuries on me. Probably as retribution for that scene with Boom Boom. She certainly couldn't admit that she'd gotten her ass kicked by the wife of the man she was sneaking around with.

Luckily, I was on the phone with my brother who was in a private room with his club members when Boom Boom's phone rang and he said it was Nova, then excused himself.

Roman looked happy and healthy, and that was all I could ask for. Seeing he wasn't in danger, I decided to listen to my survival instincts. I hadn't expected to find Reese still outside.

The man was positively insane. He had no self-preservation.

Apparently, neither did I, since I allowed him to talk me into leaving with him. The day wore me out, leaving my defenses down. I was tired and hungry, and only wanted a hot shower and food. Unfortunately, my nausea was building. Morning sickness was a misnomer. It happened any time of the day. Small meals helped, though it didn't completely alleviate my vomiting. At some point over the course of a day, I'd throw up. Early this morning, nausea awakened me, so I thought I was home free.

Not.

I packed crackers and *7Up* in my overnight bag. As soon as we got to wherever Reese was bringing me, I'd dig them out and pray my stomach settled. I refused to vomit in front of him.

We rode so long I began to worry he was taking me somewhere to harm me. It seemed the joke was on me after all because I'd once again trusted him. As we headed southwest on Monarch Highway, my anxiety grew. He exited at Idaho Road, hooked a right, then a left at Jackson and cut off onto a dark road, kicking up dust and gravel.

I swallowed, but my mouth was dry and my pulse thumped through my body. Making me disappear would solve my unwanted pregnancy. If he claimed the baby, his girlfriend might not be happy. If he didn't want the baby, it could one day pop up, asking why Reese chose abandonment.

He slowed his speed. My hand went to my .357, a gift for my eighteenth birthday. I had a permit to carry, but had I honestly graduated to a license to kill? I could always claim self-defense. However, I'd be marked for death by the Royal Bastards.

There was also the baby to consider. After weeks of debating on keeping it or aborting it, I felt insane for wanting to protect it so fiercely.

For a little while, Reese gave me hope. I still didn't know how I'd tell Roman and I still feared his reaction, but I thought...never mind. I was the idiot. Reese had already proven who he was. I'd just used the pregnancy as an excuse to see him again.

This was *my* baby. Fuck him.

My fingers closed around the grip. My life was as valuable to me as the baby's. I wouldn't fight to live for one more than the other. Without me living, there was no child.

Reese glided to a stop beside a van, the tires of his motorcycle crunching over the gravel as he eased it into place. The engine rumbled a final note before falling silent, leaving only the crackling of the chilly night air to fill the stillness. He dropped his feet to the ground with a soft thud, his boots meeting the earth with a muted finality, his movement smooth as he dismounted. The air around him seemed to hold its breath as he stood there, for just a moment, staring back the way we'd come.

A faint light broke through the blanket of darkness, flickering just ahead like a beacon. It was enough to highlight the outline of the small structure—its wooden exterior almost blending with the night. The light was sparse, uneven, reluctant to reveal too much. From this angle, it seemed distant, untouchable, like it was waiting for something or someone to approach.

The cold of the night cut through the stillness, its chill seeping underneath my clothes and into my bones. The stars above, scattered like silver dust across the velvet sky, seemed closer here—every twinkle of light vivid against the backdrop of darkness. The crescent moon, hanging low and luminous, cast a silvery glow over the landscape, a fragile illumination that barely touched the edges of the trees surrounding them. There was something surreal about the way the night felt both alive and still at the same time, as though the land held its breath, waiting.

The trees, tall and thick, stood sentinel-like around the cabin, their branches creaking softly in the wind. The forest was alive with its own sounds—an owl hooting faintly in the distance, the rustle of leaves carried on the breeze, the subtle scurry of night creatures hidden just beyond the reach of the light. For a moment, there was a fleeting sense of peace—of quiet isolation that should've felt serene. But it didn't. Instead, there was something unsettling about the silence.

The stillness felt thick and secretive. The quiet wasn't comforting. It was...*expectant*. And somehow, that tension in the air made the forest seem not just peaceful, but somehow watchful. As if the trees themselves were leaning in, listening.

Waiting.

It was the kind of stillness that made the hairs on the back of my neck rise, the kind of silence that felt too heavy for comfort.

The peacefulness that should've settled over the area, that gentle calm of being surrounded by nature, seemed like a veneer. Beneath it, there was something else—something almost forgotten, lurking in the quiet.

It was the perfect place for me to disappear, and the problem of my pregnancy would be resolved.

"We're here, babe."

"Hmmm." Sweat bubbled on my skin and my hands trembled. "Where is here?"

Before he answered, the door swung open, and I jumped.

"About fucking time, Reese," Louisiana grouched. Before I decided if his presence was good or bad, he said, "Ainsley, maybe you can talk to Jinx."

"No fucking way," Reese snapped, unaware of my entire body sagging in relief and my adrenaline crashing. "I didn't bring her here to get into your fucking drama."

"Please." Louisiana's desperation shocked me. "Jinx is leaving in the morning."

"I'm not Jinx anymore," a female voice cried. "I'm Denali."

Louisiana swore.

Reese wrapped an arm around my waist and lifted me off, then held out his hand. "Give me your gun."

"Kiss my ass." I stomped around him. "I'll be completely defenseless."

He caught up to me just as I reached the steps, but Louisiana loomed in front of me, planting himself at the top of the small porch.

"You're not coming in here armed, Ainsley."

"Guns aren't allowed in the cabin?" I asked.

"Chicks with guns aren't allowed in the cabin," he amended. "Either you give it to Reese or you give it to me."

"If you weren't such fucking assholes, you wouldn't be concerned about women with weapons," I bit out, outnumbered by dickheads. Praying I wasn't making a mistake, I unholstered my gun, turned, and handed it to Reese.

He snapped the chamber open and emptied it.

"Christ, Ainsley. You have fucking hollow point bullets?" Reese grumbled.

"Roman wanted to make sure all threats were completely disabled," I explained with a shrug, wondering how he saw in the darkness to know what ammo I had in the gun. I glanced over my shoulder and found Reese shining his phone's flashlight on the bullet.

Louisiana stepped aside. "Go in. I need to talk to Reese."

His tone brooked no argument. Now that I was unarmed, I thought it best to comply, so I brushed by Louisiana and walked inside, where a couch sat against one wall and a table with four chairs against another. A compact kitchen was on the other side of the room. Jinx leaned against the counter, arms folded, eyes puffy and red.

The moment her blue gaze landed on me, she stiffened and narrowed her eyes.

"You have some fucking balls bringing your ass here," she snarled.

Although I didn't resemble Nova, I'd leave nothing to chance. Mistaken identity had gotten more than one person fucked up. "I'm not Nova."

"I know who you are, Ainsley. You're that bitch's friend. Guilt by association."

I pressed my lips together to hold in my wince. She was right. Despite my suspicions and warnings about Louisiana, I looked the other way.

"I don't know what you expected me to do," I said in my own defense.

Tears slid down her cheeks and she swiped them angrily away. "You could've...you could've..." Her lips trembled.

"I couldn't have done anything. When I..." Well, damn. I couldn't let her know how deeply she'd been betrayed because Reese knew, too. As Louisiana's best friend, he must've been reasonably acquainted with his wife. "I-I told Nova that I thought he was married. She didn't believe me. If I'd had a way to contact you and spilled the beans, would you have believed me?"

She glanced at the floor, then turned away. "It doesn't fucking matter. I'm leaving first thing tomorrow. My father's coming to pick me up."

Opening a cabinet door, she snatched a mug and filled it with water from the kitchen sink. She stalked to the microwave and began the heating process.

She folded her arms and stalked to me. "But if he thinks I'll stay under the same roof with his bitch's friend, he's out of his fucking mind. You or me." She poked me in the chest. "If you don't get the fuck out right now, I'll do everything I'd love to do to Nova to you."

Perhaps, the stress of the day and all the turmoil got the best of me. Or my fatigue and hunger. Maybe it was a combination. I turned away from Jinx and retched a combination of dry heaves, bile, and the water I'd drank when I was home. For the first time since my pregnancy began, weakness assailed me, and I plunked on my butt. It felt as if I'd sink into unconsciousness at any moment.

Jinx knelt beside me and swiped a cold towel over my face.

"Do you have any saltines?" I asked faintly, tipping my head back and resting the towel on my forehead. The spackled ceiling was a shiny white. Cotton Candy pink would've been prettier. I closed my eyes. "And *7Up*?"

"Are you pregnant?" she asked suspiciously.

I nodded.

"Who's the daddy?"

I popped one eye open. She was resting on her haunches, waiting for my answer, her worry palpable. She probably knew Reese's ol' lady. Whatever the reason I sought him out, I didn't want to make trouble for him. "None of your business."

When she jumped to her feet, I opened both my eyes and straightened. "It's Reese's," she said flatly. "You wouldn't be here otherwise. This is my safe space, away from the Devil's Pit. A rule of mine is no one comes here besides Keir and me except Reese. It's a sacred law that's never been broken. Until now." She glared at me. "Now, I know why."

I didn't know what to say. I couldn't explain why Reese broke her rule on my account when he didn't want anything to do with me. That man was so fucking confusing.

Laying my head on the coffee table, I ignored the vomit next to me. I couldn't clean it and Jinx wouldn't. I heard cabinet doors opening and closing, ice clinking into a glass, and the fizz of a soda.

Jinx knelt again and helped me to my feet, then guided me to the sofa. Once I sat, she handed me a sleeve of crackers.

"Take little nibbles," she warned, turning on her heel and walking out of sight. She came back, carrying paper towels and dragging a mop that left a damp trail. She cleaned the vomit in silence, while I ate a cracker.

I feared eating too much. I didn't want to vomit again.

Once the mess was cleared away, she wiped her hands on her jeans and sat next to me. "How many weeks along are you?"

"About ten."

"Your ultrasound didn't confirm it?"

"I haven't seen a doctor yet," I confessed. "I didn't know if I wanted the baby. Before I made a decision, I wanted Reese to know." Not wanting to see her judgment, I lowered my lashes. "Before you say it, I know it was just an excuse to see him."

"I think you made the right decision, Ainsley. The honorable one."

A longing for my mom and the urge to cry hit me so hard. I wanted someone to talk to and celebrate my pregnancy. If Reese didn't want his baby or me, I wouldn't waste my energy trying to change his mind. Besides, if I had to do that, it wouldn't work anyway. He had to want to be a part of our lives. Not because of pressure from me, but because it was the right thing to do.

"I don't know how I'm going to tell my brother. The reason I slept with Reese was stupid and childish. It was a mistake." I swiped at an escaping tear. "No, that wasn't the mistake. Not confessing who my brother was, was the mistake."

Jinx laid a hand on my arm. Her touch was comforting and prompted me to look at her.

"When we're in the moment, we believe we're doing what needs to be done. Don't beat yourself up over what you can't change." She dropped her hand and settled it in her lap. "Do you want the baby?"

"Yeah," I whispered.

She hugged me tightly. "Then congratulations, babe. Enjoy this time because it goes by so quickly."

Resting my head on her shoulder, I hugged her back. "You've been pregnant before?"

She pulled away and leaned against the sofa. "Almost every year for five straight years. The last pregnancy went full term, but my son was stillborn. I just gave up trying. I'm thirty-one. In four years, I'll be considered even more high-risk."

"I'm so sorry, Jinx. If this is too hard on you and you prefer I leave, I'll understand."

"My pregnancy losses *were* hard, especially the last one because everything seemed fine. But the world didn't stop spinning at my pain. Life went on. I can't shit on someone else's joy." She hugged me again, this time quick and tight. "If I were staying, I'd be here for you."

"I think Louisiana..." My voice trailed off. I couldn't fix my mouth to say he loved her. If he had, he wouldn't have betrayed their wedding vows. I sipped from the glass of soda, sighed in pleasure at the ginger ale, then grabbed the crackers. "I didn't know you'd be there. Nor did I know the real reason Nova rode with me. He'd began pulling away from her, which prompted her stunt today."

"It doesn't matter. Keir knows cheating is a hard no for me." Tears rushed to her eyes again. "I stupidly believed his bullshit excuses. Repeatedly. Whenever I questioned his whereabouts, he always gave me a valid reason. How can I ever trust him again?"

I didn't have an answer.

"I've been with him since I was twenty and we've been married for ten years. I don't know why he'd ruin us. It doesn't matter. I'm done. I'm contacting an attorney the first thing tomorrow."

"I'm probably not equipped to advise you for several reasons, Jinx—"

"Denali. Jinx is Reese's nickname for me that everyone picked up."

I digested that information. "Okay, *Denali*," I amended. "If you need to leave and think things over, then you should. But don't immediately contact an attorney. Wait a few weeks. Your perspective might change."

I grabbed another cracker and took a small bite.

"How could he betray me?" she whispered in a trembling voice and began sobbing. "How could he touch another woman and then come home to me with words of love? Pretending he couldn't wait to have me."

"I'm sorry," I said. "I'm so sorry."

"It isn't your fault. It isn't even Nova's fault as much as that kills me to admit. It's Keir's. He's the married one. He took the vows."

"You're right," I said softly.

The door opened, and Reese followed Louisiana inside. Cigarette hanging from the corner of his mouth, Reese set my bag on the table.

"You two bonding?" he asked, taking cigarette in hand.

Jinx glowered at him.

Louisiana stepped next to Reese. I'd never seen him look so pitiful. Misery dampened his usual rowdiness. His eyes were black, scratches marred his neck, and bruises dotted his face.

I didn't mean to stare, but his injuries shocked me. I saw no sign of a struggle, yet they must've had an epic battle.

"Jinx—"

She growled and Louisiana held up his hands.

"Den...babe. Morning's going to be here soon enough. If you go with your daddy, you're going to take my fucking heart with you."

She wrapped her arms around her stomach. "I can't take what you don't have."

Dropping to his knees, he captured her gaze. "I'm begging you, Jinx," he whispered.

"No, you fucking asshole," she shrieked. "No, no, no. Beg, plead, cry, bleed, break, *die*. I don't care."

She jumped to her feet and disappeared down the same hallway as earlier. A moment later, a door slammed.

"Told you, fuckhead," Reese said calmly. He nodded to me. "Come on, sweetheart. Let's get you to bed."

CHAPTER SIXTEEN

REESE

Since Jinx would rather have killed Louisiana than sleep next to him and I'd put myself on Ainsley's shit list too, those two slept in the lone bed, locked in the sole bedroom. Louisiana stretched out on the sofa and I got my sleeping bag from my saddlebags and found a spot on the cold, tiled floor.

Louisiana had kept me outside, picking my brain and going through every scenario possible to convince Jinx not to leave. He was crashing out. Yet, I couldn't help him. He'd betrayed her and knowing Jinx, she'd never forgive him. Finally, he settled on begging on his knees. He'd even said he'd crawl if she gave him another chance. I told him it wouldn't work but he refused to listen. The shit went exactly as I expected.

Her refusal left him restless, which made it hard for me to sleep. Or, maybe, it was knowing Ainsley slept right in the next room, but she might as well have been back on opposite sides of the city. I fell asleep with that thought.

The creak of a door awakened me and my eyes popped open. The first rays of sunlight slanted through the window and bounced on the wall near me. The door that led to outside remained closed, so it must've been the bedroom door.

Jinx crept into the kitchen and flipped on the light. She was already dressed, so I knew she hadn't changed her mind. Sighing, I sat up and shoved the cover aside.

She glanced over her shoulder, then turned away and braced her hands on the edge of the sink.

"He loves you, Jinx...Denali," I said.

"I don't care," she said around sniffles. I wondered if she'd gotten any sleep. She straightened and started moving, opening cabinets to pull out what she needed to brew coffee. "I told Ainsley you'd given me that nickname."

I rubbed the back of my neck. "Thanks," I bit out.

She filled the glass pot with water. "It didn't faze her. Whether she figured out we had been an item, she asked no questions. I like her a lot."

"High praise from you," I said with a small smile, my anger evaporating. Jinx always gave the women I dated some sort of test. I don't remember any of them ever passing. "You fucking hated Trinity."

"Are you actually comparing Ainsley to Trinity?" She dumped the water into the coffee maker and flipped the switch. Hopefully, she'd put coffee in the basket. "You're an asshole."

"Never said I wasn't, Jinx."

She flinched. "Don't call me that. If you can't call me Denali, then I want the nickname *you* actually gave me."

"Not doing that, babe. Jinx is close enough anyway. Just a few less letters."

Not answering, she turned away again. "Daddy's on the way."

"What I'm about to ask you will be so fucking unfair—"

"Then don't do this to me, Reese. Please? I know what you're about to ask me and—"

"I'm a motherfucker, but Louisiana loves you. He said he talked to Razor. He's willing to take a few days off. Bring you to Baton Rouge. Let him do that and if he can't change your mind, then divorce him. If there's anything left, even a little spark, then start over. He can sleep on the sofa for however long it takes to regain your trust."

"You fucking assholes stick together," she cried.

I didn't say anything. Jinx and I couldn't make a romantic relationship work, but we were good friends. When her temper got the best of her, Louisiana asked me to talk sense into her. When he acted like a fuckhead, Jinx begged me to straighten him out. He'd never hurt her so deeply, but I didn't think he'd allow his affair to last so long.

I'd had to choose between Jinx and my best friend who was also my club brother. Unfortunately, she'd been the casualty.

"I swear to you I'm out of it after this," I said. "But give him this one chance. A real chance."

"Fine, you asshole." She swiped at her tears and glared at me. "By the way, I told Candy to fuck off. You're interfering in my fucking life? Here's my interference. Give *Ainsley* a chance. She's carrying your baby."

"It sounds as if you already interfered if you talked to Candy prior to this conversation."

"After Ainsley went to sleep," Jinx confirmed. "Candy said she hadn't heard from you since you fucked her, so she figured as much without me telling her. Apparently, you got your rocks off and didn't even cuddle with her. You gave her a sorry excuse and left."

"I was going to call her. Probably this weekend. Before Ainsley came back," I mumbled. The tips of my ears burned with embarrassment. Dealing with my overwhelming lust for Ainsley on my own was humiliating enough. "She's, uh, pregnant. I don't want to stress her out."

Any more than I already had. God, I needed to get my head on straight.

Cocking her head to the side, Jinx studied me. She smirked, though tears still lurked in her eyes. "You're so fucking freaked out."

"I never expected any woman to turn up pregnant by me. Especially Ainsley."

"I wasn't talking about that." She pulled two mugs from a cabinet shelf. "I don't think I've ever seen you look at a woman the way you look at her."

Fuck, was I walking the fuck around like a googly-eyed motherfucker? "I don't know what you mean."

"I call bullshit, Reese." She poured our coffees, added cream to mine, then handed me the mug. "It's okay. It's the first time you've made a connection to anyone since Trinity's death."

Tasting my coffee, I nodded.

"So it makes sense if you think about her all the time or if you missed her."

Not only that, but she'd trusted me to take her virginity. I'd made the decision to save Roman Mac on her behalf and then saw her devastation firsthand. I had that fucking picture of her. Louisiana made sure to keep me informed of her goings-on, even when I repeatedly told him to shut the fuck up. And, now, she carried my child.

I drank more of my coffee. "I don't really know her."

"Then take this time and find out about her, Reese."

"I always said I didn't want a wife or kids."

"That's why I left you." She smiled sadly. "Not that it mattered. I have a defective womb."

"Don't say that," I told her quietly. "He might have defective cum."

"It's probably good we didn't have kids."

"You promised a fair chance, Jinx," I scolded.

She sniffed. "Fair warning. Ainsley intends to go to work tomorrow, so you have to work fast."

"I don't even know where the fuck she works."

"At Magical Meadows Daycare."

I shook my head. "It figures she told you. You both like to talk, although I think Ainsley has you beat."

"I think so."

A honking horn filled the quiet surroundings, and she heaved in a breath.

"Babe?" Louisiana said from behind me. He sounded wide awake. When he walked up to me and clapped me on the back, I knew he'd heard most of the conversation.

"Give me your phone," she ordered. "Mine's in the bedroom and I don't want to wake Ainsley."

Louisiana rushed to do her bidding, sagging when Jinx called her father and told him she was staying.

"I'm so sorry, Daddy." Her voice wobbled. She really wanted to leave. "I'll Cash App you money for gas." She smiled through her tears. "I love you, too."

She disconnected the call and handed Louisiana the phone. "If I would've went outside, I would have left." Setting her coffee mug in the sink, she drew herself up. "I suggest we go back to the club and get your bike so we can hit the road before I change my mind."

I would've preferred not to awaken Ainsley, but the hustle and bustle drew her from the bedroom, so she was at my side when Louisiana and Jinx left in the van.

I guided Ainsley back into the cabin. She sat her cell phone on the table before she dropped onto the sofa.

"Are you hungry?" I asked, suspecting why she kept glancing at her phone.

She grunted. "Nauseated."

"I have to call Razor. Make sure there are no pressing matters. Afterwards, we can always take a nap."

"Roman's going to call any second," she said, confirming my suspicions. "On Sundays, I straighten the house and choose my outfits for the work week after I talk to him."

"But we're staying at the cabin today, so we can take a nap."

"If you want the bed, you can have it, Reese."

One of us needed to concede. Since I was the jackass who mentioned another woman, I suppose it had to be me. "Sweetheart, can we spend the day getting to know each other? I shouldn't have said what I did to you."

"Is it true?"

"No, Ainsley. I'm not involved with anyone." I scratched my chin, thinking of the mistrust between Jinx and Louisiana. Honesty was best. "I've slept with one woman since you and I were together."

She nodded.

"I went on a run. When I wasn't partying at the club and out on club business, I returned to my room alone. Or I watched football."

Her eyes widened. "You're part of the Kingdom, too?"

I assumed she meant Roman. "I am. Like your brother."

"That would be me. My brother loves MMA and hockey. The bloodier the sport, the more he loves it."

"Do you really like football?" I asked, afraid to believe that.

"I haven't been keeping up recently, so I forgot a game was on yesterday."

I smiled at her and she returned a shy one of her own. A moment of peace and awareness. That electrifying connection that had turned my world upside down since I met her crackled between us. She yawned.

"If I promise to stay on my side of the bed, will you nap with me?"

She nodded and I smiled at her.

Brother by NEEDTOBREATHE pealed from her phone. I shook my head. Roman had some sappy shit for her ringtone. Now this.

Ainsley jumped up. She still wore the clothes she'd had on yesterday and I wondered why.

As she grabbed the phone, various emotions flooded her face, relief chief amongst them.

"Put it on speakerphone," I told her just before she answered.

Surprisingly, she cooperated. "Hey, Ro."

"Ainsley."

At the cold greeting, she lost her smile and I stiffened.

"Uh—"

"I'm only calling because I didn't want you to worry. I'm fine. I doubt I'll call again. I'll be too busy."

"What's the matter? What's going on?"

Her panic made my blood boil.

"I have to go, Ainsley."

"No, Roman, talk to me," she begged. "What's wrong?"

"You're pregnant." His voice boomed through the line. "With my fucking enemy's baby. Reese Sinclair wants me as dead as I want him."

Horror washed over Ainsley's features. She looked at me as the color dropped from her face, and placed a finger over her lips, then gazed at the phone and said, "I can explain."

"You don't need to fucking explain. You didn't deny it, so it must be true."

Her sob broke my heart. I couldn't stand idly by while that motherfucker destroyed her.

"You're aborting it."

"I am not," she said indignantly.

"And when you do, I never want to see you again."

"I'm not aborting my baby," she yelled, shaking her head when I opened my mouth. "I'm sorry. Just let me explain, Roman. Please," she said, back to begging.

"You betrayed me, Ainsley. You betrayed the fucking club and you couldn't tell me yourself."

"Just listen to me."

"I refuse to support the kid of a motherfucker who just used you to get back at me."

"He didn't know," she said wildly, talking before I could say anything. "He didn't know we were related until the morning after."

I squinted at her. Did she realize what she'd just said? Although it deepened my anger and dislike, Roman's curse filled tirade that mentioned my grisly death and unimaginable torture to poor Monster, didn't surprise me.

"I was going to marry Dayton and I didn't want to," she sobbed. "I just wanted to give up my virginity to anyone *other* than Dayton Morgan. And-and Nova set me up with her boyfriend's—ex boyfriend's—best friend. I didn't know he was Louisiana's brother. Club brother."

Roman choked. "Nova was fucking a Royal Bastard?"

Sniffling, Ainsley nodded, although her brother couldn't see her. "They dated for two years. And...and I'm sorry I didn't tell you. I didn't know how, but I love you."

"Fuck you. You opened your legs to my enemy," he reiterated, ignoring her tears. "So what are you going to do with a baby in your belly, no ring, no decent job, nothing to your name?"

"If you don't want to help me, I'll survive. I'm going to work tomorrow and I'll clear my things out of the house afterwards."

"Fine," he said and disconnected.

Ainsley stood in stunned silence. When she raised her tearful gaze to me, I pulled her into my arms and allowed her to cry in misery.

Chapter Seventeen

Ainsley

I couldn't remember the last time I slept in. I was always busy with some activity. Until Trinity's death, I had been pursuing my degree, working at the nursery, settling into my apartment, hanging out with Nova, and being at Roman's beck and call.

Perhaps, that was a little unfair because Nova was right. My brother devoted his life to me. It was why I intended to marry Dayton and what led me to my one night with Reese. When I moved away from home, I claimed to want my independence. What I really wanted was for

Roman to remember who he was without me. I was still around him a lot. He either had dinner at my apartment or I went to the house after work.

He was kind of a neat freak, so tidying up and washing his clothes wasn't a big deal. I joked he had a uniform—jeans, T-shirt, motorcycle boots, and his cut. Unless something big was happening and then he wore his leathers. I knew better than to touch his colors. I wasn't a member, so I didn't have the right to even hold anything with the Bloody Scorpion insignia.

I had many reasons not to sleep in and a lot of them had to do with my brother. The brother who now expected me to abort my baby, just so he could cast me out of his life. Had he even heard himself? Either or would've been bad enough. But both?

Curling into a tight ball, I covered my mouth to hold in my sob. Reese had fallen asleep five minutes after we climbed into bed and an hour after Roman hung up. I'd expected him to call back, but he hadn't, which made me cry harder.

Reese held me and comforted me until my tears subsided, then he'd grabbed my hand and led me to the bedroom. While he undressed, I'd sat on the edge of the bed, wishing I'd never confided in my former friend.

Trusting her was my fault. I'd given her the benefit of the doubt because of Boom Boom's abuse. My mistake. One I couldn't undo because my life had blown up around me.

Nausea twisted in me. Groaning, I rushed out of bed and ran to the bathroom. I hadn't eaten and I wasn't hungry. Puking bile in between dry heaves left me weak and dizzy. Scooting back, I leaned my head against the bathroom wall and closed my eyes.

"Ainsley?"

Reese's voice washed over me. I just wanted to curl into him, but I wouldn't. I couldn't trust him either. He *was* the enemy and he *did* want Roman dead. I'd known that from the beginning. As I knew the opposite was true.

I opened my eyes, careful not to move my head. I didn't want the nausea to start again. His hard, muscled thighs and long legs were impressive, and I loved his ink. His stiff cock reached his navel, and I rebuked the desire pooling between my legs. Even if vomit wouldn't have ruined sex, I couldn't be with him under the circumstances.

He crouched in front of me and brushed some hair behind my ear. His tender look made my breath catch.

I went over all that had happened since I'd met Reese, especially the night Louisiana brought Roman to me. I thought about the men with him. They'd worn skull masks, but...*fuck*. Suddenly, I knew. I knew why Roman had survived and I understood why Louisiana delivered him to my doorstep. Not only had

Reese saved my brother's life, but he had been the one to take his hands. I should've been furious or hated him for hurting Roman as he had, but he'd allowed him to live.

"Did you really allow my brother to live because of me?" I whispered, the question bubbling up out of my need for the truth.

A half-smile curved his mouth. He tipped my chin up and nodded.

"You would've killed him if I hadn't slept with you?" I asked in a shaky voice.

"If I hadn't met you," he corrected, thumbing my lips. "I wouldn't have known he had a little sister. If I hadn't remembered your gorgeous whiskey-colored eyes filled with liveliness. If he hadn't asked me not to send pieces of him to you."

I let out a horrified squeak and dry-heaved. I didn't even have bile left. "You would've dismembered my brother?" I sobbed, hysteria rising in me.

He didn't answer until he'd gotten a cold washcloth and mimicked Jinx's actions from last night. Scooping me up, he carried me back to the bedroom. Once we were in bed, he pulled me into his arms and tangled his fingers through my hair.

"It isn't any different than what Roman would do to me or any of my brothers, Ainsley."

"Neither of you can kill the other," I decided around tears. "That's not how this works anymore. I'm the bridge between you and him."

"It's exactly how it works," Reese barked. "We aren't brothers. We're enemies. What the fuck is wrong with you? Just because I fucked you doesn't change the essence of me *or* Roman."

Anger doused the pain of his words. I drew myself up, ready to blast him.

"Shut the fuck up," he snarled before I spoke. "You have a head on your fucking shoulders. I admire you, but I can't believe you're so fucking naïve. Those motherfuckers, your brother's club, killed Louisiana's brother. A blood relation. Your brother killed one of my favorite club girls. Trinity. I was weeks away from putting her on the back of my bike."

I snatched myself away from him. "Roman killed her because she led him to believe she wanted him and said she carried his baby, then he found out she was fucking you," I snapped. "She was playing with fire and got burned."

He blinked, then swept me with a cold glare. "Why doesn't it fucking surprise me that you knew Roman killed her?"

"Because I was there," I said tiredly. "I begged Trinity to leave before Roman got home. We almost got into a fight. She accused me of betraying her. I don't know where Roman got the information, but it wasn't me. He really cared about her. She refused to fucking leave and told me I was the reason Roman didn't have a life." I lifted my gaze and shook my head. "And basically reaffirmed what Nova told me yesterday. I was pathetically ordinary, which I'm not, and I hung around my brother because I couldn't find a man of my own."

Reese's pulse thumped at the base of his neck and his shoulders heaved with each pant. My heart went out to him at the mix of anger and grief on his face.

"I begged her to go, Reese. Roman doesn't take kindly to being played. He thought she set him up. It was more of her affiliation to the Royal Bastards that cost her her life rather than her being a two-timing cheat." I drew in a deep breath and met his gaze. "Tell me you wouldn't have killed her yourself if you'd known the truth."

He glanced away.

"I think Louisiana saw her or her car when he picked up Nova. You're both idiots in that regard. I don't know why he'd tell Roman and not you, but that's the only explanation I have."

Jaw clenched, he stared at the wall. I don't think he could bear to look at me. I'd already told myself we couldn't be together, so I don't know why his attitude hurt me.

"Her death has haunted me," I said in a raw, wet voice. "I had to take a break from school. That was the one time Roman's temper got the best of him and he didn't shield me from the dark side."

He refused to respond. I couldn't force him to confess he would've handled the situation just as Roman had. Nor could I make his pain go away. In his mind, I'd betrayed him once again. Whether he admitted it, he punished my smallest infraction because Roman was my brother.

"When I saw your cut, I should've walked out."

"You should have," he spat. "Or you could've told me the fucking truth and let me make an informed decision."

"Why? So you could've killed me? One-upped Roman in your stupid war?"

"Did I fucking kill you when I found out Roman was your brother? Did I kill that motherfucker when I had him in my clutches? I risked a lot to save him. Our hatred isn't strictly a personal vendetta. It's bigger than him or me. It goes way back and both clubs have brought a reign of death and terror to the other. Even if I could intervene, I wouldn't. My allegiance is to my club. It isn't to a motherfucker who couldn't sit his ass down somewhere and enjoy his fucking second chance at life. Instead of patching out, what did Roman Mac do? Go on a fucking run the first motherfucking chance he got."

From what I knew of Reese, he was laid-back and chill. I'd never seen him so red-faced, angry, and almost foaming at the mouth.

"Roman didn't have a choice," I said.

"We all have fucking choices, Ainsley. He made his. I've made mine."

He was right. Not knowing what else to say, I went to the living area and curled up on the sofa, since I had nowhere else to go or no one who cared.

REESE

Motherfucking Louisiana. Trinity might've been a two-timing cunt like Ainsley said, but he saw her as collateral damage and signed her death warrant.

Would I have killed her if I discovered she was fucking Roman Mac? You bet your fucking ass. I too would've felt she was setting me up on behalf of the Bloody Scorpions.

It was just so fucking much to deal with, especially after I'd mourned her for months. I'd lived with grief and guilt. All for nothing.

Since the day I lost my family, I guarded my emotions and let only a select few in. Until Trinity, I hadn't connected with any woman since Jinx. My instincts saved me from a monumental mistake.

As much as I still cared about Jinx, neither she nor that dead bitch compared to Ainsley. I needed a moment to process what she told me. One weight lifted off my shoulder and another descended.

Trinity got what she deserved. Roman Mac saved me the fucking trouble of having to explain why I'd killed one of our girls. I wouldn't have faced censure. Just a lot of fucking humiliation that my favorite bitch was a traitor.

My issue now was Louisiana. He'd intervened on my behalf and set me up with Ainsley. I didn't know how to help his unhinged need for revenge. He wanted to avenge Kenneth so badly, he was willing to fuck up his marriage to do so. I bet he saw Ainsley as a chess piece in his fucked-up game.

I'd see that motherfucker drawn and quartered first.

This was such a clusterfuck.

Remembering Ainsley's desperation, I squeezed my temples. I thought she at least understood club dynamics. She was asking me for the moon, when I couldn't even promise her the stars if it meant guaranteeing her brother survived.

Fuck, *I* might not live before I straightened shit out at the club, so Ainsley would at least have their protection if I bit it. Razor would just as soon see her dead because of the Roman situation. I hoped her pregnancy would end his need for vengeance. I had to declare her mine to safeguard her. Suspicion would follow both of us, but I was innocent. Ainsley's only crime was loving her brother.

If Razor wanted to kick my ass for fucking up so royally and knocking up my enemy's little sister, then I'd take the beating. Ainsley needed my help. She was pregnant by me. That made me responsible for her and the baby. Even if we didn't work out, I'd always look after her. If she was happy, healthy, and stress-free, then our child would be, too.

Her immediate need was an obstetrician and a place to stay. If the cabin was closer to the city, I'd tell Jinx that she had a roommate for the time being. Louisiana might serve as another complication, though. No matter what else he said, I was convinced he wouldn't want me with Ainsley.

Growling in frustration, I yanked on my jeans and left the bedroom. At the edge of the short hallway that led to the living area and compact kitchen, I heard Ainsley's voice.

"Roman, please call me. Please. I'm so sorry." She sniffled. "I wish I could say I didn't want a relationship with Reese, but I can't. He doesn't want me. Neither you nor him can make me abort my baby. Please don't turn your back on me. Nova said this was a shitty way to repay you." She laughed nervously. "Allowing your op to make a baby inside of me. She said a bunch of things. I-I shouldn't have...I didn't have anyone else to talk to and Nova said the rhythm method worked if it came to that. Now, she told me she'd counted wrong. Please call me. Even if you hate me, don't think of my baby as the enemy. Like Nova does."

That cunt needed to die, too.

"I love you, Roman. Thank you so much for being the best big brother any girl could ask for. Bye."

Goddamn if her heartfelt words didn't touch me. If Roman didn't soften, then he was as cold as rumor always suggested.

Shoving my hands in my pockets, I showed myself.

"I'm going to look for a full-time job, so I can have health insurance for me and the baby."

I pulled out a chair at the table and sat, then lit a cigarette, waiting for her to continue. She didn't. "I would've shot the fuck out of Trinity," I conceded around a plume of smoke and watery eyes. "Roman saved me a bullet."

"Okay," she said hoarsely.

I got to my feet and flicked ashes in the sink, since I didn't see an ashtray. Then, I remembered. Jinx liked glass ashtrays. She'd probably broken every one of them in her anger, then rushed to clean up after my call. Until she talked to Ainsley, she would've considered her an outsider.

I returned to my seat.

"I never saw myself as a father, Ainsley. I just didn't want to expose my emotions to such vulnerability."

"I understand."

"No, babe. You don't."

I wanted her to. I wanted her to understand my fear of losing another family as I'd lost my parents, sister, and brother. By the time I finished, she stood between my parted thighs after running to comfort me. Dropping my arms, I took her face between my hands.

"Is there anything else I should know about your brother?"

"Just that I love him and don't want him to die."

"A life for a life, Ainsley. That's our world. I already saved him once. It can't happen again. Under any circumstances."

"Reese, please—"

"It's club business." What didn't she understand about that? "You have no say in it. I'm not the president. I can't do anything more than I already have."

"Can you try—"

"No," I said with finality. "Our clubs are enemies. *Enemies*. Mortal fucking enemies. You're the one who has to change your wrong thinking. It's been this way long before I joined the club and it'll be this way long after I'm dead and gone."

She flinched at those words. My heart did a funny little flip at the thought that my life mattered to her just a little.

I gentled my tone. "I know it's a bitter pill to swallow. One of us killing the other. You're having *my* baby, so I'm asking you to give me a chance. Give us a chance. I care about you and I missed you. Let's disconnect from the world for the rest of the day, so it's just me and you." I pressed my hand against her stomach. "And the baby."

"Were you ever going to contact me?"

"Maybe if I had a chance to miss you, but Louisiana kept me informed of your every move. As long as he did that, I convinced myself I didn't need to contact you..."

I narrowed my eyes.

Sonofabitch. He'd known exactly what the fuck he was doing.

"What?"

"Louisiana's a motherfucker."

She smiled. "Tell me something I don't know."

I'd deal with his fucking ass later. Right now, I drew Ainsley into my arms. I had to tell Razor, Bolt, and Ma Siller about Ainsley's pregnancy. Hopefully, we all survived the fallout. For Ainsley's sake, that included her brother.

CHAPTER EIGHTEEN

ROMAN

I wanted to find a moment alone to think. Since I'd talked to my sister this morning, I'd felt like a mean fuckhead. As furious as I was with her, I couldn't get over my cruelty. But did she know what the fuck she'd done? The position she'd put me in?

Ainsley was too smart to be so fucking naïve, especially toward Nova. Of all the cunts to trust, she'd gone to her with news of her pregnancy. It didn't matter if Nova fucked the entire Kansas City chapter of the Bastards. Her problem. Her life. Her father wouldn't come under suspicion. His absolute hatred of the Royal Bastards was known far and wide.

Because of recent events, I was a different story.

Sighing, I nodded to the girl they gave me as my assistant to cater to every need I couldn't handle myself. It was inevitable I give in and listen to the message Ainsley left. When she'd called me back, Kite had been in the room. He'd offered to put the phone on speaker and answer. Even if I hadn't still been livid, I wouldn't have allowed that motherfucker to hear our conversation.

Her devastation broke my fucking heart. I glanced away, not wanting the chick to see how affected I was. Every time we settled in a different place, I was given another girl. After the first two, I gave up asking their names. They wouldn't be with me long and I'd forget them sooner rather than later. This one reminded me a little of Ainsley. She was young, dark-haired, and friendly.

She'd give me pussy just like the woman who'd been waiting for me, but I couldn't bring myself to touch her.

"Do you need anything else?" the chick asked, setting my phone on the desk in my room.

I shook my head.

A knock sounded on my door before it swung open. Kite's gaze traveled between my caretaker and me, then he smirked.

"Dinner, Roman."

"I'll take it in my room," I said politely. "As I have been doing the past weeks." I didn't want anyone to see how much of an invalid I was. Usually, they honored that. "I'm not that hungry anyway."

Kite grinned. "Bash wants all of us downstairs, so Boom Boom sent me up to get your ass."

I wouldn't get around it, so I nodded curtly and stood. "Put my phone in my pocket," I said to the girl.

Once she complied, the three of us walked to the staircase and made our way down. Scorpion cutouts interspersed with American flags covered the walls in the main room. A curved bar was situated near the stage with a pole in the middle.

It was crowded, mostly with American Scorpions. Kite guided me to where four tables were put together to create one long table. Kite sat in the empty chair to the left of a motherfucker with pale green eyes, a bald head decorated with tattoos, and a face that had seen better days.

"Did I tell you to sit there?" he asked Kite.

A black dude walked up to the table. Motherfucker was huge, taller than my six feet three inches and acted as if he owned the place, even though we had the same rank—Enforcer.

"I'd hate for Cleaner to remind you of the error of disobeying me."

Cleaner the Enforcer. Interesting road name.

Kite scowled, but glared at Bash, according to his patch, and got to his feet.

"Roman is better on this side of the table," Boom Boom said. He nodded to my arms. "He needs help and that cunt you lent us has to sit next to him, so Kite should stay right where he is."

Bash sniffed, dragged on his cigarette, and smiled as he released the smoke. "Cleaner."

The girl's panic registered a moment before Cleaner shot the fuck out of her.

"Now, she's not a problem," Bash said calmly. He crooked his finger at me. "Get over here and sit."

Unable to believe he'd just shot an innocent woman, I gaped at the motherfucker.

"You heard him, Roman," Boom Boom ordered, a touch of panic in his voice.

They didn't intend to move her body. Bash beckoned me, his eyes bright with insanity.

Swallowing, I walked to the chair. She laid next to it, in a pool of blood, her eyes and mouth open. My stomach turned. Boom Boom tore off a paper towel from the roll on the table and dabbed his forehead. The Bloody Scorpions were shook. The American Scorpions continued as though there wasn't a dead woman on the floor.

I pressed my lips together.

"Boom Boom has told me everything I need to know about Nova," Bash said. "From her picture, she looks like a hot bitch. Hopefully, she has good pussy."

"Excuse me?" I pushed out when no one spoke up on her behalf. Not even her own father.

"I'm selling Nova to Bash," Boom Boom said. "Girl's more like her momma every day. A fucking handful."

She was also a traitor, fucking Louisiana and guiding Ainsley down a path of rack and ruin.

"When I realized I can't kill Nova—she's my daughter after all—I decided to show you the same grace with Ainsley."

They wanted to *sell* Ainsley? That couldn't be right. I was misunderstanding Boom Boom's meaning. Anger and resentment skewered my judgment. If he really meant to sell Nova, I couldn't have cared less. It left me disappointed, though. That bitch was at the top of my fucking death list. She'd opened her fucking mouth to Boom Boom about Ainsley *and* she'd introduced her to Reese in the first place.

Bash shifted in his seat. "Tell me about Ainsley."

My eyes flared. Fuck. I wasn't mistaken.

"Instead of making you kill your own flesh and blood, I'm selling her," Boom Boom confirmed as if he did me a great favor. "She wants to use her cunt against us? Then let her do something useful with it and make an acquaintance of mine some money. Bash will fuck her up when he's tired of her."

Bash lifted his eyebrows. "Flesh and blood?"

"That cunt is his sister," Wizard said with distaste, nodding to me. "Let our enemy knock her up."

"We don't have time for pregnant bitches," Cleaner said.

"Who asked *you*?" Boom Boom sneered.

"Your mama when I fucked her last night," he retorted.

"I take umbrage to any motherfucker talking about my momma," Boom Boom said coldly, staring at Bash. "She was a saint. Bring your boy to heel or else."

Although Cleaner looked ready to start shooting, Bash remained calm.

He tapped out his cigarette. "I'm not pointing out that boy in the context in which you say it can be taken as a grave insult."

"What's it to you, Bash?" Wizard said with a chuckle.

"A lot," Bash declared. He nodded to Cleaner. "That's my cousin you're disparaging."

I thought he was joking or even taking a dig at my heritage. Who knew what the fuck Boom Boom and company told him, but he was dead ass serious. He swept us with a cold look.

"I'm willing to overlook the affront to my family if it doesn't happen again."

Boom Boom smiled tightly. "Of course, Bash."

It surprised me *he* hadn't started shooting. Boom Boom resorted to violence at the slightest insult.

"When can we have our weapons back?" he asked.

Oh, so that explained it. The Bloody Scorpions had to give up their shit before they entered the premises. I didn't have my guns or knives any longer. They were useless to me for the time being.

"A man feels naked without at least one gun," Boom Boom went on.

"Soon," Bash promised. "Now, leave so I can talk to this motherfucker." He nodded to me. "Go to the bar. Enjoy the alcohol. We've have broads coming in soon to suck cock."

It felt as if all eyes were on my club members and I, but they cleared away without any more argument. Cleaner followed them to the bar, then returned with two glasses, poured rum in each, then slid one to me and one to Bash.

I glared at the motherfucker. "Very fucking funny."

"Flower!" Bash called.

A small blonde chick with big blue eyes and a gorgeous face walked to the side opposite the body.

"Help him to drink," Bash said. "Don't spill a drop and he better not have to ask for a sip. Got me?"

She trembled and nodded vigorously.

Whistling, Bash lit two cigarettes, then leaned over and stuffed one between my lips, holding it in place so I could take a drag, then removing it and setting it in the ashtray.

"He has a cigarette, too," Bash declared.

"I don't need it," I said. She was about to piss herself, afraid to make a mistake while serving me. "I don't know what deal Boom Boom offered, but my little sister isn't for sale."

Studying me, Bash smoked his cigarette. The motherfucker was trying to intimidate me, then he smiled.

"They're a pain in the fucking ass, aren't they?"

"What might that be?" I asked, allowing Flower to put the glass to my lips and tip it back.

"Little sisters." He tasted his drink. "We're always trying to protect their pussies and they give it up to the wrong motherfuckers anyway."

I didn't answer.

"We love them anyway, huh?" he pressed.

Right now, I didn't know how the fuck I felt. I didn't trust Bash and I already knew my own brothers were waiting for a reason to put me out of my fucking misery. All because Reese fucking Sinclair saved my life thanks to Ainsley.

I drew in a harsh breath.

"I have a huge family tree." He laughed. "Vines and brambles. This one fucked that one and that one. It makes things very messy, but I only had one sister. Only daughter Daddy ever claimed. Why? Because my aunt Kimber loved her niece. Sisters see the best in us even when we're fuckheads."

Flower served me the drink again. I sidled a glance at the dead girl.

"Do you know what I hate, Roman?"

Probably a lot. Insane motherfuckers didn't like much. "I don't know you, so how the fuck would I know that?"

He ignored my sarcasm, drained his glass, and poured another one. "I hate motherfuckers who pretend they're decent. More than I am."

"And that is?"

"A heartless murderer without a conscience, and a motherfucker who runs women, sells them, and kills them. I don't have time for their bullshit. Except Celia. My little sister."

Begrudgingly, I applauded his self-awareness. "I see."

"When Boom Boom called and said he had a deal for me, I told him to come on over. I knew it was a cunt he wanted to sell me. He told me all about her. Ainsley. She'd run afoul of the club and you would kill her as soon as you got hands. Then he said you could tell me more since you spent a lot of time with her. The one thing he *didn't* say was she was your sister."

"And that makes a difference to you?" I asked skeptically. This time, I didn't sneak a glance at the dead chick. I looked at her pointedly.

He leaned back in his chair and folded his arms. "Even if I wasn't distracted by a war with my little brother's club, I wouldn't be happy with Boom Boom."

What did a war between two small-time organizations matter to me?

Flower brought the glass to my lips again. I welcomed the burn once I tasted the alcohol.

"Christopher Caldwell," Bash said, and I choked. "Outlaw. The Death Dwellers. If it wasn't for the little cunt he married, Daddy would still be alive and we could all live happily ever after."

I stared at Bash. He was part of *those* American Scorpions? The destruction of their clubhouses, the deaths of their leaders, their near total annihilation had been fodder for the rumor mill for years. All orchestrated by Outlaw.

Bash gulped half his alcohol. "I have a contact in the club."

"You've infiltrated the Dwellers?"

He shrugged. "Don't concern yourself with that. Sometimes, seeing Christopher so happy makes me wonder if I'm missing anything. If I was just a little fucking better, would a woman love me the way his young cunt loves him?"

"Oh, he's one of those. Forty or fifty with an eighteen-year-old."

Bash's eyes crinkled when he grinned. "Meggie's in her thirties. She's been with him since she was eighteen. But she adores him. She's given him fine sons and a beautiful daughter."

"Does Outlaw have sisters?"

"He had five. Two are left. Cleaner's father had the other three killed."

Boom Boom moved restlessly on a stool at the bar and glowered at me. "I don't know what all of this has to do with Ainsley."

"I'm going to call a couple of my sons. I thought about bringing in a dumb ass who couldn't see his cock for his balls if he had fucking illustrations."

I couldn't stop my laugh.

"But he'd be more of a fucking headache. I'd have to draw illustrations for him to understand." Bash smiled and waved his hand. He dropped his voice to a confidential tone. "None of that concerns you. This is my plan: I'm going to offer to help you as a way to soothe Boom Boom's annoyance. I'd just as well kill him, but I trust you'll do that for me."

I didn't respond.

Bash sniffed and nodded in approval. "By the time you arrive home, I'll see to it you have your prosthetics." He leaned in. "Just use them wisely."

"As much as I appreciate the offer, my answer is no." I didn't want to be indebted to this psychopath.

"Your call, Roman, but my guess is you're going to need working fucking hands sooner rather than later to protect your little sister. Come on, brother. Have you ever heard of a handless hero?"

I still couldn't trust that Boom Boom hadn't put Bash up to this to test my loyalty. "Say I'd accept your offer. How much would you charge me?"

Bash drained another glass and smiled. "Not what I'd charge you. It's what I'll charge Boom Boom. He came seeking my money from the sale of your little sister and his daughter. By the time he leaves, his wallet will be much lighter."

"You're underestimating my president. He's smart."

"Perhaps." He poured another glass and tipped it to me. "But I'm smarter."

CHAPTER NINETEEN

REESE

In my adult life, I never particularly saw myself as a caregiver. When Bolt and Ma Siller's kids needed me, I never turned them down. I considered them family, and families looked out for each other.

By the time of my mother's death, she'd taught me to cook. The only woman I ever cooked for was Jinx with the singular goal of fucking her. It worked like a charm, too. She was so impressed with my meal, she considered that foreplay.

But actually cooking for her because she needed tender, love, and care? Never. It didn't cross my mind, not even when she came down with the flu.

Ainsley was different. She'd gone through so many emotions over the past two days, I didn't want her to worry about anything but rest and relaxation. I definitely didn't want her hunting for a meal or toiling in the kitchen.

Once I convinced her to take another nap, I called Louisiana to see how things were. I was concerned that neither Jinx nor he had left a message for me, but they'd stopped in Natchez, MS and would reach Baton Rouge tomorrow. He sounded thoroughly dejected, so I figured it wasn't going well.

I'd tried to talk her into giving him another chance. It was up to him to convince her it was worth a shot.

Then, I called Ma Siller. I needed her to hear from me about Ainsley's pregnancy. Once Bolt found out, he'd fly off the handle and spin shit in a completely different direction. He'd have her hating me.

The call went better than expected. She congratulated me and sounded truly happy. I hated to capitulate to her demand that I bring Ainsley around to meet her, but she wouldn't let me hang up until I promised her. If Bolt forbade me to bring Ainsley around his wife, children, and grandchildren, I couldn't go against his wishes. It wasn't necessarily a club matter, but it was about respect.

Once I finished with those calls, I checked the refrigerator. There wasn't a lot of food. Jinx spent most of her time at the club since she ran the bar for us, so it made sense she wouldn't have a lot of food on hand. I'd always wondered why Louisiana didn't buy a place for them closer to the club. I don't think he'd ever fucked over his wife before, but it made it a helluva lot easier if their home base was over an hour away.

I awakened Ainsley long enough to ask her if she wanted anything special to eat. She'd murmured strawberries and went back to sleep. She still hadn't awakened when I returned from the grocery store. I bought enough food for several days, though I knew she intended to go to work tomorrow. Hopefully, I changed her mind. If I didn't, the food wouldn't go to waste.

Because of Ainsley's morning sickness, I didn't want to make a dish too spicy or flavorful, so I settled on chicken soup. I'd never made it from scratch, so I followed Ma Siller's recipe to the letter.

While the chicken boiled to make the broth, I tossed a coin to choose if I called Bolt first or Razor. As the president, it should've been Razor, but as the man who took me in, I couldn't discount Bolt.

News like this would spread faster than my fingers could dial. No matter who I called first, everyone would know before I got the other man on the line.

The quarter had landed on the coffee table. I leaned over and saw it was heads. That meant Razor.

Fuck.

I wasn't looking forward to this call, so I didn't press number '4', Razor's speed dial placement. When I got to the second to last number, Ainsley paused at the edge of the hallway. She looked adorably rumpled.

"Something smells good," she murmured.

"The beginnings of chicken soup."

"You cook?"

I nodded.

"I'm starving," she said. "But I'm also gross. I've been in these clothes for over twenty-four hours."

"You reek," I teased. "I can barely stand it."

She flipped me off and I laughed.

"Do you mind if I clean myself up? I'll be out in time to finish our food."

"I'm cooking, babe. I want you and the little one to rest."

"Okay," she said shyly. "I'll just get my stuff for my hair and...and stuff."

"Take your time, sweetheart."

I waited until I heard the shower running before I finished dialing.

Razor answered on the second ring. "Where the fuck are you, Reese? Louisiana asked for emergency leave and now you're MIA. What the fuck's going on?"

"It's a long story, Prez."

"Start at the fucking beginning. I come to the club last night, expecting to tell you about my winning streak at the track and you're nowhere to be fucking found."

Chi Chi hadn't ratted me out. I'd remember to thank him.

"I'm waiting, Reese."

"Once you hear the current status, the beginning will be easy enough to figure out."

"Tell me something because I'm losing patience."

"Ainsley's pregnant."

Uproarious laughter floated through the phone, the last reaction I expected. My tension eased.

Razor's laughter abruptly died. "Now, tell me the fucking truth. I'll admit that was a funny joke. Bullshit's over. Where are you and what's going on?"

The words killed my relief, and I scratched my jaw. "I'm with Ainsley, Razor. She's carrying my kid."

"How many times did you fuck her?"

"I was with her only one night. It only takes one fucking time, Prez."

"That kid isn't yours. It can't be. That little cunt is up to something. Roman Mac put her up to this."

"The baby's mine," I said flatly.

"You can't be fucking sure."

I was sure thanks to Louisiana. I knew Ainsley hadn't been with anyone else. But since

Louisiana was such a motherfucking sneak and liar, fucking around with Nova for whatever goddamn reason without clueing in Razor, I couldn't admit the truth.

"I think it is mine," I said evenly. "And Roman Mac didn't put her up to anything. His level of anger when she talked to him about the baby couldn't be faked."

"Get to the fucking club, motherfucker."

"Ainsley hasn't been well, Prez. Let me look after her tonight and come to the club first thing in the morning."

"What do your colors mean to you?" he growled.

"They're everything," I said without hesitation. "But Ainsley's all alone in the world right now. Roman Mac cut her off. I'm dropping her off at his house so she can get her car. After that, I'm not even sure she'll be allowed back there."

"Surely you're not suggesting that little twat stay in your room at the club?"

I gritted my teeth, hating the fucking names he called her.

"If you are, then you've lost your fucking mind."

As president, it was his call to make. Attempting to change his mind would only make shit worse and put me under further suspicion. My next words couldn't be helped if I wanted Ainsley safe from my club members' retribution. "Ainsley's mine, Razor," I said fiercely. "That baby is mine. I claim it and her. She's off-limits to anyone who thinks she's a Scorpion spy. She's *mine*."

I couldn't have been any plainer.

"I can demand you choose between that cunt and our club." Based on his tone, Razor intended to beat the fuck out of me just as I suspected. "Are you a Royal Bastard or a Scorpion wannabe?"

"I resent that," I snarled, jumping to my feet. "You know I've dedicated my fucking life to our club." The water abruptly stopped and I drew a deep breath. Ainsley would be out soon. She didn't need to hear this. "I wanted to do the right thing and tell you what was going on, Prez. I'll see you in the morning."

Before he responded, I disconnected. Things couldn't get any more fucked up between us and my future was no longer guaranteed.

Not wanting to consider what I might face at the club tomorrow, I went to the kitchen just as the bathroom door opened. The distinctive scent of a woman, of Ainsley, wafted to me. A steamy combination of her body wash and her shampoo that hardened my cock.

Our disagreements were brushed aside, not settled. I wasn't sure how she'd respond if I approached her. Maybe later, when I was calmer, and she was fed.

For now, I focused on the soup and shoved everything else to the back burner. Reality would intrude soon enough.

Reese's chicken soup would win first place in a cooking competition. Thick and hearty with chunks of chicken, diced potatoes and onions, and sliced carrots and celery, it was the best I ever tasted. It soothed my belly and filled me up, aided by soda crackers and ginger ale.

I wanted to call Roman again, though I knew it was a bad idea. Reese's steady conversation about football, one of my favorite topics, my work, and comparing our different recipes for several dishes, kept my heartache at bay and distracted me.

Tomorrow morning, I'd know if Roman had forgiven me. If he called as usual, then it was a yes. If he didn't, I knew what that meant, too.

"Ready for dessert?" Reese asked, breaking into my thoughts.

"You bake, too?"

"You're either a baker or a cook. Not both. If you excel at one, you're shit at the other."

"That isn't true," I protested. "My mom was excellent at both. Of course, she was a New Orleans girl. She was born knowing how to make good food."

"Bullshit. You learn to *cook* good food," he said, subtly correcting me.

"Boo on you," I replied. "She made groceries, went round the corner by her mama and them—dem actually—was a Who Dat, drank Hurricanes, feared hurricanes, walked on the neutral ground, second-lined, sucked the heads and ate the tails, screamed *throw me something, mister* and didn't show her tits, ate seafood on Fridays and beans on Mondays, said novenas and kept holy water even though we weren't Catholic, distinguished the two buildings on each side of the Cathedral—the Cabildo and the Presbytère, loved Tabasco, po' boys, and anything Zatarain's put out, had a bunch of wodies, tried her best not to use the Crescent City Connection, enjoyed the Natchez, and cursed anyone who said New *Orleens*. It's New *Orluns*."

"Goddamn, all that in five breaths. Impressive, even if I don't know half of what the fuck you mean. Fuck, most of what you mean."

I smirked. "Only thing I'll tell you tonight is what it means to be a Who Dat."

"This should be good."

"You know how we're part of the Chiefs Kingdom?"

The suspicion in his eyes tickled me. What the hell did he think I'd say?

"Yeah," he said, his tone matching his look.

"A Who Dat is a Saints fan."

His perfectly arched eyebrows lifted. "The football team?"

"Certainly not a religious saint. Yes, the football team, Reese."

"Well, goddamn. And that's the only thing you'll clue me in on?"

"I'll answer one more question."

"Two." He batted his lashes at me and I giggled. "Pretty please, babe. I cooked you a delicious meal."

"Fine, *two*," I conceded around laughter.

"What the fuck is a wodie?"

"A wardie."

"Ainsley!"

"Wodie is derived from wardie."

He glared at me.

"It means friend, pardner, road dog. Usually from the same ward as you."

"Got it." He smiled at me, the tenderness in his eyes morphing into desire. "Should I be happy when you tell me you want to suck the head and eat the tail?"

"If you want to watch me eat two or three pounds of boiled crawfish, sure," I said with a straight face.

"I hate fucking crawdads," he said. "Even when my father hosted boils, I couldn't take them. I'd help cut the mushrooms and onions.

Measure the kosher salt and vinegar. Shit like that."

"What foolishness is this?" I demanded. "Mushrooms? Vinegar?"

"The recipe for boiled crawfish. You know? The usual shit."

"You're delusional," I said with a disapproving snort. "I'll admit that you had some better recipes during our comparisons, but this definitely isn't one of them. To boil crawfish properly, wodie, you need andouille, bay leaf, garlic, potatoes, corn—"

"Our recipe calls for potatoes and corn."

"Cayenne pepper, salt, crawfish boil, onions, lemons, celery, and whatever other seasoning you'd like."

Reese pushed back from his seat at the table. "No matter, babe," he said, gathering our dishes and bringing them to the sink. He walked to the freezer and pulled out a half gallon of vanilla ice cream. "Those little suckers aren't for me."

"I love them."

He scooped ice cream into two bowls, then put the container back in the freezer, grabbed a beer from the refrigerator, and brought everything to the table, setting it down. He got two spoons before he sat down again.

"Thank you," I said, accepting the spoon he handed me.

"You're welcome, babe," he said, and took a hardy sip of beer.

We enjoyed our dessert in comfortable silence, until Reese poured some of his beer over his ice cream and shoveled it into his mouth.

"I can't fucking believe you did that."

"Kills two birds with one stone. Sometimes, I don't have time for dessert and a drink. Instead of choosing, I combine it, then get to whatever I have to do." He shoved more of that foamy brew between his lips. "This is one of my more delicious concoctions."

"I'll take your word for it," I grumbled.

He winked at me, but I couldn't look while he ate his beer cream without gagging. My stomach was so easily upset nowadays. As much as I hated the vomiting, sometimes the nausea was even worse. It was usually relentless and only subsided when it was good and ready.

"Do you like to dance?" Reese asked once we finished our dessert and settled on the sofa.

"I like music, but I don't have rhythm and I can't carry a tune."

He tugged one of my curls. I'd just shampooed and conditioned my hair, then put some oil in it. I didn't bother with the flat iron.

"Shouldn't you have at least a *little* rhythm, babe?"

Rolling my eyes, I elbowed him. "Fuck off. Roman can dance," I blurted.

He grunted and dropped his hand.

"Can *you* dance?" I said, trying to cover my blunder. Unplugging from the outside world meant laying our disparities aside for now. Bringing up Roman reminded us of our differences. "What's your favorite genre of music?"

"Country," he said, relaxing a fraction. "I dance when I'm drunk."

"Do you ever slow dance?"

"Fuck no! I don't do that sappy ass shit."

"Of course not."

"It shouldn't matter if you can't dance, babe."

"It doesn't. Not really," I amended. "In our situation, it *doesn't* matter," I decided.

"Explain."

"Let me preface by saying this doesn't fit us, but I always thought I'd slow dance once with the guy I was involved with."

"Aren't we 'involved'?" he asked, using air quotations.

"Not in the strictest sense."

His look softened again, and he leaned closer, brushing his lips over mine in a gentle kiss. "We'll get there, Ainsley," he promised.

I was afraid to believe him, but for now I kept my thoughts to myself, opening my mouth to his probing tongue and sinking into his kiss. With all that stood between us, I shouldn't give in to him. Yet my attraction to Reese Sinclair burned as brightly as ever. I wanted his hands and mouth on me. I longed to taste him. He hadn't tried to get me to suck his dick. Probably because of what I told him about Dayton. I appreciated Reese's consideration. I was ready now, though.

He stood up and held out his hand. Instead of taking it, I dropped to my knees and brought my hands to his belt.

"Babe—"

"You've been more than generous to me. I want to do this."

"You're going to fucking kill me," he murmured, unbuckling his belt and opening his fly. He shoved his jeans down slightly and his cock sprang free. Precum glistened on the tip, and I swiped my tongue over it.

"Ainsley," he groaned.

Lifting my gaze to him, I wrapped my lips around his girth and took him into my mouth. Although I wanted to block out my experiences with Dayton, I drew from that knowledge, taking Reese as far down my throat as I could. When I gagged, he eased back, but didn't rush me, allowing me to take my time. Slowly, I fell into a rhythm, dragging my tongue along the underside of his cock, licking the tip when he slid almost completely out of my mouth, and taking care with my teeth when he pushed back in.

His taste and scent aroused me. Humming low in my throat, I lost myself to his moans and the way his fingers tightened in my hair. Towards the end, he let loose.

"I'm about to come, baby," he said in a strangled voice. He tried to pull away, but I sank my fingers into his tight ass cheeks. "Fuck!" he snarled, holding my head in place and fucking my mouth until he burst on my tongue and his knees buckled.

He plopped onto the sofa, his eyes closed, his chest rising and falling in hard pants.

"Did I do it right?"

Disbelieving laughter burst from him and he popped one eye open. "You did it perfect, sweetheart."

I slapped my palm against my forehead. "I forgot to fondle your balls."

Lifting his head, he threw me a dark look. "Whatever that motherfucker told you to do, throw it out the goddamn window."

"You don't like your nuts touched during oral?"

He growled and leaned forward, grabbing me by the waist and plopping me on the sofa. "I love it, Ainsley," he said harshly, plundering my mouth with a sweeping kiss that stole my breath and almost made me forget my name.

I was so glad I wore a simple romper. He was an expert at seduction, removing the onesie and kissing me as if he couldn't get enough.

Guiding me back onto the sofa, he didn't move his lips away from me as he buried himself in me and I gasped. He felt so good, thick and heavy, sliding in and out of me, and grinding his pelvis against my pussy.

I hadn't realized how much sucking him off would turn me on, but it did, and I was so hot and ready for him that I came quick, drawing another orgasm from him. We didn't stay joined long after we finished.

"Don't leave me," I whined.

He stole another kiss. "I'm too heavy," he said gruffly, bending and scooping me into his arms and carrying me to the bedroom.

Chapter Twenty

Ainsley

When I awakened and found Reese gone two and a half months ago, I thought I'd never see him again. I didn't expect that I'd end up inextricably tied to him for at least the next eighteen years of my life.

Spending time with him in a secluded cabin never crossed my mind. It seemed so far out of reach as to be impossible. But however our relationship turned out, I'd cherish our moments together when it was just the two of us with no outside interference. He told me about the deaths of his family and I described the day my parents were killed.

It was a bond I preferred we didn't have, but luckily trauma wasn't the only thing we had in common. We talked more football, guns, cooking, music, and movies. We even broached religion and politics. I discovered he couldn't sing worth a lick, just like me. We preferred beer over wine and tequila over rum. We both liked soft baked chocolate chip cookies, corn-on-the-cob, and apples over oranges. I finally told him what all the New Orleans terms meant and he said it gave him a new appreciation for the city. He liked arm wrestling to win bets and insisted on testing my strength. At the last minute, his arm slackened and he gave me the victory.

In between, we made love and he rewarded my cock suck by licking my pussy for an hour. We barely slept a wink.

As I mounted behind him on the back of his bike, I wished time could've stood still. The farther away we rode from the cabin and the closer we drew to Kansas City, the more my anxiety increased.

When we finally reached my house—Roman's house—and Reese stopped next to my car, I laid my head on his back and tightened my hold around his waist. My eyes burned and my throat ached with my need to cry.

Reese killed the engine, wrapped one of his big hands around mine, and brought it to his lips for a kiss. I sniffled.

"Hey, babe, it's okay," he swore.

It wasn't. Deep inside me, I felt the coming storm, like an unstoppable wave bringing death and destruction. He dismounted, then helped me off the bike. Taking my face between his hands, he studied me and thumbed away the tears that insisted on falling, then dipped his head and brushed his lips across mine.

Standing on my tiptoes, I hugged his strong neck, savoring the feel of his mouth. He took his time kissing me. Still, it ended all too soon.

"Come on, Ainsley. I'll wait for you to change and get some things."

Swiping at my tears, I shook my head. "I can't let you inside. That would be like a slap in my brother's face."

"He isn't my concern. You and the baby are. I'll stay by the front door while you pack a suitcase."

"I plan to come back after work," I hedged, not admitting I hoped Roman called and took back what he said, especially the part about disowning me. "I will probably be late for work today when I'm usually the first one there."

"Roman doesn't want you here."

"Where am I supposed to go, Reese?" I demanded in frustration. "Roman isn't here right now and won't be for another twelve days."

He shoved his hand through his hair. "I'm working something out for you."

"If it involves going back to the cabin, I don't accept. It's too far away."

"It's a fucking hour away, Ainsley," he snapped. "How about you get your shit, take it with you, and I'll meet you at the daycare this evening? I'll pay you whatever you'll make over the next twelve days. No, I'll triple it."

"That's almost sixteen hundred dollars."

He was silent for a moment. "Would five grand do then?"

"What are you talking about? I earn five hundred twenty dollars a week. Less than that when I'm in school because I have part time hours."

"That's bullshit."

"It's reality."

"Roman allowed that?"

"Roman couldn't strongarm a fucking daycare, Reese," I huffed. "It's a legitimate job, adjacent to the early childhood education degree I'm pursuing. It also gives me a sense of independence."

"Yeah, I forgot. You're a 21st century chick. All about autonomy."

I scowled. "I'm going to ignore that and not call you a chauvinistic fuckhead." I started around him and then halted. "We're having a baby and I've spent an entire day playing house. I'd have no problem taking money from you. When it runs out, what then? If we don't work out, what happens to us?" I laid a hand on my belly so the jackass didn't mistake my meaning. "I gave up my apartment to take care of Roman, and he's just thrown me a-away."

All the pain and heartache I'd kept at bay the past hours swarmed me again.

"21st century chicks want security but we've learned from past generations that men are the most unreliable motherfuckers around, so we earn our own bags, fend for ourselves, and have our own safety measures in place."

"I blame Roman Mac for that mindset."

"Ha!" I stomped around him and threw over my shoulder, "That motherfucker is just like you, so shut up."

Reese was hot on my heels. When I unlocked the door and tried to slam it in his fucking face, he pushed his way inside.

"Get out!" I screeched, shoving him back onto the porch. "You can't come in here, you fucking overbearing prick. Roman might hate me, but this is his house. I can't disrespect it by allowing you in. Surely, you understand that."

"Fuck Roman," Reese spat, drawing his gun. "I don't want to be in that motherfucker's house either, but you're not setting foot in there alone. Not without me checking it."

"I didn't get an alert to any suspicious activity when I turned my phone back on."

"Do you really think any one of us wouldn't know how to bypass that shit?"

I drew a deep breath.

"Do you have to be such a fucking shrew?"

"If you say you plan to tame me, I will fucking kick you."

He smirked. "Don't have to say it, since you just did."

"You like Shakespeare?" I asked dubiously.

"Can't stand his work. I find it boring or hard to understand."

The relief I felt was so absurd that I laughed. It was getting late and Reese wouldn't leave unless he had his way, so I stepped aside and signaled he go in. I thought his racking the slide a little over the top but I remained quiet.

Several minutes later, he returned and indicated the all clear with a wave of his gun. I kept the *told you* to myself. It galled me when Roman or Nova threw that at me. Reese and I were alike in a lot of ways, so I'd bet he'd be less than pleased at that boast.

He holstered his gun, took two hundred dollar bills out of his wallet, then stuffed them into the pocket on my jeans. "Check in at the hotel up there on Minnesota Avenue when you get off from work."

"Roman won't mind if I stay here."

"Will you let me stay with you?"

"You know I can't do that."

"Then until I arrange something better, check in there. It's not far from the club, so it'll be easier to get away if you need me. I'll just be a short distance."

If not for that tangle of highways all converging near the Kansas River, Reese's club would be within walking distance of the hotel.

"I'll do it tonight," I said primly, thrilled that we'd spend another night making love.

He gave me a quick kiss, then lit a cigarette. "Don't be long getting your stuff. I have a lot of shit to do today."

Curiosity almost got the best of me, but Roman had drummed it into me that the less I knew, the better. "Can I have my .357 please?"

"Shit, I almost forgot. Glad you remembered. You need the protection."

"I can't bring my gun to work, Reese." He frowned, but I raised my hands to forestall another discussion. "When I return later, I'll keep it close by."

"Fine," he grumbled, flicked ashes into the wind, and stalked to his saddlebags.

REESE

I ended up not arriving "first thing that morning" as I'd promised Razor, but I wouldn't have concentrated if I didn't assure myself of Ainsley's safety, which included escorting her to work. The key card entry and iron fencing around the play yard eased my concerns, though the niggling in my gut persisted.

If not for logistics, I would've forced her back to the cabin and handcuffed her to the bed. The only way to do that would've been to snatch her keys and strong arm her into her car. I had handcuffs in my saddlebags, but not rope, which I needed to tie her to the seat so she wouldn't escape.

Besides, not knowing the outcome of the meeting with Razor left me at a disadvantage. Even if everything fell into place and I could've gotten her back to the cabin, if Razor killed me, she'd die, too. If they went to the cabin and unlocked her cuffs, they'd kill her anyway. Chances were, they'd sentence her to a worse fate and allow her to die from a lack of water.

So I hugged her tight, kissed her hard, and told her I'd talk to her later. I should've prepared her for the worse. Except I didn't want to worry her. We were both in precarious situations, exposed and vulnerable to the wrath of the Royal Bastards and the Bloody Scorpions.

When I walked into the clubhouse and saw most of the members already seated, I winced. Razor stood at the podium glaring at me.

Knight, Bolt's son and one of our Enforcers, clicked the lock in place and nodded to the long counter running the length of the wall just inside the door. I disarmed myself and placed my guns and knives in one of the few remaining empty spots.

All eyes were on me as I headed to Razor. The disapproval and mistrust wafting in the air felt surreal. Razor and I rarely gave up our weapons. My job was to protect him. I was big and bad enough to do it with my fists, but the odd fuckhead tested my authority from time-to-time.

Pretending shit was normal, I ignored everyone and walked to my president. I wanted to take my usual spot near the podium, arms folded, gaze roaming over the membership. Razor stared at me, cold and unwelcoming, anger lighting his eyes. I waited for him to speak or to punch me, but his frozen glower and his lack of movement chilled me.

"Is it true, Reese?" Bolt finally asked.

At his distressed tone, I regretted not calling him as I'd intended. I'd been so fucking angry with Razor, then Ainsley came out and I forgot everything else.

"Yeah," I said finally, turning my head slightly but still unable to see him. "Roman Mac's sister is pregnant with my kid."

"Good job," Baron, Bolt's younger son, called. He'd always been an ally, even when Knight wasn't, which was most of the fucking time. "Let that motherfucker choke on that. Not only does he have to live the rest of his miserable existence without hands, he'll spend his days knowing that bitch betrayed him."

I stiffened, an automatic reaction at such disrespect toward Ainsley.

"Does he know?" The glee in Warrior's tone annoyed me. "I heard he's away. On a run."

Grumbles rose up at that news. My chopping his hands off was meant to sideline him so he wouldn't pose a threat to us.

"He knows," I said flatly, almost certain Razor filled Warrior in on our conversation *if* the motherfucker hadn't been listening in the first place. "And, yes, he is."

"What'd he say to that news?" Marquis questioned.

"He wants nothing more to do with her."

"Awww, so sorry. That's the breaks," Knight sneered.

Balling my fists, I gritted my teeth.

"Where'd you meet that cunt?" he went on.

"Her name's Ainsley, Knight," I snarled, unable to take it any longer. I spun around and glared at the motherfucker. "*Ainsley*. Put some fucking respect on her name. She's carrying my kid. If you don't like it, too fucking bad. It's done. Interrogate me. Beat the fuck out of me. Shoot me but respect *her*."

"Fucking make me, Reese. How fucking dare you come in here all high-and-mighty over that slut. *We're* your brothers. She's just your fucking cocksucker."

I was so fucking livid, I saw red and moved before I stopped myself, managing one good punch before Bolt and Warrior grabbed me, marched me to a chair, and shoved me down.

Warrior's punch to the side of my head left me dizzy, while Bolt's inscrutable look hurt me more than anything else.

"Tell me about her," Razor finally ordered. "Everything."

"No." Disobeying a direct order from my president was never wise, but especially under these circumstances. "I trust her, Razor, and that should be enough."

"It isn't," he barked. "You used all your fucking favors when I let Roman Mac live."

"Never mind that's the only favor I've ever asked, I understand. Let's also forget how I've never turned down anything you or any of my brothers requested of me. Big, small, dangerous, or fun. Her pregnancy was a fucking accident."

"Probably because she put a hole in the condom," Baron called.

"Really, fucker? Which is it? I got her pregnant by design or she sabotaged my cock cover on purpose? Choose, because it sure the fuck isn't both."

"Suppose you have to choose, Reese?" Razor asked. "Her or us. And, by us, I mean you make her abort her kid. No matter the paternity, it has the blood of a Bloody Scorpion. *Roman Mac.*"

"She wants the fucking baby, Razor. What the fuck do you expect me to do?"

Bolt folded his arms and lifted his brows. "Do you want it, Reese?"

Before I spent the last day and a half with her, I intended to support her because it was the right thing to do. I hoped we could co-parent if nothing else. But after our time together, when she was sweet and pliant, trusting me with her body and her emotions, I wanted her. With the baby or without.

Separately and aside from us, she carried something I never knew I wanted, a part of me. My blood, when I hadn't had that in almost twenty years.

"Yeah, Bolt."

Rocking on his heels, he nodded. "Do you want her or do you want your kid's momma? There's a distinction. One's an obligation. The other is your world. Both your responsibility, but in different ways."

"She's not an obligation. She might not be my world, but I care about her. I enjoy her company." I met his gaze and gave him a half-smile. "She likes football and hates Shakespeare."

He smiled. "She sounds like my kind of gal." He held out his hand. "Congrats, son," he said gruffly, patted my back, and placed himself between my chair and the podium that Razor stood behind. "My boy's never done nothing disrespectful, Prez. I know that Roman situation is tetchy and Reese has used up all his favors, so I'm asking you to give her a chance on my behalf."

"All the fuck you ever do is ask for favors, motherfucker," Razor growled.

"Long years of friendship'll do that, Razor," Bolt retorted. "No matter what mishap got it made, it's not the little one's fault. Those two were consenting adults. It was their responsibility to protect against this possibility. If you're still not convinced, I have a final argument."

"I wouldn't stake my life on it," Razor said with less heat. "You'll think of fifty more after this one."

"Possibly, but so far, here's my last word. By the time her baby is born, Reese will have her firmly on our side. She'll be his ol' lady instead of Roman's sister."

"Fine, you old fucking pest." Razor grabbed the gavel and banged it. "Meeting's adjourned. Reese, we leave in an hour for Wichita. Get ready."

"Are we coming back tonight?" Usually, we went for collections and stayed overnight.

"In a day or two," Razor confirmed, then walked off.

I got to my feet. "But—"

Bolt put a hand on my shoulder and shook his head. "Not now, Reese. Let it sink in before you shove her needs down Razor's throat."

I told him about Nova, how that bitch betrayed Ainsley, and my gut feeling that she wasn't safe.

"We'll sort it out when we get back," he promised. "You saw to her. Now, it's time to return to reality and take care of club business."

CHAPTER TWENTY-ONE

REESE

We arrived in Wichita much later than normal, and that meant we'd probably stay an extra day. Right before I started prospecting, the Kansas City chapter brought in the few remaining members from Topeka after the Bloody Scorpions struck and took out most of their members. I knew none of the older guys agreed with not rebuilding the ranks. It seemed like those motherfuckers had won. Besides Kansas City, we only had two other chapters left in the state—Wichita and Elkhart, which was a stone's throw from Oklahoma and Colorado.

I always liked the idea of a Dodge City chapter and another one near the Nebraska border, but what the fuck did I know? There was a reason National didn't pursue more chapters in our state and I trusted them.

As the smaller chapter, Wichita earned extra money by helping us with distribution. We did monthly runs for checks and balances, pickups and payouts, unless the boys were particularly profitable, in which case we paid an extra visit to them.

Once I grabbed some grub and a couple of beers, I texted Ainsley to let her know I'd be out of pocket for the next day or two. I would've preferred to call her and hear her voice, but she had a couple hours left until six and she told me she had her phone off at work.

Sitting at the bar in the Wichita chapter, I enjoyed the spectacle of the girls, brought out to entertain us. Months ago, I would've fucked two or three. Tonight, each time one of them brushed up against me, I sent her on her way.

My phone vibrated in my top pocket. When I took it in hand, I saw that Louisiana had sent me a message.

> Nova just called me.
> I need to talk to you

Unable to believe the audacity of either of those motherfuckers, I stared at the words. He'd claimed to want a second chance with Jinx and he was still entertaining that bitch?

I picked up the phone to shove it in my pocket when his name flashed across my screen with an incoming call.

"What?" I got to my feet and stormed outside so I could hear myself curse his ass to hell and back. "Are you out of your fucking mind? If you're calling me to ask for my help, the answer is—"

"Reese, shut the fuck up and listen to me," Louisiana growled in hushed tones. Obviously, he didn't want Jinx to overhear. "It isn't what you think. Nova texted me but I ignored it, so she called me. I knew she wouldn't relent until I answered and I'm only grateful Jinx was in a praline shop."

"Get on with the fucking story, Louisiana," I snapped.

"They're going after Ainsley."

I froze and my heart almost stopped.

"Tonight, Reese. Nova called because she feels guilty that she was mad enough to put Ainsley in this predicament and thought you and I could save her."

"I'm three hours away," I pushed out, my mind racing as fast as my heart. "Why should we believe Nova? It could be a set-up."

"I know," Louisiana said in a strained voice, no longer whispering. "But if it isn't, Ainsley's dead. If we were there, we could at least watch her from afar until we got a bead on the situation."

A shudder went through me. At least Ainsley would be at the hotel. They wouldn't find her at the house. Still, I needed information. "Did she say who's behind it?"

"Boom Boom intends to sell her and it pissed off some members. Particularly Kite and Wizard. They ordered the hit. She thinks they're going to blame us for Ainsley's death."

Bolt peeped out the door and beckoned me. "Come on, Reese. We're about to do roll call."

I tightened my grip on the phone and turned. "Bolt, we have a problem."

Around three, morning sickness hit me so fiercely, I spent the next hour in the bathroom, vomiting. Tess, the owner of the nursery, was waiting for me when I staggered out. She was an older woman with dusky skin and close-cropped natural hair. If my mom were alive, she would've been the same age as Tess. Maybe, that's why I'd taken such a liking to her. I wasn't sure when I planned to tell her about the baby, but I definitely hadn't wanted her to find out the way she did. Nor was I sure of her reaction.

She was a church-going woman who believed in the sanctity of marriage and often complained about the wildness of young people. She'd tell me and the other four girls who worked there that if she'd been blessed with children, they would've been God-fearing and respectful.

Seeing her pacing outside the bathroom door made me pause. She halted, folded her arms, and narrowed her eyes. Heat swarmed my cheeks. For a moment, I felt light-headed enough to faint. She crooked her finger at me, turned on her heels, and glided to her office. Feeling chastised to the nth degree without her saying a word, I followed her. She waited until I walked into her office before she slammed the door.

"Sit down, Ainsley."

Even if I'd wanted to stand, I felt too weak to do so. I plopped into one of the miserably uncomfortable chairs in front of her desk.

"Does Big Poppa have to pull out his shotgun and march someone down the aisle?"

I chewed on my lower lip. It always cracked me up that she referred to her husband as Big Poppa. I couldn't listen to Biggie's song anymore without going into hysterics.

"Well?"

Mr. Montgomery going after Reese with a shotgun wouldn't work out well. I shook my head.

She craned her neck, then wiggled her fingers. "Hands."

Sighing, I lifted my hands. "I don't have a ring."

"Then Big Poppa needs his 12-gauge to fire some buckshot into some body's behind."

I lifted my brows.

"How far along are you?"

"10 weeks." In four days, I'd be eleven weeks.

"Have you seen a doctor? Do you take your vitamins regularly?" She snatched her notebook from her two-tiered file holder and grabbed a pen from the middle drawer. "And I want that boy's contact information."

"I wouldn't exactly describe Reese as a boy," I mumbled.

"How old is that irresponsible fool?"

"Thirty-one."

Laying her pen down, she leaned back in her seat and rubbed her temples. "You're about to send my blood pressure through the roof, Ainsley."

"I'm fine," I rushed to reassure her. "Except morning sickness hits me at any time during the day." I slid to the edge of my seat and raised my hands in supplication. "Don't fire me. I need my job now more than ever."

"Fire you?" She gasped. "Ainsley Valois, if you know nothing else about me, you know I live by Christian tenets. It would be against everything I believe in to turn my back on you and the pickle you're in."

Nova called the baby an enemy and Tess saw it as a pickle.

I lifted my chin. "If it's a girl, I'll name her Reesette. A boy will be Reese."

She squinted at me. "The daddy's name is Reese?"

"Reese Sinclair." She wouldn't know him from Adam.

"And he approved of that stupid name for a girl?"

"He doesn't know. I just thought of it."

"Well, think again. 'Cause Reese is good for a girl or boy. It's a unisex name, although I prefer Aislynn for a girl."

"I like that name, too."

She snatched her pen again and nodded to the door. "Go home, child. Rest. Unplug for the rest of the evening. Let me make a few phone calls and get you in to a doctor."

"You don't—"

She gave me an under eyed look. "I do. Now, get."

My head was hurting and I feared another bout of throwing up hitting me. Roman's house was ten minutes away from the daycare whereas the hotel was almost twice that.

I'd go there and crash and not even turn on my phone until later. It would mitigate my expectations of my brother calling, when I knew he wouldn't. I'd hoped showing up at the house would entice him to contact me, but nothing. A nap would help me, then I'd head to the hotel and call Reese on the way there.

"Why are you still here, Ainsley?"

I smiled. "I'll return bright and early tomorrow."

"Come back bright and early *Monday*."

"As much as I appreciate that, I need the money."

"Trifling man, I swear. Just plain trifling."

"Reese isn't trifling. It's just complicated."

She snorted. "I'll advance your pay with a little extra. Pamper yourself for the next few days."

Hopefully, Reese wouldn't be opposed to returning to the cabin. Before I left, Tess squeezed me tightly and promised me it would all work out now that she was on the case.

Chapter Twenty-Two

Ainsley

Unsure of Nova's intentions, I parked my car in the garage. If she wanted to reconcile, I didn't want to be bothered. If she wanted another round of bullshit, I definitely didn't want to deal with that.

Breakfast stayed down, but it was lunch that my belly rejected, leaving me hungry, nauseated, and thirsty. I ate a few soda crackers and drank a bottle of water.

The silence of the house spooked me. I'm not sure if it was because Roman didn't want me there or because Nova had blabbed my secrets. As I leaned against the counter, the clock shaped like a chef complete with hat didn't comfort me or remind me of how much Roman balked at my themed kitchen ideas. He gave into me, and allowed me to add matching curtains, dish towels, potholders, and rugs. Although he refused my pink kitchen walls, he compromised and allowed pale yellow. I moved out two months later, so I never really got to enjoy my handiwork as a resident.

Once I finished my snack, I started to grab my things and head to the den for a quick nap. Then, I remembered overhearing Roman talking to his friend, Visor, and calling the window in his bedroom a security risk. Visor said he didn't have time to see to it just then but as soon as Roman returned from the run, he'd get to it.

Roman hadn't liked that, but he'd had no choice but to agree. I hadn't seen a problem with it. *Then.* Now? It left me vulnerable. I wasn't sure how many people knew about that window, but I did and that was all that mattered.

Digging deep and pulling my last bit of energy up, I remembered Kevin's MO in *Home Alone*. I gathered dishes, glasses, my old jack set, and a few other items from kitchen drawers and cabinets, then laid out my booby traps in Roman's room and outside his door. The noises would awaken me and alert me to an intruder.

It was the best I could do with what I had. Besides, I was on borrowed time in this house, so I had to enjoy my last time in my childhood home, which I wanted to do in peace. Worrying about intruders wouldn't relax me, although a part of me couldn't believe Nova would really ignore our years of friendship and expose me without good reason. I know she'd been angry. Yet, I wanted to believe Boom Boom coerced news of my pregnancy out of her. I was still done with that heifer but I needed to believe my life mattered to her, even a small bit.

Completed with my safeguards, I was too tired to make it up the stairs and to my room, so I grabbed my purse off the kitchen counter, walked to the den and sat it next to my .357. Yawning, I unfolded the blanket I kept on the sofa, stretched out, and fell asleep almost immediately.

A sound awakened me and I bolted upright, blinking to get my bearings.

"Hello, Ainsley."

"Proctor?" I asked groggily. He was Roman's friend, another Enforcer who'd helped me care for my brother. "What are you doing in here?"

Missile and Visor stepped next to him. When Proctor pressed his Glock between my eyes, they smiled.

REESE

I was chomping at the bit to get on the fucking road. Razor and Warrior seemed to have more questions than normal, annoying me to no end. The minute the meeting ended, I jumped to my feet to head out.

Of course, it wasn't that fucking easy. Bolt, Knight, Baron, and Marquis kept asking me questions about Louisiana's call. Razor told me not to go, concerned I was being set up. Bolt agreed.

In the end, I left against Bolt's wishes. Way to prove my fucking loyalty, but I'd get back to Wichita before our next round of meetings tomorrow evening. Razor would fuck his night away. He definitely didn't need my protection for that.

Bolt followed me to my bike and tried to talk me out of leaving. I refused to listen and asked him to join me. Those motherfuckers shouldn't have been on our side of town, but if they wanted Ainsley dead, they'd follow her wherever.

If she hadn't agreed to go to the hotel, I don't know what I would've done. It would've been difficult to do my job because I would've been so worried about her.

Still, walking away from Bolt when he ordered me to stay until someone could ride with me felt as if I turned my back on a man who'd steadied me through my greatest trauma. I just couldn't leave Ainsley on her own, even at the risk of Nova setting us up. But that cunt seemed to have a pattern. Blow up, wreak havoc, regret her behavior and apologize.

This was one time I would've dialed Roman's number if I had it. Since I didn't, I called the clubhouse and sent two prospects to the hotel, giving them Ainsley's license plate number. Even if they didn't know her room number, they'd be in the general area since guests parked close to their assigned rooms.

On the outskirts of Wichita, I gassed up and was preparing to jump back on my bike when Bean called me with news I didn't want to fucking hear. Neither he nor Chi Chi saw Ainsley's car. I told them to monitor the check-in desk and I'd be there as soon as possible.

When I turned on her street and didn't notice her car in the driveway, I breathed easier until I reached her house and saw the door stretched open and three motorcycles where her car should've been. I stopped across the street, cut the engine, and considered my options.

This was Roman's house, Scorpion territory. Maybe, it *was* a setup. I needed to get the fuck away from this place before they shot me the fuck down.

"Help me!"

I straightened at the sound of Ainsley's scream. She jetted out of the house. A motherfucker hot on her heels grabbed her by the hair and yanked her back. I took cover behind the bumper of the car in front of my bike.

Grabbing my guns, I peeped around the cage and pointed it at her attacker. He grabbed her forearms and lifted her off her feet, shielding his body with hers as if he sensed my presence. Two other motherfuckers rushed out, guns pointed at Ainsley. The motherfucker imprisoning her, cut off another scream with a hand over her mouth, and dragged her back into the house. After his friends followed him in, he slammed the door shut.

Sonofabitch.

I hurried across the street. Expecting to hear gunfire any minute pushed my heart up to my throat. I stared at the door, wondering if I opened it, would the alarm beep or announce it opened. I couldn't risk that possibility, so I hauled my ass to the side of the house and the window Louisiana boasted about slipping through. A part of me hoped Roman Mac wasn't that much of a careless jackass and had secured that fucking window immediately. But the bigger part, the frightened-for-his-woman side, prayed he'd left it alone.

Luck was on my side. The window slid open as easily as Louisiana described. I'd ream Roman's ass another time over this lax in security. Wondering why his lamp light was on, I took it as a blessing that allowed me to see various objects on the floor. Water glasses, picture frames, marbles, jacks and several balls. Weird, but whatever floated that motherfucker's boat.

I halted long enough to take my guns back in hand. It was impossible to climb through the window holding them.

Carefully stepping through the maze of obstacles, I reached his door without incident and opened it with the utmost care. I peeped out. The overhead light shone directly on a tray with plates and glasses sitting in front of the door.

What the fuck?

Gritting my teeth in annoyance, I stepped over it and took care as I made my way down the short hall. A glance revealed another long hallway with the front door squarely at the midpoint.

Why the fuck was it so quiet? Three motherfuckers and a hysterical woman created a lot of noise, but I could've heard a fucking pin drop. Finger on the trigger, I lifted my gun and rushed down the hallway where it opened up at the other end to the den. Immediately, I saw Ainsley's purse and gun. But not her and not those three fuckheads.

Laughter accompanied by heavy footsteps exploded around me. A brief moment of listening revealed the noise came from behind me. Pressing myself against the wall and appreciating the dimness of the room, I waited for my opportunity to strike because I still didn't hear Ainsley.

The footsteps drew closer, so I hurried to the other side of the table with Ainsley's things and tucked myself into a shadowed corner. Not a moment too soon either.

The overhead light flared to life. Before I considered how exposed I was, Ainsley sprawled onto the floor, either because someone shoved her or she tripped.

My guess was the former. Her feet weren't bound like her hands. Seeing the tape around her mouth explained why I hadn't heard her.

The three Bloody Scorpions trained the guns at her head. The sight fucked with me. If I pulled the trigger, I needed to be fast enough to fuck up all of them before they shot her. Two was a definite. That third fuckhead might kill her before I got to him. I couldn't take the risk of spraying them with bullets because *I* might hit her.

"Sit up, Ainsley!" the motherfucker who'd used her as a shield earlier said.

She heaved in a breath, then sniffled. To keep as clear a head as possible, I had to ignore that pitiful sound. The minute they moved their fucking guns away from her head, I intended to shoot.

They watched as she struggled to a sitting position. My attention repeatedly strayed to her. Later, I'd call myself a stupid asshole for allowing her to draw my focus away.

"I don't know if I want you to die quickly or watch you bleed to death slowly." He circled her, having absolutely no fucking Spidey senses. *Most* motherfuckers felt the presence of someone else.

"I vote for slow and painful," one of his companions said. "She's Reese Sinclair's slut."

"We'll send her tits and her lips to him."

I couldn't believe the nausea twisting in my gut. It almost overtook my fury, especially when Ainsley began trembling.

"Roman always thought your pussy was too good for one of us and look how you repay him."

Their voices were blurring in my head. Their bullshit bored me. I had to take the fucking shots and live with the consequences. I reminded myself Trinity's death hadn't been my fault, and my misplaced guilt almost ruined my life. If shit went south and Ainsley ended up dead...then I'd never fucking forgive myself.

The shortest one dragged Ainsley to her feet by her hair, keeping his gun pressed against the back of her head. The second one jammed his gun against her temple. And fuckface mouthpiece shoved his weapon against the tape covering her mouth.

Small motherfucker kissed her neck. I thought I hated Roman but it couldn't compare to the loathing stirring in me toward this motherfucker. "We might let you live if you're willing to show your appreciation."

"Wizard and Kite would take some pussy from you if you fuck good enough. But we have to sample everything."

"Just don't let Boom Boom find out. He was going to be a recurring customer."

"Motherfucker's going soft in his old age. Selling this cunt instead of putting a bullet in her brain for her betrayal."

Ainsley made a noise in the back of her throat. They laughed. She tried to talk.

"Are you agreeing to our plan?" Small motherfucker asked.

She nodded, and I went on high alert. Ainsley intended to try to save herself. If she got them to move their fucking guns, I'd applaud her. She must've been on to something because he untied her hands.

Their leader snatched his gun away from the tape. "If you try something, I'll carve out your fucking eyeballs." He ripped the tape away and she cried out. "What the fuck do you have to say?"

The third one slapped her face. "You lead us on a merry chase again through this fucking house and we'll shoot you."

"I c-can't...I w-won't be able to p-p-perform if you have g-g-guns on me."

"Do you think we're fucking stupid? You can hit a fucking apple from ten yards away. I saw it with my own two eyes. Roman been teaching you to shoot since you were ten."

Asshole slapped her again. "Answer Proctor, Ainsley Mac."

Hearing her referred to with that last name jarred me.

"I'm Ainsley Valois and you know it, Missile."

"You're anyone I want you to be," Missile snarled. "Always such an uppity cunt. You should've followed Nova's lead. She's a good, sweet girl."

"Just move your guns away from my head," she pleaded. "They might accidentally fire."

"Do you think we give a fuck about that?" Small motherfucker demanded.

"No, Visor, but you care about Roman," she said tiredly.

"We feel sorry for that motherfucker," Proctor corrected. "Such a good big brother to an ungrateful bitch."

Visor rubbed his chin. "Maybe not ungrateful? Maybe protective? All you have to say is Reese Sinclair forced you to fuck him and we'll make a call."

"We'll still fuck you, but we'll clear up everything else," Proctor said. "Don't mean another motherfucker won't come after you." He roared with laughter. "You're not well-liked right now. Don't think that'll ever be fixed. So, let's have it. Tell us how brutal Reese Sinclair was with you."

She clamped her jaw, which pissed me off. She should've said I forced her to do unspeakable acts, but it finally dawned on me that she'd never really gotten the danger. Even after her parents were killed with her in the car, she'd looked at her brother's lifestyle as just an ordinary existence. It was why she hadn't revealed who her brother was and why she expected our hatred to fall away because she carried my baby and Roman was her brother. The rivalry between us was still abstract.

"Say it, Ainsley," Proctor ordered. "Tell us how he shoved his cock up your pussy and down your throat."

The little idiot wouldn't say it.

"Just m-m-move the g-g-guns away," she insisted.

"You know what I realized, fellas?" Missile said before anyone answered her. "She never answered whether she thought we were stupid."

Fuck me.

He looked at her. "Well, do you? Cuz the way I see it, I'm thinking *you* think we're dumb assholes. Why would we move our guns away when you karate chopped Proctor and tried to send Visor's cock up through his throat a fucking half an hour ago?"

"I won't do anything again," she said in a pitiful voice.

"Answer the question, Ainsley," Proctor said, "then we'll see."

"Do I think you're stupid?" she asked.

"That's the one," he responded, and I held my breath, praying Ainsley played their fucking game.

"As a matter of fact..." Her voice trailed off and she heaved in a breath. "I think you're all fucking brainless motherfuckers. Roman has cameras, jackasses."

"You're lying," Missile said.

Ainsley pointed toward a door on the opposite side of the room. A light was blinking.

"Roman will understand your anger and outrage. He hates me, too." Another sniffle escaped her. "But he agreed to Boom Boom's plan, so he doesn't want me dead. He will fucking hunt you for the rest of your miserable lives, especially since he considered you his brothers *and* his friends. Kite and Wizard must've paid you three a lot to betray him."

"Fuck!" Visor yelled.

"It doesn't matter if you shoot the camera or kill me. He's already seen enough to know who you are."

"I told you to get Boom Boom in on this, Proctor!" Missile screamed.

"He tipped off that Royal Bastard to Roman's location, then didn't ice him when those motherfuckers let him live," Proctor snapped.

Missile scowled. "Maybe he should've ridden out to Roman's location himself instead of loud talking in a goddamn store so that motherfucker could hear. Personally, I would've shot that Bastard and then fucked up Roman if he interfered with me and my bitch."

"You wanted my brother dead?"

What the fuck was she fucking on, goddamn it? They'd broken into her house and backstabbed her brother in the process. Clearly, they weren't loyal.

"Just put the gun down," she insisted. "You wanting Roman dead isn't important. He'll overlook that."

Had the baby affected her fucking brain? They wanted *her* dead.

Proctor was the first to drop his gun, stuff it in his cut, and back away. "Fuck no we don't want him dead, Ainsley. Roman Mac's a good motherfucker. But we ain't interfering in Boom Boom's business."

The moment he nodded and Missile secured his gun at his side, Ainsley ducked away from Visor's piece and launched herself at Missile. If I hadn't opened fire with both guns blazing, Visor would've shot the fuck out of her.

Ignoring her screams, I pulled her into my arms, lifted her over the dead motherfuckers and carried her to a place where I could hold her tightly.

Chapter Twenty-Three

Ainsley

Before tonight, only three other times had my connection to the Bloody Scorpions affected me so profoundly and reminded me of the danger and darkness: my parents' deaths, Roman's capture and loss of his hands, and Boom Boom's violence toward Nova and me. I'd always mourn my parents, but I believed I'd managed to go on with my life with my brother's help. Maybe, if the Roman and Boom Boom situations hadn't happened just weeks ago, I wouldn't have been so devastated now.

I knew who Roman was. He'd made Trinity disappear and the woman who'd punched me when I was a child. Death surrounded us, stalked us, and caught up to us. It just never sank in the way it had when Proctor, Missile, and Visor broke into Roman's house and planned to kill me.

When I insisted they drop their guns, I hadn't had a plan of escape. I was playing it by ear and trying to find a solution to save myself and the baby. It was a longshot, but it was the only one I had.

I never got the chance to see if my plan worked. Reese shot them all, then carried me away from the carnage and enveloped me in his arms, whispering sweet words as I clung to him.

The sound of motorcycles seeped into my brain and I began to cry, knowing we had no chance of escape. Even when Reese tightened his hold on me and rushed toward Roman's bedroom, I didn't think we'd survive. My emotions were a never ending loop of fear, anger, shock, resignation, and hysteria. He shoved me into the room and closed my fingers around one of his guns.

"Stay here," he ordered, hovering in the doorway.

I latched onto his wrist. "No, don't go!"

Irritation crossed his face. "Stay strong, Ainsley. Don't turn into a woman and fall into hysterics right now. And, for fuck's sake, stay in this fucking room or escape through that window. Don't risk yourself and the baby."

Before I pulled myself together, he jerked from my hold and hurried away. As much as I wanted to follow him, I couldn't. Not for me, but for our child. Locking the door, I slid to the floor and drew in deep breaths, forcing myself to remember what Roman taught me. He expected me to use my brain and assess my surroundings. It wouldn't make sense to climb out of the window and right into the hands of the Bloody Scorpions.

Disbelief and fear buzzed through my veins, and I wondered if there was any way out for us. Tears slid down my cheeks. Neither could I believe how emotional I'd been. I cried at the drop of a hat nowadays. Crawling to Roman's bed, I slid under the covers and laid my head on his pillow.

The faint scent of his cologne both comforted me and reminded me I needed to change his bed before he returned home. A little sob escaped me. No, he wouldn't want me to do that.

"Ainsley, open the door," Reese ordered. He sounded fine, but I wasn't sure if I should trust that. The Bloody Scorpions might've forced him to call me. "Sweetheart, it's fine. Bolt and Razor...several of my brothers are here."

Shuddering, I closed my eyes, the warmth of my tears burning my cheeks.

"It's fine, Ainsley," Mom whispered. "It's just Wizard and several of your Dad's brothers with some of their acquaintances."

She reached her hand around the seat and my fingers touched her palm. Gunfire erupted and I flew forward.

My eyes snapped open and my breath sawed in and out of my lungs. Wizard? Had the Bloody Scorpions been involved in Mom and Dad's deaths? Or was I just panicked knowing Boom Boom put the hit out on Roman?

"Ainsley, move away from the door," Reese said again. "I'm shooting the fucking lock away."

"N-no!" I called, stumbling out of bed. At the door, I unlocked it and swung it open. "I'm fine."

He nodded, but didn't dispute me, instead sweeping me into his arms and carrying me away.

REESE

I hated cars. It was a holdover from my trauma at my family trapped in a burning house. In my head, automobiles were even more of a death trap, leaving survival chances slim-to-none. Logically, I knew people walked away every day, but it didn't matter. I preferred my bike any day.

Yet, I sat Ainsley in the passenger seat of her car, jumped into the driver's seat, and headed to Ma Siller's. Bolt offered to bring Ainsley so I could stay behind and help with the clean-up and disposal of those three fuckheads, but there was no fucking way I'd allow anyone other than me to see to Ainsley. Maybe I was cocky, but I didn't think she'd want anyone else but me.

She only knew Louisiana, and he wasn't around, so it had to be me. I wasn't sure what she wanted, so I decided to play music at a reasonable volume in case she needed to talk.

She stared out the window the entire drive. Every now and again, a sniffle escaped her. I'd reach over and cover her hand with mine, squeezing gently. She didn't pull away, but she didn't look at me either. I wanted to get into her head and erase the bad. Whatever it might've been. I wanted to know, but I refused to ask her right now.

I turned into the Siller driveway and allowed the car to idle, waiting for Ainsley to speak. Ask questions. *Say something.* She remained silent.

Sighing, I got out of the car and went around to her side. When I helped her out, she laid her head on my chest and wrapped her arms around my waist. It was all the encouragement I needed to take her into my arms, tip her head back, and slant my mouth over hers. For the first time since I received the call that Ainsley wasn't at the motel, I relaxed. She was soft and sweet, safe in my arms.

I'd never disrespected Bolt and his woman's place with even a make-out session with a chick, but I needed to feel Ainsley trembling around my cock to calm my fear and anger. Bracing her against the car, I lifted her and grunted when her legs automatically circled my waist. She moaned into my mouth, rocking against my hard dick.

I didn't want to let her go. Not to pull my cock out or deal with her jeans. The saltiness of her tears invaded my senses, and my heart fucking broke. I wanted to return to that house, reanimate those fuckheads, and kill them slowly and brutally.

She pulled away, leaned her head against my chest, and sobbed. "I th-thought the baby was dead and I-I'd never see you again." Her fingers gripped my cut, but I didn't care. "I-I th-thought…" Her voice trailed off and another sob escaped her. "R-Roman," she finished as if that explained everything.

I kissed her again, needing a moment to regain my equilibrium. Suppose I had been too late or they'd gotten the jump on me? Suppose they'd killed her in front of me? My desire faded. Memories of my devastation over losing my family crept in. Tearing my mouth away from hers, I set her on her feet and dropped my arms from around her. She didn't notice my withdrawal.

"Reese?" a voice called from behind me.

Five minutes ago, I wouldn't have appreciated Ma Siller's interruption. More than likely, I would've been mortified. Now, I welcomed it and seized the excuse to push away from Ainsley and turn around.

"Hey, Ma," I greeted.

She stood on the porch, right under the light, allowing me to see the kindness of her brown eyes, which had soothed me all those years ago. Short and plump, she had short graying hair with bangs. I don't know where I would've ended up without her. Now, she drew herself up and beckoned me forward.

I started toward her. One lift of her eyebrow halted me and I heaved in a breath, turned to Ainsley, and took her hand in mine. At the porch, I dropped her hand and looked up at Ma Siller.

"Well, are you introducing me or what, Reese?"

I shoved my hands in my pockets. "Ma Siller, this is Ainsley Valois. Ainsley, this is Bolt's ol' lady."

Ainsley didn't notice the slight. Ma Siller did and lifted her eyebrows almost to her hairline, offering a putrid look that had me feeling like an asshole. She glared at me, sniffed, then smiled at Ainsley's bowed head.

"Ainsley's such a pretty name. I'm Glinda Dorothy Siller. Mother was a fan of L. Frank Baum."

It was my turn to lift my brows. I wasn't sure if she was shitting Ainsley or not.

Ma Siller waved, but Ainsley didn't see because she hadn't lifted her head. "You can call me Ma Siller," she continued, then glared at me again. "Everybody does."

"Ainsley—"

Ma Siller shook her head.

We stood in silence for several minutes, until Ainsley heaved in a breath and lifted her bruised face. I clenched my jaw.

"I like the *Wizard of Oz*," she said finally. "Roman and me were supposed to see *Wicked*."

"Haven't seen it yet myself, but I can't help but thank heaven that it wasn't around when Mother was carrying me." She indicated herself with her hand. "Don't see myself as an Elphaba or a Theodora."

"But you're named after the Good Witch and the heroine. That wouldn't have changed."

"Mother had quite the imagination, dear. Elphaba has much more flair than Glinda or Dorothy." Smiling, she waved to Ainsley. "Come on in, hon. You've been through quite the ordeal."

Ainsley looked at me, but I remained stoic. Her shoulders slumping, she walked up the three steps to where Ma Siller stood. The moment Ainsley reached her, she pulled her into her embrace.

"I got you, Ainsley," she swore. "From here on out, if anyone wants to get to you, they have to go through me first." She offered me one last glare, clutched Ainsley's arm, and guided her into the house.

By the time Ma Siller helped to settle Ainsley in my old bedroom and came to chew my ass out, I'd seated myself at the kitchen table, heard from Bolt that Roman's house was secured and all cleaned up, and had drunk two beers. I'd just popped the top on my third one when Ma Siller stormed in, slapped the side of my fucking head, and yanked away my goddamn beer.

She set it near the sink, then took a seat at the table. "She doesn't need your bullshit, Reese Sinclair."

"You know what's bullshit? Having a girl I didn't want carrying my kid."

"If you didn't want that possibility, you should've covered yourself. *You're* the idiot, so you can't make her suffer."

"I'm not making her suffer," I argued. "I'm safeguarding myself. The twain shall never meet, Ma. She's Roman Mac's sister. Someone will always be gunning for her. Either from the Scorpions or the Bastards. Suppose I do fall in love with a dead woman walking? Then what?"

Narrowing her eyes, she tapped her fingers on the table. "You're a goddamn travesty to that patch."

I stiffened.

"Hush, or I'll call Bolt to kick your ass before I get my Colt and shoot it off." She pointed at me. "I'll do you one better. You're a disgrace to men if you can't protect a slip of a girl. Stop feeling sorry for yourself."

"Easy for you to say. You've never lost your entire fucking family."

"I'm *about* to lose a son," she snapped. "Keep talking to me with that disrespect and I'll just have to explain to Bolt why I put a bullet in you."

I glowered at her. "Ainsley has been nothing but trouble since we met," I complained.

"Trouble is as trouble does," she retorted. "You're quite a troublemaker yourself."

Scrubbing a hand over my face, I tried to control my emotions and return to the place I'd been before Ainsley leaned her head against me and sobbed as if her heart had broken into a million pieces. I glanced away.

"Fuck her. Her safety shouldn't matter to me," I said with resentment. "She's just having my kid. I don't even know if we can make a relationship work."

Sighing, Ma leaned back and folded her arms. "Knew you to be traumatized, not a deadbeat with a load of excuses."

I still wouldn't look at her. "Ainsley could've been killed in front of my fucking eyes. She made some fucked up, stupid decisions. She doesn't use her motherfucking brain sometimes."

When I searched my soul, I realized part of my withdrawal was remembering how Ainsley refused to put me down even to save her own fucking life. On top of that, she talked them into lowering their guns and then attacked as if she had a fucking chance of a fuckhead in hell to survive.

"Well, she gave you the shot you needed, Reese," Ma Siller rationalized when I explained myself. "More than likely, she was good as dead anyway."

"She should've said I was the worst motherfucker alive!" I pounded my fist on the table, ignoring the sting. "What the fuck is wrong with her? She has no fucking self-preservation. Do you think I can handle her for the rest of my fucking life without going insane?"

"Already there, boyo," she said with laughter.

Clenching my jaw, I finally looked at her again. Usually, I found her comebacks amusing, but I don't think I'd recovered from all the emotions running through me. Death was so fucking easy. Kill motherfuckers and it was over. My adrenaline spiked at the power it gave me. Either I calmed myself with bud, booze, or pussy.

Life was hard, caring was brutal, and love was torture.

Ma Siller leaned across the table and covered my hands with her own. They were warm and comforting. More than any other time, my heart cracked open and all my long-buried grief and survivor's guilt almost overwhelmed me. It was the type of pain I never wanted to experience again, the kind of heartache I never thought I *could* feel again, even during my months of sorrow over Trinity's death.

"I don't love Ainsley," I said, scorn dripping from my words. My little sister would be about Ainsley's age now. Probably just as much of a handful. Tears stung my eyes at the thought. "She's a good fuck who I knocked up. That's why I haven't stopped thinking about her." And because of motherfucking Louisiana. "Love is for pathetic motherfuckers."

"I know, dear," Ma Siller said quietly, patting my hand. "Get it out. Ainsley's alive, son. Battered, bruised, and broken-hearted because of her brother's treatment and how his friends wanted to kill her. She's all alone right now. Except for a woman named Tess, who she wants me to call." She leaned back. "Go, Reese. Ainsley will be fine with us. You don't want her? Then, fine and mighty. I'll make sure Bolt doesn't tell you about the smallest detail from here on out."

I blinked. "But—"

She nodded at the door. "Go," she repeated. "I can handle it from here."

CHAPTER TWENTY-FOUR

ROMAN

I'm not sure what Bash told Boom Boom for the motherfucker to leave me in Salt Lake City at the American Scorpions' clubhouse, but my brothers rode out this morning. I felt vulnerable and alone, and I missed my sister. Each time I thought about calling her, I remembered her betrayal. Carrying a Royal Bastard's kid sickened me on its own. Knowing Reese Sinclair was the father cut like a fucking knife.

Though Kite vied for top position on my kill list, I didn't realize how much he helped me until he left. Bash didn't send any of his brothers or a woman to help me. He didn't send in food. If I hadn't forced myself to figure out how to pull my pajama bottoms down and then use my feet to flush the toilet, I would've laid in my own waste since I went an entire day without seeing anyone. I used the shower to clean myself when I finished and sobbed like a bitch the entire way through. I gripped the towel between my elbows, staggered back to my room, because the weight of my self-pity overwhelmed me, and dropped the towel on the bed, rolling my body on it to dry myself as best I could.

By the time Bash sauntered in late in the evening, I lay in total darkness, completely naked, starving, fuming, and miserable.

He flipped on the overhead light. Other than a brief glance to identify my visitor, I refused to acknowledge him.

"I suppose you found a way to go to the shitter."

His sadistic greeting pissed me the fuck off and I stiffened. "Fuck you."

A chair scraped across the floor followed by movements that indicated Bash sat. "I'll ignore your disrespect once. Don't let it happen again if you like living."

I'd wrapped my entire life around my club and my little sister. I was useless to one and wasn't talking to the other. "Kill me. I don't give a fuck."

The smell of cigarette smoke traveled to me and my woe deepened. I would love a smoke. Food would be even better.

"I'd say you do," Bash countered, chafing my nuts.

"You don't fucking know me," I snarled, "but let me clue you the fuck in. My sister is a traitor and I'm fucking helpless, an enforcer who can't fucking *enforce*."

"You're only as helpless as you feel, fuckhead. When I didn't send anyone in to help you, you made do. You weren't fucking helpless then, were you?"

My gaze flew to him and the smirk on his pockmarked face sent anger through me. "You withheld assistance on purpose?"

He puffed on his cigarette, then took it between his two fingers. "It worked, didn't it? The more you rely on other motherfuckers, the more dependent you'll become."

"Who the fuck are you to try to save me with your fucking mind games?"

"I'm not in the saving business, Roman. But I *am* a big brother who'd do anything for his little sister. Even when Celia has pissed me off so much I want to fucking kill her."

"I don't want Ainsley dead," I said quietly, the fight leaving me. "I just feel empty. When she moved to her own apartment, I put up an argument, but she wanted her independence, so I shut the fuck up." I blinked at the ceiling. "I've heard about empty nest syndrome, you know? Never thought I'd experience it."

"It's normal. You were her primary caregiver."

I nodded. "I love that kid. *Loved*," I amended harshly, and changed the subject, not wanting to dwell on my complicated feelings. "Mom and Dad would be so proud of her."

"Would they be proud of you?"

"I hope, although I didn't do it for them particularly. I did it because Ainsley had no one else and I was her big brother. She needed me."

"Sounds like you needed her, too."

I'd never thought of it like that, so I shrugged.

Bash flicked ashes from his nearly gone cigarette. "She probably still needs you."

"Doubtful," I scoffed. "She has Sinclair." My head was starting to hurt, so I drew in a deep breath and got to the heart of the matter. "What do you want? Why are you here?"

"I'm here because this is my fucking club and I can go anywhere I please. I *want* to check on you and ask why the fuck didn't you come out to eat." Snickering, he swept my naked body with an amused glance. "Never took you for a modest motherfucker, but I suppose I understand why you didn't make an appearance."

"It's habit," I said, scorn dripping from me. "I don't want Ainsley seeing my cock." Or anyone's until she had a ring on her finger. Distaste sat thick within my gut. I moved onto another thought of how Ainsley had seen my ass on a few unfortunate occasions.

In silence, Bash finished his cigarette, then he threw it on the floor and stomped it. I remained silent, resenting his amusement at my plight, his intrusion, and his presence. He was right, though. My room belonged to him. For that matter, it seemed as if *I* belonged to him, too. All the promises he'd made about the prosthetics weren't sincere. I'd gone to bed with a modicum of hope that I would have a sense of normalcy soon. In hindsight, I expected to be left with Bash for him to help me, but I hadn't expected to be abandoned.

"Are you hungry?"

My jaw clamped. I refused to answer that motherfucker. I hadn't eaten or drank anything since yesterday.

"Do you need a smoke? A drink? A cock suck?"

All the above. I'd rather gnaw off my toes than admit that.

"Do you know why I offered to help you?"

He didn't intend to leave without my engagement. "You already told me."

"Maybe I want you to repeat it."

"Maybe I don't feel like it."

"Maybe I'll throw you out in the fucking desert and see if your fucking survival skills kick in. If you make it back, I'll really help you. If you die, then it's no more than you deserve for being such a pathetic motherfucker."

Without pondering what I could and couldn't do, I shot into a sitting position, ready to headbutt him. If not for the .44 pointed at me, I would have.

I raised my arms, unable to truly surrender. Shame poured into me and I flicked my glance over the stitches. Narrowing my eyes, I processed the fact that my bandages were gone.

"Self-pity is as soul destroying as any addiction," Bash said calmly, still holding the gun on me. "When you're pushed, you do what you must, so why not take balls in hand and make the most of what you have?"

I dropped my gaze to the floor and lowered my arms.

"I'm out of credit with most of my suppliers. I refuse to touch the club's merchandise because, well, I don't want to end up like Big Joe Foy."

Since I didn't know who the fuck that was, I didn't respond.

"Mind over matter is surprisingly effective. It's what Daddy always said. Didn't get a clue the first couple times he beat my ass for my addiction, but that last one? After I OD'd? That lives with a man. My father loved me. His brand of tough love was the wake-up call I needed. I learned to control myself when I couldn't get my hands on coke. Don't mean it don't feel like I'm crawling out of my fucking skin sometimes. It just means my father impressed upon me the necessity of mind over matter."

New form of therapy: abuse. I managed not to snort since Bash seemed so convinced his father's treatment was right.

Lowering his gun, he fell silent, allowing me to turn his words over in my head. I wasn't sure where he was going with this.

"I relieved Boom Boom of a hefty amount of cash. On behalf of you," he added with a chuckle. "Yeah, I think a man who loves his little sister as I love mine should be whole, but you disappointed me today. You turned yourself into an invalid."

"Exactly what the fuck I am. Hands are important. Physically, psychologically, socially. I didn't lose one. I lost both. I can't even surrender with dignity."

"If you feel like you're a cripple, I don't need to waste my fucking resources on you."

"Cripple is an ugly word. And it isn't your resources. It's my president's."

"Who'd just as soon see you dead."

"Did he tell you that?"

Bash shrugged. "If not you, then Ainsley."

"He walked that back and decided to sell her to you." As if that was any better. She would've been little more than a sex slave, destined for a slow, painful death. "Execution might've been better."

Not responding, Bash studied me before finally asking, "Why should I help you, Roman?"

"You took Boom Boom's money. Fucking over him is to your detriment."

"I've fucked over more than one motherfucker in my life," he countered without remorse. "Do you honestly think he cares if you get the fucking prosthetics? He left you with me with no questions asked. Methinks he's hoping I fuck you up."

I wouldn't put it past him. I still had my suspicions about how Warrior sniffed out my location, but my head was spinning. I no longer trusted my own president, or any of my brothers, and hesitated to trust Bash.

"Do you fucking deserve to have hands again if you're such a whiny bitch? Surviving means rolling with the punches. You saw no one was coming in, so you took care of business. Exactly what I expect you to do. I should've waited to see how fucking long it took you to tuck your tail between your fucking legs and come out for food, but a situation has developed that I think you'd want to know about."

"Which is?"

"First, your payment to me."

"I intend to liquidate the money I saved for Ainsley—"

"I don't want money. I want drugs. Boom Boom's payments will only get me so much when I account for the high grade and the bumps."

"I live in Kansas City. How the fuck can I deliver drugs to you on a regular basis? And I'm not a low-level dealer. I can send you money every month to pay your dealer, but I can't personally deliver them."

Bash nodded. "That'll have to do then. First payment will be tomorrow."

"Weren't you high last night?"

"Used the last of my stash." Digging into his jacket pocket, Bash pulled out my cell phone. "Who is Proctor, Missile, and Visor to you?"

"Good friends of mine. Who are they to you?"

Not answering, Bash pressed the keypad on my phone to unlock it.

"Kite gave you my code?"

"If you're in my care, I need to know how to access your shit."

When he held the phone up, I immediately recognized the app for the home alarm. Before I questioned what the fuck was going on, a scene from my worst nightmare played out and I listened to what those motherfuckers told Ainsley. I thought I'd watch her die, especially after the stunt she pulled. My first emotion at Reese Sinclair's rescue was gratitude. He'd gone against three motherfuckers to save my sister. Relief and joy hit me, until I remembered he was my enemy.

"This is only from the camera in the den during the standoff," Bash said, intruding upon my confliction. "There's footage of them breaking in and footage of upstairs when she karate chops one of the motherfuckers and almost gets away."

My gaze drifted back to the phone, but Bash pulled it away and tucked it back into his cut pocket.

"I'll ask you again. Why should I help you?"

"To fuck up Nova, Kite, and Wizard," I snarled. He was a club president, I didn't think he'd appreciate hearing I intended to kill my own. "And any other motherfucker who crossed her."

"Do you know the American Scorpions are older than the Death Dwellers by a few years?"

"Excuse me?" I wasn't interested in hearing that history, nor did I fucking care. I didn't personally know any of those motherfuckers. "And?"

"Daddy always wanted the clubs to work together. Before his death, he even considered a merger. Who'd absorb who? By the time he went to Hortensia, that idea was off the table. My uncle, Rack, started out as a Scorpion but became a Dweller. He was just in awe of Logan Donovan."

I squinted, and Bash smiled.

"You have a problem, Roman. You're all alone and the officers in your club want you dead. Whether Ainsley carries your enemy's baby doesn't matter."

"What are you suggesting?" I asked, though I already knew and the idea insulted me. "I know it isn't me flipping and becoming a Royal

Bastard. My father would turn over in his fucking grave."

"Your father isn't here to help protect you and your sister."

"I'd have a fucking bounty on my head from the Bloody Scorpions and the Royal Bastards would always look on me with suspicion."

"Say you don't flip and take out all the top motherfuckers. I'm sure you have some members who'd stand with you. There are always fuckheads who don't like their president and dream of overthrowing them or supporting an asshole with the balls to attempt a coup."

He was right. I could think of several off the top of my head.

"You'd have to get rid of all the Boom Boom loyalists. However, that would still put you at odds with Reese Sinclair."

"That motherfucker breathing puts me at odds with him."

Bash chuckled. "Doesn't change the dilemma of him dropping a baby in Ainsley's pussy."

I glared at him. He only seemed to care that I was a good big brother. Everything else flew the fuck over his head.

"He has her firmly in his corner. Once you get over your anger, you're going to want to be a part of her life. Your best shot may be to patch over to the Bastards."

"Absolutely fucking not! Fuck no. I'd rather piss on those motherfuckers' graves, than break bread with them."

"The feeling is probably mutual, but you don't have to be an empty nester. You can be a doting uncle and a loving brother."

"Or a dead one."

"Always a risk, Roman, but I believe Reese might be willing to listen and try to help you."

"You're insane. He'd want nothing to do with me, and that feeling is mutual, too. I don't understand how you reached such a fucking conclusion.

"He didn't have to risk his life to save her. Had it been me, I certainly wouldn't have. A dead cunt is a dead cunt."

"I noticed how little regard you have for women," I sneered.

"Little regard?" Bash chortled. "I *hate* bitches. Except Celia. Maybe if I had a bitch like Hopper or Kendall..." He shrugged. "Who knows? I'm a little obsessed with Meggie but for a different reason. Hopper isn't out of reach and Kendall is a kid brother's wife, who I haven't formally met. I still intend to shoot my shot but I think she's loyal to the brainless blond."

Despite my annoyance that he insisted on talking about fuckheads I didn't know, I laughed. "What does this have to do with any fucking thing? I don't know any of those people, but I know you."

"Doubtful. I'm more complex than you think. I'm not merely a mindless woman killer."

"But you *are* a woman killer?"

His look of disapproval chafed me. "Careful, or I'll think you have Johnnie's brain. Or lack of."

I lifted a brow.

"The brainless blond," he supplied. "One of my half-brothers."

"How many do you have?"

"Lost count years ago. The two that matter the most are Johnnie and Outlaw."

"Your enemies?"

"Outlaw," he said with a shrug. "Johnnie is his own fucking enemy. If he didn't think he was the sharpest knife in the drawer, he might realize exactly who he's betraying." Bash grabbed a cigarette from behind his ear, then lit it with the lighter he took from his pocket. "As for why I'm telling you all this, you're going to be here for a few weeks. I thought maybe you'd like to know a little about me." He took a drag of his cigarette and released the smoke. "Besides, I respect a man who goes to war for his sister."

"As long as I keep her away from you. If you hate women, my association to her wouldn't matter."

"She's your sister and you're my drug supplier. By the way, how tall is she?"

"Five seven. Why?"

"Thought she was tall. She's very pretty. After I saw her try to stand up to those dead fucks, I had to get my cock sucked. I love a woman with long legs, a gorgeous face, and a world of bitchiness. A woman who's a little wild and a whole lot of mean turns me on. Haven't met many of them. Most cunts look at me like I'm the big bad wolf. And small chicks just annoy me. The world's a better place without such weak cunts. They're so fucking easy to break."

I stiffened, hating the images those words provoked. I got the sense that Bash meant breaking in the literal sense.

"Have no use for little chicks but to fuck them and dispose of them," he said around a huff of smoke. "But bitches like Ainsley, Kendall, and Hopper? If I put stock into the romances I read, that's who I'd go for."

Squinting, I cocked my head to the side, sure I'd misunderstood. "You read romance novels?"

"Only place I'll ever find love."

"Maybe, if you didn't see women as fucking targets, you could've found love."

He grunted. "Love isn't in my cards. Neither are romance and marriage."

"Kids are?"

"I have a bunch of them, so I suppose so. Two of them patched in to my club. I'm like Daddy. Only recognize my sons."

"I suppose you're like *Daddy* in regard to how you feel about women?"

"He didn't have a lot of love for bitches." Bash once again dropped his cigarette to the floor and stomped it out. "Sometimes, Daddy left me with club sluts. Ten and eleven, you don't see broads one way or the other. They saw me as a fuck toy and a punching bag. Those sluts spat on me, burned me with hot water and cigarettes, fucked me, made me eat pussy. I swore I'd make every cunt pay once I grew up. I kept my promise. Daddy showed me what to do when he found out what they did to me."

I didn't know how to feel about Bash. Most of me abhorred his violence and cruelty towards women. Maybe if I hadn't had my mother until I was fifteen, I would've been a brutal as Bash. My father wasn't a cheater. He loved and respected my mother, and he adored Ainsley. He stood between me and the harsher side of club life, even when I was twenty-five.

"My father was a great man," Bash continued. "He was almost nineteen when I was born and my momma overdosed when I was two months old. Daddy took me on the road with him and kept me at his side his entire life. My father wasn't a good motherfucker to most people. Besides me, I can count on one hand the people he looked out for. *I'm* not a good motherfucker. If you don't like me, I don't care. *I* don't like Boom Boom, insisting you sell your own sister."

"He wants to sell his daughter."

"Is a daughter a sister?" he demanded, scowling.

I blinked. "It's a tad worse to most people," I pointed out.

"I don't agree. You know sisters first."

I refused to argue with a man convinced he was right.

"You're going to be here for about a month," he said, flipping yet again and changing the subject. "Weekends are packed. Weekdays are mostly regulars. The bitch du jour has breakfast on the side table by 8AM. We're responsible for our own lunch. Dinner is at 6PM. Food's out until it's gone. You miss it, you fucking starve. Church is on Wednesday evenings after dinner. Walk out this fucking room then and I have to kill you."

"I thought you had people to take care of me sooner than that?"

"Well, motherfucker, my *people* can only work within the constraints of your capabilities. Hand transplants were suggested to me, but you have to be in the headspace where taking immunosuppressants for the rest of your fucking life is something you can do. Whether you live another ten years or another fifty, it has to become just a part of your routine. And, *you*, miserable fuckhead, aren't there yet."

"You aren't inside me," I yelled. "You don't know what the fuck's going on in my head to say what I'll do."

"Don't have to be. I know what you're *not* doing, and that's getting up off your fucking ass and *trying* to take care of yourself."

Glowering at me, he got to his feet, opened the door, and yelled, *"London!"*

Footsteps clipped down the hallway and then halted. Bash snatched a girl into my room and shoved her to me so hard she fell into my arms. Indignation flashed in her long-lashed gray eyes as she scrambled out of my embrace. Long, dark hair mantled her back and shoulders. Sweet pink lips drew my attention and I licked my own.

"Tío's bitch," Bash announced, thumping her shoulder.

"You're treating your uncle's woman like this and you expect me to believe Ainsley's safe?"

"My uncle's…? Tío is my son. Named him in honor of his heritage."

I lifted a brow. "Isn't he American like you?"

"His mother was Colombian. She met with an unfortunate end within weeks of his birth, so I claimed him and named him. DNA proved he was mine."

Shifting her weight, London clasped her hands together. She gazed at my cock, suddenly erect, and glanced away, a blush creeping into her cheeks.

Pinning her with cold dislike, Bash nodded to her. "Little Miss London is a physical therapist. For the next month, she's at your beck and call, though part of her duties will be to prepare you for your prosthetics. We'll have a suitable prosthetist by this time next week."

"You can't keep me here against my will," London spat. "My job will report me as missing."

Bash balled his fist but I moved quicker than I had in days and took the blow meant for her. It landed on my chest, whereas he meant to knock her out with a hit to her head.

"Awww, such a gentleman. London," he continued without missing a beat, "you've made Tío very unhappy. Maybe you can absolve yourself and get back into my good graces if you help Roman. You can suck his cock. Give him pussy and you're dead. Your cunt, like you, belongs to my son."

"She won't help me if she's here under duress."

"Then she dies," Bash said simply. "So I suggest you two follow my orders. You'll get back to your sister and London will breathe another day."

CHAPTER TWENTY-FIVE

REESE

"We'll be gone for about ten days," Razor said, concluding his announcement of a run to the Provo, UT chapter. Luckily, it was voluntary since it was more of a social visit.

Zombie, their president, invited us to The Metal Shop, the club's music venue, to see Vengynce. Normally, I'd go because I loved partying with them. Not this time. Besides, that didn't concern me. It was the shit that happened *before* that had me up in arms.

Jameson, our National President, approved of the money we were bringing in by working so closely with the Wichita chapter. Topeka's loss was a blow, but we'd recovered. Now, he'd assigned us a big shipment of guns to move to the southern border so we could funnel them to the cartels. We were expected to leave in two days. I couldn't see any way around that decree. At the same time, I couldn't see myself leaving Ainsley.

In the week since that nightmare at her brother's house, I'd seen her once. She didn't take my calls, so I knew Ma Siller told her what I said. She liked Ainsley and didn't want my assholery to hurt her in the end. A couple of hours ago, Ainsley texted me and asked me to come with her to her first doctor's appointment tomorrow afternoon.

I'd agreed without second thought, not considering the possibility of a run when Razor called emergency church. There were a lot of calls to make and logistics to arrange. Louisiana had returned two days ago, although I hadn't seen Jinx. He was tight-lipped and angry, so I suspected she'd left him. I had my own shit to deal with, so I couldn't bring myself to placate that motherfucker when he facilitated his own fucking misery. I hoped he had his head in the right place, since he and Bolt had to plan the routes.

"Any word on Boom Boom and company?" Warrior asked, his gaze on me.

Folding my arms, I shifted my weight and held in my glare.

"Heard they're back," Marquis said, bored.

Snickers rose up.

"Yeah, without Roman Mac," Knight added. "Pieces of that motherfucker is probably strewn over all the places they went."

So much about me had changed since I met Ainsley. I'd found a smidgeon of humanity. Any other time I'd be high-fiving and celebrating right along with my brothers. Now, her devastation ran uppermost in my head.

"I'm fucking jealous," Warrior grouched. "I should've cut that fucker's head off when I had the chance."

I scrubbed a hand over my face. As much as I detested the Bloody Scorpions and would celebrate the complete and total annihilation of the entire organization, I'd wanted Roman to escape for Ainsley's sake. I wondered if she knew of her brother's death or if she just chalked it up to his anger.

Legalities needed tending to. The house needed vacating. If he had a will, it needed to be probated. I didn't want the Bloody Scorpions laying claim to anything that rightfully belonged to Ainsley. Whatever she wanted, she'd have come hell or highwater.

"You don't seem too happy about Roman's death, Reese," Razor observed.

What did he expect me to say? I shrugged.

"Tomorrow, we need to head on over to the garage," he continued. "I need to pick up their balance sheets. Make sure it matches my numbers."

"What time tomorrow?"

"Whenever I say," Razor said sharply. "I'm thinking around two. You got a problem with that?"

Sonofabitch. Ainsley's appointment was for two. She wanted me there as much as I wanted to be with her. "Ainsley sees the doctor for the first time tomorrow."

Razor lifted a brow. "That's my problem how?"

"No way, Prez," I answered without hesitation. "But she's carrying my kid. My first one. I want to be there."

"Your first?" Jester asked. "You planning on having more?"

"It depends," I responded.

Warrior snapped his brows together. "On?"

"It doesn't matter," I said defensively, although it did to me. I hadn't planned on one child and if Ainsley and I didn't work out, I wouldn't have any more. If we did and she wanted the kid to have a sibling, then I'd have more. "First kid is special."

"It would be special if that little cunt didn't have Roman Mac *and* Bloody Scorpion blood in her," Razor growled.

"You allowed Bolt and several of our brothers to help me when she was in trouble."

"Wrong. I allowed them to infiltrate Roman's home. If he's having a shit fit that she's pregnant with your kid, then when he realized Royal Bastards were in his place, I hope it tormented him in his final hours."

"He might not have seen the footage," I reasoned, disheartened by everyone's firm stance on Ainsley. Since we met, I'd spent half my time defending her and the other half either avoiding her or chasing behind her. If Razor had relented, I could've brought her to the clubhouse temporarily. "Even if he did, I don't think he'd care we were there because we saved Ainsley."

"You sure put a lot of faith in our enemy," Knight said.

"I cut off his fucking hands, bro. What more do you want from me?"

"You know he killed Trinity," Knight said bitterly. "You know he's one of their top enforcers. Makes a man wonder about your allegiance."

"You have one more fucking time to question my loyalty, fuckhead," I snarled, annoyed and fed-up. "I'll beat you into the fucking ground." I turned to Razor. "Very few of us have ol' ladies, but we respect them and give them the benefit of the doubt."

"Confirm her brother's death and then we'll see," Razor said.

"How the fuck am I supposed to do that?" For that matter, how was it my fucking problem, since they were the ones stuck on bullshit and spewing rumors about me. "I know about as much about that motherfucker as you do."

"I've met Ainsley, Prez," Louisiana inserted. "She's harmless. Her only crime is Roman. Other than that, you should give her a chance for Reese's sake."

Louisiana met my eyes. His expression was still unreadable, but I appreciated his putting in the good word for her, so I nodded.

"When Jinx was pregnant the last time, you all were as happy as me," Louisiana said quietly. "Shouldn't we do the same for Reese?"

"We like Jinx," Marquis said. "We don't like Ainsley."

"You've never met her," I snapped. "Do you know why? Because none of you want her here."

Razor glowered at me. "I got one question for you."

"If it's about Roman Mac, I don't have an answer yet, Prez."

He stepped from behind the podium and walked over to where I stood. His pats to my jaw felt more like hits. "Get it soon, Reese. But that's not what I want to ask you."

I didn't like his diabolical smile. "Okay." What the fuck else could I say?

"Do you love this cunt? Do you plan on keeping her? Do you see forever with her?"

Bolt tugged at his long beard. "Ain't that three questions you asking my boy, Razor?"

"All in the same family, so I count it as one," Razor said calmly. "So give me the answer to my *one* question in three parts to address everything."

My mind scrambled for answers. Ma Siller and I had a similar conversation. I was convinced it was a fucking conspiracy.

I'd already claimed Ainsley, thinking to protect her, but it wasn't enough. What more could I say? I liked Ainsley a lot and had been deeply in lust with her since the moment she walked up to my table. I never counted myself as the jealous type but she gave me a piece of herself that only I got to have. It meant more to me than I wanted to admit, then or now, though I just had. Now that she carried my baby, I wanted more with her. However, I don't think I loved her—I hadn't known her long enough. I wanted her and that should've sufficed.

"I've aged ten goddamn years waiting for your fucking answer, Reese," Razor growled, forever a surly motherfucker.

"What do you want me to say?"

"Start with the truth," he ordered. "From my vantage point, if you bring her here and it don't work out, then what? Does she have any other connections in that fucking club that would want to hit us because of her?"

I didn't think so, but without being one hundred percent sure, I couldn't answer the question.

"What about if you take her as your ol' lady?" Razor pressed. "I don't care if *they* want her dead, we'd still be encroaching on one of their princesses. That would put a target on our backs because of your fucking cock."

"What the fuck do you want me to do?" I yelled, at the end of my rope. "Ainsley's twenty-one-years old, pregnant, and alone. How the fuck can I find out anything if Ma Siller has all but barred me from the fucking house because I vented over Ainsley's recklessness and you won't let her set foot in the fucking club? This is all bullshit. I don't have a fucking answer to any of your questions, Razor."

My less-than-respectful tone deserved Razor's wrath. I knew better, and yet, it infuriated me that if Ma Siller wasn't barring me from visiting Ainsley, then something came up at the club.

Razor punched my jaw. I reeled back, pain streaking through me and stars dancing in front of my eyes. His gut punch doubled me over. Through a haze, I listened as he banged the gavel and adjoined the meeting.

I wasn't sure why I invited Reese to the doctor's appointment. Ma Siller told me to give him space to get his head on straight. She insisted I content myself with seeing Reese when I saw him and warned me not to chase him because that would only drive him away.

I'd been so sure Reese would prove her wrong. I thought he'd want to see me and talk to me, yet he only showed up once. After he left, Ma Siller asked me if I'd come out of the room the night we met. I hadn't. Once she left me, I called Roman and left a message for him. Eight days later, he still hadn't called me back.

Ma Siller went into great detail about her conversation with Reese. It crushed me, but then she walked it back a little by saying he felt something for me and that had him running scared. Hearing her perspective about Reese as a brokenhearted thirteen-year-old left me hurting for him as much as I did when *he'd* told me about the loss of his family. I understood his grief and fear, but where did that leave me and the baby? He was emotionally scarred so he rejected anything that might bring him pain.

Ma thought Trinity's death also played a factor. She made it sound as if they had something deeper than Reese led me to believe. By my second day with her, I didn't know if she liked me or wanted answers to pass along to the club.

She grilled me about everything from my parents to Roman to my friendship with Nova. It exhausted me. Tess and Big Poppa's visits lifted my spirits. Every day, she brought something for me to eat, usually broth-based and hearty.

Once they left, Ma Siller got back to her interrogation. When she ran out of questions, she had her daughters come and take up where she left off. Sometimes, I heard myself answering the same questions.

Reese visited on the fourth day, although Ma Siller didn't give us a moment alone so I could ask him about his conversation with her. After a couple of hours, she put him out. When I awakened, three days ago and went to the kitchen for a glass of water and saltines, a completely different woman greeted me as if she'd had a personality transplant. Ma Siller was solicitous, kind, and affable.

During Tess's lunchtime visit yesterday, she told me she'd made an appointment for me with an OB. Tess and Big Poppa were going out of town for their anniversary, but she promised to check on me every day. Meanwhile, Ma Siller offered to come to the appointment with me.

Instead, I told her I'd invited Reese and I wanted to drive there on my own. Although he hadn't responded to my text, I thought maybe he'd come, but as my name was called and the nurse took my vital signs and my history, he still hadn't contacted me.

"Here's a hospital gown and a sheet," the nurse said. "Dr. Purdue will be in shortly."

As I lay on the table, I didn't think the doctor knew the meaning of shortly since I'd been in the room for forty-five minutes before he walked in with the nurse following behind.

He was tall, blue-eyed, and handsome with a bedside manner that I immediately liked. During the pelvic exam, I pulled the sheet over my head in embarrassment, but he explained everything calmly and gave no indication he saw my action as anything but mature.

"Everything is fine. Nothing to worry about," he said, sliding off his gloves and washing his hands. He nodded to the nurse. "Arthel will get you ready for your ultrasound."

She led me from the exam room to where the ultrasound machine was via a connected door. Once she typed in my name and date of birth, she left me alone.

Which was exactly what I was—alone. Never more than in that moment when I expected the father of my baby to suddenly arrive because, as far as I knew, it was his first child, too. Or just because of me.

He didn't have to want *me*. He just had to care.

I blinked at the ceiling, wondering what I'd gotten myself into. I didn't have anything, so how could I take care of this baby? Why did I even want it? It was an unplanned accident that happened because of my misguided stupidity. Listening to Nova about the rhythm method and how I didn't want my first time to be so impersonal. I was just lucky that Reese didn't have an STD, like Louisiana swore.

From the beginning, I'd set myself up for this massive failure.

Even if Dayton had lived, I would've still ended up pregnant. That would've gone over as well with him as it had with my brother.

My tears didn't surprise me. They were my new normal and went right along with that stupid morning sickness. Ma Siller said carrying babies was hard on a woman in every way.

The door opened and I didn't bother lifting my head, regretting so much, including not allowing Ma to come with me.

"The doctor will be with you shortly," Arthel said.

"He doesn't know the definition," I mumbled just as Reese said, "thank you."

I stilled, afraid to believe he was here and afraid to lift my head and discover he wasn't. My skin prickled and my heart sped up. The smell of cologne and motor oil invaded my senses. I ignored the slight nausea.

"Are you going to talk to me?"

The sound of his voice washed over me. His uncertainty surprised me.

"Ainsley?"

"Have you done anything where I shouldn't talk to you?"

"I know Ma Siller told you what I said."

I'd gone through too many emotions today to get into this conversation right now.

"Can I at least explain myself?"

"Not here," I said tiredly.

"I'm sorry."

"Until the next time."

"Can I take you for a ride after we leave and we can talk then?"

"I have my car and Ma Siller is cooking a nice dinner for me." Her words, not mine. "You can follow me there, then I'll go for a ride with you after we eat. If I'm not too tired. You'll just have to come back tomorrow, if I am."

"I won't be here tomorrow. I'm going on a run for two weeks."

My heart sinking, I sat up. Reese stood a few feet away, staring at me, as handsome as ever. His gray eyes searched my face.

Before I formed a response, the door opened and Dr. Purdue walked in, followed by Arthel, prompting Reese to finally close the distance between us. Grabbing my hand, he kissed my forehead.

"Are you ready, Ainsley?" Dr. Purdue asked.

Reese's brows snapped together and he scowled at the doctor. "Who the fuck are you?"

Immediately, his attitude raised my hackles. I shoved aside my fear that he'd go on a run and drop out of sight like Roman had. "My doctor," I gritted, snatching my hand away, unconcerned about Arthel's gasp and the doctor's stiffening. "You know? Identifiable by his lab coat and badge."

He scowled at me.

"Save it," I ordered, holding my hand up to ward off his response. "You don't get to come in here and act like a jackass after ignoring me for days, baby daddy. You didn't even have the decency to respond to my text. You just left me wondering if you'd show up."

"Did you just call me baby daddy?"

"Is it not what you are?" I asked sweetly. "And it's better than sperm donor."

Swearing under his breath, he clenched his jaw.

"You're here, Reese. Act like you have sense, respect my doctor and his nurse, or get out. You're not ruining this moment for me, jerk."

"It's my moment, too. This is my first kid."

I studied my nails. "I can't tell by your deadbeat behavior, so let's cue the violins that you're so put upon."

He pinned me with a severe look, then glowered at the doctor. "Can we get on with it?"

Dr. Purdue searched my face. "Would you like to proceed with him in the room or should I ask him to leave?"

Reese balled his fists at his sides. "Wait a damn minute. This is my baby, too."

"That *I'm* carrying, Reese. You aren't responsible for it, me, or the bills."

"Did you even put me down as the father?" he snapped. "Or are you erasing me there as well?"

"Ha. You've erased yourself. And, yes, I put you down, although I don't know anything about your family's medical history. I needed you here to fill that part out."

Some of the fight left him and he swore again. "I'm sorry, sweetheart. I'll tell you whatever you need to know. Or I'll fill out the paperwork myself."

"Why don't you do that while I complete Ainsley's ultrasound?" Dr. Purdue suggested. It was obvious he didn't want Reese in the room. Not that I blamed him, considering how much of a fuckhead he'd been. "We won't be long."

"Is that what you want, Ainsley?" Reese asked, a note of vulnerability creeping into his voice. "You're right. You're carrying our baby. It's about you, not me."

"I want you here with me." I didn't think about my answer; I just blurted my deepest desire. It was an illusion that reality would burst the moment we walked out of this room. For now, I could pretend that his plaintive note really meant he'd lowered his guard enough to truly consider me. "Just behave."

He gave me a half smile. "As you wish."

Reese sat on a rolling stool while Arthel had me lift my gown and lower the sheet to reveal my belly. Its flatness disappointed me. By now, I'd hoped to see a bump.

"This is going to be cold," she advised, shaking the bottle of gel and then coating my skin with it.

The uncomfortable chill lasted a moment, disappearing when Dr. Purdue spread it around with his doppler. He stared at the screen as he continued moving the little device. Reese also focused on whatever was on the monitor so I turned my head and saw absolutely nothing but black, white, and shades of gray.

"There's your little one right there," Dr. Purdue said, pointing and continuing to move the doppler. "It's about four point five centimeters and ten grams."

I'd repeatedly gone through this moment in my head. The visual confirmation of the baby inside of me. At times, I'd felt indifferent. I already knew I carried a child. How would seeing it make a difference? Other times, I felt alone, overwhelmed, and fearful. Visible verification would make it real and remind me of my plight. I'd remember how stupid I was to trust Nova. Suddenly, none of it mattered. Not the hows, whys, or maybes. Only it and its well-being counted.

"Can you tell the sex?" I asked, staring at the oddly shaped head that seemed to make up half of what the doctor identified as a baby.

"I can take a guess, but it won't be as accurate as it will be if we wait another couple weeks."

"What do you want to do, Reese?" I asked shyly. "Do you want Dr. Purdue to take a guess or should we wait?"

He dragged his attention away from the screen, got to his feet and brushed his lips over mine. "Whatever you want, Ainsley," he said softly. "But I prefer certainties."

"Okay." I looked at the doctor. "We'll wait."

"Can you do that 3d ultrasound, doc?" Reese asked, as if he hadn't acted like a raging asshole. "I looked it up when I got a moment last night. I thought she'd have that."

"She can," Dr. Purdue responded, allowing bygones to be bygones, "but there isn't a need."

"Neither is there the money," I said, keeping it real.

I know I wasn't supposed to bring up money, especially in mixed company, but if it wasn't for Tess bumping up my pay, I would've had to wait until my insurance kicked in, which would take another three weeks. Although I still hadn't returned to work, I was now a permanent full-time employee, and eligible for all benefits.

"I'll pay for it," Reese said.

Arthel sniffed. "My sister, Big Poppa, and Glinda are dividing the bill."

"What?" Reese's strangled cough drowned out my gasp. No wonder Tess had gotten me in so quickly. Arthel was her sister. "I have money to pay."

"Billing isn't our department," Dr. Purdue said sharply, giving his nurse a warning glare. "You'll have to talk to them."

Folding her arms, Arthel gave Reese the stink eye. I wondered what she'd heard about him. It couldn't have been any worse than his display when he first arrived, which served to underscore his bad behavior.

"I will definitely talk to them," Reese said. "This is my baby. I'll do the paying."

"Are we ready to hear the heartbeat, Ainsley?" Dr. Purdue cut in, his movements stiff and jerky. He obviously didn't like Reese, either.

"Can you confirm how many weeks she is?" Reese demanded, the feeling of dislike mutual.

It was a typical question, so I shouldn't have put much stock into it. Given his recent behavior, however, I couldn't help but feel a way about it.

"She's eleven weeks and four days. Estimated due date is June 28th."

Reese nodded, though his expression remained unreadable.

Turning back to the job at hand, Dr. Purdue nodded. Arthel immediately squeezed more gel onto my belly. He slid the doppler around a moment, then turned a dial on the machine.

The heartbeat rose strong and loud in the silence of the room. If I'd repeatedly imagined visual confirmation, hearing the beat of its heart was *unimaginable*. I'd never considered how it would feel to have Reese's watery laughter, tight hug, and quick kiss. I didn't think about how I'd suddenly feel so attached to him and our baby, and long for us to be a couple and then a family. And I definitely didn't expect awe and joy to course through me so fiercely that I burst into tears.

Reese leaned in and drew me into his arms. Just then, I didn't care that he didn't love me and didn't want the baby. In the here and now, I felt safe and wanted. I buried my nose in his strong neck, breathing in the faint scent of leather, grateful he'd come to experience this with me.

He whispered sweet nothings and comforting words to me.

"Your baby looks perfectly healthy," Dr. Purdue said into the silence, punctuated only by my sniffles. Not even the baby's heartbeat rose up anymore. "Arthel will give you your lab slip for bloodwork, though I don't expect any abnormalities and I'll see you back in four weeks. Any questions?"

I swiped at my cheeks. "I don't have to see you every week? Four weeks is a long time between visits."

"You're young and healthy, and your baby looks fine," he said with reassurance. "Unless complications arise, the typical schedule is every four weeks until the twenty-eighth week, then every two weeks. Once you hit thirty-six weeks, I'll see you weekly."

"You'll be my attending physician?"

I'd read stories where an OB sometimes sent in one of the associates in their practice, especially if they weren't on call.

"Even if I'm not, the doctors in this practice are more than capable of taking care of you and the baby."

"I don't know them. I know you."

"We'll talk about it closer to your due date. Why don't you get dressed so you can check out? There's still time before the lab closes to get your bloodwork."

"Dr. Purdue, right?" Reese demanded, not giving the doctor a chance to respond before saying, "I'd like to talk to you while Ainsley dresses."

The doctor made a show of looking at his watch. "I don't have time at the moment."

"I'm not asking. I'm *telling* you, so make the fucking time. I need to talk to you. It'll be two minutes, then you're free to see Kingdom Come for all I fucking care."

Most people would've been mortified at Reese's threatening demeanor, but most people hadn't had Roman as a brother. I wondered how either of them would react if I ever pointed out how similar they were in so many ways.

Pretty sure, neither of them would appreciate that observation, which just confirmed how alike they were.

CHAPTER TWENTY-SIX

REESE

I had to all but do fucking handstands for Razor to give me time to come to Ainsley's ultrasound. One thing that was becoming abundantly clear was they were pushing my back against the wall and forcing me to make a choice. I told Razor, Jester, Warrior, Bolt, Louisiana, and almost all the officers and the brothers I was closest to that I understood their position. I said it so many fucking times I thought maybe I'd turned motherfucking blue.

Only one thing mattered to them—Ainsley's relationship to Roman. Not a goddamn thing else. Not the respect the Bastards had for their brothers' ol' ladies. Not my years of loyalty and service. And not me.

Frankly, the argument was tired. I stood on one side and they were determined to draw a line and stand on the other, daring me to attempt to bridge the divide. When we returned from the run, I intended to turn in my patch. I wouldn't desert my club at the last minute, but Ainsley needed me. She wouldn't have invited me to the ultrasound if she didn't, so fuck anyone who stood in my way.

I walked into the office with a sense of obligation. She wanted me there and by a miracle I arrived in time. Didn't expect to find a surfer like motherfucker about my age as her doctor and I acted like a jackass, especially after reading some women crushed on their physicians. I wasn't jealous—that wasn't me. I was more like...*outraged.*

As usual, Ainsley checked my bullshit. I loved the way she stood up to me so fiercely. I'd already fucked up enough, so I stood down, intending to serve as her support.

What I didn't expect was my reaction to seeing the baby on the ultrasound. I didn't expect to feel a depth of tenderness for her unmatched to anything I'd ever experienced. Seeing a little blob in grayscale shouldn't have shot desire and protectiveness into me. I wanted to fuck her with the same fierceness I wanted to keep her safe. She carried a part of me I lost inside her. I needed a moment before I heard the heartbeat. Of course, my question came across as asinine. Still, I could've had a month and it wouldn't have prepared me to hear the baby's heartbeat.

It was no longer an abstract little being that had turned my fucking life upside down. It was my child.

For Dr. Purdue to brush Ainsley off when she requested his assurance he'd be her attending physician during the delivery pissed me the fuck off.

The doctor guided me into his office and closed the door. I ignored his fancy degrees, expensive furniture and expansive view of downtown.

"Name your price," I said. "However much it takes for you to be the one to deliver the baby, I'll pay it. I'll have someone drop off half tomorrow and half after the delivery."

"That isn't the way this works, Mister…?"

"Sinclair," I supplied. "Money talks, so it's exactly the way it works. Point me to your billing department by the way. The only one who's paying for Ainsley's care is me."

"You can request to talk to the manager at checkout. I don't take payoffs, Mr. Sinclair. I took the Hippocratic Oath because of allegiance to my profession and my patients."

"Don't consider it a payoff," I said flatly. "Consider it a fee. It's important to Ainsley, so it's important to me and I don't intend to leave until you agree to do what she wants."

"Security might say differently."

"Security might find your fucking body floating in the river, too."

He drew himself up and I raised my hands.

"I'm not here for a fight, Purdue. I'm here to give Ainsley what she wants."

"Ten grand tomorrow and fifteen grand after she delivers, in addition to my normal fees."

"Done. We can't have a paper trail for obvious reasons, so I trust you like living. Don't fuck over me and this will be an easy transaction."

Not answering, he opened the door. "The deal is made, so leave."

"You got it."

As much as I loved Ma Siller, I was sick of her interference, too. Ainsley and I needed to talk before I left. I was in enough shit at the club without insulting Bolt's ol' lady. If it came to that, I'd just have to do it. Ainsley was near her second trimester and I was done with the fucking games.

We weren't chess pieces to be moved around the damn board at everyone else's beck and call.

I didn't doubt Ma Siller liked Ainsley, but Bolt told me today the grilling she and the girls subjected Ainsley to. He wasn't sure if Ainsley would mention it, so he wanted to head off the drama.

"Ainsley passed Glinda's tests with flying colors."

So fucking what? She shouldn't have been tested in the first fucking place.

When Ma Siller opened the door and I guided Ainsley into the house, she suggested Ainsley change into something more comfortable.

"No," I said. "Ainsley and I are going for a spin after dinner. Her jeans are just fine."

Ma Siller lifted a brow at Ainsley. "Are you up to it?"

"I'm fine. Reese and I need to talk." She smiled at me so sweetly. "But I'm going to take a quick shower. I won't be long."

True to her word, it took her twenty minutes for her to return to the kitchen, smelling like flowers and wearing another pair of jeans and a black long-sleeved T-shirt.

"Is dinner ready? I'm starving," Ainsley said. She looked between Ma Siller and I. "Now that I'm freshened up, what can I help with, Ma?"

"Nothing, child. Take a load off and sit down. I'll heat the chicken and rice while we have the pear salad."

"I love pears!" Ainsley gushed, although I foresaw disaster on the horizon.

Pulling Ainsley's chair out, I waited until she situated herself at the table before I took my seat. "Have you ever had Ma's pear salad?"

"Nope, but she's cooked goulash, stewed chicken and noodles over mashed potatoes, cheesy potatoes, and a snack of shredded turkey with cream of chicken soup served over white bread." She leaned closer. "Tess brings me a lot of food, but Ma cooks all the time, and I don't want to insult her."

"It's fine, Ainsley," I told her in low tones. "Eat the food you like the best."

"So far, I've liked it all."

She smiled at me and my heart melted. Her trust in me had been shaky at best. After Ma Siller told her what I said, it was probably non-existent. I wouldn't have a lot of time with her because I still had a lot to do, but I had hope that she'd at least hear me out.

Ma Siller sat a plate in each of our places, then seated herself, and demanded we say grace. When I first moved in, I resented the order until I realized it was a small price to pay for her kindness to me. Even if they were just words I said to make her happy.

On cue, Bolt walked in. He always managed to miss the blessing. He swore it wasn't on purpose, though I called bullshit. Dutifully, he washed his hands, kissed Ma Siller's cheek, before grabbing his own plate of pear salad and sitting at the table.

Glancing from Bolt to me, Ainsley shifted, then cleared her throat. "I've already thanked Ma Siller, but seeing as how I've barely seen you since I moved in, I want to thank you, too."

Bolt grunted.

"Are you looking forward to your run?" she pressed.

"Might be if my dang gonnet ride wasn't giving me shit."

"The chain again?" I asked, lifting my brows.

Worry creased Ma Siller's face. "I thought you had it completely replaced, Siller."

"I did, Ma," he said gruffly. "But that sumbitch's flapping around again. How the fuck can a new chain do that when I only been riding it from the club to here? Don't make sense."

"Have you checked the sprockets?" Ainsley asked. "I know those aren't cheap, but that could be the issue."

Bolt, Ma Siller and me looked at Ainsley. She'd mentioned Roman taught her about bikes, but I'd brushed it off. At the time, it wasn't important in the scheme of things.

"Louisiana said the same thing," Bolt confirmed. "But I checked those motherfuckers myself. They looked fine."

Ainsley squirmed, looked at me, then at Bolt again. "My brother has a club member named Wizard," she started hesitantly. "I'm not supposed to know this but he got his road name because he's a wiz with bikes but he also seems to teleport wherever he pleases." She pursed her lips, lowered her lashes, and squirmed again. "Do you think your bike could've been sabotaged in some way? Maybe, acid instead of the proper chain lube? It would corrode the links. Depending on what's used, it could happen quickly."

Bolt's hard stare raised my fucking hackles. I slid my chair closer to Ainsley and draped an arm over her shoulder. Sliding his pear salad aside, he rested his arms on the table.

"Reese, Louisiana, and me spent yesterday evening checking everything. On my ride over here, I thought I'd have to pull to the side of the road and call someone."

"Then, you should have," Ainsley said. "A faulty chain can be deadly. If it isn't the lube, then perhaps the axle nuts or chain adjusters were loosened. It is definitely something Wizard would do. You helped Reese save me—"

"Reese saved you," Bolt growled.

"You still went there and cleaned up. You're a target as much as I probably still am. As much as Reese is."

"We have guards at the gate," Bolt said, with a smidgeon more civility. "Wizard would have to get on the grounds to tamper with my bike."

Ma Siller shook her head. I hadn't seen the fear in her eyes in quite a while. "Yeah, Ainsley. Siller's bike don't have bells and whistles."

Ainsley drew in a deep breath. "I know you see me as little more than the enemy and you don't have to answer me. I shouldn't say anything because I don't know where Roman is. If you strike the Scorpions, then Roman might be the casualty. You're a valuable part of the Royal Bastards. Do you really think Wizard wouldn't know your bike and that of Reese's and the rest of the officers? Don't you know theirs? Know everything about your ops. Enemies 101."

"Know what I think, Ainsley?" Bolt said.

"I can't read minds, so that's a no."

Bolt chuckled. "You're a little smartass, aren't you?"

Sniffing, she sidled a glance at me. "So I've been told by one or two people."

"I'm sure Reese and Roman don't see eye-to-eye on a lot, but they'd agree about that," he speculated.

Ainsley shrugged.

"Here's what I think," Bolt said, scratching his jaw. "You're a keeper. Any woman who knows her shit about bikes is a prize in my book."

I'm sure she'd won him over because of more than that, but the breath I'd been holding whooshed out.

"Let's eat," Bolt declared, and pointed to the stove. "Ma, bring out your chicken and rice for Ainsley. Give her extra helpings. She has that little one to feed." He pulled his plate to him, picked up his fork and dug in, scooping up a piece of pear, mayo, and cheese and shoveling it into his mouth. "Delicious. One of my childhood favorites."

Ainsley smiled and picked up her fork. "It looks delicious," she said, breaking off a piece. "I would've thought pears, whipped cream, and toasted coconut was more of a dessert than a salad."

"Ainsley—"

She shoved the fork into her mouth and began to chew, then abruptly stopped and gagged. Her eyes watered and her normally gorgeous skin tone turned a hideous green.

I grabbed the napkin off my lap and brought it to her mouth. "Spit it out."

She complied and gagged again. "What was that?" she cried.

"Southern Pear Salad," Ma Siller said calmly, sitting a plate of boiled chicken and rice in front of Ainsley. "I forgot your aversion to mayo lately. Can't remember if the pear salad is a southern thing or a black thing. You're covered either way."

Ainsley jerked her horrified gaze away from the main course. "A black thing?" she asked, appalled. "I know you're fucking lying, Ma. *And* southern has no color."

"She's probably right, Ma," Bolt said, leaning across the table and pulling Ainsley's pear salad to him. "We had it at our church socials when I was growing up. Whenever Ma Siller serves this, it's like a piece of nostalgic heaven." He shoved half the pear salad into his mouth and talked around globs of cheese and mayo. "I could eat this every day."

Ainsley clapped a hand over her mouth, jumped to her feet, and rushed to the sink to vomit.

It was time for us to go.

I'd been craving barbeque for days, but after Ma Siller tried to murder me with her food, I thought soup and a sandwich might be best, so we stopped in a little shop not far from the Sillers' place and grabbed a bite to eat. Reese didn't say much. He barely paid attention to me for all the texting he was doing.

My emotions were still raw from the ultrasound. Added to that was worry that Wizard was up to fuckery. I had no doubt Boom Boom ordered the sabotage, which got me to think about my brother. If Wizard and the others were back, where was Roman?

He wanted nothing to do with me. However, if he was back, he would've called and demanded I clear all my things from his house. His radio silence didn't make sense.

Until it hit me: Roman was dead. They'd taken him on the run and killed him. The realization sent me rushing to the diner's bathroom and throwing up everything I'd just eaten. The sobbing that accompanied my vomiting left me weak and miserable.

"Ainsley?" A knock accompanied Reese's call. "Open up, babe."

I covered my mouth with my hands.

"We need to leave, baby."

Imagining Roman discarded like a piece of trash turned my stomach again.

"Open the door, Ainsley," Reese coaxed. "We have to leave."

Stumbling to the door, I unlocked it, then went to the basin, splashing water on my face and rinsing out my mouth, while Reese hovered in the background.

"I can stop at a convenience store and get you crackers and *7Up*," he said quietly.

"I can't eat anything else." It wouldn't stay on my stomach. Not because of the baby, but because of my brother.

I covered my face with my hands, not protesting when Reese pulled me into his arms.

"What has you so upset, sweetheart?"

"Roman's dead."

Reese went still, then tightened his hold on me. "You don't know that," he said gruffly.

"They're back," I said, not bothering to lift my head. "I thought I saw Kite near Dr. Purdue's office, but I wasn't sure, so I brushed it off. Listening to Bolt confirmed their presence. Wizard is behind whatever is wrong with his bike."

"Our grounds are secure, Ainsley. Besides, Bolt has been having an issue with his chain for weeks now." He pulled away and grabbed my hand, tugging me back into the restaurant and heading toward the door.

I wasn't sure where we were headed until I saw the signs for Monarch Highway and I knew we were going back to the cabin. Around us, the sounds of nature rose to a fever pitch and a billion stars gleamed from the night sky.

I half-expected Louisiana to open the door with Jinx inside, but that didn't happen. Reese pulled out a set of keys and unlocked the door to let us in.

Everything that had personalized it and gave it a homey feel was gone. The furniture was there, but everything else had been cleared away.

"Jinx left him," I said woodenly, stumbling to the sofa and sitting.

"Jinx filed for divorce," Reese corrected. "Louisiana was served with the papers today. She cited irreconcilable differences. There are some developments that have taken place in the last couple of hours that she isn't happy about."

More of Louisiana's fuckery. "I'm sorry. I hoped they would've worked it out."

"Me, too," he said quietly. "She loved Louisiana a lot and he betrayed her."

"I feel somehow responsible."

Reese nodded. "So do I," he said, sighing. "I knew he was fucking over her and I looked the other way. Louisiana's fucking insane behind Jinx and I thought..." His voice trailed off. "I'm not sure to be honest."

"I brought Nova with me. If I hadn't believed her lies, Jinx wouldn't have found out."

Reese finally moved from where he'd been standing in the middle of the floor and sat next to me. He tried to draw me into his arms, but I shook my head and he respected my wishes.

"It isn't your fault. That secret was a ticking timebomb, bound to see the light of day eventually."

"I suppose you're right."

He took my hand in his and brought it to his mouth, kissing each of my fingertips and igniting a fire deep inside me. But it would forever be this way between us if I allowed it.

Reese would fuck up, he'd apologize, promise to do better, and make love to me. I tugged my hand away and settled it into my lap.

"It's okay, Reese," I said, empty and lost, feelings I'd become all too familiar with since I discovered my pregnancy. "You don't have to tell me pretty words or romance me. If you want sex, be honest, and let me decide."

"Would you say yes?"

I wanted to, deep down in my soul where no one could see all my hopes and fears, dreams and disappointments. But I didn't know what to do or how to respond. It was just a question, so I didn't have to say anything.

"I was angry with you," he said, when he realized I wouldn't answer.

"Ma Siller told me. It still doesn't make it right. You can't shit on me and then correct it when you're over your anger. You should've shouted at me."

"Would my words have been any better had I said them directly to you?"

"It would've been in the heat of the moment. Not over an hour later when you had a chance to think about what you were saying but said them anyway."

"That was unworthy of me."

"I disagree. It was unworthy of what I supposedly meant to you after our time together here. It was exactly like you because you've done it since we met."

Reese shoved a hand through his hair and gritted his teeth. "I care for you so fucking much."

"Words are cheap. Not only don't most of your actions exhibit care, but most of the time I don't even think you like me."

He gave me an incredulous look.

I'd gone through so many emotions today that I didn't think I could handle any more.

"I'm thinking about patching out," he announced, that bombshell grabbing my attention like nothing else. "You and I will never have a fair shot as long as I'm a Royal Bastard."

His expression gave nothing away. I didn't know if he genuinely wanted to do this or if he felt obligated to do it.

"Razor kept throwing shit my way today. That's why I was late to the ultrasound. It's a collective effort to keep us apart."

I leaned my head against the sofa and stared at nothing in particular, just seeing my brother in his cut and riding his Harley. To the end, Roman loved his club and would've been lost without it. I don't think he could've given it up, even for me. Like Reese, he might've tried out of a misplaced sense of duty, but it would've slowly eaten him up and our relationship would've been damaged long before now.

Somehow, I managed to hold my tears at bay. Reese and I needed to have this conversation. The moment I got back to my room at Ma Siller's, I'd give into my grief. I hadn't even gotten to tell Roman goodbye. Worse, he'd died angry at me—*hating* me.

I swiped at the tears sliding down my cheeks. "Babies are little monsters," I sniffled. "I didn't cry this fucking much when *I* was a kid."

"Ainsley, I would like you to stay here while I'm gone."

Frowning, I lifted my head. "Why?"

"Ma Siller has places she can go. If those Bloody Scorpion motherfuckers are back, you need a safe space. This is it."

"It's in the middle of fucking nowhere. I don't have clothes or food or my car."

"I'm going to get three of my brothers to help me. Two of them will have twelve-hour shifts guarding you and one will run errands for you. You can't have your car. It might have a tracker on it. Whether because of Roman or one of those other motherfuckers, I don't know."

"Couldn't your brothers lead the Bloody Scorpions here?"

"I'll be gone for two weeks. So far, we're having a pretty mild autumn. They'll camp outside."

That sounded gross, but what did I know? "One Arctic blast can change that."

"Hopefully, it doesn't. As for the one who runs errands for you, I'll make sure he takes different routes every night when he returns."

"Why can't I go with Ma Siller?"

"We're going to take measures to keep all of you safe—"

"Wouldn't that be easier in one fucking place?"

Reese rubbed the back of his neck. "Louisiana's bringing Jinx here. Ma Siller..." His voice trailed off and he shrugged. "We don't know if she'd hide Jinx not only from the Scorpions but from Louisiana, too."

"You assholes are using me to hold Jinx hostage?"

"Of course not," Reese said in exasperation. "You're pregnant, so she won't desert you."

"No. Fuck no! Absolutely not."

"Ma Siller *might* hide Jinx. If she doesn't, she certainly won't stop her from walking out if that's what Jinx wants."

"You're so unfair," I cried.

"Another thing? I need your phone. We're leaving it at the Siller place to test our theory."

I rubbed my eyes. "How will I communicate or play games or watch a movie? If I stay, there's nothing to do here without a phone."

"If you have your phone, there may not be anything to do. Cell phone reception is shitty without the antennae and signal booster. Louisiana removed it when Jinx left."

"Why in the world would he do that?"

"He had it up for her. She's gone, so it's gone."

"Can he put it back?"

"We can't have anyone pick up on the cell phone signal."

"You have all the fucking answers," I grouched.

He grinned, and I pretended it didn't affect me.

"We don't have much longer, sweetheart. Louisiana is stopping at Ma Siller's for some of your things, then he's heading this way with Jinx. But I have a proposition for you."

Judging by his husky tone, I knew he wanted sex. Once before, he'd proposed we lock out the outside world and focus on the two of us.

"Since I saw our baby on the ultrasound, knowing *I* put it inside of you, I've wanted to make love to you. I know we have so much unresolved and I'm showing zero skills of seduction."

"Zero rizz," I corrected. "Charisma, for the unknowledgeable like you."

He smiled and laid his palm against my face. "Let me make love to you, Ainsley."

My head told me to decline him. Logically, I knew he didn't mean any of what he said. He might've believed it in the here and now, yet when it came time for action, he always failed. But my heart? My body? Both craved him fiercely. In different ways and for different reasons. My heart bought into his promises, believed that somehow and some way, love would prevail. My *heart* beat hard and fast whenever he turned his gray gaze to me and transfixed me with a look. My heart remembered the shared experience of hearing our baby's heartbeat for the first time.

My body craved his touch. Craved *him*. His lips on mine—his lips all over me. His cock pulsing inside me and sending me over the edge before he lost all control.

Without me saying a word, he knew I'd given in. He pulled me into his arms and covered my mouth with his firm lips. I had to satisfy myself with what he offered me while I carried his baby. Once I delivered, my hormones would settle and I could put our relationship, and my entire life, into perspective.

He didn't want to hear about Roman or my grief over his death. That was okay. I'd mourn my brother alone, though I knew I had to keep myself together for the baby. My emotions affected it.

Reese tore his lips away. "You're overthinking this."

I didn't want to talk anymore. He had a barrier in place. No matter the reason, whether from the loss of his family or because of me, it made it impossible to resolve our differences. Pushing away all thoughts but Reese's touch, taste, and scent, I threaded my fingers through the hair at his nape and kissed him. I kissed him for everything that could've been and everything that would never be.

I kissed him because I loved him and, just for tonight, I didn't care that he'd always see me as Roman's sister and the girl who he'd accidentally gotten pregnant.

The biker saw our one night together as a mistake. I saw my one night with the biker as a blessing. He'd assured me I'd never be alone. I wouldn't have him or Roman, but I'd have my son or daughter. I would survive and thrive by hook or crook and give my child a good life.

His kiss turned hot and frantic, and he tore his lips away to stare into my eyes with wild intensity. He kissed my chin, my jaw, and down my throat, growling when I threw my head back to give him easier access.

My pulse quickened, and a flutter I couldn't ignore rose in my chest.

His hand slid down my arm, his fingers tracing patterns on my skin. His thumb brushed the sensitive spot on the inside of my wrist and my breath hitched.

"Ainsley," he said, barely above a whisper. "I dream of having you in my arms."

Before I responded, his lips were on mine again, soft and insistent. This kiss was slow, deliberate, as if he was savoring the moment. His hand moved to my waist, pulling me closer, until I could feel the heat of his body. I melted into him, my senses overwhelmed by his taste and scent.

His fingers slid under the hem of my T-shirt, his touch sending sparks of desire through me. I gasped as he pulled the shirt over my head, tossing it aside without breaking our connection.

"Reese," I breathed.

"Shh," he whispered, his lips finding mine again.

His hands were everywhere, both gentle and demanding. He unbuttoned my jeans, sliding them down my legs, leaving me in nothing but my bra and panties. For a moment, doubt crept in, and I felt exposed and vulnerable, but the way he looked at me like I was the most desirable thing in the world broke through my defenses and exhilarated me.

"You're perfect," he said, his voice thick with desire.

His hard cock pressed against me as he trailed his lips down my neck, his teeth grazing my skin.

My heart was racing, my body aching for him.

He swept me into his arms, cradling me against his chest. I wrapped my arms around his neck, my legs around his waist, as he carried me to the small bedroom where we'd found our own slice of heaven the last time we were here. The room was dimly lit, and the bed was inviting. When he laid me down and pulled back the comforter, the sheets were soft and cool against my skin.

He unhooked my bra, tossing it aside, cupping my breasts, and brushing my nipples. Moaning, I arched into his touch as pleasure coursed through me.

"You're so responsive," he murmured, brushing his lips over my collarbone.

His kisses continued down my body, his hands moving with him, exploring every inch of me. He paused at my panties, his eyes meeting mine as he hooked his fingers in the waistband, sliding them down my legs.

Then his lips found the sensitive skin of my inner thigh. I squirmed, aching for his touch, for the release that I knew was coming.

"Reese, please."

He looked up at me with hungry eyes. "Please what?"

"Touch me," I whispered. "I need you."

His fingers trailed up my thigh, his touch feather-light, until he reached the core of my desire. He slipped a finger inside me, and I gasped. He added another finger.

My head fell back against the pillow as yearning built within me. His fingers moved in rhythm, sending me spiraling toward the edge. I cried out, my body tensing as my orgasm washed over me, wave after wave of pleasure crashing into me.

He dipped his head, his tongue flicking over my clit. His mouth was hot and wet, his fingers inside me, stretching me, filling me. I was lost in the sensations, my body arching off the bed, my hands clutching at the sheets.

"Reese, I'm—"

Another orgasm exploded, a wave of pleasure that left me shaking, my body convulsing. When I finally came down, he was hovering above me, his eyes dark with desire, his cock straining against his jeans. I reached for him, my hands fumbling with his fly, desperate to feel him, to taste him.

"Slow down," he warned, hoarse. "Let me take care of you."

But I wasn't in the mood to be slow. I needed him, now, and I wasn't going to wait. I pushed his jeans down, freeing his cock, and wrapped my hand around it, marveling at the heat, the thickness, the way it twitched in my grip.

"Ainsley," he groaned, his head falling back as I stroked him, thumbing the tip. "Fuck, that feels good."

A wicked smile curved my lips, and I leaned down, taking him into my mouth. He tasted like salt and man, like desire and need. I moaned around him, the vibrations making him curse my name. I sucked him deep, my tongue swirling around the head, my hands gripping his thighs to keep him steady.

"Stop," he gasped, tangling his hands in my hair. "If you keep doing that, I'm not going to last."

I pulled back, licking my lips, and gave him a sultry grin. "Then fuck me, Reese. Show me what you've got."

He shed his clothes, his eyes never leaving mine. He was a vision, his body hard and muscular, his cock thick and long. I reached out, running my hands over his chest, feeling the warmth of his skin, the hardness of his muscles.

When he was naked, he returned to me, positioning himself between my legs, his hands on either side of my head. I reached down, wrapping my hands around his cock, feeling its thickness, its hardness. He hissed, his eyes closing as he savored my touch.

"Tease," he growled.

I smiled, stroking him. "You like it."

He groaned, his eyes opening. "You're so fucking sexy like this."

A flush swept over me. He poised himself at my entrance, his cock teasing me, sliding along my seam.

"Ready?"

I nodded and rolled my hips. "Yes."

His eyes locked on mine as he thrust inside me in one smooth motion. I gasped at the fullness, the way he stretched me, filled me, claimed me. He moved slowly at first, giving me time to adjust, his lips brushing mine with each thrust.

"You feel so good. So tight, so wet. You were made for me, Ainsley."

I wrapped my legs around his waist, urging him deeper, faster. He obliged, his thrusts becoming more urgent and demanding. The bed creaked beneath us, the comforter long forgotten as we moved together, our bodies slick with sweat, our breaths coming in short, ragged gasps.

"Tell me what you want," he demanded, low.

"You," I whispered, my hands roaming over his back, tracing the contours of his body.

His weight was both comforting and exhilarating, a reminder of his strength and the power he held over me.

"Say you want me again," he ordered in a rough whisper. "Tell me you're mine."

"I'm yours," I breathed, lost in the moment and wishing it were true.

"How do you want me to fuck you?"

"Harder," I demanded, my nails digging into his back. "Fuck me harder, Reese."

He growled, a primal sound that sent a jolt of pleasure straight to my core, and slammed into me with a force that made the bed bang against the wall. I cried out, my head thrown back, my body trembling on the edge of another orgasm.

"Come for me. Let me feel you fall apart around my cock."

His words were my undoing. My orgasm crashed over me, a tidal wave of pleasure that left me screaming his name, clenching around him, milking him, drawing him closer to the edge. He thrust one last time, his body stiffening as he came, his seed spilling deep inside me, his name a hoarse whisper on my lips.

We collapsed together, our bodies still joined, our hearts pounding in unison. Reese's breath was hot against my neck, his arms wrapped tightly around me, as if he was afraid to let me go.

"That was..." I started, but words failed me.

"I know," he murmured, his lips brushing my hair. "It was everything."

We lay there in silence, bound by the intimacy of what we'd shared. Even if it faded the moment the outside world intruded, for now, I'd cherish it and pretend it would last forever.

CHAPTER TWENTY-SEVEN

ROMAN

Despite being an enforcer, patience had never been my forte. It was a skill I was forced to hone to survive and serve my club, not one I naturally possessed. There was an art to being a good fucking killer, and perfecting it took time.

Yet, it was an art that required goddamn hands, and those had been stolen from me.

Being dead would've been better, an opinion that was reinforced when I discovered Ainsley's betrayal.

And yet, even with my life out of fucking whack—in part because of my little sister—I couldn't bring myself to hate her. I was so pissed and hurt, I didn't know whether to shit or go blind. But she was still my only relative, my baby sister who I'd spent a decade protecting and loving. Without her in my life, the Earth itself seemed to be tilted off its axis.

The road to recovery hadn't been easy. I still wasn't whole, but now, I was back to having hands. Medical technology has made major advancements, enough so that I didn't need to walk around looking like a damn pirate with hooks for hands. Thanks to Bash, I'd acquired an array of prosthetics. Functional hands, blades of all kinds—and yes, a hook. I still hadn't gotten the hang of my robotic hands, but my arsenal of attachable weapons meant I wasn't entirely helpless.

It was two weeks away from Thanksgiving and, after nearly two and a half months, I was finally near my hometown. Last night, Bash's two sons, Easton and Tio, stopped to rest in Topeka. If it'd been up to me, I would've powered through, but I wasn't calling the shots. I was reliant on them for everything, and while Easton wasn't so bad, Tio made my ass itch. He was an asshole, and how he pulled someone like London, I hadn't a clue.

She was an angel, while he was one of Satan's cruelest demons.

As much as I disdained the perilous situation she was in, her fucked-up relationship wasn't my priority at the moment. Tio had spent the day sleeping off a hangover and a night of loud sex. I was in an entirely separate room, and it kept me up. I didn't want to think about how Easton, who shared a room with his brother, fared.

Again, something else that didn't matter to me. What did matter was the fact that Tio had given us a fifteen-minute notice of when we'd be riding out. Though he was the younger brother, we played by his rules. I was too helpless to pitch a bitch about it.

My annoyance was overridden by my anticipation. In an hour, I'd be back in Kansas City. That meant I could start crossing names off my list.

At the top of it? Nova fucking Wren.

I gripped a burner phone in my faux hand, the simple task requiring an embarrassing amount of concentration. Navigating it was even harder, making my movements clumsy and shaky, but I managed. London—sweet, beautiful, *trapped* London—had stayed by my side for two weeks, helping me get used to my prosthetics and giving me basic exercises to do.

Unfortunately, we'd been forced to part ways, but her guidance had helped me feel somewhat normal again.

That simple text had taken over a minute for me to write, frustrating me to no end. I didn't intend to carry out the conversation via messages; they were evidence, and a pain in the ass. I just needed confirmation that I had the right number, which came just minutes after my initial message.

Who the fuck is this??

I scoffed at the reply. Her bitchiness was her one constant, and what damned her to a death sentence. But in this instance, it proved useful, allowing me to confirm I had the right girl.

Louisiana? Is this you?

My brows snapped together.

Nova and her Cajun side piece were the ones who set Ainsley up with Sinclair, causing this whole mess.

Nova was a dumb bitch, to still be communicating with a motherfucker from a rival club—something she'd condemned Ainsley to die for. Rage swept through me, knowing she'd snitched on my little sister for the same thing she'd done. It made me more eager to snuff out her life.

Fortunately for her, I wouldn't share my revelation with her father, but it reinforced my need to end her miserable existence.

I took several deep breaths, needing to *sound* calm before I continued. When I was sure I wouldn't cuss her ass out the moment I heard her voice, I pressed the call button, and three rings later, she picked up.

"Listen, asshole—"

"It's me," I said, interrupting whatever insult she was about to spew.

"Roman?" she asked, the venom leaving her tone. "What do you want?"

Her dead. To get to her, I'd let her think she'd finally ensnared me in her trap.

"I-I want to see you," I answered, the words tasting like ash on my tongue. "The last several weeks have been hell, and fuck, babe, I need some comfort. I'll be home in about two hours. You free?"

Her blood coating my flesh would comfort me like nothing else.

She was silent for several seconds, and I feared that her desire for me had fizzled out.

"I understand," she replied, her voice breathier than before, her excitement almost tangible. "With all you've gone through, losing your hands, Ainsley betray—"

"Don't," I growled, clenching my jaw so hard, I almost cracked a tooth. "Don't bring her up."

My reaction could've blown my cover, but mercifully, she was too stupid to realize my anger was directed at her.

"I'm sorry," she said quickly. "It must be rough to hear about her right now, knowing what she did. But yeah, I'm free. Come to my place, and I'll make you feel so much better. A good blowjob will have you feeling brand new."

"Not your place. We need to be discreet."

"Right. I'll text you the address to my favorite motel. It isn't in club territory and there aren't any cameras except the one at the front desk, so you don't have to worry about Daddy ever finding out."

The slut snuck around enough to have a favorite motel?

"All right, baby. I'll see you tonight," I said, then hung up the phone before she responded.

Five minutes later, the address came through. Already, I knew what knife I'd use on her. I was nearly buzzing with excitement, more than ready to do what I did best.

Kill.

Riding my bike was still too big of a risk, so for the time being, I took my cage. London found it easier to teach me to use my prosthetics for driving in such a short time. Besides, she didn't ride.

Thankfully, traffic was light, so any accidents my less than stellar driving might've caused didn't occur.

I glanced at the motel's sign to confirm I had the right place, then checked the texts to see what room she was in.

Room 192 :)

I nodded, and pocketed my phone. The room was located under the staircase that led to the second floor, and the furthest first floor room from the office. It only had one neighboring room, which seemed vacant. I wanted to laugh at how easy she was making this for me; Nova's survival instincts were nonexistent. Boom Boom should really be fucking ashamed of himself.

I knocked twice. The door swung open before I pounded on the flimsy wood a third time. Nova stood there, her blonde hair thrown into a ponytail, her lips a glossy pink, and her body exposed by black lacy lingerie.

"Roman," she purred, her gaze sweeping over me as she stepped aside. "Come in."

Wordlessly, I entered. The minute she closed and locked the door, she wasted no time grabbing my shirt and pulling me close. Standing on her tiptoes, she pressed her lips against mine. I barely responded to the kiss, much to her chagrin. Huffing, she pulled away.

"There's no need to be shy—"

"Get undressed," I interrupted, not intending to dwell here longer than necessary.

Before I killed her, I had a point to prove.

Her blue eyes widened, her sultry grin reappearing. She made a show of removing her garments. Seeing as she only wore two things, it didn't take long for her to be standing butt-ass naked. She spun in a circle, ensuring I saw every inch of her nude body.

My eyebrows rose at Nova's pierced nipples. I reached out and brushed my thumb against the metal, her obnoxiously fake moan destroying any arousal I might've begun to feel.

"Do you like what you see?" she breathed.

She sounded so desperate for my approval; it was pathetic. I wouldn't give it to her.

"On the bed," I ordered.

Again, Nova scrambled to obey, crawling onto the bed and going onto all fours. She spread her legs wide, falling onto her elbows for a deep arch. A hand snaked between her legs, her fingers gliding through her slit, sinking into her pussy. She whimpered, pumped a few times so I could hear how soaked she was, then withdrew from her core.

My cock didn't even twitch at the show. My disdain for her made a hard dick impossible.

"I'm so wet for you," she crooned, wiggling her slender hips. "Come feel for yourself."

I unbuckled my belt and unzipped my pants. Approaching the bed, I pulled my jeans and boxers down just enough for my cock to be visible.

"Face me," I said. Though my hard tone didn't dissuade her, my soft dick did.

She looked up at me with furrowed brows, glancing between my eyes and my exposed manhood.

"Oh," she muttered, realization finally sinking in. "Roman, I—"

"Save it," I barked, moving to make myself decent again.

She grabbed my wrist, and I paused. Apparently, she took that as a signal to continue, but when her hand found my cock, I recoiled.

"What the fuck are you doing?"

"It's okay if it's hard for your dick to rise. You're getting up there in age. If you need some time—"

A disbelieving laugh left me. "You think that's the issue? No, sweetheart, I have no problem getting hard."

"Clearly, you're fucking lying, because you're soft—"

Putting my cock away could wait. It wouldn't be the first time I killed someone with my balls out.

Using my hands was still difficult, but I managed to wrap one around her throat and squeeze. Not as hard as I would've liked, but enough for her to get the goddamn message.

She squeaked, falling silent as her eyes grew to the size of saucers.

"You know why my dick is soft, bitch? Because I feel nothing for you. You're a backstabbing little cunt that's a waste of oxygen," I growled, tightening my grip around her throat out of sheer willpower.

She choked and sputtered, clawing at my hand as she tried to squirm away. I pressed my knee down on her stomach, keeping her still as I choked the life out of her.

"Ainsley trusted you, Nova, and you repaid her by blabbing your big fucking mouth and sentencing her to die."

Just the thought turned my stomach. Ainsley would still be safe and sound had Nova shut the fuck up. My little sister would've told me of her pregnancy eventually, surely before she entered the second trimester. It would've been early enough for me to convince her to abort it, without every Bloody Scorpion in Kansas City wanting her dead.

Would I have been happy? Fuck, no. Would this rift between me and her exist? Also, no. Once my anger cleared, I would've apologized for whatever ugly words I'd spewed.

"And let's not forget," I continued, a cruel smirk spreading across my face as her movements weakened. "This was after you punched her for whatever goddamn reason. I don't know why, because unlike you, Ainsley is loyal. She never told me what the hell went down to lead to you laying hands on her."

After Ainsley's revelation, I suspected it had something to do with Louisiana. I could use this time to confirm my theory and find out how long Nova had been pitching pussy to a Royal Bastard. But I wasn't interested. I didn't care since I wouldn't do anything with the information. I certainly wouldn't tell Boom Boom or any of those motherfuckers in my club. They'd tried to kill Ainsley. I'd never forgive them. I felt no fucking allegiance to those assholes any longer. If Bash wasn't a psycho woman killer, I'd prefer to throw in my lot with him. As it stood, I didn't belong anywhere any longer.

"Roman." Nova sounded pitiful. She'd perfected her manipulation tactics. "I'm s-sorry."

"No, you aren't, so don't fucking lie when you're just moments from facing Judgment." No matter what she said, she wouldn't be leaving this motel room alive. "If Boom Boom was a motherfucker to you, you should've come to me for help. You didn't have to betray Ainsley."

"I had no choice!"

"Not at the club," I agreed. "While we were on the road, you voluntarily called Boom Boom and revealed Ainsley's pregnancy."

An idea came to me, one that had me stepping away from the bed and releasing her.

She scrambled back, rubbing her neck as she looked at me with wide, terrified eyes. The tears streaming down her face didn't move me.

"I'm sorry," she whimpered, her voice hoarse. "I'm sorry, I-I didn't mean—"

"You never mean to do shit, Nova. Ever since you were a little girl, you'd get into all sorts of trouble and fuck over people and then be too much of a pussy to own what you did."

A coward was one of the worst things in the world, right up there with snitches, badges, and abusers.

"I'm feeling generous tonight," I continued, her sniffles grating on my nerves. "You have five seconds to leave the room. If you survive, keep your fucking mouth shut."

With that, I began to count. She tripped over herself exiting the bed, scooping up a white robe I hadn't noticed before. It was covering her body by the time I reached three, and she made it to the door by the time I reached five.

But it wasn't open, disqualifying her from living.

I tsked; she sobbed, fumbling with the bolt lock as I dug into my pocket. My blade was in my hand by the time she unlocked it, and lodged between her shoulders before she could open it.

A sharp cry left her throat, and she collapsed onto the carpet floor.

"Shit," I murmured, walking to where she lay and pulling the blade from her back.

She barely twitched.

I'd meant to hit the back of her neck, but I still had yet to perfect throwing with my new hands. The fact that the knife had sunk into her flesh was a miracle, so I suppose I couldn't complain too much.

She'd bleed out if I left her now, but I was never one to leave a job unfinished. So, I corrected my mistake and drove the knife into the side of her neck, ensuring Nova Wren was among the dead, so I could scratch her name off my list.

Chapter Twenty-Eight

Ainsley

If anything good came of days in the cabin with Jinx, it was solidifying our friendship. We talked, laughed, and cried together. She helped me through some of my darkest days of missing Reese and mourning Roman, and I listened to her grief over Louisiana's betrayal. I sensed she still loved him, but she couldn't trust him, so she didn't see any way forward for them. On the other hand, she gave me hope that perhaps Reese would put things into perspective while on his run and finally admit he had real feelings for me.

A week before Thanksgiving, our errand guy came early in the morning with news that the guys were back. Jinx was wanted at the clubhouse and Ma Siller awaited me.

Jinx had been so good to me; it was my turn to return the favor. We'd been planning for this announcement for three days, ever since Tyson and Fox re-installed the antennae and signal booster. We figured the guys would return soon and Louisiana expected Jinx to have changed her mind.

"Chi Chi, we weren't expecting to go back today," I said, exchanging a glance with Jinx and smiling at the prospect. "We had a spa day planned."

He was a skinny guy with huge gauges in his ears and piercings covering his face. Tattoos decorated his arms, neck, hands, and fingers. I was quite sure he had a crush on Jinx.

"But Reese and Louisiana—"

"It would make me so happy, love," Jinx said with a little pout.

Blushing, he took in her pink hair, touched upon her face, and studied her lips.

She twirled her hair around a finger. "Send Tyson and Fox away, then you and I can go pick up some supplies for Ainsley and me. Oh fuck. Never mind. That means you'll be the only guy here stuck with us."

"You all didn't know they were coming home today," he said quickly. "You've got the right man for the job. I have two sisters, so I know how girls like to pretty themselves up. Leave it to me—"

"I don't want to be alone in this cabin," I inserted. "Once Tyson and Fox leave, let Jinx go pick up what we need, while you stay with me."

"Uh—"

"Ainsley's a good friend of mine," Jinx said. "Like a sister. If you get them away from us and stay here with her, I promise I won't be long."

"*Ainsley* will be more protected at the cabin than you will be on your own going from place to place. Shit's about to hit the fucking fan because my cousin told me a little while ago that Nova Wren's body was found a few days ago."

Gasping, I stumbled back as if I'd been shot. Even Jinx paled, but Chi Chi kept on talking.

"Those Bloody Scorpion fuckers are blaming us. That cunt wasn't even on our radar right now. Why the fuck would we want her dead?"

My head was buzzing and it felt as if a piece of my chest had been ripped away. Nova had proven herself not to be a true friend, but that didn't stop grief from overwhelming me for the person I *thought* she'd been.

Jinx folded her arms. "I thought you were supposed to take different routes every day so no one would follow you?"

Even in my shock and misery, unease slid into me. Reese promised we'd be safe because two of the guys wouldn't leave and one would take different routes every day to check on the four of us and deliver supplies. Chi Chi apparently hadn't listened.

Unconcerned at the risk, he shrugged. "His old man's gas station is a rinky dink old place that belongs in another era, but we go there to help the family keep it going since it's so important to JT." He smiled. "Sometimes, I even get your stuff from there if it isn't too much. It isn't too far from the club, so there's no danger. Bean heads over to the gas station after his overnight gate duty shift. I stop in on my way here every morning. I have to go back, though, because the news threw me off and I forgot gas."

"You can get gas somewhere else," Jinx said firmly.

Chi Chi shook his head. "Nope. I can hang out a little longer with Bean. JT might still be there, too. Old man's a funny motherfucker. Anyway, we need to hit the road so I can update Prez about that dead cunt, and he can let everybody else know what's going on. Bean told me to let them know ASAP, since he'd just found out from a chick that stops in sometimes. Apparently, she was a school friend of Nova's."

"Bean should've brought his ass back to the fucking club and told Razor," Jinx yelled.

"Bean thinks Razor likes me more than him and he'll receive the news better from me." Chi Chi threw his hands up in the air and blew out a frustrated breath. "Chances are another motherfucker told them that bitch got iced."

Unable to take it any longer, I staggered to the sofa and sat, doubling over and bursting into tears.

"Asshole," Jinx hissed. She stomped toward me, sat down, and hugged me. "I didn't like that bitch, but I know she was your friend. I'm so sorry, Ainsley."

"We grew up together," I sobbed. "I was done with her. She'd changed so much. I didn't want her dead, though."

Chi Chi's eyes widened and he scrubbed a hand over his face. "Uh, wait. Your Nova is *that* Nova?"

"If you mean the daughter of the Bloody Scorpion's president," I said sadly and wondering what rock he'd been under, "then yes. They are one and the same." Imagining what she must've suffered, the fear she'd probably experienced, made me cling to Jinx and ignore Chi Chi's gasp. "I'm sorry. I know...she's the reason you and Louisiana...I'm sorry," I rambled, devastated.

"It's okay, sweetheart."

"Now, they're blaming the Royal Bastards for something Boom Boom did." I told Jinx about what happened to Nova on her father's orders. "He sacrificed her to come after Reese and Louisiana."

Jinx froze.

"He probably would've blamed my death on the Bastards, too."

Pulling away from me, she took my face between her hands. "We have to go to the clubhouse, Ainsley. You have to tell Razor before Keir ends up dead. Not that I care," she added quickly. "I want to kill him myself. I'm more concerned about Reese."

I searched Jinx's face and saw her panic. I knew it was partly because her plans were going up in smoke, but mostly because of Reese and Louisiana's safety.

"We can stick to our plans," I whispered, swiping my cheeks. "I'll go."

She hugged me again. "You're the sister I never had. I'll find another way to escape," she said in the same tones. "Right now, we'll go together."

REESE

We ended up staying a week longer than expected because once we finished our work and went to Provo for the concert, Razor insisted we stay an extra few days to help out Zombie at their salvage yard, Outlaw Towing, which also served as their clubhouse. While we were there, Bolt replaced the sprockets on his bike and the chain adjusters. The trip ended up being an all around success, except for the fact that I couldn't talk to Ainsley. She stayed on my mind. After our last night together, I'd become a little obsessed with her.

Chi Chi gave me a daily update and it impressed me how she'd not only won the guys over but solidified her friendship with Jinx.

As soon as Jinx arrived, I planned to head to the Siller house and tell Ainsley I wanted us to move in together. Razor warned me not to interfere with whatever Louisiana had planned for Jinx, but I didn't think the asshole would win fucking points with her by kidnapping her and holding her hostage until she changed her mind, which was exactly what the fuck he planned to do.

Razor said it was their business. I called bullshit and wanted to save Louisiana from another monumental mistake with Jinx.

To pass the time until she arrived, I sat at the bar next to Louisiana, looking at apartment listings. We were road weary and a little dusty, but we needed to unwind from the exhilaration of our trip, so we were all hanging around.

"No! No! No!" Louisiana suddenly shouted, drawing my attention. Losing all his color, he jumped to his feet.

"What's the matter, Louisiana?" Warrior asked from where he sat at the table with Razor, Jester, and Bolt.

Louisiana's hands were trembling as he stared at his phone in horror. "No! This can't be true."

"What?" I demanded, truly intrigued now.

Marquis, Knight, and a couple of other guys gathered around us.

Louisiana raised his gaze to me, but I wasn't sure he actually saw me, so I snatched the phone from his hand

A photo of Nova greeted me, along with the caption that her body had been found five days ago. According to the short article, there were no suspects.

I wasn't sure what to make of Louisiana's reaction. He'd claimed not to have any real feelings for her, but then he seemed on the verge of losing his shit. Her death didn't matter to me. She'd fucked over Ainsley too many times. As far as I was concerned, she got what the fuck she deserved.

Razor walked over and snatched the phone from my hand. A look of momentary confusion dropped into his face, then he set the phone on the bar and stared at Louisiana.

Before anyone said anything else, the door opened and one of the prospects guided Jinx and Ainsley in. If not for the outrage rising in the room, I would've thought she was a figment of my imagination.

"Jinx, is this some kind of a fucking joke?" Razor demanded, glaring at Ainsley.

The roar tore Louisiana out of his shock and he hurried to Jinx, though his scowl to Ainsley raised my fucking hackles.

"I'm sure Ainsley talked Jinx into bringing her here to see Reese," Louisiana said.

I stalked to Ainsley's side and tucked her against me as Jinx shook her head.

"That isn't true, Keir," she said tightly, evading his hands when he tried to draw her to him. "Tell them—"

"What can she say?" Louisiana asked. "That she betrayed her friend and got her killed?"

Louisiana and I were brothers and my loyalty was to him and everybody in our club. *They* superseded all else, but I'd be goddamned if I allowed him to fuck over Ainsley, especially because of Nova.

"Let's take a walk, brother, so we can talk," I said coldly.

"Talk about what, Reese? I was hiding in Roman's closet when Ainsley came in the day Boom Boom beat her up because Nova punched her after Ainsley exposed my marital state."

Jinx choked, and all I could do was gape.

"Do you hear what the fuck you're saying?" I demanded.

"What? That I dropped Nova when fucking Boom Boom called me trying to figure out my identity after he found my fucking number on her phone? I didn't want her but I sure the fuck didn't want her dead."

"How the fuck is that Ainsley's fucking fault?" I snarled, fed up with motherfucking Louisiana and his saga of two women. One who all the brothers liked and agreed he'd been a jackass not to use any means possible for Jinx to never discover he'd fucked over her; and the other who needed a fucking bullet in her head because she abused Ainsley's trust.

"I didn't want her dead, either, Louisiana," Ainsley said quietly. She licked her lips and looked at Razor. He was a fearsome motherfucker, but she kept a respectful distance and spoke calmly. "I'm almost positive her father killed her. He wants a reason to come after...after..." She glanced from Louisiana to me and back to Razor. "I'm sure he killed Roman and..." Her voice broke, but she drew in a deep breath, swallowed and forged on. "Boom Boom wants me dead, too. Missile said otherwise, but he wouldn't like that I carried Reese's baby. He's going to make his brothers believe Nova and Roman's deaths are an egregious affront that has to be avenged."

Razor gave her a severe look. "Who introduced you to Reese? Was it Louisiana? Was it because he was fucking Nova and you were her friend?"

"What?" she whispered.

I tightened my hold on her.

"Answer here or in the pit," Razor growled.

A little tremble surged through her. I didn't want to give up my best friend either. If Razor was interrogating me, I'd find a way to save Louisiana, even if it was him who'd kicked off this latest round of bullshit by fucking Nova.

"I'm counting to three, then I'm snatching you from Reese," Razor warned.

I hated the panic on Jinx's face and the resignation on Louisiana's. They believed Ainsley would give him up to save herself. I merely wondered what the fuck was Razor's end game: branding Ainsley a traitor no matter how she responded or finally accepting her if she gave the right answers.

"We met at a Cajun restaurant. At the bar," Ainsley added. "I don't like sitting at a table alone, so I was going to have a daiquiri and my food at the bar. Reese...Reese was by himself, too. He, uh, he said his friend liked the place but he was a no-show."

"What is Nova Wren to him?" Razor pressed.

Pursing her lips, Ainsley rocked on her heels. "I wasn't aware Reese knew Nova."

In all fairness, he *could've* meant me, but we all knew he wanted information about Louisiana and Nova.

"Oh, I'm sure he did," Razor declared, glaring between Louisiana and me. "Those two stick together." He glowered at Ainsley. "So tell me just how deeply involved was my road captain with the daughter of my club's biggest enemy?"

Ainsley shifted her weight.

"Answer me."

He roared those words he seemed to be stuck on so fucking loud, we all fucking jumped.

"Prez, ease up on her," I said. "She's pregnant."

"Shut it, Reese," Razor ordered. "If I take her downstairs, you won't be around while I get my answers."

I glared at Louisiana, hoping he'd speak the fuck up and save Ainsley, but he turned his head. Fucking asshole.

"Now, talk, Ainsley," Razor said.

"I don't th-think Louisiana…" Ainsley swallowed and tried again. "He didn't have a relationship with Nova," she whispered.

Razor gave her a nasty smile and my fucking heart dropped. "I don't believe you. He just freaked the fuck out over her death."

Louisiana drew in a deep breath and Jinx's face crumpled.

"I've heard bits and pieces about the war and the rivalry," Ainsley started. "I know the Bloody Scorpions shadow the Royal Bastards and pop up in the same cities your club has claimed territory in. And I know there's been a lot of death on both sides. My parents included. If Louisiana was with Nova, it wasn't because he wanted her. We had a conversation when he brought Roman to me and I've thought about it. I think Nova was a means to an end."

"If that's the case, why is he so fucking upset over her death?" Razor asked. "You want to psychoanalyze? Do that one. But you standing there lying isn't helping his case or *your* case. I was suspicious of Reese, when it should've been this motherfucker." He pointed to Louisiana. "That baby's in your belly because of him. That bitch is dead because of him."

"First? *Ew.*" Laughter rose up at Ainsley's dramatic shiver. Even Razor smiled. "*Reese* is the reason I'm pregnant. Not Louisiana. Perish that fucking thought. Second, Nova's death..." Sadness pulled her features down. "If Roman was still alive, I'd think he killed her. She's the one who outed my pregnancy to her father and marked me for death. Roman wouldn't have taken kindly to that. It wouldn't have mattered what I said, she would've been dead."

Razor folded his arms. "Killing his president's daughter would've been a death sentence for him."

"Do you really think he would've cared about that?" Ainsley responded. "They tried to kill me. Roman would've seen that as the ultimate betrayal."

"Look me in the fucking eye and tell me Louisiana didn't have anything to do with you meeting Reese," Razor demanded. "Tell me he wasn't fucking your best friend. Repeat what you said to me about meeting Reese at a fucking bar." He locked gazes with her. "Don't drop your fucking gaze. Don't flinch. Don't stutter. Just tell me the fucking truth."

"The truth?" She looked at Louisiana, then me before raising her gaze to Razor again. "The truth is Louisiana loves his club and he's loyal to his patch. The truth is he ended up caring about Nova but always put his wife first. It's why he disappeared for days at a time and didn't want Nova calling him. The truth is he wanted Reese to stop grieving for Trinity and I swore I only wanted no-strings attached sex. The truth is Louisiana probably saw it as a grand joke that he set up his best friend to take the virginity of a Bloody Scorpion's sister. The truth is Roman turned down Nova's advances five months ago because he only saw her as my friend and another sister. It pissed her off, so she set me up. The truth is *I* was blindly trusting and very naïve and should've been honest with Reese."

"Why weren't you?" Razor said, though he'd lost some of his edge.

"Because I trusted Nova and Louisiana, and I thought they were right that Reese was perfect for my first time. But it was simply because I was attracted to him. He captivated me within minutes of meeting him."

Razor looked at me. "You can move her to your room for now. Get shit sorted."

"Thanks, Prez."

"I can stay with Reese?" Ainsley breathed, not giving Razor a chance to answer before she launched herself against him, stood on tiptoe, kissed his cheek, and hugged him. "Thank you."

Razor grunted. "Louisiana, do what you have to with Jinx, then report to the pit. I'm beating the fuck out of you."

Louisiana nodded, lifted Jinx into his arms, and started carrying her away, ignoring her curses and struggles.

All my happiness fled.

"Where's he taking her?" Ainsley demanded.

"It's not our concern," I said in warning. Better me than Razor. I understood Ainsley's outrage, I was feeling a good dose of it too, but she was my main concern, which meant she couldn't interfere with Jinx and Louisiana any more than I could. "Let me show you upstairs—"

"Jinx didn't come here to be manhandled," she cried.

"It's between Jinx and Louisiana," I said flatly. "I'm going to have Chi Chi take you back to Ma for right now. I'll pick you up later."

She gave me an incredulous look that I ignored. She'd just gotten on Razor's good side. It was so new, he'd revoke his good will at one little misstep. Certainly, she knew better than to interfere in any club business, especially between a brother and his ol' lady.

She scowled at me, turned on her heel, and stomped away.

CHAPTER TWENTY-NINE

ROMAN

As an enforcer, there were times when I couldn't just shoot, stab, strangle, or kick a motherfucker to death. Hits were always so easy, especially when Boom Boom ordered me to make the problem go away without bringing heat to us. If we were trying to make a point—mainly with the Royal Bastards—I had to get creative and invent ways to kill fuckheads.

In the case of those motherfuckers who'd fucked with Ainsley—also known as my brothers—it helped that I'd known most of them for years. For instance, every weekend, Vector went to his ex's farm and helped her with the chores. According to him, she was a nut job with good pussy. He kept her at arm's length and fucked her in exchange for his 'help'. On Saturdays, Vector rode the entire property, searching for issues, and then he'd spend Sundays correcting whatever problem he found. More than once, I'd helped him.

How'd he repay my generosity? Leaving me with a psycho in Salt Lake City and targeting my little sister by helping Kite and Wizard with their plans, which was proven to me when Bash brought messages he'd gotten after Easton DeLuca hacked their phones.

I rode solo when I killed Nova, but this time, DeLuca helped me. We camped out on the far edge of the property. Around noon, Vector rode into view on an ornery horse not too fond of people. He always swore he had an understanding with the beast.

I waited until Vector guided the horse to a patch of uneven ground, dotted with old concrete that should've been removed years ago. It remained. Grass grew around it, creating an even more perilous situation.

At my nod, DeLuca fired the shotgun we'd brought just for this purpose. The horse reared, but Vector surprised me by not falling off. Just when I thought we'd have to fucking shoot him and possibly blow my cover, the horse bucked, and Vector tipped over. His boot caught in the stirrup.

"Now," I whispered to Easton, pointing my chin at the flailing fucker.

DeLuca fired again, sending the horse into a frenzy that Vector had no hope of surviving. When his shouts abruptly stopped, we walked to where the pickup was parked underneath a tree, half a mile away.

Bones was next on my list. The lazy fuck liked stinging insects, despite being allergic. Stupid fucking move that I teased him about when we were cool. Now, it provided me with an opportunity to snuff out his life.

Tio and Easton didn't like my idea of leaving a big jar of yellow jackets on Bones's doorstep, then shooting it to release them once he came outside. *I* didn't want Boom Boom to know I was back. Once Nova turned up dead from stab wounds, if I killed Vector and Bones the same way, he'd know they were taken out. He might not suspect me but a rival club, one in particular. Since Ainsley was connected with those fucking Royal Bastards, I didn't want to endanger her any more than she already was.

"And who the fuck will be collecting the damn bugs?" Tio hissed, in a shitty mood from whatever Bash had told him.

He took daily calls from his father. Not only to give his old man updates, but to hear about London. She'd been left behind at the American Scorpions' clubhouse, since bringing her on our killing spree would've been a hindrance.

DeLuca snickered. "Don't tell me you're scared of bugs?"

"You must be too, asshole, because you're sure as hell against it," Tio rebutted.

DeLuca shrugged. "Because it's a stupid ass Looney Tunes' death."

I glared at both brothers. They shat on my plan, without presenting a discreet, alternative method.

"It's a creative way to take out a damn target, you scary little bitches," I growled, more than willing to go solo. "If you two are too pussy to help me, I'll do it on my own."

Tio scowled. "Is that supposed to be a threat? Because I don't give a fuck what you do. Go ahead, get yourself killed because you're too fucking hardheaded."

Unsurprisingly, Easton spoke up for me. Of the two, he was far more agreeable and locked in an endless rivalry with his younger brother.

"Bash told us to give you whatever help you fucking need, Roman, so we'll do it your way," DeLuca said before I could reply to Tio. "You just better know what you're doing."

His wary look made me snicker. "You underestimate me, motherfucker."

With Easton finally on my side, the plan went off perfectly. As far as anyone would know, Bones had brought a jar of yellow jackets home and then dropped it, causing it to break and the notoriously aggressive insects to attack. Once the wasps fucked off, we retrieved the bullets used to shatter the jar and went on our merry way.

Next on my list was motherfucking fuckhead *Kite*. Then, before I moved onto the clubhouse and Boom Boom, I'd get Wizard. They would have personal treatment.

Five days after Nova's death and two days after Vector's, I tossed aside the newspaper with the article about her and went after Kite bright and early. His house was laughably easy to break into. The lock on his front door was fucked up, his windows weren't secured, and he had no security system. Motherfucker must've thought living in the middle of nowhere made him safe. If he wanted seclusion to be enough, then he shouldn't have crossed me.

I slipped in through the backdoor—which also had a fucked up lock—and crept to the hallway leading to his bedroom. His ol' lady left him a decade ago, taking their brood of children with her. Kite bounced between his aging two-story home and his room at the clubhouse. Luckily, tonight, he was in his room, letting a slut that looked eerily like Ainsley ride his cock.

It pissed me off.

I moved quickly, yanking the girl off Kite and tossing her aside. I tried to avoid handling women so roughly, but the bitch was in my way. She screamed, and Kite's eyes flew open.

"What the fuck?" he screeched, scrambling to pull up the covers to conceal his wrinkled cock, as if I hadn't seen his balls a dozen times before. His eyes went wide as he realized my identity. "R-Roman. You're alive—"

"Yep," I replied simply, then used my hook to slit his throat.

His hands flew to his neck, trying in vain to staunch the blood flow. He gurgled as blood overflowed from his mouth. A minute later, he was slumped over and dead.

With that taken care of, I turned my attention to the girl. She was curled up in a ball and crying, shaking like a fucking leaf. Sighing, I wiped my bloody hook on Kite's sheets, then used my prosthetic hand to beckon her to her feet. She stood in an instant, covering her chest with her arms. The longer I studied at her, the younger she looked, and the more her resemblance to Ainsley became clear.

It made me regret killing the perverted asswipe so quickly.

"What's your name?" I asked her, retrieving the dress on the edge of the bed and holding it out to her.

She took it immediately, wiggling into the garment. "Cyndie," she whispered, looking at me as if I'd attack her at any moment.

Which, was a reasonable fear, considering I just killed a motherfucker in front of her.

"That Volkswagen Beetle parked out front, is it yours?"

A single nod was my reply.

"Well, Cyndie, I'm feeling nice tonight. Hop in your car, get the fuck away from here, and don't tell anyone what you saw."

Niceness wasn't the only reason I was letting her go, but also just how much she reminded me of my little sister.

"Oh, and look in the bottom left drawer of his dresser, sweetheart," I instructed, recalling that Kite kept cold hard cash in his sock drawer.

He always relied on the club girls to clean his house, and more than once, I'd heard them gossip about the amount of money he kept in that particular drawer. *He* wouldn't have use for it anymore, and Cyndie needed an incentive to be quiet.

I cocked a brow when she didn't immediately comply. "Go on, open it."

Her bottom lip wobbled, and I'm sure she thought someway, somehow, I was setting her up. Still, she complied, gasping when she stumbled across the money. She looked back at me, completely bewildered.

"D-do you want me to hand it to you?"

I chuckled and shook my head. "Nope. It's yours."

Some of her fear faded. After a moment of hesitation, she took as many bands as she could.

"What's the catch?"

"Your silence, because taking that money means you're now an accomplice. Now run along, sweetheart, before I change my mind."

She didn't have to be told twice, taking the rest of her belongings, the money, and hurrying the fuck out of there.

A minute after she left, I exited the same way I entered. DeLuca was waiting with the getaway ride, while Tio had stayed behind at the motel. He'd been arguing on the phone, screaming at London, after Bash informed him of another escape attempt. Mentally, I applauded her guts but also worried about the consequences. Tio cared enough about her to not want her dead, but he wasn't above laying hands on her. Nor was Bash. His violence towards women was my biggest gripe with him.

Perhaps when I blew up the Bloody Scorpions, I'd add their names to my list. Immediately, I dashed the idea, knowing that it'd be a suicide mission. I might've had a few screws loose, but Bash and Tio were on another level.

"Took you long enough," Easton mumbled as I slid into the passenger seat.

I rolled my eyes as I buckled up. "I was gone less than ten minutes."

"Who was the girl?" he asked, changing topics.

"Some chick Kite was fucking. Paid her to keep her mouth shut."

He glanced at me, something like respect brewing in his gaze. "You don't kill women."

"Don't like harming those weaker than me," I replied, fishing my phone out of the cupholder.

There were some exceptions to that rule, almost always because of Ainsley. No one fucked with her without consequences.

DeLuca fell silent and turned up the music's volume, allowing Michael Jackson's vocals to echo through the vehicle. Surprisingly, Easton was a huge fan of the King of Pop. I didn't mind one bit, as his choice of music reminded me of my mother. She, too, was a Moonwalker.

Bobbing my head to the beat, I opened up the app that allowed me to peer into my home's camera. Ainsley hadn't returned since those fuckers had broken in. No one else had infringed on my space, but I was still glad that she was gone. It burned me up knowing she was under the protection of a Royal Bastard, the hatred of their organization ingrained in me, even as I worked on destroying the Bloody Scorpions.

And yet, I felt gratitude for Reese Sinclair, thankful that someone was looking out for Ainsley. As long as he kept her safe and provided for her, I'd accept him into our family once I made up with my little sister. I wanted what was best for her, and if that was Sinclair, I'd give my blessing.

Chapter Thirty

Ainsley

Chi Chi was waiting for me in the van. I don't think he ever got out, not that it mattered to me. I was too angry to care. After Jinx set aside her plans for Louisiana and I tried to save him on her behalf, he betrayed her.

A few minutes later, Chi Chi pulled into a little gas station with a small store and old pumps. "I still got to get gas, Ainsley," he reminded me. "Do you need anything? I'm getting myself a pop. Want one?"

"I'll have apple juice or orange juice. If they don't have that, I'll have milk."

He smiled. "Okay—"

A bullet to the head cut him off. His eyes rolled back and he fell against the door.

I screamed, intending to make a run for it, but Wizard opened the passenger side door, jammed the gun against my head, and snatched me out.

REESE

Instead of remaining on premises and interfering in shit I'd been warned away from, I waited until I was certain Chi Chi and Ainsley left before heading to my bike.

I hated feeling so fucking inept, which clung to me in the wake of Jinx's curses and her demands that Louisiana let her go. More than anything, I felt as if I'd let Ainsley down—*again*. Once the heat of the moment cooled, I digested Razor warming to Ainsley and set aside my relief. She took it as a kindness, but I knew his gesture wasn't as heartwarming as he made it seem.

I'd bet all my fucking money not only had he known about Nova's death, but he'd suspected Louisiana was fucking around with her. He'd tested Ainsley's loyalty to me, *us*. If she gave any of us up to save herself, I could only imagine how that would've turned out.

Fuck, I didn't want to imagine.

Heading to Ma Siller's, my plan to ask Ainsley to come with me to tour a couple of apartments I'd chosen played in my mind. She'd probably have a ton of questions, especially about the status of our relationship, so I worked out the conversation as *I'd* make it go.

It might be hard because Ainsley was so stubborn, but I just wouldn't respond to anything that took us off-topic.

"Reese, I know you don't love me. However, we're having a baby together, and I'm so attached to you that, of course, I'll move in with you."

She didn't really have to say the words, but she would. How many times had she said how much she liked me? Every time I wanted to make love to her, she gave in. *And* her response to Razor when he said she could stay at the club told me everything I needed to know.

However, Ainsley resisted me at every fucking turn. Fuck if I didn't enjoy matching wits with her, but I intended to have my way this time.

"Ainsley, babe. What's love anyway? You and I have a connection, something special. I

feel it as much as you do. We should live together. One, you'll need someone to rub your back once you get further into your pregnancy. Two, you'll be able to fuck me any time you want. I've heard pregnancy amps up a woman's sex drive."

Information courtesy of Louisiana, and something I never thought I'd need to know.

"But, Reese, I just love you so much. We share more than sex. I want to have your name. I want our son to have your name. Let's get married."

My heart skips a beat, and tender satisfaction wells inside me. "You're having a boy?"

Her whiskey-colored eyes are soft and sweet as she looks at me. "Dr. Purdue hasn't confirmed it, but what else could your seed make, Reese?"

I puff out my chest.

"What do you say?" She smiles in adoration and drops to one knee.

Ainsley and her 21st-century values would make her jump the gun and forget that I was the one who proposed.

She grabs my hands. "Reese Sinclair, will you do me the honor of becoming my husband?"

"Oh, sweetheart. You do me the greatest honor, but marriage is just a piece of paper. I know this crushes you. However, I can't marry

you. If that ever changes, I'm the one who'll propose."

Her eyes are huge and vulnerable. "I love you so much, Reese. You're like the stars and the moon combined, shining brightly in my life."

"I know, babe. I know." I drop to my knees and pull her into my embrace. "Always remember, I got you. We don't need marriage. We're moving in together and we'll live happily-ever-after. You'll do as I instruct and know that I always have your best interests in mind."

She kisses the bridge of my shoulder tenderly and nods. "Yes, Reese. Whatever you want, I'll do."

Okay, so maybe the conversation wouldn't go *exactly* like that, but a guy could dream.

Somehow, I made it to Ma Siller's place without wiping the fuck out. When I saw the pickup in her driveway, I scowled. I wasn't up to socializing today, which she'd expect me to do until her guests left. But the Utah plates suggested they might be here for a couple of days.

Fuck. I almost called Ainsley and told her to come outside so we could grab a bite to eat. Ma wouldn't question that.

However, as I bounded up the steps, a motherfucker that looked uncannily like Channing Tatum and wearing an unfamiliar cut walked out of the house and onto the porch, stopping inches from me.

"Roman sent me out to make sure you're unarmed."

I stiffened, and my hand immediately went to my gun.

"This is about Ainsley," the motherfucker said quickly, raising his hands. "You didn't get the messages?"

Ma Siller rushed out, tears in her eyes. "Bean called right before Easton—" she nodded to the motherfucker, "Tio and Roman showed up."

Bean was a prospect who was Ma's cousin so many times removed that I didn't think they were really related. She did, and that was all that mattered. His father owned an old gas station that the club frequented to help him out.

"JT's dead," she sobbed. "B-Bean went to relieve his father after he finished his gate duty." Tears fell fast and furiously. "He went to the bathroom and...and..."

Roman Mac walked out of the house, followed by a tan motherfucker I didn't know— Tio, I presumed. He wasn't my concern, though. *Mac* was. He should've been a fucking ghost. He was *supposed* to be bug food, but there he was, recovered and as lethal as ever, judging by his leather duster, a prosthetic hook he wore in place of one hand, and a mechanical hand for the other.

He was once again a threat. I should've shot him on that principle, but his eyes were tormented. When he looked at me, it wasn't the stare of a man examining an enemy, but one in need of help.

This wasn't some sort of ploy or revenge plot, which let me know something was very, very wrong.

"I've been tracking Wizard," he said hoarsely. "But I got there five minutes too late. Bean hid around the side of the building and saw that motherfucker come out of the store, shoot one of your guys in the fucking head and take my sister. I couldn't fucking save her."

The pain in his voice reflected my own. The only time I felt such anguish was during the immediate aftermath of my family's death. Then, I'd been a grieving child, alone in the world and terrified of what the future held for me. I was an adult now, who'd been too cowardly to man up and stand by the side of the woman who carried my child, a woman I'd grown to care for deeply.

I might never get the chance to correct my mistake, and the crushing regret added to my torment.

"No," I croaked, my head filled with horrific images of what she might go through at those fuckers' hands.

They'd make her suffer before they killed her, that I was sure of. The Royal Bastards showed no mercy to enemies, and we were even more ruthless with those who betrayed us. Razor didn't allow rapists among our ranks, but everything I knew of the Scorpions told me they didn't have such rules. Violating someone so intimately was a surefire way to break them.

Combined with the beatings and torture they would inflict, the Ainsley I knew and cherished could forever be gone, even if we saved her. Mental scars were harder to heal than physical ones, and her brutal treatment might render her a shell of herself.

But, fuck, at least she'd be alive in that scenario.

"Where'd they take her?" I pushed out, trembling from the rage and fear coursing through me.

Ainsley's only crime was expressing her autonomy and allowing me entry into her bed. She'd been too naïve to grasp what a grave offense that was to the Bloody Scorpions, one she might pay for with her life.

"If we knew that, why the fuck would we come here?" Tio asked, his bored tone pissing me off.

"Tio, shut the fuck up," Easton ordered, looking between Roman and me. "One motherfucker can't take on an entire club."

Fucking try me. I didn't care who or how many I had to kill to save Ainsley.

"Even if I stand with Roman, *two* aren't a match against those fuckheads either," Easton continued.

"That's why I'm here," Roman said, the dejection in his tone nothing like the man I knew. "I had a fucking plan to avenge Ainsley and punish the assholes who harmed her. Can't do that with her gone. I don't know where she is, and I can't get her back on my own."

"You won't," I vowed, my dislike of him lessening.

He wanted to save Ainsley, and right now, that was the only thing I gave a damn about.

CHAPTER THIRTY-ONE

REESE

Ainsley had been missing for two fucking days. In that time, I hadn't eaten and had barely slept. Once Easton called the president of the American Scorpions and Bash explained the situation, Razor, Jester, and Warrior eased up and allowed Roman Mac on our property. They made him remove that fucking hook but let him keep one of his prosthetic hands because he still couldn't shoot a gun.

We were all up in arms over JT and Chi Chi's deaths, and Ainsley's kidnapping. Louisiana divided his time between the main room and wherever the fuck he was holding Jinx.

Easton and Bash contributed to our planning. Roman sat at a corner table, alone. Not speaking. I didn't think he'd eaten anything either. I damn sure knew he hadn't slept. None of us knew what the fuck was going on in his head. It wasn't good. I knew *that*. I understood, too. If Ainsley was alive, they were probably torturing her. I would give my own life if it meant saving her.

All the times I could've gotten off my fucking ass, I'd ignored her. Ignored my own feelings. Now that she might be gone, I admitted to myself how much she meant to me. I'd lusted after her at first, then I'd spent time getting to know her, sleeping next to her, having her in my arms, and I loved everything about her.

I loved *her*.

I just prayed I'd get the chance to prove to her how much.

"*Roman!*" Bash's voice cut through my pain. "Come to this phone motherfucker."

"I can hear perfectly well from where I'm at, so talk," Roman said flatly.

Easton sat his phone on Roman's table.

"I'm not there to shoot your ass off for your disrespect, but my boys are, so I suggest you tone it the fuck down."

"Let them shoot me and put me out of my goddamn misery," he growled. "I've failed Ainsley."

"Nope, but you *are* failing her with your pathetic whining," Bash snapped.

My snicker joined my brothers' and Easton's. Roman glared at the phone.

"I hope I didn't waste my money on a pussy."

I looked at Roman, wondering if those words would get a reaction. He gripped the table and gritted, "What do you want?"

"You've done an admirable job of crossing names off your kill list," Bash said, sounding as proud as any father.

I merely exchanged glances with Razor, Bolt, and Louisiana.

"But the job isn't finished. Remember? If she's dead, Boom Boom still needs to die."

Roman scrubbed a hand over his face. I swore his eyes watered. *I* barely heard anything past *if she's dead*, and I'd only known her for a short amount of time.

"If she's alive, you can make up with her," Bash continued. "Boom Boom was on your fucking list too, so you'll hit the jackpot. To complete your kill list, fuckhead, get your head out of your fucking ass."

"Really?" Roman pounded his fist on the table. "Your sister is safe and sound. Mine is..." He drew in a deep breath. "The last time I talked to her, I was a supreme motherfucker to her." He glared at me, the first time he'd engaged with me since we arrived.

"In the eight days you've been home, how many motherfuckers have you killed, Roman?" Bash asked.

"Nova, Vector, Bones, and Kite."

Fuck, that motherfucker moved fast.

Shifting, Louisiana stared at Roman. If he saw, he didn't react.

"I didn't ask for names. I asked for a number."

"Count them," Roman said flatly. "That's quite fucking easy."

Bash growled. "You're working on my fucking nerves, asshole."

"It doesn't fucking matter, Bash. I spent my fucking life protecting her only to fail her and…" He pressed his lips together and shook his head. "I'm going to the clubhouse and kill Boom Boom. I don't give a fuck anymore."

"If you walk out that fucking clubhouse where you're at right now, Easton is shooting you," Bash barked. "Then he's bringing all those prosthetics to me so I can get a fucking refund."

I lifted a brow at the phone. Roman shrugged and gave me a small smile.

"That's not how that works," he said, "but whatever."

"I'm asking you *one more fucking time*, what will you do about Boom Boom?"

"I've just fucking told you," Roman said.

"No, you just said you were committing suicide. Nothing else."

"I'm not blowing up the clubhouse," Roman announced.

I think everyone stopped breathing. I sure the fuck did because that motherfucker was certifiable. He'd intended to blow up his own brothers?

"So you rode from Utah to Kansas with motherfucking explosives for no goddamn reason?" Bash demanded.

"Ainsley might be in the clubhouse, Bash," Roman said in a voice so filled with pain, I turned away, finally getting what he meant. Blinking, he glanced at the ceiling. "I want to get her back. Give her a proper burial."

A buzzing started in my head, and it felt as if my muscles atrophied.

"Roman, I respected you because you're a good big brother," Bash said, unmoved by Roman's revelations. "You're still her fucking brother. Get your fucking ass to that clubhouse. Not for a suicide mission, but to stick to the fucking plan we crafted before you left Utah. Tio's already in position. When you get inside, Easton will talk to the two fuckheads patrolling the place. Tio will pick off fuckhead on gate duty. Easton will take care of the other two."

"That's where we come in," Razor said. "Some of our Wichita guys are coming up. That's the last component we're waiting for before we ride. They should be here in the next twenty minutes. While Reese searches for Ainsley, Roman Mac can take care of Boom Boom. If Roman gets fucked up—" He shrugged.

More than likely, he would. The Bloody Scorpions wouldn't go down without a fight.

Whoever killed their leader might meet a brutal end if they weren't careful.

A silent battle raged within me. I wanted to find Ainsley myself *and* take out that motherfucker.

"Now, I have another question, Roman," Bash said.

"You're just full of them," Roman sneered.

"That I am. Did you fuck London?" he demanded without missing a beat.

Who the fuck was London and why the fuck was that important?

"No."

Roman's one word came out in a hard tone that should've been hard to dispute.

"I think you did," Bash said, proving me wrong. "For the record, I don't give a fuck. If my son wasn't so into her, I would've taken her pussy, too."

The distaste on Easton's face registered and I got the feeling Bash meant he'd take it, even if she wasn't willing to give it. Roman's anger backed up my theory.

"But she's Tio's cunt, which means her pussy's off-limits to anyone but him. Am I fucking clear, Roman?"

"I didn't sleep with her," Roman growled, glaring at the phone. If possible, he looked a little more unhinged. "We're friends, Bash. I don't knowingly fuck another man's woman." He scowled between Louisiana and me. "And I especially don't force myself on a woman, fuckhead."

My eyes widened. It didn't matter if I didn't care for Bash. He was a fucking president, and Roman was not only disrespecting him but calling him out in front of strangers.

"You know, Roman, you're showing yourself to be amazingly ungrateful," Bash said with a long-suffering sigh.

"So sorry," Roman said with sarcasm. "Every time I think I like you, I remember what a misogynist you are."

"You're a stupid motherfucker if you like me at any time," Bash said flatly. "Did you think I was blowing smoke up your ass when I said I fucking hate women?"

My skin prickled.

"You do know your sister is a woman?"

Ice cubes clanked against a glass. "What a brilliant fuckhead you are to let me know a bitch with a pussy who shot out of my father's nuts like me is my sister. Thanks. I'll make sure to tell Celia this stunning development the next time I see her."

Roman growled. Fuck, I didn't blame him. I wanted to bang my head against a fucking wall. This conversation wasted precious time. Every second counted as long as Ainsley was missing.

"Now, back to sweet London," Bash said.

Distaste swept over Roman's face. "She's my physical therapist, Bash. I was hoping she'd continue working with me."

Bash laughed. "Since when, fuckhead? Just a few minutes ago, you were on a suicide mission."

Roman glowered at the phone.

"You do know she's here with me, right?" Bash goaded. "At my mercy. Meaning, if I think *you're* lying about fucking her, I'll take out my anger on *her*."

"Yeah, because she's a weak, defenseless woman," Roman snapped. "That makes you a coward. I doubt you could kill a man."

"Ahhh, this drink's delicious," Bash said, smacking his lips together. "Believe what you will, Roman. I don't like broads. It doesn't mean I won't shoot the fuck out of a motherfucker. Or cut his fucking head off. Didn't you like the skulls on the terrarium? From two fuckheads who double-crossed me."

This motherfucker continued shocking me. My eyes widened again and Roman gaped at the phone, then lifted his gaze to Easton, who gave a curt nod. If I had been in Razor's position, I wouldn't have ordered Easton to disconnect either. It was a fascinating glimpse into a man we'd long considered an enemy and a motherfucker who could be a worst motherfucker than Boom Boom ever hoped to be—all things considered.

"I hate to burst your bubble, Roman," Bash went on. "But this isn't a romance novel. One of my favorites, *Wills and Throttle* by Daria Monroe, is about an attorney who's married to a biker but falls in love with the president of an enemy club. Her husband's a fucking stupid dickhead, but she's still his. Fucking over him is a death sentence for her and the motherfucker she's cheating with. Get my fucking drift?"

"Reading romance novels are for pussies and bitches," Roman said, though amusement threaded through the words.

Bash snickered. "I'm not wasting my fucking breath defending my reading choices, fuckhead. You neither pay for them nor have to read them, so shut the fuck up."

"Touché." Roman leaned forward. "What can I do to protect London?"

"Oho, here we go," Bash chortled. "Finally, getting to the heart of the matter."

Easton pressed a button on his phone. "Offer to buy her," he ordered.

I choked.

"Excuse me?" Roman asked.

"You want her, buy her," Easton said flatly, then pressed his phone screen again, and I realized he'd muted the conversation.

"I'll give you fifty grand for her," Roman blurted.

"In addition to the rest of the money you owe me for my help?"

"Yes."

"And our other agreement?"

"Yes."

"I think you did fuck her," Bash said. "No man's paying that much for a cunt that's not giving him pussy."

"Tio doesn't want her, Bash," Easton said. "We both know that."

"I was hoping some of her goodness would rub off on your brother," Bash admitted, sighing. "I'd hate for that little motherfucker to end up like me, all alone and wishing he had a bitch to love him no matter what."

Roman shook his head in disbelief. "You're insane."

"Maybe, but who gives a fuck? Can't have a bitch who loves me if I don't like bitches," Bash said. "Since I like you so fucking much, Roman, this is my offer. I'll keep her safe until you get Ainsley back. Once that matter is taken care of and Ainsley is with you, dead or alive, you have a week to bring me two hundred fifty thousand dollars *plus* what you owe me—"

"You want a quarter of a million dollars for London?" Roman demanded, sounding as appalled as I felt.

"If you don't survive," Bash continued, ignoring Roman's question, "or if you take longer than seven days, I fuck her then return her to Tio."

"I don't have a quarter of a million dollars, Bash," Roman said. "But I can get you a supply of coke by tonight that'll last you for a week. It was our original deal. I can get you fifty grand when this is settled."

"I might slap her around anyway," Bash declared. "At the least, she sucked your cock and you won't make me believe otherwise."

"You said she could," Roman said. "Although she didn't. She never offered and I would've declined if she had."

Bash growled. "You're a fucking liar."

"She has a brother, Bash," Roman said in a patient tone, not addressing Bash's accusation. "He's five years older than her and she misses him but doesn't see him because he hates Tio and your kid threatened to kill him. She wants to protect her big brother."

"Are you shitting me?" Bash asked with suspicion.

I thought Roman was lying too, until he shook his head and raised the mechanical hand as if Bash could see. "I swear on my father's grave. She's someone little sister."

"And motherfucking Tio kept her away from her brother?" Bash demanded.

"He did," Roman said, lowering his hand.

"That little motherfucker. Fine. I accept your deal. Easton, call with an update as soon as you can," Bash ordered, and disconnected.

"You just got Tio's ass beat, Roman," Easton chided.

"London's miserable because she can't see her brother," Roman said flatly. "Fuck Tio. I'd just as soon break that fuckhead in two."

Easton sighed. "Not many people want smoke with my little brother."

Roman got to his feet, and some of the younger members shifted. Instead of going for their weapons to shoot an enemy down, unease wafted from them. Ainsley's brother was a tall man who could easily intimidate the inexperienced. He smiled viciously. "Not many people want smoke with me, Easton," he said in a deadly tone, and started off.

Louisiana planted himself in front of Roman, blocking him from walking outside.

Roman lifted a brow.

"You killed Nova," Louisiana accused.

And? She was a bitch to Ainsley and almost ruined his goddamn marriage. What did her fucking death matter?

"She hurt Ainsley," Roman said simply.

What more did he have to say? Those three words spoke volumes.

Louisiana stepped out of the way and Roman continued outside. I followed him. Ainsley adored that motherfucker. Talking to him might help me. Everyone else seemed so calm when all I wanted to do was leave.

Roman leaned against a post near the entrance. He glanced over his shoulder, then turned away again.

"What do you want, Sinclair?"

"Ainsley thought you were dead." Accusation laced my tone. "You could've clued her in. She was devastated."

"I thought it was better. I didn't want Boom Boom catching wind of me being alive."

"Were you really planning to blow up your own fucking clubhouse?"

"What's it to you? They're your enemies. Be fucking happy."

I stiffened. "You're my goddamn enemy as a Scorpion enforcer. You spend a lot of time at that fucking clubhouse from what Ainsley—"

"It's not my clubhouse," he interrupted on a growl. "Once I get Ainsley back, I will blow it up. Hopefully with whoever's still breathing after we're done."

"You're not one of us," I said sharply.

"Didn't ask to be, but Ainsley's *my* little sister. I get to say what happens to her once she's recovered."

"Bullshit!"

"You didn't marry her. That makes me her next of kin."

"Shut the fuck up, Roman. Ainsley sang your fucking praises about all that you taught her and you've just given up on her? Already concluded she's dead? Fuck you." I suddenly wanted to beat that fuckhead to the ground. "Fuck you," I shouted again. "If Ainsley were dead, I'd know. I'd feel it somehow."

"So, she wasn't just a piece of ass to you."

I growled.

He sidled a quick glance at me. "Trinity wasn't that for me. I cared about her. I thought she was pregnant by me."

"Ainsley told me," I gritted.

"For what it's worth, I don't make a habit of killing women. Trinity two-timed me and disrespected my sister, who, by the way begged for Trinity's life."

"I know the fucking story. What's your point, motherfucker?"

"Did you love her?"

"Did you?"

"I cared about her." Sighing, he finally faced me. "But relationships don't work out for me. I'm done with them. If I survive today, I'm freelancing."

"A gun for hire?"

He gave me a sardonic grin and lifted his bionic hand. "Haven't quite learned to shoot again. I've been wondering if I could find someone to make a prosthetic that fires bullets."

"You're crazy," I said around laughter.

"*Iron Man* vibes," he said. "One of Ainsley's favorite movies."

"I know," I said quietly. She'd told me during our overnight stay at the cabin. I hated that I didn't immediately catch the reference. "We discussed our favorite movies."

His look of approval surprised me. "Then you took time with her. Got to know her a little."

I suddenly felt sick, remembering how special I thought she was, how special she made me feel. I nodded, unable to do much more.

"Then she must've talked a lot." Roman laughed sadly. "Say one thing and she talked for hours."

Bowing my head, I blinked and smiled. I'd made a similar observation about her.

"Do you know why I keep talking about my little sister as if she's already gone?"

What little peace I felt while Roman discussed her abruptly fled. I didn't want to hear that he'd given up on her. Or anything that would confirm I'd never see her again or hear her laughter. Hold her in my arms or match wits with her.

"I'm trying to prepare myself, Reese. Psych myself up if she really is dead, but I've been afraid to move from the table, afraid I'd break my..." He shook his head and gave a short laugh. "My whatever. I've been trying to will her to fight. To stay alive. I want to hug her tightly and apologize to her. I want to tell her about the girl I met. If I still believed in love, I might..." His voice trailed off again. "It doesn't matter. London has enough problems without me adding to them."

"Ainsley's alive." She had to be. I couldn't imagine my world without her. "And when I rescue her, if you don't apologize, I'll cut off your fucking feet and cut out your tongue."

He smiled and clapped me on the back. "I'm going to hold you to that," he said and walked back into the clubhouse, leaving me alone.

Chapter Thirty-Two

Ainsley

I never considered all the creature comforts such as food, water, and a soft, warm bed that I enjoyed for as long as I remembered. They just were and I took them for granted. But when one languished in a cage in the trailer of a dead ex-friend those things tended to be missed.

Wizard threw me in the back of the van, shoved Chi Chi aside and drove us back to the Bloody Scorpions' property. I didn't want to consider what they'd done to Chi Chi's body. I'd liked him a lot. We'd gotten to be friends over the three weeks he delivered things to Jinx and me and checked on us daily even when he had nothing to bring.

Gradually, the images of Chi Chi's death faded into a haze of exhaustion. By the second day, the truth was inescapable. I wouldn't make it out alive. Nor would my baby. I'd never see Reese again or admit that I loved him.

I hoped Jinx got away from Louisiana. She deserved better than to have his will forced upon her when he'd fucked up so badly. Seeing my parents and my brother, and introducing my baby to them, was my only consolation. I hoped Roman forgave me in the afterlife.

The opening front door pulled me from my lethargy. I was thirsty, hungry, and achy. I couldn't even raise myself on my knees because the cage was too small, so I remained in a tight ball. Yesterday's vomit and pee were dried and a sour ammonia smell permeated the room.

The cage door clanged open. Rough hands grabbed my ankles and jerked me onto the floor. Nova had kept a very neat house. She'd liked cleanliness and pretty things. Now, she was gone and what she liked no longer mattered. The world wouldn't know how much I'd valued her and her friendship. Her death wouldn't matter in the big scheme of things.

Perhaps, death was good. I was so tired of losing the people I loved. I was still grieving my brother, wishing I could see him...

"Get up, Ainsley."

Asshole couldn't be serious. "I don't think I can, Wizard."

He kicked my back and I cried out in pain. "Stand up."

"Can't you just kill me?" I asked tiredly. "Abuse my body afterward."

"I won't be able to hear you scream my name."

"You're insane if you think I'll scream in pleasure while you assault me."

"Scream my name to beg me to put you out of your fucking misery," he corrected. "Wouldn't put my cock where a Bastard's been. I'm too good for that."

In his own miserable mind.

By now, Reese and the rest of the Royal Bastards must've realized I'd been taken. Chi Chi hadn't returned with the van. I'd hope they would storm the place on my behalf, but it was all a pipe dream.

I was the one who hadn't been living in reality.

"It's because of the fucking Bastards that Nova is dead," he spat, delivering a kick to my thigh and then starting to pace. "They're the reason my brothers are dropping like flies. They took your brother's hands, slut, and you were still fucking one of them. If Roman hadn't been made a cripple, he might still be fucking alive. And you're delusional enough to think I'd want to fuck a Bastard's whore? Bitch, please."

The callous way he talked about my brother's death made my heart ache. I was so thirsty, my throat hurt. I assumed dehydration was setting in, and yet, tears slid down my cheeks at confirming Roman had been betrayed by his own brothers, men who were supposed to protect him until the end.

"Is that why you killed my brother?" I rasped. "Because he was no longer useful to you? That's how you repaid his years of service?"

"As if you care, you two timing cunt," he barked, yanking me up by my hair. I whimpered at his rough handling and my scalp burned. "But for your information, we didn't kill him. We don't know what the hell happened to him. We left him in fucking Utah over a month ago, and he ain't shown up. That can only mean one thing."

His words should've dejected me further. Instead, they gave me a glimmer of hope. Time and again, Roman defied the odds. He had real-life plot armor, seeming to always escape the most perilous of situations. If no one knew what happened to him, he could still be alive. And if he were alive, assuming he had his freedom, he would've seen the video of Proctor, Missile, and Visor breaking into his house and tormenting me, acting against his wishes and Boom Boom's.

All the pieces fell into place.

It wasn't the Royal Bastards waging war against the Bloody Scorpions, or Boom Boom trying to reignite the feud. Roman was alive and well, and taking his revenge on anyone who'd wronged him, who'd wronged *me.*

My survival wasn't guaranteed. In fact, I'd likely die horrifically. But if Roman was killing people on my behalf, certainly, he didn't only feel hatred for me. Somewhere in the past few weeks, he must've found it in himself to forgive me, and that brought a smile to my face.

Wizard's slap quickly wiped away my grin, the backhand making spots dance in my vision and blood fill my mouth.

"The fuck you smiling for, bitch?" he roared, his rancid breath fanning over my face and fueling my nausea.

With my empty stomach, it was easy not to vomit. It was harder not to cower, but I wouldn't play into this fuckhead's wishes and show my fear.

"Roman isn't dead. He'll make you pay," I stated plainly, narrowly avoiding a kick to my stomach.

Roman wasn't dead. I let that sink into me. He'd want me to utilize the skills he'd taught me and try to escape.

For me and my baby to have a shot at life. For me and Roman to make up. For Reese and I to give our relationship a chance, to explore the complicated feelings between us. I wouldn't go out without a fight. In a them or me situation, Roman taught me to choose *me* and worry about guilt, fear, horror, or any other emotion later.

"Roman isn't dead, Wizard." Reese said I couldn't kill in cold-blood and that taking a man's life for the first time stayed with you. I didn't doubt that, which was why I hoped Wizard listened to reason. "If you help me, he'll remember that. He'll spare you."

Wizard chuckled with zero humor, shaking his head as he approached again. "You've always been a stupid bitch, living in your own world. Roman is dead. There's no one in this world who cares about you, so give the fuck up, Ainsley. Do yourself a favor and stop fighting."

Ha.

As if.

My response to his words was to grab his ankles, using all my strength to yank. He howled as he landed on his ass. By sheer will, I made it to my feet, wobbling to the gun that lay abandoned on Nova's kitchen island. Why Wizard would be dumb enough to remove his weapons, I didn't know, nor did I care. His stupidity gave me the shot I needed.

"I'll cut your fucking baby out, you stupid whore!" he snarled, his voice too close behind me for comfort.

I cried out as his fingers tangled in my curls, but not before my hand grasped his gun. Wizard was too enraged to notice, a mistake on his part. He threw me onto the floor and loomed over me. Intense dread washed over me at the menacing look in his eyes. Before he could strike, I aimed the gun and fired.

Depravation of food, water, and comfort meant I couldn't shoot as well as I typically could. My goal was to hit a vital location, and I did. Yet, instead of shooting his head, heart, or stomach, the bullet lodged in his scrotum. I'd never heard such a pained yowl. His hands clutched his injured crotch, tears streaming down his face as his legs gave out.

"Fucking hell!" he screeched, his shaky voice an octave higher.

I scrambled out of the way, not wanting to be pinned under him. He was losing blood quickly; hemorrhaging would finish him off if I didn't. But Roman had taught me to never leave an enemy breathing. With his advice in mind, I forced myself to put the gun to Wizard's head and pull the trigger, putting an end to his cries. The gunshots in the small trailer made my ears ring and my stomach heave at the blood and gore. Wizard stared sightlessly up.

The oppressive silence sank in, as did the knowledge that I'd killed a man. Dully, I realized Reese was right. This would haunt me.

My entire body trembled, my shaky hands making it difficult to hold the gun. A sob tore from my throat, and when I made the mistake of glancing at Wizard again—a man I'd known since I was a child—my stomach turned.

I'd *killed* someone, and because of me, blood and brain matter were all over the walls of my dead best friend's home.

The thought made me hunch over, the gun clattering to the floor as I dry heaved. My stomach was empty, but the stench of the room, the gore surrounding me, and the knowledge of what I'd just done made me retch for minutes. When I finally got control of myself, I grabbed the gun from the ground, though I hadn't stopped shaking, nor had my tears ceased.

Pocketing the weapon, I pinched myself, praying this was just a nightmare. My surroundings staying the same caused me to cry harder, and I jumped at the sudden yells in the distance.

Fear assaulted me, and I took the pistol back in my hands, whimpering as gunshots joined the ruckus. Shit was popping off outside, and as the noise drew nearer, I knew it wouldn't be long until I found out the source of the commotion. The gun was my only chance, but even still, I'd be outnumbered. One girl could only do so much with one gun, especially against several armed men.

I glanced at the cage and considered crawling inside to hide. My vomit and piss made me dismiss the idea. Instead, I hurried to Nova's bedroom. Her bed was low to the ground, but I could crawl under. It was a tight squeeze; however, after time in the cage, it was nothing.

My hiding spot wasn't the best, but it was better than being a sitting duck in the open. Now, the only thing I could do was formulate a better plan, and hope I made it out alive.

CHAPTER THIRTY-THREE

ROMAN

I never thought I'd be considering Ainsley's funeral.

Then again, I never thought my hands would be chopped off and replaced by prosthetics, that I'd turn against the club I'd grown up in, that a man I once idolized would become someone on the top of my kill list. Clearly, my life had changed a lot over the past several months. Ainsley was at the center of these changes because without her relationship with Sinclair, I'd be dead.

But because of it, she might be.

I'd long ago stopped believing in any God, but as I walked into the clubhouse of the Bloody Scorpions, I prayed we'd *rescue* Ainsley and not recover her body. However, I knew the chances of that were slim, and it tore me up inside that she died thinking I despised her.

Was I pissed at her? Like all hell.

Did I hate her? Impossible.

I nodded to those who greeted me, but in reality, I barely registered their words. If—*when*—Ainsley's body was brought to me, I'd give her a proper funeral. Not many people would show up, as most people we'd been close to were Bloody Scorpions. Yet, I'd still make sure I'd honor her life, before laying her to rest with our parents.

When that was done, I'd drink my sorrows away and drown in pussy. I'd pay for London's freedom, my last act of goodwill. Then I'd spend my final day riding on my bike and listening to my favorite songs, until I arrived somewhere peaceful and pretty, somewhere fitting as my final resting place. I'd drink that expensive bottle of liquor I'd been planning to gift Ainsley when she graduated from college—a little liquid courage—then shoot myself in the fucking head.

I'd be all alone in the world, and a world without my little sister wasn't one worth living in.

"You look well, boy," Boom Boom greeted as I approached his table. "Bash hooked you up good."

It took everything in me to return his smile. "Sure did."

If he realized how much effort it took for my civility, he didn't say anything. Instead, he looked at Easton, who was flanking me. Tio was somewhere nearby, up high with a sniper rifle, waiting to pick people off.

When he crossed that task off the list, he'd drive the van full of explosives onto club grounds.

"Your daddy told me he had a deal, Easton. Any clue what it is?" Boom Boom asked DeLuca.

Remaining silent, Easton shrugged in response.

"Ainsley," I said simply, getting to the heart of the matter. The sooner I brought her up, the sooner we'd get the show on the road. If I had to smile in his fucking ugly mug a moment longer than needed, I'd lose my shit and ruin everything. "Bash is offering monetary compensation in addition to a deal you will find very beneficial if you give her to me."

"All well and good," Boom Boom said after a moment. "*If* I had her."

Hate was too mild a fucking word for what I felt for Boom Boom. I despised him. I wanted to cleave him in fucking half and second line in his fucking blood. I wanted to twist his fucking head off and throw his corpse into fucking flames. Ainsley hated that scene in *Twilight*. Since she made me watch it with her over and over, I found something to look forward to.

That was one of the best fucking scenes ever when that tracker motherfucker met his demise.

I covered my face with my hands and heaved in a breath, my heart shattering as the reality hit me. Boom Boom had probably already dismembered her. My stomach heaved and I turned, not caring any more.

"What makes you think that cunt's here?" Boom Boom's voice broke through my devastation. "She probably went to Sinclair and he buried her. Like he did Nova."

My nostrils flared and I opened my mouth to spit in his fucking face and tell him I killed that bitch.

"I need to talk to some of your boys," Easton inserted, throwing me a look of warning, forever a discerning fuckhead.

Boom Boom's eyes flickered between us. "Which ones?"

"Motherfuckers on gate duty," Easton answered without missing a beat. "If you didn't know Ainsley is here, then someone betrayed you and took her without your knowledge. Bash wants her soon. He paid you well for her."

"He did," Boom Boom agreed and looked at my prosthetics. "Although he managed to get most of it back for Roman's care, I can see my money didn't go to waste."

He looked at me, and I nodded, knowing he expected allegiance and appreciation. I'd stomp his fucking corpse.

He rubbed his chin. "There's more money involved, Easton?"

"A lot more. More than you can imagine. In fact, Bash has an unexpected bonus thrown in. I just need to talk to the ones on gate duty," he repeated.

To my ears, DeLuca sounded like a phony motherfucker, one worthy of suspicion. But Boom Boom—a man I thought was so goddamn brilliant at one time—just nodded.

"All right, boy. Go do what you need to do. See if Ainsley's here and let me know what you discover."

Easton and I exchanged a look. Even as a kernel of hope unfurled in me, I wondered if he was setting us up, but as DeLuca left, nothing happened. I considered following behind him. Not to act as a bodyguard, but to kill those assholes myself. Some blood might get my head in the game. Yet, I knew that would also show our hand too early. To the knowledge of the Bloody Scorpions, I was still one of them.

"Sit down, boy," Boom Boom ordered, waving at an empty seat at his table. I obeyed, though sensation traveled down my arms, my nerve endings twitching to fuck him up. "How long do I have to deliver that cunt to him?"

I gritted my teeth, hating how he referred to my little sister.

"As soon as possible. Where is she?"

His expression grew steely. "I don't know what you mean, Roman. If she's here, it isn't by my doing."

The Bastards weren't far behind us. Once the gate was open, they'd flood the place, and the siege could begin.

"I know you took her, Prez." It took great restraint to keep my tone even, when all I wanted to do was cuss that motherfucker out as I gutted him. "I want to deliver her to Bash personally since he was so instrumental in fast-tracking my mobility. So, where is she?"

He studied me for a moment, examining my face, looking for any signs of deception. I wasn't sure if he liked what he saw, and I didn't give a damn. If I kicked the bucket now, as long as Easton, Tio, Reese, and everyone else did their jobs, Ainsley still had a chance.

"I've been reconsidering the sale," he announced, leaning back in his chair and taking a swig of his beer. "Might just send him a different bitch. Two, maybe, to apologize. He lost Nova too, so it's only fair."

My emotions went into a tailspin again and dipped to the lowest of the low. The smidgeon of hope disintegrated and I felt like weeping. Anger at my own thoughtlessness swirled in me.

Had women always been treated with such disregard at the club? Was I that fucking blind?

I wasn't the most progressive man, but I didn't harm a woman without cause. My father beat my ass if I showed any disrespect to my mother, who I loved dearly. And from the moment Ainsley was born, I adored her. When I became her guardian, I couldn't hang around the club as much, too focused on raising her and teaching her important life skills.

Because some of the other members helped me with getting Carol to safety, I believed that Boom Boom's abuse was the exception, a fluke that wouldn't happen again.

I'd been wrong, and if I had noticed it earlier, Ainsley might still be here.

"Bash paid for Ainsley. He doesn't like being double-crossed," I said, knowing fucking with that madman was a death sentence.

"Your whore of a sister got my baby girl killed, Roman," he growled, goading my temper. "Death is what she deserves."

Mercifully, the sounds of gunshots reached me. It had every member of the club on high alert. I mimicked those around me, looking around and standing, pretending to be as clueless as everybody else. When those motherfuckers pulled their pieces, so did I. I'd been practicing for this moment. My aim was no longer as solid as it once was, but it was decent enough, despite what I said to Sinclair.

The moment the club doors burst open and Royal Bastards flooded in, I shot the assholes surrounding Boom Boom.

I wanted to save him for last.

The shock on his face, the betrayal that flashed in his eyes, made me want to laugh.

"Surprise, motherfucker," I said, smirking at him, though I felt nothing but rage.

His flicker of fear satisfied me, but I didn't have time to savor it. Chaos erupted, and he disappeared into the crowd.

No matter. I'd find him later and make him pay.

For now, I'd kill as many assholes as possible, then blow this bitch to smithereens.

REESE

If I wasn't out of my mind with fucking worry over Ainsley, I might be concerned about Roman. He was a goddamn lunatic, plain and simple, who didn't seem to fear a thing. Fear, while a hindrance in some situations, is ultimately meant to keep you alive. It's your instinct's way of warning you that something is wrong and your fucking life may be in danger. An absence of fear, therefore, made you a loose cannon with no regard for life, yours or anyone else's.

A fucking fitting description for Roman fucking Mac. The only person he gave two shits about was Ainsley. His love for his sister drove him to plan the slaughter of his own club brothers and risk his life trying to retrieve her.

Even if it was only her corpse.

The thought of Ainsley dead nearly sent me into a frenzy, filling me with unmatched sorrow and grief. Unlike Roman, I couldn't psych myself up. Once again, I noted that I had nothing to compare to Ainsley's loss. Not my family's or Trinity's. There had been a wall between Trinity and me. Deep down, I knew we weren't meant to be, and my *instinct* prevented me from lowering my guard. Just as I'd done with Ainsley, except this time, she was carrying my child and it was my fear of intimacy that created the wall. I hadn't wanted to face losing her as I had my mother, father, brother, and sister. I hadn't wanted to commit myself as her man and the father of her child because I was a coward.

Now, I might never get the chance to be the man she deserved or the dad my father had been. If she wasn't alive, then neither was our baby.

I felt sick, terrified, and so goddamn regretful, it physically pained me.

"Let's move!" Razor's voice broke into my thoughts. "The gate's open."

I forced myself back into the moment, barely able to wait until Louisiana twirled his hand in the air and gave the signal to ride.

He'd threatened to handcuff Jinx to the bed, but Razor intervened by threatening her father. He'd secured her agreement that she'd return to work at the bar. *Or else.*

Loyalty to our club and the brothers came above everything for Razor. Louisiana wanted Jinx and that was all that mattered.

We blazed onto the Bloody Scorpions' grounds, kicking up dust and rocks. The scent of exhaust fumes and motor oil were like a drug to me. I was amongst the first to dismount. I turned, just in time to see Louisiana roll over one of the fuckheads Tio had brought down with a headshot.

He rode to me as my brothers dismounted and began rushing into the clubhouse. "I'm getting the van and bringing it onto the grounds so we can transport Ainsley once we find her." He didn't give me a chance to respond before he sped away, heading toward the gate, then circling around the perimeter as if I couldn't see.

I suspected he was going rogue and off script to kill some Bloody Scorpions before their motherfucking clubhouse was blown off the face of the goddamn Earth. Risky fucking move, but one I couldn't care about right now. My only concern was Ainsley.

Bolt shoved me and shot some fuckhead who appeared from nowhere, the sound of the gunfire forcing me to focus. If he hadn't been there, I might've got my head blown the hell off.

"Pay attention, boy," he barked.

I swallowed and nodded, reminding myself what was at stake. "Sorry," I mumbled, feeling like a scolded child at Bolt's annoyance because of my near-fatal mistake.

"Don't apologize, just keep your head in the game," Bolt ordered. "Stick to the fucking plan! Let's go."

Two minutes after we headed deeper onto the club's property, we ran across another fuckhead, and I slammed my pistol against his temple. Time was of the essence, but I needed to get some of my aggression out.

"Fuck!" he hollered, the force of my blow dropping the motherfucker to the ground.

Before he had another chance to react, I shot him. Bolt didn't say a thing, understanding how I felt and seeing all Bloody Scorpions as the enemy. We started off again, moving toward where we suspected she was being held captive.

We had a rough idea of her location. Thanks to Easton, we'd been able to tap into the Bloody Scorpions' CCTV. Their security measures were laughable. Cameras were only located in a few select areas, none of which contained Ainsley. The clubhouse was ruled out entirely. Her most likely location—if she hadn't been disposed of— was the small trailer park on the back side of the property. Only the front of the club had cameras, so we couldn't confirm our guess. The grounds of the Bloody Scorpions' club were compact and square, nowhere as big as the Royal Bastards'. There were only so many places she could be, so sooner or later, we'd stumble across her.

The trailers were in sight. We were getting closer to Ainsley, to saving her from the torment she must've endured. We just had to stay alive to do so.

The screams and gunshots echoing from the clubhouse assured me Roman and his allies were doing their part just fine. Failing to do my part would let them down and put our lives at risk.

More fuckers spilled out from the side and back entrances, too pussy to fight back. Bullets were punishment for their cowardice. Bolt and I mowed them down before they had a chance to pull their weapons. None of them was Boom Boom. Their Prez had left them to hang, and now, he was hiding like a pussy.

After I completed Ainsley's extraction, I'd hunt that motherfucker down and give him special treatment. Our chapter didn't breach many enemy clubs, but I kept my Glock 17 with extended magazine for any tense situation. Couldn't run out of fucking bullets in the middle of a fire fight.

Killing Scorpions was second-nature to me, a knee-jerk reaction I didn't think about.

However, as we neared the trailers, I realized that reaction would make our job harder. I needed one of them to talk and point me in the right direction. So, when a young, lanky motherfucker stumbled in the same direction we were heading, his shoulder oozing blood, I pistol whipped him. But this time, when he dropped to his knees, I didn't shoot, though he held a gun in each hand.

"Drop your weapons," I ordered, ignoring Bolt's confused look.

The kid was no older than twenty-five and scrambled to obey.

I waved my gun at his hands and he popped them into the air.

"Scoot back," I said, another command he immediately listened to.

"I-I'll do whatever you want, man, just chill the fuck out," he stammered, his eyes nervously darting between Bolt and me.

Perfect.

"Where's Ainsley?"

"Nova's place," he answered without a second thought. "It's the central white trailer with pink decorations outside." He swallowed. "That's where Prez said she is when he sent me to kill..." His eyes bulged. "I-I m-mean I-I haven't touched the bitch, man, I swear. Only officers are allowed in there right now, and I don't even fuck Black girls, so—"

My bullet interrupted the bullshit he spewed. His eyes rolled back, and he crumpled to the ground. He'd proved useful, but the way he'd spoken about Ainsley infuriated me. I gave his side a good, hard kick, ruing that he was too busy being dead to feel anything.

"Let's go," I said to Bolt, setting off before he responded.

Time seemed to simultaneously speed up and slow down as I neared the white trailer. Pink flamingos and a pink doormat identified it as Nova's place. The door was locked, but old and flimsy. Kicking it down was a breeze. The stench of an array of bodily fluids turned my stomach. The strong odors circulating through the small space were a noxious blend that challenged the strongest of fortitudes, including Bolt's. I heard him gag behind me, and I couldn't blame him one bit.

"Holy shit," I breathed as my eyes landed on the dead Bloody Scorpion laying in the living room.

Blood pooled under him, and brain matter splattered the wall. My gaze swept over the rest of the room. When it landed on the cage, piss and vomit on the bottom of it, rage filled me. If the dead fucker's words were true, it didn't take a genius to figure out that's where Ainsley had been held.

The question was, where the fuck was she now?

"Someone got to the fucker before we did," Bolt said, nudging the body with his boot.

I couldn't bother to respond. Worry clawed at my throat. Had the little fucker lied to me? Maybe he'd said what he thought I wanted to hear, in a desperate attempt to save his own life, unaware he was fucked regardless.

"Search the place," I growled, unable to accept that we'd been led on a wild goose chase.

Scouring the tiny trailer wouldn't take long. Bolt got to work immediately, while I remained rooted in place, the possibility of Ainsley being truly gone becoming more likely.

I hadn't claimed Trinity, something that turned out to be a good thing. Still, I'd been given a second chance at finding love, of having a family after mine was stolen from me. And for a second time, I blew it. The adage that the third time's a charm floated through my head, but I didn't want to go through another tragic heartbreak for my happily ever after. The only woman I wanted was Ainsley, and if she'd met a grizzly fate, then I'd commit myself to a lifetime alone. If I couldn't protect the beautiful mother of my unborn baby, then why doom another woman? It seemed that falling in love with me was a death sentence, and I wouldn't curse another soul.

A hulking figure darkening the door interrupted my brooding and reminded me just how vulnerable I truly was. I raised my weapon, but it was too late. Boom Boom's giant ass stood there holding a shotgun, aimed at my head.

Trapped in a standoff, neither one of us pulled the trigger.

"Prince Charming here to save his little slut; how fucking sweet," he sneered, his eyes burning with fury.

"Where is she?" I demanded, uncaring of the gun pointed at me.

If he was going to shoot me, I wouldn't go out like a pussy, pleading with a madman for mercy. I'd stand my ground and use my last bit of consciousness to fire my piece.

He looked at the cage and shrugged, his nonchalance pissing me off, and contrasting with his manic gaze. "Fuck if I know. She escaped her cage." He looked beyond me, zeroing in on the body before scowling at me. "Took Wizard out, too. Wondered if he got to try her pussy before the cunt killed him. He'd been chomping at the bit to sample her."

He was goading me, trying to rile me up, so I'd make a mistake. I knew his game, but I couldn't help but react.

"Shut the fuck up," I barked, my fury making me tremble.

He laughed, the sound mocking and grating. "When I find her, I'll fuck her before slitting her—"

I reacted on impulse, pulling the trigger and drowning out his threat. The bullet landed in his chest, but not before he fired the shotgun. Luckily, some higher power was looking out for me, giving me the speed to avoid the pellets, but just narrowly. A mere centimeter stood between me and death as I dove out of the way and hit the floor.

My heart pumping, ears throbbing, and adrenaline high, I made my way to where Boom Boom lay bleeding. I didn't think he was breathing. His eyes were wide open, and he wore a horrific death stare that made him even uglier. However, I wouldn't take my chances, so I placed my pistol in his mouth and pulled the trigger.

For a moment, I just admired the masterpiece his blood created, breathing heavily. Bolt's voice jolted me out of it.

"Reese, she's in here!" he called from the bedroom.

My feet were moving before my brain had processed the words. The relief in his voice hinted that she was alive, but I wouldn't feel better until she was back in my arms.

The bedroom was as pink and orderly as the rest of the house. The décor didn't matter to me, only the fact that Ainsley was there, huddled on the floor with Bolt's arm around her. She looked like she'd been through hell and back but appeared to have no extensive injuries. The bruises I saw pissed me off, though with time, they'd fade.

When Bolt saw me, he stepped away. I dropped to my knees, pulling her into my arms as emotions swamped me.

"You're alive," I croaked, my eyes watering, relief like I'd never felt before slamming into me.

She clung to me as if I were her lifeline, burying her face in my neck. She released a watery laugh. "You came."

Exhaustion laced her tone, and I wondered if she'd slept at all. Based on her chapped lips and raspy voice, they'd deprived her of water, likely food too. It was risky for her and the baby, but a day or two in the hospital should get her back to normal, especially if the baby was fine.

"Of course I came, sweetheart," I said, holding her close to me, rocking her gently. "I thought I'd fucking lost you. I-I'm so sorry, Ainsley. For not protecting you, for taking you for granted, for—"

It all spilled out, and before I could ramble anymore, she pulled back.

"Hush," she whispered, her eyes growing droopier. "I forgive you. Just...get me out of here, please."

Her voice cracked on the last word and my heart ached. Holding her tightly against me, I stood up. As we walked out of the trailer, I was faintly aware of Bolt trailing me, but my primary focus was Ainsley. I cradled her as if she were the most precious thing in the world.

Which, to me, she was. And once she recovered from this ordeal, I'd spend the rest of my life proving it to her.

Chapter Thirty-Four

Ainsley

My three-day stay at the hospital was uneventful. I needed an IV for dehydration, and was given pain medications that wouldn't harm my baby. Who, fortunately, had survived the ordeal. My little gift was a fighter, and the doctors predicted there'd be no long-term side effects from my beating or stint in the cage. They'd stressed that it'd been a miracle I hadn't miscarried, giving me the perfect name for my child.

As a kid, I adored the *Sims* franchise, something Nova used to mock me for. When I entered college, I was unable to play the game as frequently, and I stopped entirely when Trinity was killed. But my years-long obsession meant I'd researched a fair number of names to bestow on the *Sims* I created within the game. Confined to a hospital bed, I had little else to do but watch TV and consider what I'd name my baby.

I'd settled on two—Mavisha for a girl, Bennett for a boy. Both meant miracle, with the former being of Arabic origin, and the latter being of Anglo-Saxon origin. Mavisha would have Nicolette as her middle name, while my son would have Bennett as a middle name, with his given name being Reese. I'd considered my son having my father's name as a middle name—Cedrick—but decided I liked the ring of Reese Bennett better.

I would've loved to get Reese's input, but unfortunately, both he and Roman made themselves scarce.

Each had visited only once. Yesterday afternoon, Roman came with a big bouquet and a teddy bear and apologized for his behavior. I'd forgiven him without a second thought, and he'd sworn we'd talk things over when I was released from the hospital. Last night, Reese brought flowers and chocolate. We hadn't said much. At my request, he just crawled into my bed and held me. The intimacy immediately lifted my mood. His phone ringing interrupted our moment, and since it was Razor on the other end, he had to leave. His parting gift was a kiss, and a declaration of how overjoyed he was that I'd made it, how proud he was that I'd fought.

Just the thought made my heart flutter.

My steady stream of visitors included Ma Siller, Bolt, Tess, Big Poppa, Jinx, and Louisiana. Jinx said she'd decided to stay and refused to tell me what changed her mind.

Neither Roman nor Reese was available to bring me home, so on the day of my release, Tess and Big Poppa did the honors. I was itching to see the two most important men in my life. Reese had instructed me to go to Roman's house. Surprising, but it seemed the two had settled their differences, which was all I ever wanted.

Big Poppa sat my things right inside the door, kissed my cheek, and went back to the car, while Tess hugged me tightly, promised to visit the next day and shooed me inside.

The moment I walked through the front door, a strong pair of arms engulfed me. I melted into Reese, savoring his scent and closeness. He buried his nose in my hair, inhaling deeply, which heated my cheeks.

"I stink," I complained. Although I'd taken a quick shower this morning before my release, I wasn't able to do my normal routine in the hospital. I didn't have the body wash and hair products I used.

"You smell amazing," he mumbled against me, sniffing again to prove a point. "I missed you so fucking much."

"You saw me last night," I reminded him, ignoring the butterflies fluttering in my stomach at his words. "A few hours ago."

It was just his relief talking. As much as I wanted to be his, my kidnapping didn't change the status of our relationship.

But boy, did I long for something more than the endless hot-and-cold.

I wouldn't chase him, nor would I push him for more. That didn't mean fantasies didn't live in my head about us becoming something concrete, a unit that'd raise our baby together. But after seeing Chi Chi killed in front of me, and being beaten, starved, and held captive, I was forced to confront how short life was. I wouldn't live the rest of my days in regret, wondering what could be with a man who didn't want more.

The thought crushed me, but hey, it was what it was.

"Hours too long." He punctuated his sentence with a kiss to my head.

He only pulled away when Roman cleared his throat. The sound drew my attention to him. Emotion overcame me when I took in my beloved brother's presence, standing tall with prosthetic hands, his expression neutral, but his eyes filled with love and admiration. Best of all, he was alive, the rumors of his death fortunately false. A silly part of me wondered if his visit to the hospital had been a fever dream, something I hallucinated due to exhaustion and medication.

It wasn't, and the giant smile on my face betrayed my joy.

"Hi," I said simply, not knowing what else to say after a month of no contact.

He grinned, softening his features. "Hi," he mimicked.

Reese placed a hand on my lower back and lightly pushed, encouraging me to go closer to my brother. I obeyed, and as soon as I was in arm's length, Roman took his turn hugging me.

"I'm so goddamn sorry, Ainsley," he said with feeling, repeating his words from the hospital. "I was such an asshole to you."

"You were," I agreed, just the memory of his anger cutting me. "But it wasn't without cause."

"Didn't make it right," he said with a sigh, releasing me from his hold and stepping back. He ran a hand through his hair, his curls flowing freely for once. "I wish I could take back what I said, but it's too fucking late for that. Just know I regret my words. I'll be the best damn uncle to your baby, and if you want Sinclair in your life, then you have my blessing." He looked over my shoulder, pinning Reese with a hard stare. "Just don't hurt her, or that'll be your ass."

I couldn't help but giggle. He'd forever be overprotective.

"I won't," Reese vowed, making me look back at him, the hope blossoming within me a scary feeling. He shifted his focus to me. "I made some mistakes with you myself, sweetheart. But when you were taken...I...fuck, I thought I'd lost you, and I realized what a stupid motherfucker I'd been by pushing you away."

"Understatement," Roman whispered.

I shot him a glare over my shoulder. Seeing as he hadn't been there for me, he didn't have a damn thing to say.

"Can we have a moment alone, Roman?" I requested, knowing things would go smoother if he were absent.

"Let him stay," Reese said, interrupting whatever reply my brother would've had. "I want him to hear what I'm about to say, so I have a witness to hold me to my promises."

"Make sure you don't make promises you can't keep," Roman warned, earning another nasty look.

"Your commentary isn't needed," I sniffed, crossing my arms over my chest.

He just shrugged. With an eyeroll, I looked back at Reese, my heart pounding in my ears as I waited to hear what he'd say next.

"I love you, Ainsley Valois," he declared, stealing my breath away. "So damn much."

Words eluded me, and I wondered if I'd heard him correctly.

"I want to make an honest woman out of you, to stop fucking around and do right by you. Maybe not now, but—"

"Before the baby is born," Roman interjected.

Despite him being the one to insist Roman stay, annoyance flashed across his face.

"We'll see," I said quickly, my arms dropping to my sides. I gave Roman a pointed look. "I-I love you too, Reese, and I'd love a future with you. But I don't want to rush things, or for you to feel obligated to marry me. I want to be a wife one day, but at our pace, not because of others' expectations."

At the big, goofy grin on his handsome face, I wondered if he heard a thing I said.

"You love me," he repeated, as if he hadn't been the one to say it first.

"You wouldn't be standing here if she didn't," Roman said.

I whirled around to face him. "You have one more thing to say before I lose my goddamn mind, Roman. I love you, but please, be quiet right now."

As happy as I was that we'd made up, he didn't get to abandon me in my moment of need, then shit on the man who'd been there to protect me. Sure, Roman made up for his mistakes with the blood of those who'd wronged me, but it didn't fully erase his initial reaction.

He'd earned my forgiveness, but forgetting would be another matter entirely.

Roman was silent for a moment. Then, he nodded, sighing as if the simple task pained him. "Fine. I have a phone call to make anyway about an important matter."

He and Reese exchanged knowing looks.

My curiosity removed the shock I felt that Roman had actually given in, but he was gone before I questioned him.

"What was that about?"

Reese shrugged. "I'm not sure," he said, though I suspected otherwise.

He navigated me to the living room couch. Once he sat down, he gripped my waist and pulled me onto his lap. I gasped and giggled at the bold move.

"The moment my brother leaves, you pounce," I joked, relaxing against him.

"Can you blame me?" he quipped, settling his hands on my hips as I straddled him.

I had nothing inappropriate in mind, besides looking into his gorgeous eyes. Although, I'd be a lying heifer if I said the feel of his dick twitching to life didn't send heat rushing through me.

"Did you mean what you said?" he questioned, caressing my sides, his gentle touch sending a shiver down my spine. "When you said you loved me?"

I nodded, leaning forward to nuzzle my nose against his. "Every word. Did *you* mean it?"

"Yes," he said without a moment of hesitation. "When the assholes took you, I was out of my fucking mind with worry, and so much regret, I could hardly breathe. I've been a bastard to you, and I'll spend the rest of my life making it up."

I wondered if I was dreaming, because the declaration sounded absolutely perfect—almost too good to be true.

Without a second thought, I kissed him. He groaned, wrapping an arm around my waist to pull me closer. I took the opportunity to ease my tongue into his mouth, deepening the kiss and worsening my growing arousal. Only when his hand grabbed my ass did I remember Roman's presence, and as much as it pained me, I pulled away panting.

"We're going for a ride later," I decided, needing to be truly alone with him to show exactly what he did to me and how much he meant to me.

"Any destination in mind?"

"Somewhere with a bed."

He chuckled, though his eyes darkened at my brazen words. "That can be arranged."

We fell silent, basking in each other's presence, savoring the closeness. Reese spoke first.

"I don't have a ring right now, and don't know when I'd get one, so this isn't a proposal," he said, the clarification making my eyebrows raise. "But I wasn't kidding when I said I want to make you my wife, Ainsley. I want our child to have my name, and I want my ring on your finger and a cut on your back, showing every motherfucker around that you're mine."

The thought of wearing a 'Property of Reese,' cut made me swoon. Not only would it show others I'm taken, but it'd be an official claim, a tangible sign of who I belonged to.

"I want that, too," I breathed.

"Then you'll have it," he swore, the adoration in his eyes making me feel like the luckiest woman alive. "I'll give you the moon, the stars, and anything else you want."

"I never took you for a poet, Reese Sinclair," I mused, threading my hands through his hair.

"You bring it out of me, baby."

"Well, I can't say I hate it," I replied with a giggle, leaning down and kissing him again.

It was brief and chaste but still left me swooning.

In that moment, all the pain and chaos of the last several months faded, as did the thoughts of the torment I endured during my kidnapping. The tears, the fear, the sadness, the anger —none of it mattered because it'd led me and Reese to where we were: in love and planning a future together. My one night with the biker flipped my world on its head, and despite the ensuing madness, I wouldn't have it any other way.

If you're familiar with the Death Dweller books and the Bridge Series where Bash makes his first appearance, then I would like to clarify the timeline. The events in *One Night With The Biker* coincide with the timeline in the latter part of *Reckless*. Although it's implied that Bash knows Kendall here, he has been stalking her.

Wills and Throttle by Daria Monroe refers to my character in *Bounty*.

Much love to everyone and I hope you enjoyed Reese and Ainsley's story.

Thank you for reading One Night With The Biker.
If you enjoyed it, please consider leaving a review at
your point of purchase and on Goodreads. It means a
lot to me to hear what you think. You can also check out
other books in the series here:
https://www.royalbastardsmc.com/

Website: https://katckelly.com

Email: katkelwriter@outlook.com

Snail mail: 24200 Southwest Freeway, Suite 402, Box
#353, Rosenberg, TX 77471

Amazon Author Page: https://sqr.co/Follow-Kat-on-
Amazon/
Website: https://www.katckelly.com
Dedicated Series Website:
https://deathdwellersmc.com

Facebook:
https://www.facebook.com/kathryn.kelly.336717
Twitter: https://twitter.com/katkelwriter
Blog: http://kathrynkellyauthor.blogspot.com
Pinterest: http://www.pinterest.com/kathrynkelly336/
Goodreads:
https://www.goodreads.com/author/show/7422779.Kathryn_Kelly
Instagram: https://www.instagram.com/katkelwriter/
YouTube: https://sqr.co/Kat-on-YouTube/

Crimson Syn, thank you for allowing me to be a part of the Royal Bastards MC. I have long admired the series, and I am excited to add my story.

Natasha Hooks, you're the best and I appreciate how much you help me.

Cathi, thank you for riding up to support me at the book signing. That meant so much to me.

Kat's Krewe, y'all rock and keep my going, even when I'm at my lowest. Thank you for your support.

Mama, thank you for being you.

Kate, I appreciate you allowing me to ride with you until your besties get back in town.

Zoey, Lucian, and Garrett, I miss you all so much, my loves.

Alegra, I love you.

Royal Bastards MC
One Night with a Biker

Mayhem Makers
Bounty

Death Dwellers MC Legacy
Reckless
Restless
Relentless
Ruthless
Remorseless
Ruptured
Rampage
Revenge

Phoenix Rising Rock Band
Inferno
Incendiary
Scorched
Inflame

Dirty Boy Studios
Dirty Boy

Death Dwellers MC
Misled
Misappropriate
Misunderstood
Misdeeds
Misbehavior
Misjudged
Misguided
Misalliance
Misconduct
A Very Christopher Christmas
Misfit
Mistrust
USA Today Review

Misgivings
An Outlaw Valentine
Misrule
Death Dwellers: The Complete
Set
Outlaw's Dictionary

Single Titles
Captivated
All My Tomorrows

Kathryn C. Kelly is a New Orleans native who has called southeast Texas home since 2005. She had intended to travel the world but always return to her beloved New Orleans. Hurricane Katrina had other plans. She is the mother of three beautiful daughters and the daughter of one gorgeous mother whose footsteps she followed in by becoming a writer.

Kathryn is the former owner and editor of Inside Rose Rich Magazine. She and her mother have been published by Jove Books as Christine Holden. The books have long been out of print but they got the rights back to the five novels and have plans to re-release them soon.

Kathryn is a cancer survivor. In 2010, she felt a small lump in her breast. In 2015, at the urging of her mother, she went in for her bi-yearly mammogram and was diagnosed with Stage 2b/3a HER2 positive breast cancer. On November 30, 2016, she rang the bell. During her treatment, she was also diagnosed with Li-Fraumeni Syndrome.

She is hard at work on her next book.

In her head, she is a biker babe with a Harley in her garage, waiting for her to hit the road. In reality, she has yet to hop on a bike and ride. She loves Cards Against Humanity, has strong opinions that she keeps to herself, must take her time when she talks in public so nothing untoward pops out, and always strives to see the best in people and in life.